CRITICAL ACCLAIM FOR SCOTT CARPENTER'S
THE STEEL ALBATROSS

"Adventure and authenticity superb. . . . I had a sly sensation I was reading highly classified material with every turn of the page."

—Clive Cussler

"Mr. Carpenter writes with an easy, light touch, with just the proper blend of technology and plot to guarantee that the reader will turn the pages, race to the end, and then wish for more. . . . *The Steel Albatross* is a first-rate techno-thriller."

—*Dallas Morning News*

"Carpenter puts the importance of individual ingenuity in the forefront. . . . A gung-ho tale. . . . *The Steel Albatross'* strengths are in the gadgetry and the author's solemn respect for the military virtues. . . ."

—*Philadelphia Inquirer*

"*The Steel Albatross* [shows] comprehensive knowledge of naval routine, as seen from the vantage points of the lowest seaman and the highest Pentagon officials."

—*The New York Times Book Review*

"Mr. Carpenter sprinkles fascinating underwater scenes and details about deep-sea diving through a skillfully unfolding plot."

—*Washington Times*

"As high-tech as they come. . . . A fast . . . entertaining read."

—*Denver Post*

Books by Scott Carpenter

The Steel Albatross
Deep Flight

Published by POCKET BOOKS

For orders other than by individual consumers, Pocket Books grants a discount on the purchase of **10 or more** copies of single titles for special markets or premium use. For further details, please write to the Vice-President of Special Markets, Pocket Books, 1230 Avenue of the Americas, New York, NY 10020.

For information on how individual consumers can place orders, please write to Mail Order Department, Paramount Publishing, 200 Old Tappan Road, Old Tappan, NJ 07675.

SCOTT CARPENTER

DEEP FLIGHT

POCKET BOOKS

New York   London   Toronto   Sydney   Tokyo   Singapore

The sale of this book without its cover is unauthorized. If you purchased this book without a cover, you should be aware that it was reported to the publisher as "unsold and destroyed." Neither the author nor the publisher has received payment for the sale of this "stripped book."

This book is a work of fiction. Names, characters, places, and incidents are products of the author's imagination or are used fictiously. Any resemblance to actual events or locales or persons, living or dead, is entirely coincidental.

An *Original* Publication of POCKET BOOKS

POCKET BOOKS, a division of Simon & Schuster Inc.
1230 Avenue of the Americas, New York, NY 10020

Copyright © 1994 by Scott Carpenter

All rights reserved, including the right to reproduce this book or portions thereof in any form whatsoever. For information address Pocket Books, 1230 Avenue of the Americas, New York, NY 10020

ISBN: 0-671-75903-5

First Pocket Books printing August 1994

10 9 8 7 6 5 4 3 2 1

POCKET and colophon are registered trademarks of Simon & Schuster Inc.

Cover art by Bohdan Osyczka

Printed in the U.S.A.

DEEP
FLIGHT

The small boat slowed until the noise of its meticulously muffled outboard motor was softer than the slap of the waves against the bow. The two divers in matte-black wet-suits that covered everything except their faces knelt on the duckboards. They finished strapping on their rebreathers, affectionately known as O-two rigs because they delivered only pure oxygen to the diver. Though highly prized in clandestine underwater operations because they left no telltale exhaust-bubble trail, the rigs did have a down side: swim with this scuba below sixty feet for more than three or four minutes without intricate precautions and highly specialized training, and you're dead.

At a signal from the helmsman, the taller of the two frogs hauled in on the line to the swimmer delivery vehicle, an SDV-4 Mk III. He barely broke the water, which had been under tow behind them, and made it fast alongside.

The divers looked around to get their last visual bearings. It was a moonless night, but the starlight was bright enough to show most of the horizon as a ruler-straight line between the navy blue of the sky and the inky blackness of the ocean. To the northeast loomed Mount Lamlam, the tallest point on the island of Guam, with the headland of Facpi Point to its left. Just to the left of that was the silhouette of an odd-

1

looking ship with a tall, lacy framework amidships. It looked to be about three miles away. That was their target.

The diver looked down at the instrument strapped to his wrist and took a bearing on the ship. He cast the deep-dive unit free, touched his partner's arm, and nodded. The two adjusted their facemasks and mouthpieces, attached their buddy line, and slipped noiselessly over the side of the boat. In a few moments the bow of their tiny submersible swung away as it picked up headway and slowly disappeared below the surface. The swimmer delivery vehicle then reversed heading and made its own departure, leaving nothing but a dark, calm sea and a silence broken only by the purr of distant surf.

Meanwhile, two fathoms down, the divers leveled off and took up the heading to the ship. The diver in the front seat of the submersible kept careful track of their heading, depth, and elapsed time. He knew that navigation of this sort involved major unknowns and many approximations, particularly at night. Small errors in estimating initial position and determining speed through the water, coupled with instrument reading errors and such vagaries as the speed and direction of the current, could easily amplify one another, leaving the divers far from where they expected when they surfaced.

The lead diver checked the luminous instruments on the panel in front of him and on his wrist. Then he reached back and squeezed the arm of his companion. Each attached a tether line to the little boat and swam cautiously to the surface. The ship was just fifty yards away. Its hull loomed up from the water, sheer and high as the wall of a prison.

Ship's officer T. J. "Tommy" Brashford hated standing the midwatch. From midnight to zero-four-hundred was when he ordinarily got his best sleep. Left to himself, he always fell asleep promptly at ten o'clock and woke up just as promptly at five-thirty the next morning. Ever since high school, that had been his normal rhythm. Which just proved, he thought sourly, that there was nothing normal about shipboard life.

Underway it wasn't so bad, as there were always a hundred details to keep him from nodding off. In port or at anchor, it was a different story. This made the second day in a row that they had been swinging around the hook, and the biggest excitement they'd had in all that time was watching the seabirds dive for garbage.

He yawned widely, cracking his jaw, and glanced at the ship's clock. Just over an hour until his relief would show up and he could hit the sack. He took a sip of coffee and made a face. It was thick, bitter, and just barely warm. He picked up a dog-eared sports magazine and flipped through the pages, glancing at the photos.

Tommy's eyelids were drifting toward closed when a gong sounded three times, paused, and sounded three more times. He sprang up out of his seat and studied the readouts on the large black console on the afterbridge bulkhead. Then he grabbed the handset of the intercom and punched in a four-digit number.

"Jansen?" Tommy said. "The bridge. We've got an intruder inside sixty yards off the starboard quarter. Yeah, I know it's probably a dolphin, but your guys had better check it out. Rules is rules."

He hung up and went to the starboard wing of the bridge, where the elevated position let him see the whole length of the deck. Three men appeared from somewhere forward and hurried in his direction. One was carrying a portable searchlight. The other two held what he knew were Armalite semiautomatic rifles. Aft at the railing, they took up positions about six feet apart, the one with the searchlight in the middle.

The intense beam of the searchlight speared out and downward, sweeping the water close to the side of the ship. The two armed men stared down, their rifles at the ready.

On the bridge, Tommy nodded with satisfaction. Jansen's security guys were on the ball, even if this was a futile exercise. Then he glanced at his watch and made a face. He should have noted the time of the original contact, of his call to Jansen, and of the moment when the security team appeared on deck. The skipper would read him off in the

3

morning for sure, unless he made up a time for the original contact and entered it in the ship's log. What harm could that do?

The fact was, their new, fancy-shmancy intruder alarm was more of a nuisance than a help. As Jansen had said, most of the time it sounded off for porpoises and the occasional shark. Sometimes it went off for no reason that anybody could figure. And why did they need it, anyway? Was anyone really expecting an underwater demolition team to mount an assault on a ship peacefully engaged in deep-ocean mining? Not likely. And an attack by Malay pirates wasn't in the cards either, not this far from Malaysia. No, chances were someone on the project, in a position of some authority, had a relative who worked at the lab that had developed the gadget and had made a nice piece of change when he'd authorized its purchase, on a sole source basis, for the ship.

"Over there!" someone shouted. "I just saw something!"

The searchlight beam swung to the left. Half a second later Jensen's men opened fire, with a sound like ripping cloth amplified a hundred times. Ten seconds later, the Armalites fell silent.

This time Tommy remembered to check the time: 0302.

The man stood motionless in the shadows. The deck patrol, walking at a leisurely pace in the direction of the bow, had passed his position two minutes before. He checked his pack of cigarettes and lighter. If they came back this way before the plan went into action, and if they spotted him, he was ready to say that he had come on deck for a smoke.

He glanced at his wrist. The radiant minute hand was nearly vertical. The next few minutes would tell.

From somewhere behind him came the muffled sound of a gong. He straightened up and took a deep breath, then turned his face away as the three-man patrol hurried aft. The moment they were past his hiding place, he walked quickly across the open deck to a steel structure that looked like a shipping container with windows and a door cut into its sides.

Mounted on the wall next to the door was a keypad that controlled the door lock. The combination was changed every day. The man took out what looked like a pocket calculator, attached its magnetic probes to either side of the keypad, and lightly pressed each of the keys in order. The numbers on the calculator's LED screen changed wildly for a few seconds, then stopped at 5483. He pressed those four numbers in order, and the lock clicked open. The man put the instrument back in the inside pocket of his jacket and stepped through the door, carefully closing it behind him.

He took out a small flashlight and switched it on. The lens had been covered with black friction tape, except for a tiny space at the center, so the light beam that emerged was no wider than a pencil. He moved it slowly around the interior of the room. The walls were lined with racks of electronic gear. At the far end was a computer console. A tiny red light on the power control center next to it indicated that the central processing unit had been left on. That was normal; switching it on and off every day put more stress on the circuitry than leaving it on all the time.

The man sat down at the console and switched on the monitor. He was prepared to find his way through the log-on procedures if he had to, but he lucked out. The screen came up showing the DOS C> prompt.

From his pocket, he took out a diskette and slipped it into the disk drive. Using just two fingers, he typed

```
DEL C:\ROVER\*.*
```

and hit the return key.

Are you sure (Y/N)? the screen demanded. He hit the Y key. The screen blanked for an instant, then returned to

```
C>
```

With a grim smile, the man typed

```
XCOPY B:\ROVER\*.* C: /S
```

The tiny green light on the disk drive shone. Words scrolled up the screen, moving almost too quickly for him to make sense of them:

```
Reading source file(s) . . .
B:\ROVER\TELEMTRY\ATTITUDE
B:\ROVER\TELEMTRY\CLARITY
B:\ROVER\TELEMTRY\DEPTH
B:\ROVER\TELEMTRY\INTERNL
B:\ROVER\TELEMTRY\SALINITY
B:\ROVER\TELEMTRY\TEMP
. . . .
                47 File(s) copied
   C>
```

The man held down the Return key until nothing showed on the screen except a long vertical line of C> prompts. He switched off the monitor, retrieved his diskette, and walked silently to the door. Cracking it open a half inch, he listened carefully, then slipped out. The door locked automatically behind him. Moments later, he was safe in his cabin.

The tiny sub broke the surface and the lead diver scanned the faint horizon. According to his calculations, they should have been close to the pickup point. But where was the boat? He raised his mask, removed the mouthpiece, and reached back to do the same for his partner, who was too weak from the shock of a shoulder wound to take care of it himself.

From a sheath on his left calf, he removed his Beady Eye, the nickname for the American SEALs' NRQ-1 infrared night signaler. Its light was as invisible to the unaided eye as the coded blinks of a TV remote controller. The crew on the distant ship would be unlikely to notice it—ordinarily. But, as their reactions had shown a few minutes earlier, these were not ordinary times. The ship's crew was alerted now. Their lookouts might easily be using the new model image-intensifying snooperscopes. If so, the IR glow would stand out like a railroad flare.

He held the light so that his body was between it and the ship, but before he could turn it on, he caught sight of the outline of the boat, darker against the midnight-blue sky. It was no more than a hundred feet away. He resheathed the light, powered up the tiny sub, and made way for the pickup boat. There was a first-aid kit on board and good medical care available soon. He was pretty sure his partner would be all right.

"Yes, sir, I'm sure!" the guard said, for what seemed like the dozenth time. "It was somebody in a wetsuit and a face-mask! I only saw him for a split second, but I know what I saw."

"Tex" Jansen turned to the other guard and said, "And you didn't see him, is that right, Bowie?"

"Well, sir," Bowie replied slowly, "I saw *something*. But it went under just as I caught sight of it. It was big and black, that's all I can say."

Jansen sighed in frustration and put his pen back in his pocket.

"Okay," he said. "We'll leave it at that. The captain will want to hear your stories himself after I fill him in. Then again, maybe not. Whether you were shooting at a frogman or a porpoise, we don't know for sure. Either way, there's no sign of it in the water near the ship."

"Sir, I'm sure I—" Bowie began to say.

"I know," Jansen said wearily. "You're positive you hit it, whatever it was. Don't worry, I'll include that in my report. Now you guys had better get back to your patrolling. Just be glad there was no harm done."

CHAPTER 1

RICK TALLMAN'S TAXI TURNED ONTO KALIA ROAD AND cruised past the four huge towers of the Hilton Hawaiian Village. Moments later it came to a stop in front of the Hale Koa Hotel. Rick climbed out and stretched. The seat he'd occupied on the five-hour flight from Los Angeles must have been meant for a dwarf or a small child. Certainly not for someone who topped six feet.

He paid the driver and added a reasonable tip. The man grinned and said, *"Mahalo."*

Rick, like most Navy men, made it a point of pride to know at least a few words of the language of any place he spent time. A tour of carrier duty in the Pacific had given him the chance to pick up a little Hawaiian, and his shipmates, who had served all over the world, had passed along handy words in Japanese, Tagalog, and a few other languages spoken widely around the Pacific Rim.

"You're welcome," he replied. He grabbed his two bags from the backseat and nudged the door closed with the one in his left hand, then turned to look around. His hotel, open only to active or retired military personnel, was on the grounds of Fort DeRussy, a U.S. Army base plunked down right in the middle of some of the most expensive real estate in the world.

Not far from where Rick stood was a coastal battery, part of the old naval defense works that ringed Honolulu and Pearl Harbor. Once the battery's twenty-foot-thick concrete walls had sheltered immense guns that could hurl shells carrying a ton of high explosives each at enemies fifteen miles at sea. Now the guns were gone and it housed a military museum.

Beyond the coastal battery loomed the close-packed hotels of Waikiki. Each of the tall towers was angled to make as many rooms as possible face the ocean. Of course. Tourists who came to Hawaii from all over the world did not want some view of the golf course, the zoo, or the skyline of downtown Honolulu. They expected to look out the window of their room—or, better still, step out onto their private *lanai*—and see a white sand beach, deep blue water, and the moon rising over Diamond Head. Not to mention swaying palms and beautiful *wahines* in see-through grass skirts, dancing to the sound of ukuleles and Hawaiian guitars.

Rick thought that he'd do without the view of the beach and all the rest if someone would just point him in the direction of one of those *wahines*.

He carried his bags into the lobby, where the Army spec/4 behind the front desk looked up and said, "Yes, sir?"

"You're supposed to be holding a room for me," Rick said, putting his ID card on the counter. "The name's Tallman."

The man glanced at a folder, then at the card. "Oh, right, Commander," he said. He took down a key from the board behind him and pushed it across to Rick, then added, "There's a message for you too, sir."

Rick knitted his brow as he took the envelope and tore it open. How could anyone have known that he would be passing through Honolulu? It was only three days since he had unexpectedly received orders calling him off medical leave and sending him to Guam.

The note was short and to the point:

Ricky,
Come see me as soon as you're settled in. Room 342.
                                                    Will

Rick felt a grin spreading across his face. Wilson W. Ward,
Captain, USN (Ret.), was Rick's godfather. He had always
taken his duties seriously. It was he who had introduced
Rick to fishing and scuba diving, and he who had paddled
Rick the one time he overheard him talking back to his
mother. More recently, Ward had designed and built the
Steel Albatross, the revolutionary, sonar-proof stealth submarine that plumbed the deeps with the silent ease of a
sailplane soaring the sky. Rick had given the *Steel Albatross*
its name and been its first pilot.

Rick stuffed the note in the pocket of his aloha shirt,
followed it with his room key, and carried his bags over to
the elevator. Two minutes later, he was looking out at a
prospect that included Waikiki Beach, a wide expanse of
blue sea, and, off to the left, across Mamala Bay, the glori-
ous silhouette of Diamond Head. No rising moon or dancing
girls, but maybe that was too much to expect in the middle
of the afternoon.

Behind him, the phone rang. He picked it up, then held
the receiver away from his ear.

"Where are you, goddamnit!" a familiar voice roared.

"I'm right here," Rick replied, grinning to himself.

"Well get your butt over here, *wikiwiki.* You think I came
halfway across the Pacific just to admire the view?"

Still grinning, Rick hurried down three flights and
knocked on the door of Captain Ward's room.

"About time," the older man rumbled, pulling Rick inside
and shutting the door. As they shook hands, Rick noticed
more gray in the tangled black brow that topped Captain
Ward's piercing blue eyes. Not much else had changed in
the year since they'd last seen each other, though. Ward still
reminded Rick of a fireplug: short, solid, and made of the
best cast iron. Even at ease, he stood with the ramrod pos-
ture he had learned during his first year at Annapolis, when
upperclassmen had ordered him to "brace." The aloha shirt

he was wearing over his khaki British Army shorts was a '40s-vintage "silkie" that depicted the Aloha Tower against a pinkish-orange sky, with a purple Diamond Head in the background.

Rick pretended to shield his eyes.

"Enough clowning around," the captain said, slapping Rick's hand down. "We've got work to do."

"I don't suppose you'd care to tell me what kind of work?" Rick replied. "Three days ago I was lying on the sand in Palm Beach, convalescing. Now I've got these weird orders sending me to Guam. Not that I've got anything in particular against Guam, you understand. But I wouldn't mind knowing why some dork in BuPers decided to send me there."

Captain Ward crossed the room to a small refrigerator. "You want a beer?" he asked, pulling the door open.

"No, thanks. I washed down my airline lunch with California champagne," Rick said.

The captain gave an exaggerated shudder and unscrewed the cap on a bottle of Coors. He took a swallow, then said, "Rick, my boy . . . the reason you're here is a long story, and there's nothing for me to do but start at the beginning. As you know, for the last few years I've been playing around with some pretty far-out ideas for submarine propulsion. The *Steel Albatross* is one, of course, but I've also got a real soft spot for what I call ELMAHYDYD."

"Oh, sure," Rick said with a grin. "I used to have an elmahigh-dyed T-shirt."

The captain looked at him blankly. Then he caught the joke, and growled like a bear whose alarm clock had just gone off in the middle of February. "In the old days men were keelhauled for lesser offenses than that," he barked.

"Sorry, sir," said Rick. "You were going to tell me about your new propulsion system."

"ELMAHYDYD. Stands for *ELectro-MAgnetic HYdro-DYnamic Drive.* I can't go into details, but it works on the principle of Lorentz forces. You take ionized seawater and use a powerful electromagnetic field to push it through a big duct, the same way a shrouded propeller does. But this system is very efficient, gives you lots of thrust, and it's very quiet. Most important, there's no propeller cavitation. That's what puts an upper limit on the speeds you can get with big ships, you know. Over a certain number of revs, a prop creates so much turbulence that it can't get a bite on the water."

"Sounds like a naval architect's dream," Rick commented.

Ward nodded. "Just about. You can vary the duct diameter through a wide range, so this scheme should be able to answer any imaginable marine propulsion requirement. There's no reason why it shouldn't work. As a matter of fact, a Japanese team just finished sea trials on an experimental craft that uses a similar system. The problem is, the only way the cost-yield energy calculations come out looking okay is if you assume that your electromagnets are made from superconductors, materials that have essentially no electrical resistance."

"And that's impossible, from what I've read," Rick said. "Don't you have to cool things down almost to absolute zero to get superconductivity? That's hard enough in a top-level research lab, let alone on a warship. Seems to me that's a real mountain to climb."

"That's what I thought too," Captain Ward said. "That's why I put ELMAHYDYD on hold and turned all my energies to *Steel Albatross*. But more recently, I've turned them back again. As a matter of fact, keep this strictly to yourself, but I installed a small prototype of the drive in *Albatross*."

Rick stared, amazed. "You're that far along?" he exclaimed.

"Yes and no," the captain replied. He walked over to the window and stood there, hands clasped behind his back. "The drive works, all right, but only on an emergency basis. The cooling system has to chill the superconducting magnets down to about five degrees Kelvin, which uses up energy like there's no tomorrow. That's why ... Have you ever heard of scandium?"

The abrupt change of subject made Rick feel like a contestant on a quiz show, one that didn't give prizes to winners and made losers feel like assholes. "Scandium," he repeated.

"It's an element, I know that much. One of the rare earth metals, I think."

"Right. And it may—just may—have an important role in developing practical high-temperature superconductivity. For security reasons, I won't go into any more detail. You understand."

"No, I don't," Rick protested. "I have just about every kind of clearance there is. You know that."

"I know you do," the captain agreed. "I took a peek at your folder a couple of days ago, just to make sure there wasn't anything new in it."

"That's illegal," Rick said. "Those files are supposed to be strictly confidential. You're not even on the active list anymore."

Captain Ward gave him an ironic look. "Tell me about it, sonny. The point is, you may have a Q clearance and all that, but you don't have a need to know. At least that's what the pencil pushers would say. I don't necessarily agree, but that's neither here nor there."

"Okay," said Rick. "I can live with that. Can you tell me where you *get* scandium? And can you also tell me why I care?"

The captain rubbed his chin. "I'll tell you why, later, but getting it, that's the problem," he admitted. "It's not all that rare, relatively speaking. The sun happens to be loaded with it. But here on earth, it's a bitch to get at, and a bitch to refine once you do. That's the reason ..." He broke off and studied Rick. "Does the name *Glomar Champion* mean anything to you?"

Rick thought for a few moments, repeated the name, then snapped his fingers. "Wasn't that a ship that Howard Hughes built, about twenty years ago? The story was that the ship was going to revolutionize deep-sea mining. Then later it came out that the whole story was just a cover. The cloak-and-dagger boys had been in charge of the project from day one. The ship's real mission was to try to recover a Russian sub that had been sunk somewhere in the middle of the Pacific."

"About 750 miles northwest of here, and over three miles

down, to be exact," the captain amplified. He walked over to the table near the window, pulled out one of the chairs, and sat down. Rick followed him.

"It must have been quite an operation," he continued, looking out at the water. "They had a giant grappling hook mounted on the end of a string of drilling pipe. They planned to lower it down to the sub, grab it, and haul it up. Just like the Lucky Dip at a carnival midway. But there was a hitch. According to the official story, the sub—PL-722, a diesel-powered Golf 2–class boat carrying three SSN-5 ballistic missiles tipped with thermonuclear warheads, to be exact—broke her back on the way up to the surface. The team salvaged the bow section and learned a hell of a lot about Russian torpedo technology. But they lost the big payoff, the boat's missiles and codebooks, which were in the stern section."

"The 'official story'?" Rick repeated. "Is there another version?"

"Some scuttlebutt," the captain admitted. "Supposedly the spooks recovered the whole boat, gave it a very careful look, then fed it to a compactor and gave the pieces the deep-six, then invented the story about the sub breaking in half because they wanted the job to sound as tricky as possible. That way the Navy wouldn't scream as loud when it got the half-billion-dollar bill for the project."

"Half a *billion,* for half a sunken sub?" Rick gave a snort of disbelief. "That doesn't sound like much of a bargain. Was it worth it?"

Captain Ward shrugged. "Who knows? If the Navy kicked about the price, it was done very much behind closed doors. And maybe the spooks were telling the truth after all. A couple of years ago, they handed over to the Russians a videotape, showing the burial at sea of six sailors they found in the sub. They did it proper too—Soviet Navy flag and all. Anyway, once the project's cover was blown, the *Champion* was mothballed in San Francisco Bay, not far from Treasure Island. It never was used for deep-sea mining. Until now."

Rick made a guess. "The scandium?"

"Bull's-eye," Captain Ward replied. "But with a new

twist. *Champion* was supposed to go after manganese nodules, or manganodules, that show up on the ocean floor. Manganodules contain a bunch of other useful, scarce, and extremely valuable metals as well, including cobalt, but they're damned hard to harvest. For a start, they usually turn up at depths of twenty thousand feet or so."

Rick whistled. "Not your ordinary backyard duck pond."

"No. Another problem is that most of the prime manganodule deposits, such as the Clarion-Clipperton zone a thousand miles northeast of here, are in international waters. The regulations about mining in international waters are still pretty iffy, so no one wants to pour money into a project that might sink without a trace at any moment."

"I can understand that," Rick said. "But where's the twist you mentioned?"

"About ten years ago, marine geologists discovered new undersea deposits of manganese and other minerals," Captain Ward replied. "Seamount crusts, they're called. It seems that the underwater slopes of many seamounts, ridges, and islands are covered with a layer of ferromanganese that's extraordinarily rich in cobalt—five times as rich as manganodules—and rich in other rare minerals as well."

"Including scandium, I bet," Rick said.

"Give that man five silver dollars," the captain said. "Best of all, the thickest deposits are found only six or seven thousand feet down. That's still not a duck pond, but it's a helluva lot closer to the surface than twenty thousand feet. *And* some of the richest concentrations fall within the exclusive economic zone, or EEZ, of the United States. So we can go after it without setting off all kinds of international hoopla. That's why *Champion* was recommissioned late last year. She's now on station off Guam."

"I had a hunch that Guam was going to come into this story sooner or later," Rick said. "But I still don't see where *I* come into it. Or you either, for that matter."

"Simple. They need us," the captain replied. *"Champion* has been fitted with a new version of that unmanned, remotely controlled, underwater machine the guys at Scripps and Woods Hole developed a couple of years ago. With a little Navy help, I might add. What it's supposed to do is scan the ocean floor, find the deposits of crust, then scrape and vacuum them up. It worked well in testing, they tell me. But now it's developed some mysterious glitches at depth. Whenever they bring it back on board *Champion,* all the systems check out fine. But below about 1000 fathoms the thing goes ape on them. They might as well be sending down an old clapped-out Volkswagen, for all the good it's doing. And the only way to identify the problem is for someone to go down there and watch it working ... or not working. But taking a technician a mile down to the bottom of the Pacific is a tall order. Or it would be, if it weren't for us."

Rick didn't try to hide the excitement in his voice as he asked, "Does this mean I get a chance to get back in the *Albatross* again?"

"Well now," Captain Ward said, suddenly cautious, "that depends. How's that arm of yours these days?"

Two years before, just as he was on the point of finishing the Navy's Top Gun course for advanced fighter-weapons training, Rick had run his motorcycle off the road and into a tree. His broken arm had healed, but it had left him with what the doctors called a cross-union, a bump where the break in one of the bones in his forearm had healed, that drastically cut down on the rotation ability of his wrist. That had been the end of his career as a fighter jock.

Two Navy surgeons had told him the damage couldn't be repaired. A third, Dr. Sam Deane, thought an operation might help, but he doubted whether Rick would have the discipline to follow through with the necessary therapy afterward. It turned out that the "Sam" in "Sam Deane" was short for "Samantha." When she met Rick, while he was going through the SEAL training course at Coronado, California, she changed her mind—about the operation, and about a lot of other things concerning Rick as well.

Rick held his elbow pressed against his side and slowly rotated his fist. He was pretty sure that Captain Ward couldn't sense the jabbing pain the motion caused him. The last couple of months had given him a lot of practice at hiding it.

"Better than it was," he said, in a level voice. "Not quite back to normal yet, but I'm getting improvement every week."

"Well, that's good, Ricky," the captain said. "Did Sam do the operation herself?"

Rick shook his head. "In the end, she decided we knew each other too well for her to operate on me," he replied. "But she chose the surgeon, briefed him, and watched over his shoulder the whole time he was working on me. He wasn't too thrilled, but it obviously did the trick."

"So now you're fit for active duty," Captain Ward continued. *"Very* active duty."

"The Navy thinks so. For what it's worth, so do I."

"That's good enough for me. Okay then—*Berkone* sailed for Guam two weeks ago, with the *Steel Albatross* Mark II aboard. Officially, she's under charter to an outfit called SeaVenture, Inc. That's the corporation that took over and reactivated *Glomar Champion*. We'll both be on the SeaVenture roster as consultants. Your orders should be waiting for you on Guam."

"This isn't a Navy operation?" Rick demanded. "Why not? I know they held back from financing *Albatross* in the first place, but I was sure that after she'd done such a great job of proving herself they'd see reason and take the project over."

"That's what I thought too," Captain Ward said bitterly. "But with all the cuts in military spending, the last thing anyone in BuShips wants to hear about is another project of any kind, no matter how important or how cheap. Thank God there are still one or two agencies in Washington that can see farther than the tips of their noses."

Rick studied the captain's face. He knew that Ward, like most line officers of the regular Navy, was deeply wary of getting involved with the shadowy world of espionage. He also knew that sometimes the spooks were the only ones with enough foresight, or money, to get behind any idea the least bit out of the ordinary.

Captain Ward apparently read Rick's thoughts. "I know, I know. I don't like it any better than you do. But the country needs the scandium, and the people who are going after it need us. And it'll give us a chance to field test the improvements I've made on the *Steel Albatross*. It's no skin off our butts if they just want to use her as a glorified taxi."

The captain pushed his chair back and stood up. "You're probably feeling a little jet lagged," he said. "Better get some rest. We take off for Guam at 0800 tomorrow."

"I'm booked on an afternoon flight," Rick said as he got to his feet.

"You mean you *were*," his godfather said. "I changed it. We'll meet for breakfast at 0630."

Rick had learned one or two things at Annapolis before he set a new class record for demerits and bilged out on disciplinary grounds. There was only one acceptable response when a senior officer—even a retired senior officer—made a statement like that. He snapped to attention and said, "Aye, aye, sir."

"Get your butt out of here," Captain Ward barked. But Rick saw the glint of amusement in his eye.

CHAPTER 2

Bᴀᴄᴋ ɪɴ ʜɪs ʀᴏᴏᴍ, Rɪᴄᴋ ᴋɪᴄᴋᴇᴅ ᴏꜰꜰ ʜɪs sʜᴏᴇs ᴀɴᴅ ʟᴀʏ down. As he stared at the ceiling, his hands clasped behind his head, he could feel the debate beginning again. The same debate that had been raging in his mind since even before the operation on his arm. What future now for Tallman, Richard B., LCDR, USN?

Should he request a return to flight status? He had good reason to think that the request would be granted. Sam— Dr. Samantha Deane, MC, USN—had assured him that his arm would pass the medical exam. She ought to know. Part of her job, as one of the Navy's orthopedic specialists, was screening applicants for strenuous duty. And once he was back on flight status, he could ask to be assigned to fighter planes again. He could even go back to finish the Top Gun course at Miramar. They wouldn't turn him down, he was sure of that. Before that damned motorcycle crash had pulled his plug he had been a contender for the top scoring trophy.

As always, the thought of once more being in control of an F-14 Tomcat filled him with a longing that he could hardly bear. He had dreamt of being a fighter pilot ever since he was five years old. His mother still kept the rubber-band-powered model of a World War II–vintage Grumman

Hellcat he had painstakingly built, from balsa and tissue paper, when he was nine. A plastic model, the kind his friends were assembling, would have been easier to put together, but it wouldn't have flown, and that was the point.

Much later, after many twists and turns, Rick had actually made it to flight school, carrier duty, and finally Top Gun. Then, in a single blink of an eye, it had all been taken away. Now he had a chance to win it back. How could he hesitate, even for a moment?

But ... At a point when his future in the Navy looked about as promising as a Red Sox victory in the World Series, he had been volunteered—a better word was "shanghaied"—into the Sea Air Land Team training course at the Navy's Special Warfare Center. The SEALs had the reputation of being the toughest, meanest, dirtiest, and most dangerous guys in the whole damn Navy, and the training course that produced them was even worse. Of the picked recruits who entered it, barely one in three graduated. And Rick had had a harder time than most, after the senior instructor, Lieutenant K. W. "Kiwi" Kraus, had decided that he had a personal mission to run Rick out of the program.

Rick had stuck it out, mostly through sheer cussedness. He had even begun to get a grim pleasure from taking everything Kraus and his fellow instructors could dish out. Then a group of renegade hard-liners in the Kremlin had set in motion a plot that threatened the safety of the United States and the entire world. The job of sinking the scheme had fallen to Rick, Kiwi Kraus, and the *Steel Albatross.* They had succeeded, but by the time Rick had recovered from the ordeal, his classmates had already finished their training and pinned the pistol-and-trident insignia of the SEALs on their uniforms.

Rick had run into Kiwi in the lobby of the Del Coronado a couple of months later, just before the surgery on his arm. "Hey theah, you ol' son of a hawah!" Kiwi had bellowed, in that Down East accent that had always sounded phony to Rick. "I was expectin' to see your name in ouah next class. You turn lazy on us or what?"

A woman in her forties, with perfectly styled blond hair

and perfectly styled resort clothes that had probably come from Bergdorf's, had turned and given them an icy stare. She had seemed deeply offended by the way they were lowering the tone of the place. Rick had given her a wink and turned back to Kiwi.

"They're going to do some work on my busted wing," he had explained, tapping his arm.

"The hell you say," Kiwi had said, grinning. "I didn't see it keeping you from doin' a whole lot. You ask me, you just wanted an excuse to get away from us lowlifes in the Teams. But get this, mister, and get it good. We already spent a shitload of Uncle's bucks on your training, and we expect you to finish it, soonest."

He had reached over and tapped the Naval Aviator's wings on Rick's uniform shirt. "I'm not saying a word against flyboys, you understand," he had continued. "But you're just this far away from winning the right to wear a badge that means a helluva lot more than that one. You don't want to be turning down that chance, now do you?"

"I really don't know," Rick had confessed. "I have to see how the operation turns out. And then . . ."

"And then you'll come back and finish the program," Kiwi had said. "And I swear I'll push you even harder than last time."

"Sure, you do that," Rick had replied. "It'll do you just about as much good as last time too. They don't call me Ironman for nothing."

"They don't call you Ironman at all, boy!" Kiwi had thrown a mock punch at Rick's shoulder that Rick easily blocked.

As they were saying goodbye, the SEAL instructor had added, "Just remember, Tallman. You come back to finish the program, you'll be dealing with me. But you *don't* come back and finish, you shawnuff gonna be dealing real heavy with me!"

So there it was, Rick thought, sitting up on the bed and looking out at the beach. Top Gun or SEALs? Forty thousand feet above sea level, or a few hundred below? Mach three, or only as fast as his fins would push him? He didn't feel any closer to an answer than he had months before. But he now knew that the pride he felt at being accepted by the men who were SEALs, the unmet challenge of completing the Team training and being counted as a member of that elite group, would count for a hell of a lot when it came time to choose. Maybe this mission of Will Ward's was a Godsend. At least it would let him put off his decision a little while longer. And at best, he might come out of it with a clearer idea of what he should do.

That might take care of his professional future, but what about the personal side? What did he really feel about that beautiful, wonderful lady named Samantha? Attraction, yes, an abiding, weird, and powerful attraction. And a deep affection that included her six-year-old son, Billy, as well.

Could he really be in love with Sam? Did she love him? And even if the answer to both questions was Yes, what then? Was he really ready to marry and settle down, to accept responsibility for a wife and child in one fell swoop? What if there was a better choice out there somewhere, maybe just around the corner, some wonderful person he hadn't yet met? How the hell was a man supposed to know these things for sure?

It was too much to deal with. Put it aside and live for today. Tomorrow would take care of itself.

Snapping back to reality, he glanced at his watch: five-fifteen. Plenty of time to do a little shopping before the stores closed. He needed a present for his mother, and one for Sam, and something very special for little Billy. Billy had never known his dad, a Navy pilot killed in a training accident, and for now Rick was the closest thing he had to an uncle. Rick hadn't exactly asked for the role, but now that it was his, he meant to live up to it.

The crowd on Waikiki was beginning to thin out as the dinner hour drew near. Rick strolled along the sand, pausing for a moment to admire the giant orchid mosaic on the bottom of the beachside pool of the Halekulani. When he reached the Royal Hawaiian, dwarfed by its more recent neighbors but still as dignified as ever, he turned in and walked through the palm-shaded gardens toward the shopping center on the other side.

Old Navy men of his father's generation, guys who had done tours of duty in the Pacific Theater during World War II, still talked about their shore leaves in Honolulu, when the "Pink Palace of the Pacific" served as a Navy billet. "Those were the days," they would say, shaking their heads. "A dollar a night for a room right on the beach, and beautiful girls who saw cheering up lonely servicemen as their patriotic duty!"

Rick was halfway across the garden when he thought he heard a muffled cry. It seemed to come from behind a row of tall bushes covered with fragrant pink and white flowers. He ran along the walk until he found an opening in the bushes, then pushed his way through and looked around. About fifty feet away, four burly Japanese in jeans and T-shirts were struggling with a tall, slim woman. One of them was holding her by the elbows, and a second had his hand clamped over her mouth. As Rick sprinted toward them, the second man let out a loud hiss and jerked his bleeding hand away from the woman's teeth. The woman opened her mouth to scream, but another of her attackers quickly thrust a wadded-up cloth in her mouth.

The fourth member of the gang must have heard Rick coming. He whirled around and dropped into a stance with his left leg forward, the toes just touching the ground, and his bent right leg back. Rick realized instantly that he was going to need his knowledge of full-contact karate for this little encounter. Silently blessing the name of Sergeant Shigeo Matsunaga, USMC, who had spent so much time teaching Rick his skills in unarmed combat, he bore down on his opponent, feinted a left jab to the head, and followed it immediately with a hook-kick to the ribs. The blow connected, but not with enough force to end the fight. The guy rolled with it and came back with a *mawashi-geri*, or roundhouse kick, aimed at Rick's neck. Rick blocked it with his left forearm, then launched a blunt-lance blow at the point just below his opponent's breastbone.

"Ouf!" Clutching his chest, the guy sat down hard. Rick

had no time to gloat, however. From the corner of his eye, he saw a handsword chop coming at his neck. Rick dropped and rolled, dodged a footsword sidekick, and drove the point of his elbow into his attacker's crotch as he sprang to his feet. The guy staggered backward, cupping his groin with both hands, but after his initial gasp he didn't make a sound.

Rick grabbed a quick deep breath and looked around. Another of the gang, the one with the bleeding left hand, was moving warily toward Rick, circling to his left as he came. The almost imperceptible tensing of the man's lower body gave Rick the split-second warning he needed to block a powerful side jump-kick. He moved in, managed to grasp the front of his attacker's shirt, and used the man's own momentum, Aikido-style, to send him sailing across the narrow clearing.

At that point Rick's luck ran out. Strong hands grabbed him from behind and held him. He tried a backward jab to the solar plexus with the point of his elbow, but the other guy knew that one. Another of the gang, the one who had gotten an elbow in the family jewels, charged in, arm held high, ready to strike. He obviously intended to demonstrate *Tameshiwara,* using Rick's neck for the more usual stack of boards or bricks. Rick pretended to cower away, then at the crucial moment he launched a murderous shin-kick at the man's crotch. Once burnt, twice shy: In his haste to avoid the kick, the guy tripped over his own feet and cannoned into the path of one of his partners, who was running over to help out.

The guy holding Rick hadn't loosened his grip one bit. Rick tried to hook his captor's ankle while throwing his own weight backward, but the guy knew that one too. In response, he dug his chin deep into Rick's neck, below and behind his left ear. Rick's left arm went numb.

"Aiee!"

At the stifled cry, Rick whipped his head around. The woman at the center of the ruckus had just brought the Cuban heel of her right sandal down, very hard, on her captor's toes. For one instant he loosened his hold on her right arm. In that one instant, her hand dived into her purse and came out holding a small, shiny automatic. As another of the gang made a dash in her direction, she aimed it at him and pulled the trigger.

The little gun made less noise than a champagne cork, but it had a big effect. The guy holding Rick spoke urgently in Japanese. A moment later the whole gang was running toward the street. Rick was glad to see that one of them was limping.

"Hey, what's going on?" someone yelled from the other side of the line of bushes. "That sounded like a shot. Somebody call the cops!"

Rick turned. The young woman was running over to him. She stopped two feet away, giving him a moment to notice her long, pale blond hair and the sky-blue eyes that seemed too large for her face.

"You must help me," she said quickly, in a low, slightly accented voice. "Please, take this! Hide it!"

She thrust the pistol in his direction. Her forefinger was still inside the trigger guard, and the chromed barrel was pointed straight at Rick's belly button, or even just a tad south of there.

"Sure," Rick said. He spoke as if he were trying to calm a spooked horse. He reached over and grasped the receiver of the automatic, shifted its aim toward the ground, and gently took it from the woman's hand. "Er, why?" he added, holding back a relieved sigh.

"I am not American," the woman replied. "If it is discovered that I was armed, they will bar me from the country. That would ruin me."

A babble of voices was drawing nearer. Rick heard someone with a Midwestern accent saying, "In there, Officer. I'm sure it was a gunshot. I'm from Chicago, I should know."

"Everything's all right," Rick called out. He flipped the safety on and tucked the tiny automatic into his waistband. The tails of his aloha shirt would hide it. Then he leaned over and dusted off his slacks. If anyone patted him down, he was in big trouble. Still, he never could resist a lady in distress—especially if she was beautiful as well.

"You in there, this is the police. Come out with your hands up," an authoritative voice said. "And do it slowly."

Rick led his companion toward the break in the hedge. On the other side, they found two uniformed police officers, .38s at the ready, flanking the opening. A growing crowd of gawkers stood a cautious distance down the path.

"Okay, what's the story, fella?" one of the officers demanded.

"I'm a naval officer," Rick said. "I was crossing the gardens when I heard this young lady call for help. Some men were attacking her. When I showed up, they ran away."

"That is right," his companion said breathlessly. "They tried to take my purse. I was very frightened. But this gentleman rescued me."

The second police officer, a broad-shouldered guy with thick black hair and strong Polynesian features, stepped forward. "You folks have some ID?" he asked. He kept his pistol at the ready while Rick reached slowly into his hip pocket and produced his wallet. He took Rick's identification card with his left hand, glanced at it, and added, "Okay, thanks, Commander. Are you at the Hale Koa?"

"That's right."

"And you, Ms. . . . ." He took her passport and flipped it open with one hand. "Ms. Yussupov? Where are you staying?"

"At the New Otani Kaimana Beach," she said. She put her fingertips to her forehead, in a gesture that looked so phony that it might have been real. "Please, sir, may I go? I am very upset by what has happened. I want to go back to my hotel and rest."

The policeman holstered his revolver and exchanged a look with his partner. "Sorry, ma'am, but we'll have to ask you a few questions first. Can you tell us anything about the men who attacked you? What they looked like? What they said to you? Anything else?"

She shifted her hand to the base of her neck and said, "No, nothing. Nothing at all. I was much too frightened to notice. They were three or four, that is all I know."

The other policeman leaned forward. *"Haole? Pake? Kanaka?"* he asked.

"I don't understand."

"He's asking if they were Caucasian, Chinese, or Hawaiian," Rick said.

"Not Caucasian, I think," the young woman said. "But as to the rest, I cannot say."

"Do you think you would recognize them again?"

"No, I am sure not. I have no recollection of their faces."

"How about you, sir?" the policeman continued, turning to Rick. "Did you get a good look at them?"

Rick shrugged. "I'm sorry. They turned and ran when I came on the scene. All I can tell you is that they had black hair and were wearing T-shirts and jeans."

"Like half the boys on Kalakaua Avenue," the policeman said in disgust. He turned a suspicious look on Rick, then on the young woman.

His partner hastily said, "It's too bad this happened, Ms."—he took another glance at the passport, still in his hand—"Ms. Yussupov. I hope you won't let it spoil your vacation in Hawaii. Are you here for much longer?"

"A few days," she replied.

"And you, Commander Tallman?"

"Just a one-night stopover, I'm afraid," Rick said.

"Oh? Too bad. You should plan to stay longer next time. By the way, you two didn't happen to know each other before this incident, did you?"

Rick glanced over at the young woman. She was a stunner, all right. "I wish I could say Yes," he replied, grinning. "But now that we've met, would you like me to take you back to your hotel?"

"Oh yes, please," she said, grasping his arm. "If you're sure you don't mind."

Rick met the policeman's amused glance. "That's okay, isn't it, Officer?" he asked.

"Well, unless Ms. Yussupov wants to file a complaint. . . ."

"Oh no, please! All I want is to forget this ever happened!"

"In that case . . . have a nice evening, Commander." He

didn't actually wink at Rick, but he looked as if he wanted to. As he handed back her passport, he added, "And once more, ma'am, we apologize for what happened this evening. There's a few bad apples in any barrel."

"It could have happened anywhere in the world," she replied. "Thank you for your help."

She and Rick started up the path toward the avenue. He was sure he could feel the gaze of the two policemen drilling into his back and the sharp edges of the .25-caliber automatic drilling into his stomach. What kind of mess had he gotten himself into *this* time?

At the avenue, they turned right, in the direction of Diamond Head. The sidewalk was packed with tourists. Underfoot, earth-tone tiles formed patterns that looked like Polynesian tapa cloth. As they passed the entrance to the International Market Place, with its huge, spreading banyan tree and its little stalls selling local crafts and souvenirs, Rick remembered that he was supposed to be shopping for presents. That could wait, he thought, pushing the image of a reproachful Billy and an even more reproachful Sam out of his mind. He would find plenty of gift shops and curio dealers on Guam after all.

His companion cleared her throat and said, "I have not yet thanked you for helping me, Commander. It was a very gallant act on your part. And you fought magnificently."

Rick felt his cheeks get warm with embarrassment. He felt a mad impulse to say "Aw, shucks, ma'am, 'tweren't nothin'," in his best Jimmy Stewart accent. He fought back the temptation and said instead, "I'm glad I could be of help, Ms.—"

"My name is Natalie," she replied. "Natalie Yussupov."

"And I'm Rick Tallman. Yussupov ... is that a Russian name?"

"Originally, yes. But I am not Russian. I am a French citizen. Mr. Tallman—"

"Rick."

"Rick. Will you think that I am very forward if I invite you to be my guest at dinner this evening? As a way of thanking you for your gallant intervention?"

Rick glanced over at her. A pink hue was spreading across her high, strong cheeks. Her eyes were directed downward, toward the sidewalk. For the first time, he noticed her long, delicate lashes. They seemed to belong to a different face than her full red lips. But both held out their own brand of promise.

"Thanks," he said simply. "I'd like that."

CHAPTER 3

RICK LEFT NATALIE ON THE SIDEWALK AND STEPPED OUT into the avenue to flag down a taxi. Natalie's hotel was five minutes away, at the far end of Waikiki, practically in the shadow of Diamond Head. As they walked into the open and airy lobby, Rick felt himself start to relax. The place seemed more informal, more laid back, than the huge, high-rise hotels nearer the center of town.

"Will you excuse me for a few moments?" Natalie asked in a low voice. "I must return to my room, to shower and change. After what happened, I feel soiled. It is as if the filthy hands of those terrible men are still touching me."

"Oh, sure," Rick replied. "No problem. And maybe, as long as you're going upstairs, you'd like to take your property with you. I'd just as soon not have it on me." He lightly touched his waistband.

"I am sorry, I didn't think," she said. She glanced both ways. So did Rick. No one was paying them the slightest attention. Suddenly she took a step closer and pressed herself against him. "Please, hold me," she breathed into his ear. "Tightly."

He didn't need to be asked twice. As he wrapped his arms around her, he felt a hand snake under the front of his shirt. The unexpectedly intimate touch on his bare skin made his

31

stomach muscles ripple wildly. A moment later the hand withdrew, taking the tiny automatic with it.

Rick gave Natalie an admiring glance. He had to work hard not to burst out laughing. Anyone in the hotel lobby who had noticed their embrace might have gotten a lot of ideas about what they were up to but would certainly never have suspected that they were exchanging a pistol.

"I will return very soon," Natalie said, taking a step back and holding her purse closed with both hands.

"I'll be out on the beach," Rick replied. "It's too nice to stay indoors."

Nice for more than one reason, he thought as he strolled out onto the sand and sat down near the base of a coconut palm. Late as it was, there were still lots of sunbathers out. Both males and females were showing off their painstakingly perfect figures and equally perfect tans, in bathing suits that were exactly the minimum allowed by law and custom. Wasn't this the stretch of Waikiki that locals called Dig Me Beach? He could see why.

Fifty yards out, just beyond the first line of breakers, three windsurfers zipped by. Their colorful close-hauled sails were silhouetted against the evening sky. They made a perfect picture—so perfect that Rick cynically wondered if they were employed by the State Tourist Office, or maybe by Kodak, to cruise up and down along Waikiki Beach for the *malahines'* cameras.

Was it time to start thinking about what he had gotten himself into? Or could he put that off until the morning? Natalie was young, beautiful, and sympathetic, and her distress had been real. Her attackers had been mean, ugly, and very aggressive. It had been easy to choose sides.

But now what? What should he do with this intriguing, exotic beauty who had come into his life? Just walk away? Fat chance!

On the other hand, young and beautiful damsels in distress didn't usually carry handguns in their purses. That .25-caliber Beretta she packed might look and sound like a popgun, but at short range it could make some pretty impressive holes in you. He could think of a lot of questions to ask her. But did he want to start down the path of asking them? Maybe not. Not yet, anyway.

From close behind him a voice said, "You are a brave and foolish man, Lieutenant."

He looked around, then scrambled to his feet. Natalie had changed into a pale yellow dress that hugged her figure in all the right places and revealed the shape of the firm nipples on her high, ample, and well-formed breasts. A yellow and green *pareu*, the length of cloth that Hawaiians used for everything from a stole to a beachrobe, was tied casually around her shoulders, and she had tucked a yellow orchid behind one ear. She looked as if she could have stepped out of an old movie about the South Seas.

"Hey, you look terrific," Rick said. "But why do you say I'm brave and foolish? Because I took you up on your invitation?"

She gave him a teasing look. "One of the most important rules to learn in this part of the world is never to sit under a coconut palm. One gust of wind, and *boom!* A coconut descends, very fast, and you are there beneath it. I once knew someone in Papeete who was almost paralyzed in that way."

"Thanks, I'll remember," Rick said. He couldn't help looking upward as he followed her away from the tree. A dozen or more coconuts hung there, in three groups. Nature's cluster bombs.

Natalie rested her left hand lightly on his arm. He glanced down and noticed that she wore a large gold sealring on her index finger. It was deeply engraved with what looked like a coat of arms. Of course, that didn't necessarily mean she was an aristocrat. During Rick's junior year at Princeton, before he'd dropped out to go to flight school, a guy in his dorm had tried to talk him into buying a gold class ring with the college seal. It had looked at least as impressive as Natalie's. The only way Rick had managed to get rid of him was by ordering a beer jacket with his name and class numeral painted on the back.

"I reserved a table for us at the Hau Tree Lanai, here at

the hotel," Natalie said. "I think it has the most beautiful setting in Waikiki, and the food is not at all bad."

The restaurant was outdoors, right at the edge of the beach, in the shelter of a grove of trees—*not* coconut palms. The pastel tablecloths sparkled with china, crystal, and silver. The maitre d', in black slacks and a blue and green aloha shirt, hurried over to them.

"Good evening, Countess," he said. He bowed slightly, then gave Rick a curious glance. "It's nice to have you with us again. Your table's ready."

He led them to a table set a little apart from the others. A hibiscus bush gave it a feeling of privacy, without blocking the magnificent view of Diamond Head in one direction and the sweep of the bay in the other.

Rick accepted a menu from the host and waited for him to leave. Then he said, "Countess? I'm impressed."

Natalie blushed. "Once, long ago, my family had a certain standing in Russia," she said. "That was before the Revolution, of course."

"Then you really are a countess?"

"Well ... yes, if you like. But truly, it means nothing, only that I sometimes get a better table in a restaurant or a nicer room in a hotel."

"It sounds as if you travel a lot," Rick said.

Before she could reply, a waiter interrupted with a plate of bite-size hot appetizers and two tall chilled glasses with slices of fruit on top.

"I hope you will not mind that I ordered for both of us," Natalie said. "They make a very good mai tai here."

Rick would have preferred something less sticky-sweet, but he smiled and lifted his glass. "I'll drink to that," he said, and took a sip. She was right, it *was* good—unusually tart, with a strong flavor of rum.

"Have you looked at the menu?" she continued, setting down her glass. "The *mahimahi,* grilled over a fire of kiawe wood, is very fine. And to start, perhaps *opakapaka* with sliced mango."

"Sure," Rick said cheerfully. "Though if you ask me,

tapaka-tapaka sounds more like the engine on a lawn mower than something you'd want for dinner."

"It is a kind of fish," she explained. She didn't seem to have caught his joke. "And *mahimahi* is a fish also, a fish called a dolphin. When I first heard that I was very upset. I thought they meant the mammal dolphin, that very beautiful, very intelligent creature that is not a fish at all but a creature like us. But no, it is only a fish that bears the same name."

Rick had a soft spot in his heart for dolphins and porpoises. As a boy in the waters off Florida, he had sometimes played games of tag with them. He had often thought of how the landlubbers, who so admired the feline grace of their house cats, would be blown away by the surpassing grace of the porpoise—and of the sea lion, for that matter—in the water.

"I'm glad to hear that," he said, coming back from his underwater reveries. "I'd hate to think I was eating one of Flipper's cousins."

"Yes. Then you are in accord? Good. And with dinner, they have a Macon-Lugny that will stand up well to grilled fish. Unless you think it is your patriotic duty to drink a wine from California."

Clearly, Natalie was used to having things her own way, Rick thought. Not that he was going to let that get to him. His own mother was the same. After fighting back blindly for most of his teenage years, he had learned to accept whichever of her plans he could live with and pretend not to hear the others.

"No, that sounds great." He sat back and took another sip of his mai tai while she gave the waiter their order. Once they were alone again, he said, "You seem to know Hawaii pretty well. This can't be your first visit."

"Oh no, I am often here, on business."

"Pretty long trip from France," Rick observed. "Is there a direct flight, or do you have to come by way of the States?"

Instead of meeting his eyes, she seemed to look over his left shoulder. "I don't know," she said. "I have not been back to France since I finished university. I live in Tokyo now. I own an art gallery there."

Rick shook his head. "Really? How does a French citizen who's also a Russian countess end up in Tokyo?" he asked.

"That is a long story. My grandmother was French, you see. But when she was just a girl, she lived in Peking. Her father was with the French legation. There she met my grandfather, a dashing young cavalry officer who had led his regiment of Cossacks against the Reds during the Civil War in Russia, then gone into exile in China after the Red victory. They fell in love and married. Later they moved to Hanoi, in what was then French Indochina. My father was born there."

"Let me see if I'm still with you," Rick said, smiling. "Your father was half-French and half-Russian and born in Indochina. How about your mother?"

"She is all French and born in Algeria," Natalie said. "My father met her there when he was doing his military service. I told you it is a long story. And complicated as well. Perhaps I should wait," she added, glancing around. "I think this is our *opakapaka*. I hope you do not find that it tastes like grass clippings."

Son of a gun, Rick thought. So she *had* heard his joke about a lawn mower, but she'd kept a poker face. This lady had some unexplored depths!

The sommelier brought over a shiny urn on a stand. The neck of a bottle, wrapped in a white napkin, stuck up out of the crushed ice. He lifted the bottle out just enough for Natalie to scan the label. She nodded, then watched as he cut the foil and pulled the cork. Rick watched her. Her features and expressions sent such conflicting messages that they might have been borrowed from different people. Was she direct or devious? Timid or forward? Passionate or coolly manipulative? Or all of the above? He couldn't tell. But whatever her character, she was simply gorgeous. Maybe he should let it go at that.

Natalie sniffed the cork, took a sip of the wine, then nodded again. The waiter filled their glasses halfway with a pale gold liquid that captured a hint of rose from the setting sun. Rick lifted his glass and said, "Here's looking at you, kid."

Natalie smiled and touched her glass to his. "Here's looking at *you*," she said softly. As she met his eyes, he caught his breath. It was like looking into an endless pool of blue water, or looking up at the sky from the bottom of the sea. He even imagined a faint flicker of stars beyond the blue.

She took a small bite of her *opakapaka*. Rick looked down at his plate. The light, delicate slices of fish were arranged in the center, decorated with mango slices so thin that he could see through them. A flaky puff pastry that looked a little like a Middle Eastern dessert sat to one side. He left it there and took a bite of fish. He liked it.

After another sip of wine, he said, "What about you? Were you born in Algeria too? Or in France?"

"Neither. I was born in Phnom Penh."

"Cambodia?" Rick whistled softly. "When was this? The '60s? That wasn't one of the more peaceful corners of the world!"

"No. But after my father died, we went to live with my Uncle Germain on his cattle ranch near Nouméa, in New Caledonia. My mother lives there still."

"Is that where you grew up, New Caledonia? I've never been there. Did you like it?"

Natalie looked off into the distance. "Very much," she said softly. "The climate is like the best of the Côte d'Azur, and the countryside is full of drama. In my dreams I still see the cliffs at the foot of Mount Humboldt, plunging down to the sea. And the Isle of Pines, just south of Grande Terre, must be one of the most beautiful spots on earth. But it is the same story all over again, like Indochina, like Algeria. The Kanaks, who lived there before the French came, a hundred fifty years ago, call us foreigners and say they will make us leave. Men like my uncle declare that they have run for the last time, that they will die first. It will end in blood, as it always does. That is why I left."

Rick frowned. "Those men who attacked you today," he said. "Do you think they had something to do with these people you're talking about in New Caledonia?"

Natalie looked so startled that Rick wondered if she had forgotten the attack in the Royal Hawaiian gardens. "Why—" she stammered. "No. No, not at all. It is not possible."

"Do you have any idea who they were then?"

"No, of course not. But I have had nothing to do with la Nouvelle Caledonie since I left to go to university in France. I have been back once or twice, to visit my family, but that is all."

"Those guys looked and sounded like Japanese to me," Rick observed. Without seeming to, he watched her face closely.

"Oh?" she said, trying to look completely uninterested. "You may be right, I cannot say." She turned her head and signaled a waiter to remove the plates from the first course.

Rick waited until the waiter had left to say, "If your gallery's in Tokyo, most of your dealings must be with Japanese. Can you think of anyone who's mad enough over anything to send a gang of hoods after you?"

"My clients are people of wealth and culture, not gangsters," she said with a tinkly, unconvincing laugh. "What you are suggesting is quite impossible. You have been watching too much bad TV."

"Then who do *you* think those hoods were?" Rick demanded bluntly.

Natalie shrugged, as if the question didn't concern her. "Local criminals, perhaps," she said. "Or . . ."

"Or?"

"In my business, I often have to deal in large sums of cash."

"Really? Why?"

"The recordkeeping is much easier," she said blandly. "And some of my clients may prefer to carry an easily transported work of art—a seventeenth-century ivory *netsuke,* for example—rather than a heavy suitcase full of paper money."

"And people with suitcases full of cash sometimes get the wrong kind of attention from customs agents and police," Rick pointed out. "Not to mention holdup men."

"That may be, but it is no concern of mine. I do not work for the tax authorities. Am I shocking you? I apologize, but this is the world. Perhaps the fact that I sometimes carry much cash became known to the wrong people. I will be sure to take more care from now on."

"Once the word gets around that you're an Annie Oakley, junior grade, maybe they'll leave you alone."

She looked at him with bafflement.

"Annie Oakley was an old-time rodeo star," Rick explained. "A sharpshooter."

Natalie's face turned bright red. "You must have a very strange impression of me," she said. "I do not carry that . . . that object as a rule. I happened on it, among some bric-a-brac I had bought, and put it in my purse without thinking."

Sure, thought Rick. And you managed to draw, flick off the safety, and fire without thinking, too. Uh-huh.

The waiter brought their main course and refilled their wineglasses, then withdrew.

"But we have talked much, much too much, about me," Natalie said, hurriedly bridging Rick's silence. "I want to know all about you. I know you are very brave and very gallant, and I heard you tell the police that you are a naval officer and you are leaving Honolulu tomorrow. Is the ship you are serving on about to sail?"

"Not exactly," Rick replied. He smiled to himself at the thought of using the word "ship" to describe the *Steel Albatross*, which was smaller than the average stretch limo. "I'm a Navy diver. I'm flying to Guam tomorrow, to take part in a research project nearby."

"Really? That is fascinating. Those waters are full of sunken ships from every period of history. The most wonderful artifacts turn up now and then. If you should happen on any, I hope you will keep my gallery in mind." She found a business card in her purse and wrote a number on the back, then handed it to him. "This is the address and number of the gallery, and this is my personal number."

As he tucked the card in his shirt pocket, Rick thought of saying that the ethics of taking souvenirs from submerged wrecks was the subject of a lot of controversy. In many places it was strictly illegal. But what was the point of telling her that? She probably knew it as well as he did. And he suspected she would go on running her business exactly the way she wanted to, whatever he said. Why spoil their dinner with a sermon? He wasn't her chaplain.

Instead he asked, "Is that what you mostly deal in? Antiques?"

"More or less," she replied. "Over the last hundred years, countless antiquities and works of art have left Japan. Some were bought by foreign visitors, some were taken abroad and abandoned by Japanese soldiers, and some were 'liberated' by those who occupied Japan after 1945. I specialize in finding such objects and returning them to their place of origin."

"It sounds like interesting work," Rick commented. "You must have to be more of a detective than an art dealer."

She smiled, and her face, which had been still and withdrawn while she was telling her family's history, lit up. "Anyone who deals in art must have a little of the detective," she said. "How long will you be on Guam?"

"Questioning a suspect?" he said with a laugh. "The answer is, I don't have any idea. Why?"

"I pass through Guam from time to time, and it would be pleasant to think that I might call on a new friend the next time I am there." She lifted her fork and added, "I apologize, I am keeping us from this delicious meal."

By the time they'd finished their dessert of chocolate pâté with crushed macadamia nuts, a gibbous moon was rising, just to the right of Diamond Head. Its light paved a gleaming highway across the swells of the bay.

"What do you say to a walk along the beach?" asked Rick as he pushed his chair back and got to his feet.

"Thank you," Natalie said with a faint, beguiling smile.

Rick picked up the *pareu* from the back of her chair and held it for her. As she pulled it around her, his hands rested on her shoulders. She leaned back against him for just a moment, then straightened up and looked around.

"The beach and the moonlight are waiting," she said, meeting his eyes. "And if you are interested in Japanese art, perhaps you would like to come to my room after our walk. I have located some very unusual scroll paintings on this visit, the sort that are rarely seen outside of private collections and almost never put on public exhibit. You will understand why when you see them."

Something in her expression told Rick exactly what sort of Japanese scroll painting she was talking about. He felt the inside of his mouth turn dry and his breath come a little faster. As they started toward the beach, he slipped his arm around her waist. She moved closer, until he could feel the warmth of her body through his thin shirt.

"I can hardly wait," he said.

CHAPTER 4

Tom Fitzhugh shifted his weight from one side of his butt to the other. The move didn't help. The cotton pad under him wasn't much thicker than his jeans. Not only was his ass falling asleep, now his left calf was threatening to cramp. All the others in the room looked as if they were used to sitting cross-legged or hunkering on their heels. He definitely wasn't.

There was another reason he felt uncomfortable. His was one of only three white faces in the room. The others were mostly Japanese, with a sprinkling of native Guamanians, or Chamorros. Tom had been wandering the Western Pacific for six months now, living the life of a scuba bum. He had often found himself the only white in a cafe or outdoor market or on a beach. It had never bothered him before, and it had never seemed to bother anyone else either.

Here it was different. There was an intensity in the room that he didn't understand but couldn't ignore. Why wasn't anyone chatting with his neighbor or looking around at the others? Everyone seemed wrapped up in his own thoughts. But what were they all thinking about? He had no idea. He felt as awkward and out of place as a wetsuited diver at a Wild West show.

He glanced over and caught the eye of Kazuo Takauji,

who was sitting next to him. Kazuo gave him a faint smile, then turned his face forward again.

Tom had first met Kazuo only two days before, at Apra Harbor. Or, more exactly, thirty feet down in Apra Harbor. He'd been on his way down his descending line to explore the wreckage of the *Cormoran,* a German cruiser scuttled during World War I, when Kazuo swept by him on the way up, moving with the lazy grace of a skilled diver. Later, on the dock, Tom had recognized the other diver's distinctive wetsuit and said hello. Over a beer, Kazuo had told him a little about a group he belonged to, called Project Ocean Friends, and invited him to come to a meeting and find out more. Tom had said yes, partly because the project sounded intriguing, but mostly because he had already felt a bond of friendship starting to form with Kazuo and hadn't wanted to let it slip away.

Kazuo nudged him and pointed with his chin toward the far end of the room. A shoji screen slid aside. A young woman stepped through the opening and paused for a moment. Tom sat up straighter, and his breath caught in his throat.

His first thought was that she was barely in her teens. But that illusion, created by her slim figure and the childish bob of her gleaming black hair, didn't survive a second look. Her oval face and high cheekbones had the eerie perfection of a porcelain doll. Her full red lips seemed almost painted on. Her eyes burned with a dark fire made more noticeable by the paleness of her skin. She was wearing pants and a tunic of black silk, cut something like a martial arts uniform. Her feet were bare.

"That is Hoshi Ito," Kazuo whispered, leaning closer. "She is our director."

"Hoo boy," Tom whispered back. Kazuo frowned, seemingly offended by his lack of seriousness.

The young woman walked slowly to the center of the room, faced the audience, and bowed. Then she sank gracefully to her knees and sat back on her heels. Her head turned, deliberately surveying the two dozen people facing her. As her eyes met Tom's, he felt the back of his scalp tighten. In anticipation? Dread?

"Welcome," she said. Her low voice had the smooth, velvet texture of chocolate pudding. "The reason you are here is that you are already friends of the ocean. Tonight you will find out what it is to make yourselves part of the work of Ocean Friends. Some of you, not all, are ready to hear. For you, this will be the most important night of your life, because it will give your life the meaning and purpose it was always meant to have. But I warn you: The course is not easy. Only those with unusual courage and vision can follow it to the end."

A scoffing voice in the back of Tom's mind said, "Terrific. All we need is a few shouts of 'Hallelujah!' or maybe 'Banzai!' to make the evening complete."

At that moment, Hoshi Ito paused. She turned and looked directly at him. He saw in her eyes that she had somehow sensed his skeptical reaction, as clearly as if he had spoken aloud. When she spoke again, he knew she was speaking directly to him.

"All people have the ability to hear the call of our mother, the ocean. But first they must let themselves," she said. "Few open themselves completely to her. And fewer still understand the urgency of her plea for help, for rescue. All over the globe, our fellow humans are raping and killing that which gave us life."

Tom was astonished to realize that his eyes were damp. What was going on? Sure, he loved the ocean. He always had. He could still recall his first trip to the beach at the age of four or so. He had scared the bejesus out of his parents by dashing straight into the surf, then howling his heart out when they had dragged him out and made him play on the sand instead.

Since then, all his moments of feeling truly alive had been by, on, or under the sea. But he was no flaming eco-freak. He was just an ordinary guy who loved diving more than anything else.

Hoshi was still speaking. "The ravishers of the ocean call their ignorance and greed common sense, or even human nature. But we know better. We know that respect and love for our Mother Ocean are the signs of a higher form of humanity. We know too that the ravishers are our enemy, and everyone's. We are few now, but we know that our numbers will grow, and that in time we will win. We must. Otherwise our planet and our species are doomed."

Her eyes surveyed the listeners once again, and once again they came to a stop at Tom.

"Our tasks are many and difficult," she said in a lower voice. "Anyone who joins us will find important and fulfilling work to do. But our greatest need, our Mother Ocean's greatest need, is for those who know her best to come to her defense. Those who heard her call and struggled to learn the skills they need to explore her wonders. Those who are now as much at ease beneath the water as on the land. To them, I say, Join us. Join us now. You will be in the very first rank of the friends and defenders of our Mother Ocean. Your courage will bring glory to all of us, and your deeds will be remembered forever."

Tom was breathing shallowly now, through slightly parted lips. He could not escape the thought that, if he tried to shut his mouth, the passion inside him would force itself out, like froth in a shaken bottle of warm soda or nitrogen in the blood of a diver who returned too quickly from the depths. It was as if everything he had ever done or thought or felt had been bringing him to this particular place and time.

He forced himself to sit still, to keep his face impassive. But when he met the gaze of the young woman seated in front of them, he saw a spark of satisfaction in her eyes.

He could tell she knew that from this moment on, he was hers.

Two days later, Tom took Kazuo up on his invitation to visit the Ocean Friends compound. They met in Agana and drove down along the coast. A couple of miles south of Agat, Kazuo turned the Land Cruiser off the highway, onto a narrow lane paved with crushed shells. A few yards in from the turn, a high gate topped with nasty-looking coils of razor wire blocked the lane. The top of the wall on either side of the gate glittered with shards of broken bottles set into mortar.

Kazuo leaned out his window and inserted what looked like a credit card into the slot of a steel box mounted on a pole. The box gave a click, and the gate swung open.

Tom looked around as Kazuo drove through the gate. From high on a nearby palm, a TV camera was tracking them. "Pretty tight security," he commented.

"Oh, yes," Kazuo replied. "We need it. Our work is opposed by very powerful interests. Some of them would do almost anything to stop us. So we are very careful."

The lane curved through a dense band of bushes. On the other side, on a gentle slope with a sweeping view of the ocean, was a sprawling one-story house encircled by a veranda. A web of paths linked it to half a dozen smaller outbuildings. At the foot of the slope, a wooden dock reached a finger out into the water. A beamy ship the size of an ocean-going tug was tied up at the end of the dock. The bow was built very high, but at the stern, the gunwales descended practically to the waterline.

The pilot house was set far forward. Just behind it, the radio mast bristled with antennas. Tom identified the interlocked circles of a radio directional finder, several whip dipoles for low-frequency transmission, three rotatable radar antennas, two small dishes, probably for spread-spectrum satellite communications, and a GPS antenna. Amidships, a pair of articulated deck cranes crouched like twin praying mantises. Each of them clutched a big Zodiac rubber boat in its claws. Just aft of them was a small helicopter landing pad. And at the stern, just in front of a tall A-frame boom, was the tarp-shrouded shape of a submersible craft.

"Wow!" Tom exclaimed. "That must be the ocean research ship you were telling me about. That's some fine rig you've got there!"

"That's it," Kazuo said proudly. "The RV *Ocean Friend*. Thirty-eight meters long, three hundred fifty tons displacement, and built to weather any kind of sea. She was a gift to the Project from an anonymous friend."

"You've got some very rich friends. Can we go aboard?"

"Of course." Kazuo guided the Land Cruiser down the hill and parked. A razor-wire-topped hurricane fence blocked access to the dock. Tom noticed that the fence was attached to its posts with white porcelain insulators. A bluff? Or was the fence really electrified?

Kazuo used his credit card again, grabbed the heavily insulated handle, and held the gate open for Tom.

"With these cards we can change access to any part of the Project instantly," he explained as they walked down the dock. "We also know exactly who has been through which gates and doors and at precisely what time. If a problem arises, we can study the computer records and discover who could, or couldn't, have been responsible."

Tom wasn't as thrilled by this news as Kazuo seemed to expect. In fact, he thought, glancing up at yet another remote-controlled video camera, all these security measures made him very antsy. Of course, if they needed them, they had every right to put them in. Still, he wished they hadn't. Holing up in an isolated compound surrounded by barbed-wire fences wasn't his idea of how to run an idealistic campaign to save nature's balance.

He followed Kazuo across the gangplank and stepped down onto the steel deck. A few feet away, two crew members were scraping paint from a section of the deck. They glanced up as Kazuo walked around them, but no one said a word.

As he passed between the two deck cranes, Tom looked over one of the Zodiacs. It was easily an eighteen-footer, fitted with a 150-horsepower outboard.

"You dive from those?" he asked.

"Yes, as a rule," Kazuo replied. "We also use them for deploying equipment and ferrying supplies. You notice the davits? They use special winches and a newly developed dynamic damping system to control pendulum action. This gives us the capability to launch and recover the Zodiacs safely, even when the seas are high and the ship is rolling and pitching."

He flashed a smile and added, "We prefer to operate in

calm seas, of course. But we do not always have a choice. The Project is more important than our likes and dislikes. Come, I will show you our new submersible. We are just beginning her sea trials. We have not yet named her, but in my mind I call her *Ocean Child*. Who knows? Perhaps you will have the honor to go down in her one day."

Kazuo led him back toward the stern and pulled the canvas covering off the front of the submersible. Like other undersea craft Tom had seen, it resembled a twenty-foot-long metal boiler to which a bewildering assortment of tanks, pipes, and Plexiglas bubbles had been attached. Two jointed arms with claws protruded from the front. The craft rested on sturdy metal runners that held the little sub about four feet off the deck. A circular structure ringed with small Plexiglas viewing ports sat on the top, a few feet back from the bow.

Amidships, extending below the hull and between the runners, was another vertical cylinder about three feet in diameter. Tom assumed it was the underwater entrance trunk.

"Is that a lockout chamber?" Tom asked, pointing to the structure.

"Yes. Up to two divers can leave and reenter the craft underwater once the air pressure inside is made equal to the water pressure outside," Kazuo replied.

"How deep will she go?"

"The builders rate her for 800 meters, but there's a large safety factor, and we've exceeded that depth many times."

Tom whistled. "You mean you could tool around at nearly half a mile down if you wanted to? For how long?"

"The life-support system is designed for 1000 man hours, at sea-level pressure," Kazuo said proudly. "And that does not include the mixed-gas supplies for divers and the lockout chamber. We are also planning to install a rebreathing apparatus that works on an entirely new principle."

"What about electronics?"

For the first time, Kazuo hesitated. "Well, there are the standard fathometers, side-looking sonars, pingers, scanners, directional hydrophones, and other locating devices, of course. We are also trying out a new underwater telephone

48

that will permit simultaneous communication between *Ocean Friend, Ocean Child,* and the divers."

He scanned the horizon, then began to pull the tarp back over the craft. Had he just heard something?

Tom looked around. There was nothing in sight. He must have imagined the change in Kazuo's manner.

His eye fell on another piece of equipment, sitting to one side of the submersible. This too looked like a steam boiler with various tanks, pipes, and fittings attached to it, but it was only about eight feet long and five feet in diameter. At the rear were the wheel, hinges, and dogs of what he presumed to be the door to the outer lock.

"Is that what I think it is?" Tom demanded.

Kazuo looked over his shoulder. "That is our hyperbaric chamber," he replied. "*Ocean Child* can do everything that this chamber can do, of course, and much, much more. But it is always nice to have a—what do your NASA people call it?—a backup, or a redundant system, in case the primary system fails."

Tom studied the recompression chamber more closely. Now he noticed shackles welded to its top surface and a heavy cable from the chamber to the take-up reel of a powerful winch. A thick neoprene hose was attached to a complex of valves and pipes.

"I get it," he said excitedly. "You send the whole chamber down to diving depth. That way, if something happens to the sub, the divers can transfer to this chamber and be brought back to the surface still at bottom pressure. That's a great idea!"

"It has been used before," Kazuo admitted. "We have found it very practical. Come, we should be going."

On the way forward, Tom paused to look through the porthole of the cabin just below the bridge. It looked like a booth at a marine electronics show. Three big color monitors hung from the ceiling, just over a panel of radar and sonar screens. An equipment rack in one corner was loaded with radio gear. Next to it was a VAX minicomputer, the size of a refrigerator, and its workstation console. In the center of the room was a big flatbed plotter.

Kazuo noticed that Tom had stopped. He hurried back. "Our Project is very complex," he said, taking Tom's arm and turning him away from the porthole. "Naturally, our equipment must also be complex."

"Oh, sure," Tom said. "But still, this is really an amazing setup. The one thing I don't understand is, what's the point?"

"The point is to rescue our mother, the ocean," Kazuo said solemnly.

"Sure, right. I'm with you all the way. But do you really need all this for that? Or that ultra-high-tech rebreathing apparatus you mentioned? Or a million-dollar research vessel, stuffed with more electronics than the Super Bowl blimp? I just don't get it."

Kazuo put his hands on Tom's shoulders and studied his face for a long time. Then he nodded. "You are right," he said. "There is more, much more to our Project than we have yet told the world. Hoshi said that you would ask. She always knows. It is her place to answer your questions."

Kazuo glanced at the big stainless-steel Rolex diver's watch on his wrist and added, "We will find her at the house, I think. She will be getting ready for tonight's Project meeting."

On the veranda of the house, Kazuo slipped off his shoes and added them to a row of shoes next to the door. Tom did the same with his tattered sneakers. Inside, Kazuo turned left, down a long hallway, and stopped in front of a closed door. He tapped once, lightly, then opened it and stepped inside. Tom followed.

Originally, the room must have been a bedroom. Now it felt almost like a shrine. The walls and ceiling were pure white. Louvered shutters filtered the light from the tall windows in the long wall and the French doors set into the end wall to the left. The floor, of some exotic reddish-purple wood, was as smooth and highly polished as a finely wrought cabinet. The only furniture in the room was a black lacquer chest, about the size of a footlocker. On it sat the only decorations in the room, an antique fan painting of a storm at sea and a small green vase that held a single white chrysanthemum.

Hoshi Ito was kneeling on the floor, facing slightly to their right. There was a sheet of rice paper on the floor in front of her, and she held a wire-bound brush lightly in her hand. She did not look up when they came in. Slowly, intently, she dipped the brush in a small porcelain ink cup, then leaned forward to draw three large characters on the paper. As she did so, the lapels of her white silk tunic gaped open, giving Tom a glimpse of the upper slopes of her small, firm breasts. Along with a stir of excitement, he felt a flush of shame, as if he had just been spying on his sister.

Hoshi studied her work for another moment, then put the brush down, sat back on her heels, and raised her head. As her eyes met Tom's, he once more had the uncanny feeling that she was reading his thoughts, as easily as he would read a newspaper. He looked away, then, defiant, almost angry, met her eyes again. The faintest trace of a smile crossed her face. She waved her hand to invite him and Kazuo to sit down.

Kazuo sank to his knees in a single graceful movement. Tom stooped down, using one hand to let himself down onto his butt, and crossed his legs. Clearly, he was going to have to practice this floor-sitting business, unless he wanted to go on feeling like a clumsy, unmannered oaf.

"You have seen our research ship," she said, in that low, soothing voice he remembered from the meeting. "What do you think?"

"It's fantastic," Tom replied, a little too loudly. He stopped, cleared his throat, and added, "It's a diver's or oceanographer's dream, easily the best setup I've ever seen or even heard about."

"But it left you with questions."

"Well ..." He glanced over at Kazuo, who seemed to be staring at the vase with the chrysanthemum. "To tell you the truth, I don't understand what you need all that for. I mean, from what I heard the other night, what you're trying to do is make people more aware of how pollution and all are destroying the ocean. Is that right?"

"Yes."

"Then why put all that money into a research vessel? Why not use it to—I don't know—produce a TV show on ocean pollution and broadcast it by satellite to every country in the world? Or get millions of people to mail little bottles of toxic waste to the heads of companies that pollute?"

Hoshi nodded her head a fraction of an inch. The rest of her body was as still as a marble statue. "These are good ideas," she said. "Or they would have been, once. Now it is much too late for them. The world is very quickly approaching a crisis. There is no time to convince the millions, no time for them to organize and act, even if they were able to. No, the future, if there is to be a future, must rest in the hands of those few who are ready *now* to understand and to act."

Tom's head was spinning. "Understand *what?* Act *how?*" he pleaded.

Hoshi looked at him in silence. He could almost feel her eyes boring into his skull.

Finally, she said, "There are some truths that everyone can know, that everyone *must* know. In our public campaigns, we try to make people aware of these. But there are other truths, secret truths, that are much too dangerous to be entrusted to the ordinary person. Only certain very special people have the mental strength to take them in without harming themselves. When I saw you, I knew at once that you were one of those special people."

"I still don't—"

Hoshi held up a hand, and he fell silent.

She looked past him, with a gaze that seemed to travel into the far distance. "In many cultures, there are ancient stories of a time when the world was destroyed. They tell how a small remnant of humanity survived to continue our race," she said. "Few understand that these tales are in a sense true, and that we ourselves carry a genetically encoded trace of real events that happened in the dawn of our species. Even fewer realize that the tales are also prophetic of events still to come."

Tom shook off the spell of her voice enough to say, "Prophetic? Come on, you don't expect me to believe that a bunch of folktales foretell the future, do you?"

"Not in a literal sense, no. But for those who know how to read them, yes. Why is that so difficult to understand? Our species, and other species before it, have a history that encompasses millions of years. That history, with its triumphs and failures and catastrophes, has left its mark on us. We do not have to learn everything anew in each generation. We can call upon the hard-won wisdom of our ancestors, if only we are willing to listen and to make the effort to comprehend. Are *you* willing to make that effort? Think carefully before you give me your answer. A great deal— perhaps even your life—depends on it."

Tom turned the question over in his mind. Hoshi's earnestness impressed him, but he was also a little disappointed by the direction she was taking. He had expected to learn about the Project's research goals, not to listen to stories about Noah and the Flood. Still, he didn't have much choice. Either he listened or he got up and left, and he didn't want to do that. He was astonished by how much he didn't want to do that.

He took a deep breath and said, "I'll try. But I'm not making any promises that I'll succeed."

"Are you familiar with the research on global warming and the destruction of the ozone layer?" Hoshi asked.

Tom blinked in surprise. Where was this going? "I guess so," he replied. "Well, not really familiar, but I've read a little about the subject."

"This must go no further," she said, fixing him with her gaze. "We, together with a small, secret group of oceanographers and climatologists who have access to the most powerful supercomputers in the world, have created a model of world conditions over the next few years. We've discovered that the threat is much more grave than the public, or even most of the scientific community, realizes. In fact, the very future of our world is at stake. The global warming trend created by the greenhouse effect, and other contributing factors, now has us at a precipitous point of no return. The unpleasant truth is that we have already done irreversible

damage to our home planet. One of the results of our depre-
dations is the impending rise in sea levels, which will flood
most of the world's population centers and most fertile crop
regions. Whole nations such as Bangladesh will simply cease
to exist. People who flee to higher ground will escape the
flooding but not the searing levels of ultraviolet radiation
that will no longer be filtered out by the ozone layer."

She paused and looked down at her clasped hands. "All
this has been said before, though not enough people have
listened." She continued, after a moment, "But there is
much more. With global warming and the extension of the
oceans over millions of square miles of what was formerly
dry land, the tropical ocean currents will flow much farther
into the northern and southern temperate zones and be
warmer as well. Do you see what that means?"

Tom shook his head.

"Warm tropical currents provide the energy that powers
cyclonic storm systems," Hoshi said. "Already, the destruc-
tive force of a typhoon or hurricane is far greater than our
puny thermonuclear weapons. And according to the computer model, these storms will grow steadily more powerful,
until they reach the point that nothing—no plant, no animal,
no building on the face of the earth—can stand against
them."

Tom believed her. From the little that he already knew
about the subject, the grim picture she was painting made
sense. But more than that, she was presenting it with such
utter conviction that he couldn't imagine *not* believing her.

"Then it's hopeless," he said. "There's no way out."

Her eyes flashed. "If I truly believed that," she said
sharply, "I would . . ." Her clenched hands made a slashing
motion from left to right at the level of her waist.

Tom fought down a feeling of nausea as he imagined her
committing hara-kiri.

"But there is hope," she continued. "More than hope, a
certainty. Our mother will give us shelter from even the
fiercest storm."

For a moment, Tom thought she must be quoting poetry

or a line from a hymn. Then he remembered all the times she had referred to the ocean as "our mother."

"Of course!" he exclaimed, as the pieces of the puzzle dropped into place. "Once you're thirty or forty meters down, it could be dead calm or blowing at gale force on the surface, and you wouldn't know the difference. But whatever vessel you're using for a tender sure would."

"No tender," Hoshi said. "Nothing on the surface, at the mercy of the winds. Nothing at all."

"Then how . . . ?"

Kazuo spoke for the first time since they had entered the room. "We are planning to build a habitat," he said. "A self-contained, self-sustaining environment. An ark, carrying with it everything our kind needs to repopulate the earth after the crisis passes."

"I told you that the old stories contain a secret truth," Hoshi added. "Now you understand. When the time comes, the chosen few will enter the habitat and cut themselves off completely from the growing disaster. They will be superbly trained, thoroughly prepared for their mission. They will have the strength to survive and thrive, even as the surface world enters the convulsions of ecological death."

"But what's the point?" Tom asked. "If the whole world is going to be destroyed, why bother hiding out on the bottom of the ocean for a few months or years? You're still dead the minute you return to the surface."

Hoshi shook her head. "No," she said. "The ecological crisis is like a fever, which rids the sick person of his disease, then passes. The computer projections are very clear on this. The death of so much vegetation, killed by the higher levels of ultraviolet radiation, will create vast new deserts throughout the world. What will happen when those deserts are swept by the great winds of the cyclonic storms?"

Tom frowned, then exclaimed, "Duststorms! Sure! And once all that dust gets up into the upper atmosphere, it will start cooling things off, the same way that the dust from the eruptions of Mount St. Helens or Krakatoa did."

"Exactly. And with the cooling, the terrible tropical storms will begin to die down and the polar ice caps will start to reform. The ozone layer, no longer preyed upon by fluorocarbons and all the other exhaust gases of our technological and overpopulated civilization, will replenish itself. Gradually, the earth will become ready to welcome life once more. And at that point, just as in earlier beginnings, life will come forth from our Mother Ocean. But this time it will be very different. We will renew the world, yes, but starting from a level higher than that reached before the disaster, because we will know the mistakes of our ancestors and not repeat them. And ... because the chosen few will represent only the very best of the old, dead world."

"Now you can see why *Ocean Friend* is equipped with such advanced electronic devices," Kazuo said. "Its real mission is to map the ocean floor and the deep currents, to locate the perfect location for the habitat. We know this is the place to look, because our studies show conclusively that here, in the vicinity of the Marianas Trench, is the most richly endowed of all the world's oceans. Here is to be found everything we will need to sustain us for as long as the rebirth will take. For that reason, we are working in finer detail than anyone has ever before attempted at such depths. Every time our soundings suggest an important feature of any sort, someone must go down and examine it firsthand. This makes the mapping extremely slow, but it is necessary. So much depends on our decision."

Hoshi struck in. "We hope that you will join us. Your diving skills will be very valuable to our work, of course. But that is not the important point. I see in you a possibility. Do you have the inner strength to become part of the team that will enter the habitat, when the time comes? If you wish, and you are ready to commit yourself to the work, you may begin the program of mental and emotional training at once. Very few are given that chance. But I must warn you. In the end, only the very strongest, the most stable, will be chosen. The success, even the survival, of the team will depend on the total preparation of each member. Are you willing to become a candidate?"

Tom stared at the floor and tried to bring some order to his thoughts. What did Hoshi see in him that he himself didn't see? He could never live up to her expectations. But did he have the right to say No, to turn down her offer? The Project needed him, and the Project just might be the most important thing in the world. He had a duty to give it everything he could. And even if in the end he failed, he would fail knowing that he had been part of it.

He raised his head and met Hoshi's eyes. He saw that he didn't need to announce his decision. She knew it already. She had known it long before he himself had.

"You will live here, with the others in the group," she said. "Someone will go for your bags. Tomorrow, *Ocean Friend* sails to continue its work. You will be aboard. And when you return, your training will begin. Welcome to your new life."

Somewhere in the house, a door closed loudly.

CHAPTER 5

THE YOUNGER MEMBERS OF THE DEPARTMENT USUALLY
referred to Ken Kirby's office as "the rat's nest." This had
nothing to do with his character or temperament. Everyone
admitted that he was a hell of a nice guy, on those occasions
when his mind wasn't several thousand miles away. No, the
name was given in recognition of a state of disorder that
seemed more fitting for an elderly recluse than for the leading economic analyst in a government organization so obscure—or so secret—that even the people at the National
Security Agency, who liked to claim that NSA stood for
"No Such Address," simply called it "that bunch of nuts
in Bethesda." Its official name was the Office of Research
Coordination, which had the advantage of seeming to mean
something without saying anything at all.

Newspapers from capitals all over the world went through
the door of Ken's office every morning. Most of them stayed
there, stacked in tall piles that leaned against each other for
support and grew faster than a bamboo grove. Magazines
too, in polybags and plain brown wrappers, that ranged from
Forbes and *Business Week* to *Sea Technology* and *Holly-
wood Reporter*. These competed for space on a wall of metal
shelving that looked as if it had been salvaged from the
parts department of a Studebaker dealership.

Most of Ken's desk was given over to stacks of newsletters. These offered, in breathless paragraphs filled with boldface and italics, the latest inside information on such topics as recent occupational safety regulations, parallel processing software, and new developments in guano mining. Two computer terminals—one networked with the rest of the department and the other hard-wired to the leading financial database—took up the rest of the desktop.

The only horizontal surface in the office that usually stayed reasonably clear was a battered Samsonite bridge table with folding legs. Ken stood next to it now, tapping a thick deck of index cards in his left palm and whistling "Près des remparts de Séville," from Bizet's *Carmen*. From her desk just outside the open door, his secretary, Joyce North, heard and smiled. The only time Ken whistled tunes from *Carmen* was when he was hot on the trail of a new idea. When he was simply reading or thinking, he was more likely to favor "Michelle" or "Ruby Tuesday."

Ken began to lay out the index cards in rows and columns. Some were pink, some yellow, some pale blue and green. Soon the entire tabletop was covered. He scratched the back of his head and gazed down at the array, then picked up several cards and put them down in a different place. An untutored observer might have thought that he was involved in an obscure variation on solitaire.

After more head-scratching and gazing, Ken swept all the cards into an untidy stack, straightened them, and began to lay them out again. Some went down quickly. Others were shuffled to the bottom of the stack for later consideration.

At eleven o'clock, Joyce brought in a cup of steaming chicken bouillon and made space for it on the desk. Ken was still hovering over the bridge table, selecting index cards one by one and whistling "Toréador."

He looked up blankly. Then his eyes refocused and he smiled at her. "Oh, thanks," he said. He picked up the bouillon and took a sip, then added, "Do you know if Harley's around?"

"I saw him in the hall a little while ago."

Ken's glance wandered back to the bridge table. "Good.

Tell him I need a few minutes with him in his office, will you? In, say, half an hour?"

Forty-seven minutes later, Ken was still rearranging his index cards. The phone rang. It was Ramon Tejerina, Harley's secretary.

"The director has to leave soon for a luncheon appointment," Ramon announced. "I understand you wanted to see him?"

Ken looked over at the bridge table. The pattern was close enough to complete. "Sure," he said. "Tell him to hang on, I'll be right over."

At Harley's office, Ramon silently buzzed Ken in. Harley was standing by the window, hands clasped behind his back. He turned and waved Ken to one of two black leather Barcelona chairs, then took the other one himself.

Harley Cassell had first come to Washington fresh from Boult Hall, UC Berkeley's law school, as executive assistant to a new congressman whose district was redistricted out of existence fourteen months later. The ex-congressman had gone back to the Bay Area and joined his uncle's law firm. Harley had stayed in Washington, gliding from one government organization to another, with occasional, very profitable, interludes in the private sector.

For almost two years now, he had held the title of director of the Office of Research Coordination. He liked to tell friends that in reality he was a nanny, like the one on "Muppet Babies." The most important part of his job was to keep an eye on his brilliant but peculiar colleagues and see to it that they didn't stray into too much trouble.

"Well, Ken?" he said. "What have you got?"

"Oil."

Harley waited a few moments before saying, "What about it?"

Ken thumbed through his index cards. "Some funny things seem to be going on. The way it looks to me, somebody is betting a lot of money—a *whole* lot of money—that the price of oil is going to fall."

"He's got a fifty-fifty chance of being right," Harley

pointed out in a dry tone of voice. "The price is bound to go either up or down ... unless it stays the same, of course."

Ken brushed this comment aside. "Do you know anything about commodities futures?" he demanded.

"Enough to make me stay away from them."

"Yeah, me too. They're a terrific way to make a bundle, as long as you don't mind the risk of losing your shirt. My oldest will be ready for college in two years, so I mind."

"Somebody else doesn't mind, I take it."

"Well ..." Ken pulled one of the index cards and studied it. "Futures prices are usually pretty predictable. You've got seasonal factors, of course. But if oil for March delivery is going for nineteen bucks a barrel, the price for April delivery will be in the same ballpark, a few pennies higher or lower maybe, depending on whether the market thinks the supply-demand relationship is heading up or down."

"But—"

"Here, take a look." Ken handed Harley a blue index card. "Those are yesterday's New York Merc futures prices for crude oil. What do you notice?"

Harley studied the columns of numbers. "From now until September, the price climbs slowly. Then it slides fast."

"And autumn is when the price usually climbs, because of heavier anticipated demand during winter," Ken pointed out.

"What's this last column?" asked Harley.

"Open interest. That's basically the number of outstanding contracts for that month that aren't covered by off-setting contracts."

"That has an inflection point in September too. The last three months, the numbers increase steadily. What do you think that means?"

Ken shrugged. "Ordinarily, the farther away the delivery date, the smaller the number of contracts written, covered *or* uncovered. But someone is going short on September, October, and November contracts. In other words, they expect a significant fall in oil prices after the summer. If that happens, they cover their short position at the spot price

61

and make out like bandits. If prices don't drop, they walk home wearing a barrel to cover their asses."

"Um-hum. What kind of money are we talking about?"

"That's very hard to say. For one thing, Mister X seems to be selling contracts in London, Tokyo, and Hong Kong as well as New York. For all I know, he's writing them in Abu Dhabi, Buenos Aires, and Capetown too, just to hit the beginning of the alphabet. If I had to make a wild guess, I'd say his exposure is in the neighborhood of eight or nine figures."

Harley stared. "That is a very high-rent neighborhood you're talking about! As much as a hundred million or more *at risk?*"

"More, probably," Ken replied calmly. He sorted through his cards and plucked out a yellow one. "Someone is apparently shorting ELF-Aquitaine, Royal Dutch Shell, Oxy Pete, and Exxon stock too. There may be some others I overlooked."

"Who in hell— Never mind, we'll get to that in a minute. First off, what do you think all this means?"

"I already told you. Somebody is betting on a big drop in oil prices after the summer. Why? I can't tell you that. Adam Smith would say that Mister X is expecting either a big rise in supply or a big drop in demand. Or both, of course."

"We can cross off a drop in demand," Harley said, shaking his head. "The whole world runs on oil. But what about an increase in supply? Maybe your Mister X has advance word of an important discovery, something on the order of the North Sea or Prudhoe Bay. Anything in that?"

"It's always possible, but . . ." Ken broke off and searched through his cards again. "The number of drilling rigs in use is at its lowest in five years. With oil at less than twenty dollars a barrel, the word in Houston is that exploration isn't worth a bucket of warm spit. The geologists say there's probably a big new field right off Baja California, for instance. But no one wants to invest the money to prove it out, not without some hope of turning a profit."

"Okay, not a new discovery, then. How about an old one?

What if one of the major producers—Iraq, Indonesia, hell, even Nigeria—is planning to break ranks with OPEC and open the spigot a turn or two? They might even figure to make some extra change on the side by going short."

Ken shook his head. "That occurred to me too. But our Mister X is betting the ranch on a price drop of more than ten percent. If that happened, an oil-producing country would have to increase production by more than ten percent just to stay even. And that's assuming they found buyers for all that extra oil."

Harley threw up his hands. "Any other ideas?" he demanded.

"Maybe someone thinks he has an infallible system for long-range weather prediction," Ken suggested. "If he's dead sure we're in for a mild winter next year, shorting oil would be pretty smart."

"You're joking, right?"

"More or less. But just to repeat myself, he has to be counting on a big change in supply, or demand, or both."

Harley drummed his fingertips on the top of his desk. "Let's try from another angle. Who exactly is your Mister X? Is he a person, or a group, or a company, or maybe even a country? A hundred million dollars must leave one hell of a trail."

"Yes and no. I got on the phone this morning and called in one or two favors. So far I have the names of four different firms that have recently sold futures contracts for September, October, and November oil at bargain-basement prices."

"Well, all right!" Harley exclaimed, sitting up straighter. "Did you recognize any of the names?"

"Yes and no," Ken repeated. He pulled out a pink index card and read, "Beaumont Brothers, Baku Ventures, Ploesti Partners, and Maracaibo P.L.C."

"Those are all places where big oilfields were found," Harley said with a frown.

"Uh-huh. Which gives us a lead. I can't believe that four independent firms independently chose names that are so obviously connected. I'd say we're dealing with somebody who knows the history of the oil industry inside out and who has a weird sense of humor."

"And a lot of money. Anything else?"

"Well, yes, actually." Ken grinned. "All four firms have their home offices at the same address. In Georgetown."

"In Georgetown? Right here in *Washington?*"

"No, I'm afraid not. That would make life too easy for us. Georgetown, Grand Cayman Island."

"Oh, shit," groaned Harley. "The money laundry of the West Indies. A population of twenty-five thousand people, most of whom work for banks that are pledged to absolute secrecy!"

The telephone buzzed. Harley picked up the receiver, listened for a moment, and hung up.

"Sorry, Ken," he said. "I'm late for my lunch date. What's your feeling: Do we hang on to this for now, or share it with Langley?"

"Give me another day or two," Ken replied. "I'd like to see what I can find out before anybody else gets a chance at muddying the water."

"Okay. But keep me in the loop. If this is as big as you say, we don't want it going *bang!* in our hands."

Three days later, Ken walked into Harley's office with a smile on his face and a new stack of index cards in his hand.

"Bingo," he said.

"You got something."

"Um-hum. Quite a lot. But damned if I know what it all means."

Harley waved him toward the Barcelona chairs. "Coffee?" he asked.

"Sure."

Harley spoke into his phone. Ramon must have anticipated the request; two minutes later he slipped in carrying a tray with two cups and saucers, sugar, cream, and a small porcelain pot of coffee. He set it on the glass-topped table between the two chairs and slipped out again.

"Well?" Harley said, after pouring the coffee.

"First of all, I came across half a dozen more companies

registered in Grand Cayman with names like Athabaska, Brent, Permian, and Santa Barbara. I probably missed some."

"Does it matter?"

"Probably not. The pattern is clear enough." Ken put his coffee cup down and sorted through his index cards. "The companies I found all belong, in different proportions, to three holding companies: one in Panama, one in Liberia, and one in Macao. And all three of those are wholly owned subsidiaries of an outfit called Globamundi, headquartered in Vaduz, Liechtenstein."

Harley sighed. "Somehow I knew we were going to wind up in Liechtenstein. The favorite financial haven of cocaine billionaires, African dictators, and tax evaders of every nation. A place whose secrecy laws make Swiss bankers look like a bunch of contestants on 'To Tell the Truth.' So we hit a dead end."

Ken's smile widened to a grin. "Well, no. Not quite. Ten percent of the shares of Globamundi are registered to one Karl Rothart, a Vaduz lawyer who is also listed as general secretary of the corporation. I imagine he's a nominee for the other shareholders."

"A front man, you mean."

"Same thing. The rest of the shares are evenly divided— forty-five percent each—between E. A. 'Red' Bell and Cui-chi Nishimura."

Ken sat back and waited for a reaction from Harley, who put his hands together, steeple fashion, and tapped his front teeth with the nails of his index fingers.

"Bell I've heard of," Harley finally said. "Big oil money. Tulsa, is it?"

"Right."

"He's the one who was in all the papers a couple of years ago, right after Desert Storm. Some kind of patriotic stunt."

"He gave T-shirts with a big American eagle on them to every schoolkid in Oklahoma," Ken replied. "He tried to get people in other states to do the same, but it didn't catch on."

"Thank God," Harley said with a snort. "Can you imagine every kid in the country wearing the same T-shirt? Straight out of an old episode of 'Twilight Zone'! How about the other guy though? What do you have on him?"

Ken pulled out three or four green index cards and scanned them. He knew all the information on them by heart, but he had learned years before that most people put more trust in someone who consults his notes, instead of seeming to talk off the top of his head. A case of the pen being mightier than the tongue.

"Cuichi Nishimura," he repeated. "Industrialist and financier, which means that he has a finger in lots of different pies. The core of his empire is an electronics manufacturing company. No one's ever heard of it, but its TVs, VCRs, and personal computers sell by the millions under dozens of different house brands. His net worth doesn't quite put him in the same class as the Sultan of Brunei, but he'd make anybody's list of important fortunes."

"Important enough for him to be able to risk losing his half of a hundred million dollars?" asked Harley.

"Only a Congressional appropriations committee could mislay that kind of money without hurting," Ken replied. "But he'd still be left with more than enough for a rainy day. Or even a whole monsoon season."

Harley gave him a searching look. "You've got a kicker up your sleeve, don't you? Come on, out with it."

"Nishimura is apparently a very private person, almost a recluse. A reporter once called him the Howard Hughes of Japan. By the way, right after the story appeared, the reporter was suddenly transferred to the Japanese equivalent of East Armpit, North Dakota. I managed to track him down. I had to swear that not a word he said would ever be made public."

He paused and gave Harley a querying look.

"No problem from my end," Harley said.

"Okay. First of all, there's some mystery about Nishimura's past. The earliest official record that this reporter could track down was from 1948, when Nishimura was already in his thirties. No birth record, no war record, nothing from before then."

"Everybody leaves a paper trail. Didn't anybody ever ask him about his past?"

Ken nodded. "Sure. My reporter friend did, for one. Nishimura's reply makes him sound like that character in the comics who brings disaster wherever he goes. Nishimura's whole family died in the flu epidemic when he was a little kid. His army unit was sent to the jungles of Burma and didn't come back. Oh, and he was born and had all his schooling in Hiroshima."

"No records, then," Harley said in a cheerful voice. "None at all. You'd almost think he didn't exist. Interesting ... How did he make all his money?"

"He got in on the ground floor of the Japanese miracle, making cheap transistor radios and those little cameras they used to give away for four cereal boxtops plus twenty-five cents shipping and handling. He ploughed all the profits back into upgrading his plant and his product line. Keep that up for almost forty years, and if you've got a minimum level of smarts and luck, you too can be a billionaire."

"What about politics?"

Ken nodded slowly. "Very interesting, that. Like any Japanese businessman, Nishimura forks over a lot of money to the party in power, the Liberal Democrats. They're roughly similar to our Republican party. Some of the money's over the table, some under. That's the usual thing too. But according to my source, he is also the secret sugar daddy for some of the fiercest far-right groups in the country. Real up-with-the-Emperor and down-with-the-filthy-foreigners-and-all-their-toady-henchmen stuff, complete with private militias in samurai costume."

Harley gazed at the ceiling. "As you say, very interesting. But I'm not sure how much it really means. Everybody needs a hobby. I knew a fellow in high school whose father believed that people who pay more taxes should have more votes, since it's their money that the government is spending. He even set up an educational organization to preach the message to the rest of us. Tax-exempt, of course. Still, I admit that our Japanese friend makes a curious partner for

'Red' Bell. Samurai costumes and Desert Storm T-shirts don't seem to go together, somehow."

"Something brought them together," Ken pointed out. "And I find it hard to believe that it was simply money. They both have more than enough of that already."

"If you believe that, Kenneth, you'll never be rich. People who found great fortunes don't believe there is such a thing as *enough* money, let alone more than enough."

"I'll keep that in mind. Do I keep digging?"

"Of course," Harley replied, with a small smile. "So far all we have are some odd facts that might or might not form a pattern and some very engaging speculations. Until we stumble over something that I feel I simply have to pass along to our colleagues in Langley, I think we'll just follow our own path and see where it leads us."

CHAPTER 6

THE SOUND LEVEL INSIDE THE CABIN CHANGED SUBTLY. Suddenly alert, Rick opened his eyes and sat up. Then he relaxed. No emergency, and in any case, he wasn't in the pilot's seat. He was just another tired, grubby passenger with the smell of recirculated air in his nose. He yawned and stretched. The movie—Chevy Chase's latest try at a comeback—had just wound down to an end. The 747 was beginning its descent toward Guam's Agana International Airport.

He checked his watch. Two-seventeen P.M., Honolulu time, which meant . . . He did some quick calculations, then backed up the hands to read 10:17 A.M. He was about to push the stem back into place when he remembered that he had to change the date as well. Most of a day had just been stolen out of his life. Luckily he would get it back the next time he crossed the International Date Line going the other way.

In the next seat, Captain Will Ward stirred. He gave a loud snort, then opened one eye and looked at Rick suspiciously.

"We're nearly there," Rick said.

The captain opened his other eye. "Uh-huh. By the way, I called your room last night, more than once. Something I

69

wanted to talk over. None of my business, but would you like to tell me where you were until after three?"

"Er . . . no," said Rick. He kept his eyes pointed straight ahead.

"Tomcatting around, I suppose," Captain Ward grumbled. "I thought you'd put all that behind you after you and Sam . . . Still, I suppose that's none of my business either."

"Well . . . no," Rick repeated, then hastily added, "sir."

"Belay that," the captain snapped. "Do you think I spent a lifetime in the Navy without learning to tell the difference between respect and insolence?"

Rick tried to figure out if the proper answer was Yes or No, then gave up and settled for a grin. Captain Ward replied with a "Hmmph!" that was more amused than anything.

Outside, a few thousand feet below, regularly spaced cumulus clouds paced across the sky like a platoon of cotton balls. The water surface, a deep, flat blue, looked almost purple where their shadows fell. Toward the horizon, a faint white line marked the passage of a small interisland freighter.

Ward's questions about Rick's night had bothered him a little. Not that he was ashamed of it; he and Natalie were both adults, after all, and what they did together was strictly their own business. Besides, it had been terrific for both of them. Still, the captain's probing made Rick recall another wonderful evening, not with Natalie but with Samantha Deane.

It was Halloween, and Sam had invited Rick over as a break from the pressure cooker of SEAL training. Sam's brother, Mac MacDougall, already a legend in Navy underwater circles, had been there too. The three adults had helped Sam's kid, Billy, carve a really wicked-looking pumpkin, then Mac had offered to take Billy on a nice long tour of trick-or-treating.

It was the first time they had been alone together, and Rick had had no idea what to expect. He certainly hadn't expected to end up lying on the sofa next to Sam, panting like an asthmatic steam engine. And when Sam had gasped,

"No, Rick, please! Not here!" he had been sure she was about to order him out of the house. Instead, she had added, "Let's go to the bedroom."

Captain Ward shifted in his seat, bumping Rick's elbow and breaking into his reverie. Rick suppressed a sigh and turned back toward the captain.

"Where are we going to be staying?" Rick asked. "The visiting officers' quarters at one of the bases? On board *Berkone?*"

"Not my problem," the captain replied. "It's up to the people in charge to figure out where we stay. I just hope they don't stow us in a VOQ. I'm too old and stiff to like sacking out on a metal-spring bunk that thinks it's a hammock."

"They're not like that anymore," Rick assured him. "In the New Navy, when you put up at a VOQ, you'd think you're at the Holiday Inn. Individual telephones, color TVs, the works."

The captain snorted. "New Navy, my hairy ass! Don't talk to me as if I was a Congressional committee, sonny. And if I'm going to think I'm at a Holiday Inn, I'd just as soon hold out for the genuine article. I'm a sucker for those shoe-shine pads in little foil packets."

The Fasten Seatbelts lights came on, followed closely by No Smoking. A few moments later, one of the flight attendants marched down the aisle, glancing at the tray tables and seatbacks to make sure they were in the proper position. The big airliner banked a few degrees to starboard, then leveled out for the approach.

The airport's perimeter fence appeared under the wing. The tires hit the concrete, and the pilot slammed the engines into reverse thrust. After a 6000-foot jaunt down the runway, the plane came almost to a stop, then made a leisurely turn onto a taxiway that led to the terminal.

Rick looked over at Captain Ward, expecting the look of relief he saw on his godfather's face.

"Well, we made it," the captain said, with a smile. "But I got to tell you, Ricky, speaking as an old submariner: The whole time we were up there, I never once put my full weight down!"

Inside the terminal, they spotted someone holding up a card that said SEAVENTURE. They made their way through the crowd to him.

"Captain Ward? Commander Tallman?" the man said. He stuck out his hand. "I'm Ray Lapham. Welcome to Guam."

Lapham was about fifty, with prematurely white hair, pale blue eyes, and a deep tan. He was wearing jeans faded almost to white, a white polo shirt, and deck shoes with no socks. A pair of Serengeti sunglasses was propped up on his forehead. Rick thought he looked as if his real home was at the wheel of a racing ketch. Or at least that was the impression he wanted to give.

"Thanks," Captain Ward said, after shaking his hand. "Glad to be here. You're the project coordinator here, aren't you? How come the big enchilada is reduced to meeting planes?"

Lapham smiled. "Security, Captain. I didn't want the news of your arrival to get around ahead of time, so I decided to pick you up myself. I have a car outside," he continued. "Is that all your luggage?"

"No, we've got more coming," the captain replied. "Why don't you go after the car, while we wait for the bags?"

"No need. The car is right by the main entrance. I'll wait and give you a hand with the bags. Oh, and while I think of it, if you find out that you need anything you forgot to bring, just let one of my people know."

They turned and started toward the baggage-claim area, then stopped as a crowd of about fifty people streamed past. At their head was a man in a dark suit, holding a furled umbrella high in his right hand.

"You notice anything about that bunch?" Lapham asked.

"They're all Japanese," Captain Ward said.

"Correct. What else?"

"They're all young," Rick pointed out. "And it looks like they're all couples, except for the guy with the umbrella."

Lapham nodded. "One hundred percent correct, Commander," he said. "They're honeymooners, down here on a package tour. Umbrella-san is the group leader. In the past ten or fifteen years, Guam's become the Niagara Falls of Japan, or maybe the Miami Beach. It's pretty close to Japan, pretty warm, pretty cheap, and just plain pretty. It's also a duty-free port. You can pick up a new Nikon here for a lot less than in Tokyo. They come by the 747-load. Great for the economy, but not everybody's so happy about it. People on Guam were put through a lot during the Japanese occupation in World War II, and many of them still remember."

They retrieved their bags, and Lapham led them outside, to a four-door Chevy that was sitting squarely in a no-parking zone. Rick glanced around. Practically every other car in sight was made in Japan or Korea. They put their bags in the trunk and Rick climbed into the front seat, leaving Captain Ward the back.

Leaving the airport, they turned onto a four-lane road lined with tire stores, carpet outlets, and banners announcing 59-cent hamburgers. Rick found himself thinking of Route 17, a few miles south of Patterson, New Jersey.

"Glomar Champion is in port for the moment," Lapham explained. "The seas are a little too rough to deploy the seabed crawler. But according to our weather people, we should be able to get back to work by Thursday. In the meantime, you'll have a chance to get acquainted with the rest of the bunch. We've taken over one wing of a hotel on Tumon Bay as headquarters for the operation. You'll be comfortable there."

"What about *Berkone?*" asked Captain Ward. "Has she made port yet?"

"I understand she's still three or four days out," Lapham replied.

"Any problems?" the captain demanded, with a hint of alarm in his voice.

"No, no. Not that they've told us about, at least."

Rick felt a sense of relief wash over him. If something had happened to the *Steel Albatross,* before he had even gotten another chance ...!

After a couple of miles, Lapham turned onto a winding road lined with royal palms. Ahead was a long white six-story building shaped like a pair of boomerangs laid end to end. Balconies, with openings like half moons, lined each floor. They drove past a set of rust-colored composition tennis courts and stopped under the canopy at the front door. A bellhop, in black trousers and a red jacket that reminded Rick of Sergeant Preston of the Yukon, hurried over to open the car doors and take their bags.

"Come along," Lapham said, turning the car over to another member of the hotel staff. "It's nearly lunchtime. We'll probably find some of our people at the pool. Oh, and if you don't mind, I won't use your ranks. Security, you know."

Rick looked over at Captain Ward with raised eyebrows. Security? Aside from Lapham's decision to meet them at the airport, this was the first sign of any. No one would guess from his manner that he and his co-workers were engaged in an important national project. Was the purpose of their mission so highly classified that they themselves didn't know what they were doing or how important it was?

The hotel pool sat in the middle of a green lawn that sloped down to a narrow white sand beach. Beyond, the waters of the bay shaded from pale green to the intense blue of open ocean. A dozen white-painted tables, each with its own brightly colored umbrella, were lined up on the grass near the edge of the pool. A few yards away, the service bar, disguised as a thatched hut, was already doing a steady business dispensing fruit punches served in coconut shells.

Lapham led Rick and Ward to a table near the end of the row. The man and woman sitting there looked up as they drew closer. The man had long brown hair, pulled back in a ponytail, and a close-cropped full beard. His thick gold-rimmed glasses gave the impression that he was peering at the world from a great distance.

As for the woman, Rick couldn't help smiling as he met her curious, open gaze. *Just what I needed,* he thought. *Another attractive woman to keep my mind off my work.*

He took a closer look. Feathery locks of jet-black hair framed her round face, just as long jet-black lashes framed her dark blue eyes. A light dusting of freckles topped her cheeks and her small upturned nose. He could easily imagine her dressed all in green, playing impish tricks on travelers who made the mistake of crossing her woods after nightfall, like the Leprechaun or his Hawaiian cousin, the Menehune.

The guy with the ponytail got to his feet, interrupting Rick's survey.

Lapham said, "I'd like you people to welcome Will Ward and Rick Tallman, who'll be joining our motley crew. Will, Rick, meet Eloise Jackson and Dave Collier. Eloise is a marine geologist."

From the shade of the umbrella, the dark-haired girl smiled and raised a hand.

"And Dave is the guy who designed our crawler, the one we're having all the problems with. We also think of him as our resident hippie."

The fellow with the ponytail scowled at Lapham, then looked over at Rick and Captain Ward and said, "Hi." He sounded cross. Rick hardly blamed him. If someone had introduced Rick in those terms, he would probably have left the gathering with fewer teeth than he'd arrived with.

"Hello," Rick said, at the same time as Captain Ward.

Lapham dragged a couple more chairs over to the table. "An aperitif before lunch?" he asked, beckoning the waiter.

"Not for me, thanks," Captain Ward said, taking a seat next to him. "We're still stuck in yesterday. Or is it tomorrow?"

The others laughed, and Eloise said, "I still haven't worked all that out. All I know is that whenever I call a friend back in the States, it's never what time I expect it to be, and sometimes it's not even the right day."

Rick sat down next to her. "A friend of mine bought a watch that can be programmed for six different time zones," he said. "The only problem is, he either forgets which is which or he forgets where he is."

"And sometimes both, I bet," Lapham said. "Well, all I can say is, it's nice to have you guys on board. We've all heard a lot about you both, but Will, you're a legend in your own time—"

"Save the butter for your biscuits," the captain growled, though Rick could tell that he wasn't really displeased.

"And we've heard a few stories about you too, Rick," the project coordinator continued, with a sly expression. "We can't figure out if we should believe them or not."

Rick gave him a quick smile that didn't travel past his lips. Which stories had they heard? How Fuck-Up Rick Tallman had bilged out of the Academy, left Princeton without graduating, been busted from Top Gun after wrapping his Harley around a tree, screwed the pooch royally in the Persian Gulf, and missed just enough of his SEAL training to keep from graduating? Every guy in his Year Group knew at least some of those stories, and he could think of a few of them who would jump at the chance to spread them.

"If they're to Rick's credit, you'd better believe them," Captain Ward said, in a tone that left no room for disagreement. "And if they're not . . . well, I guess you'd better believe some of those too!"

Everyone laughed, even Rick. Well, not quite everyone. When he glanced over at Dave Collier, he found the reputed hippie studying him with a look of dislike that bordered on hatred. Rick tried to think of anything that might have set him off, but he came up empty-handed. He gave an inner shrug. Maybe Dave was simply pissed off because his bottom-crawler wasn't acting the way it should, and further pissed off that Rick and the *Albatross* had been called in to help. If so, it was a clear case of tough shit. Rick hadn't asked for this assignment, but now that he had it, he meant to carry it out as effectively as he knew how. If that put a bee up Dave Collier's butt, too bad for him.

"Where do you hail from, Rick?" Eloise asked, lightly touching his arm. Something in her face made him wonder if her interest in talking with him was more than casual.

As he thought over how to answer that question, Rick was also wondering about her accent. It was too faint for him to be sure, but his best guess was East Texas or Louisiana.

"I'm a Navy brat," he explained. "So we lived lots of places when I was little. Then my mom settled down in Palm Beach, Florida. I guess I'd call that home as much as anywhere."

"Really? I know Palm Beach," she said. "We used to go visit some real good friends of the family, who moved there after he retired from the oil business."

She pronounced it *bidness,* and Rick narrowed his guess down to East Texas. He was about to go on record with it when she added, "Did you ever spend any time in Houston? That's where I grew up."

"I've visited there," Rick replied. "But that was a while ago. I don't know the place well." He thought of telling her that his father had trained as an astronaut at NASA's Manned Spacecraft Center in Clear Lake, just a few miles outside Houston. Rick was just finishing high school at the time, and he had spent an endless, boring, and excruciatingly painful spring vacation at his dad's bare bachelor studio in an apartment complex just off the Gulf Freeway. The place had been miles from anything that might interest a seventeen-year-old, even one who was in the mood to let himself be interested. Which Rick hadn't been. He had spent half his time hating his father for dragging him away from all his friends in Palm Beach, and the other half hating himself for not having whatever it would take to make his father like and respect him.

He didn't say any of this to Eloise. He wasn't used to talking about his father to anyone, except, very occasionally, Will Ward or Sam Deane. Instead, he said, "You're a marine geologist? I'm surprised you didn't stay in Houston."

"I grew up there," she repeated with a grin. "That kind of takes away the romance. Not that there was ever what you'd call a whole lot of romance about Houston to begin with. And anyway, offshore exploration in the Gulf has never really been the same since the last big drop in oil prices, back in 1985. Not that I mind that much. There's a lot more to marine geology than finding that stinky black stuff, and I like working within hollering distance of the cutting edge. I've got a feeling you're the same way. Am I right?"

"Hey, Rick!" Captain Ward called from across the table. "Wake up! The man wants to know if you want anything."

Rick looked around. A waiter with Polynesian features was standing just behind his chair.

"Oh—just a cup of coffee, with cream," Rick fumbled. The waiter smiled and nodded, then walked away.

Ray Lapham leaned forward. "I was just asking Will to tell us a little about what the SA-1 can do," he said.

For one moment, Rick didn't recall that SA-1 was the official designation of the *Steel Albatross*. Then he opened his eyes wide in disbelief. The very existence of the *Albatross* was classified information, and its capabilities were top secret. People on the deep-sea mining project, people like Eloise, probably needed to know a little about the revolutionary submersible, at least enough to show them why the *Albatross* was being called in to help. And Dave was actually going to be a passenger in the craft. But to talk about the subject in public like this? He must be off his nut!

Captain Ward stepped in. "I think that's a conversation we should save for another time and place, Ray," he said smoothly.

A startled look crossed Ray's face. He glanced around, then said, "Oh, of course. You're absolutely right."

After a short but awkward silence, Ray continued, "Did you know that practically all the native birds of Guam are extinct? It's true. They're all gone: the Guam broadbill, the *koko,* the rufus-fronted fantail—"

"The *what?*" Eloise demanded. "You made that one up!"

"No, I didn't. And the weird part is, nobody could figure out the reason for their extinction. Different experts blamed pesticides, predators introduced from off-island, sport hunting, loss of habitat . . . you name it. Some people even tried to say that the noise of jets taking off from Anderson Air Force Base was scaring the birds so badly that they wouldn't mate."

"Those Air Force jet jockeys do get pretty noisy at times," Rick observed. "Especially around six o'clock, at the bar of the officers' club. But I never heard that it kept anyone from mating."

The look Ray gave him made Rick decide to keep his jokes to himself for a while.

"Did they ever figure out the reason?" Eloise asked.

"Oh, yes," said Ray. "It turned out that a very common snake, that everybody had been calling a Philippine rat snake, is really a tree-climbing snake from New Guinea that lives on birds and eggs. Nobody knows how it first got here—stowed away on a copra trader, probably—but once it was here, it was in snake heaven. All of its natural predators were still back in New Guinea, you see. And the birds of Guam had never come across snakes before, so they didn't have any defenses against them."

"Huh!" Dave said, straightening up in his seat. "That's an interesting story, Ray. And there's a moral to it too. The snakes came from another country to a place that didn't belong to them, and as usual, it's the natives who got the shitty end of the stick. You work it out," he added, glancing over at Rick with a look full of challenge.

CHAPTER 7

THE HELICOPTER BANKED TO THE LEFT AND BEGAN TO FOL-
low the coastline toward a ship anchored in the middle of
the bay. Rick studied the ship through the small window
next to his seat. He knew that the *Glomar Champion* had
been specifically built for its deep-ocean retrieval mission,
but to the casual glance it looked like a total kludge. Someone with a strange sense of humor had apparently taken a
600-foot container ship and stuck a huge oil derrick onto it,
more or less amidships. Then, to add to the joke, he had
cantilevered a big helicopter landing pad out over the stern.

As the chopper settled toward the landing pad, Rick
turned to Dave Collier and asked, "What do you use that
derrick for?"

Dave gave him a sidelong look. "Do you know anything
about *Champion*'s checkered history?" he asked.

Rick nodded.

"Okay. Then you know that originally the plan—the *announced* plan, I should say—was to use what amounted to
a huge vacuum cleaner head mounted on the end of a long
string of pipe to scoop up the manganese nodules. The point
of the derrick was to assemble the pipe string, the same way
they do on drilling platforms. Then the nodules would have
been forced up the pipe and caught in a giant sieve on board

the ship. There were some big problems with that approach, though. A three-mile-long string of drilling pipe with no lateral support is more rigid than a strand of spaghetti, but not by a whole lot. So you lower the thing and hope it goes somewhere close to where you want it to be. Which it might, *if* you can keep the mother ship exactly on station, and *if* the pipe doesn't get whipsawed by competing currents at different depths. Then, of course, you hope you find what you're looking for on the bottom, because if you don't, you have to pull the string, shift the ship to another position, and go through the whole procedure again. It made just barely enough sense to be a good cover story for the cloak-and-dagger stuff that was the ship's real mission—as long as no one looked at it too hard. Which no one did. The great American public can't seem to shake the habit of swallowing whatever lies Washington decides to hand out."

Rick bridled. The public, American or otherwise, certainly got misled from time to time by its leaders, and he wasn't ready to defend fooling people, even if it was supposed to be for their own good. On the other hand, he sensed that, given the chance, Dave would talk about the United States Navy with exactly the same tone of supercilious contempt. And in any case, Dave had to know that SeaVenture, Inc., his supposed employer, masked some sort of covert government operation. Didn't he owe any loyalty to the people who paid his salary?

The helicopter touched down. Rick decided to save his remarks for another time. He and Dave had to work together on this mission. Rick couldn't let his personal reactions to the engineer and his wacko opinions get in the way.

Dave was the first one out of the chopper. Rick let Captain Ward go ahead of him, then he too climbed down. A dark-haired man of about thirty, in sharply creased khakis, stepped up and introduced himself as Jack Mathieson, the ship's second mate. As their little group followed him forward, Rick noticed two burly guys, obviously iron-pumpers, standing with folded arms on either side of the companionway, watching them intently. In spite of their dungarees and T-shirts, they looked more like hired muscle than seamen.

An unauthorized visitor would have a lot of trouble getting aboard the *Champion*.

The undersea vehicle that Dave had developed was sitting in a cradle next to the portside gunwale, just forward of the huge, looming derrick. Rick was surprised at how small it was. He had been expecting something along the lines of a small submarine, but this looked more like an overgrown torpedo. It was about twenty-five feet long and no more than four feet in diameter. At the rear, vertical and horizontal fins were arrayed around an uncaged three-bladed propeller. The sleek metal skin was interrupted at several points by what looked like attitude-control thrusters.

"So this is your baby," Captain Ward said to Dave. "How about a rundown on what she can do?"

Dave's face lit up. "Sure," he said. "First of all, I call her 'Rover.' It's not very original for a *R*emotely *O*perated *V*ehicle, but I like it. As you can see, the heart of the vehicle is a pressure hull with hemispherical endcaps. Inside the pressure hull, we've got the video and communications equipment, the instrumentation, and the control system, which is built around two 80386 microprocessors. We can preprogram the system, before launch, but usually we'll control it from up here."

"What do you use for power?" asked Rick.

"She draws her power from the ship, by way of an armored cable. But I also designed in a bank of silver zinc batteries, just in case," Dave replied, sounding irritated by the interruption. "Rover's designed to operate at slightly negative buoyancy. Two independent ballast tanks, in the bow and stern, gives pitch control, and there's 300 pounds of lead shot in a hopper amidships that we can drop for quick ascents."

Something about the craft was bothering Rick. He looked it up and down with narrowed eyes. Then it came to him. "I thought this vehicle was supposed to operate on the bottom," he said. "I don't see any runners or caterpillar treads. How do you manage?"

"Aha!" Dave said. "Come meet Junior!"

He took them to the bow of the craft, where an aluminum

frame held what looked like a cross between a bulldozer and an old-fashioned Electrolux vacuum cleaner. Two small halogen lights were mounted on its front, just above a valved opening that resembled a mouth. It looked like a face wearing an expression of malevolent glee.

"We originally designed Rover to make very low-altitude surveys of the ocean floor," Dave explained. "She was never meant to touch bottom. That's Junior's department. He's tethered to Rover by a hundred-yard umbilical cable that supplies power and control, as well as by a flexible hose. As you see, he's got treads as well as thrusters for maneuvering. The idea is that Junior breaks up the cobalt-rich crust with his 'dozer blade, then passes it back to Rover and the pipe to the surface."

"I see," Captain Ward said. "So Rover tugs the main pipe into approximate position, then Junior ranges outward from there."

"Correct," said Dave. "Junior's a lot more maneuverable than Rover, who's going to be dragging around the lower end of a big-gauge rubber hose that's over a mile long. We've made the hose neutrally buoyant, but it's still a lot of mass to mule-haul around. We think it's a workable solution, but this is really just a feasibility study. The system that's eventually used for full-scale mining may look a lot different."

"So what's the problem?" Captain Ward asked bluntly. "There must be one, or they wouldn't have called us in."

"There isn't any one particular problem," Dave replied, looking away. "Some of the time, all the systems work exactly the way they're supposed to. Then, out of nowhere, something screwy happens. Most often it's just a little something, a funny signal, a blip in the readouts that shouldn't be there. But not always. One time Rover lost attitude control and nearly stood on her tail. Another time Junior refused to deploy. On our next try Junior deployed all right but got fouled on the bottom and wouldn't come back on command. We were starting to think we'd have to cut his cable. That would have set the project back at least six months."

"It sounds like a programming problem," the captain observed.

Dave nodded. "I know. That's what I thought too. But I've checked over every line of code five times, and so have a couple of my people. When we run the programs in simulation mode, no hassles, but once Rover gets down to operating depth . . ."

"What do you expect to accomplish by going down for a look?" asked Rick.

"I need to see what actually happens when I send Rover or Junior a command. As it is, all I have to go on is the telemetry, and sometimes it just drops out for reasons we simply can't figure out. It's no more reliable than anything else."

"What about your previous experience with these two craft? Have you taken them deep before this?" Rick realized even as he spoke that his question sounded more like a challenge to Dave than he had intended, but it was too late to call it back.

Dave's expression hardened. "I've had both of them down to 1500 meters," he said, "and they worked just fine. I know, because I went down aboard the submersible *Ulysse* and watched, close at hand. Is that deep enough for you?"

Rick gave Captain Ward a look of surprise. Fifteen hundred meters was over 4500 feet—almost a thousand feet deeper than the deepest Rick had ever taken the *Steel Albatross*.

"When we started having problems, I asked Ray if we couldn't get *Ulysse* out here," Dave continued. "Just put her and her control van on a C-130 and fly her out. He was willing to consider the idea, but Washington wouldn't go along—too expensive, maybe, or maybe they just didn't want any *furriners* poking around their precious project. I even put in a call to Toulon on my own hook and told the people there what my problem was, but they couldn't help. It turns out that *Ulysse* is completely booked up for at least the next three months. A team of marine archaeologists managed to persuade some rich foundation to give them the money to search for a Minoan war fleet from 1500 B.C. somewhere off Cyprus."

"*Ulysse* is a fine craft," Captain Ward said. "I was down in her once myself. But I think you'll find that *Steel Albatross* is every bit as capable and then some."

"*Steel Albatross?*" Dave repeated. "Is that your name for the SA-1? How about that! You know what they call albatrosses around here, don't you? Gooney birds. The clowns of the Pacific. So now I'm going to have to deal with another clown," he added, giving Rick a sly glance.

Rick felt his jaw tighten. Why was this guy needling him?

Captain Ward sensed the tension. He took a small step that put him between Rick and Dave.

"I've spent a lot of time on Midway and I know about gooney birds," the captain said calmly. "I've seen how silly they can look on land. But you know as well as I do, son, they don't look or behave one damned bit silly once they're in the air. And the SA-1 doesn't look or behave one damned bit silly once she's in the water."

From the look on Dave's face, he had bitten off a little more than he was prepared to chew. "As long as she can do the job," he mumbled, turning away. "That's all I care about."

"Don't worry," Captain Ward said grimly. "She will."

Ray was waiting for them when the helicopter returned to the hotel.

"Good news," he said loudly, over the noise of the rotor. "I just raised *Berkone* on the radio. They gave me an ETA of 0700 tomorrow. And the forecast is for a rapid improvement overnight. With any luck, we can get in a test dive sometime in the next forty-eight hours."

"Does that mean we have the afternoon off?" asked Dave.

"Feeling overworked?" Ray replied, with a wicked glint in his eye.

"There's more to this island than beachfront hotels," Dave said. "And as long as we're here, I'd like to get to know some of it. Do you mind?"

Ray shrugged. "It's none of my business. Just don't get lost or tangle with one of those bird-eating snakes. Oh, and if you go up into the hills, watch out for Sergeant Webb."

"Who's Sergeant Webb?" asked Rick.

Ray shrugged again. "A local legend. More like a joke, really. Have you heard about the Japanese soldier who holed up in the interior from the time of the U.S. landing on Guam, back in 1944, until 1972, when he finally surrendered?"

"I remember when he turned himself in," Captain Ward said. "I saw photos of the guy. But I never heard of a Sergeant Webb."

With a laugh, Ray said, "The story goes that one Sergeant Cletus Webb, who took part in the landing, went on reconnaissance and got separated from the American forces. He's been hiding out ever since, because every time he starts to come down out of the hills, he sees so many Japanese that he figures we lost the war."

Everyone laughed, except Dave, who said, "I don't think much of jokes like that, Ray. The local economy depends on Japanese tourists. If we're willing to take their money, we ought to be willing to stop telling jokes about them."

"Lighten up, for chrissake," Ray retorted "Get that chip off your shoulder. And anyway, if you don't like the story about Sergeant Webb, take it up with some of the Chamorros who told it to me. And while you're at it, ask them what it was like here during the Japanese occupation, when everyone on the island was herded into concentration camps."

"I'm not saying the Japanese are angels," Dave said. "But we're not either. What right do we have to call Guam American territory? Who told us we could grab all the best land on the island for Air Force and Navy bases?"

"We can hold off discussing that until another time," Ray said, just as Captain Ward was taking a deep breath and getting ready to let out a blast. "Go take a hike, if that's what you have in mind."

"These issues won't go away just because we refuse to face them," Dave insisted.

Maybe they won't, but I will, thought Rick. Aloud, he said, "Ray? any problem if I get in some snorkeling this afternoon? I'm feeling a little stale. Don't worry, I won't go far."

The project coordinator said, "No problem as far as I'm concerned. Just keep an eye out for ski-boats and water-skiers. Some of them aren't as watchful for divers as they ought to be."

Captain Ward walked back to the hotel with Rick. He was steaming. "If I hear any more unpatriotic crap from that little pissant," he muttered, "I'll personally flatten his ugly nose."

"We all have to set aside our personal feelings and work together for the good of the project," Rick said virtuously. Then he grinned.

"You know what?" he added. "I think we're borrowing each other's lines!"

After lunch, Rick went back to his room, put on his trunks, and grabbed his fins, mask, and snorkel. As an after-thought, he picked up his double bungee spear gun.

He was particularly proud of that spear gun. He had used it to provide himself and his friends with many good meals. It provided him with a lot of personal satisfaction too.

He had wondered about that satisfaction from time to time. Part of it was a matter of fulfilling the traditional male role of hunter and provider. But there was also the pride that came with owning something that he had personally customized and made one of a kind. It bore the distinctive mark of its owner in the eight-inch bayonet that he had permanently affixed to the front of the aluminum stock. The idea had come to him after listening to a Tinian spearfisher-man tell of losing his spear when a large grouper he had hit broke the line. The encounter with the mako that followed would not have been nearly so dicey had he been left with a stand-off weapon that had more reach than his knife.

Rick headed down to the beach. On a towel near the water, Eloise was sunning herself—*lots* of herself. Her pale blue one-piece suit was cut high over the hips, and she had rolled the top part down to her waist. Her breasts were small but perfectly shaped, and nearly the same shade of tan as her shoulders. She was apparently in the habit of sunbathing topless.

Rick paused to appreciate the scene. Eloise's skin glistened in the bright sunlight, and the sea breeze carried a whiff of coconut oil.

Eloise sensed his presence, looked around, and sat up. "I know I should know better than to lie here like this," she said, pulling up the shoulder straps of her suit.

"Don't mind me," Rick said with a grin. "I'm not offended to find you here like that. As a matter of fact, I enjoyed it. But then, that suit is just about as revealing on as it was off."

Eloise raised her oversized sunglasses and propped them on her forehead. "I'm happy to know I meet with your approval, sir," she said in a lilting voice. Then she continued, less frivolously, "Goodness knows I have read enough articles about the dangers of too much sun. The magazines are full of them. But they all sound too much like my grandma. She used to have a tizzy when she'd catch me sunbathing. She herself had about the whitest skin you ever saw, in spite of living out in the middle of nowhere her whole life, forty miles from the nearest shade tree."

"What was her secret?" asked Rick, intrigued.

"Straw hats with big brims and blouses with long sleeves. And she never, *ever*, went out in the heat of the day—which to her meant between about seven in the morning and five in the evening—without her parasol."

Rick grinned at the picture Eloise was presenting. "Times have changed," he remarked.

"Yes, but I'm afraid they're changing back again," Eloise said. "That's why I'm out here, bagging all the rays I can, before having a tan becomes so unfashionable that I don't dare show up with one in polite company."

"You could always tell people it was bronze makeup," Rick suggested with a laugh.

"Sure," she replied. "Or I could put white-face on over my tan. Oh well ... have a good swim."

"Thanks, and you have a good tan. See you later." Rick

walked out into the surf. When the water was waist deep, he slipped on his fins. Then he spit into his mask, rubbed the spit around on the inner surface of the glass to keep it from fogging, and put it on. He slipped the soft rubber mouthpiece into his mouth, took a couple of breaths, and he was off.

Long easy strokes of his fins drove him quickly across the bay, as he headed out toward open water. His SEAL training had honed an already-strong swimming technique into one of efficient and effortless grace. He had learned a secret known by all good underwater men: how to relax in the water.

Four and a half minutes out from the beach, he was over an outcropping of chalice coral, pale green and looking a lot like a pile of sponges. A huge school of three or four thousand anthiases streamed by. The tiny fish, each no more than three inches long with rose-colored flanks and a lavender stripe along its dorsal surface, wheeled to the right like a precision drill team and disappeared. Rick always wondered what sort of a signal it was that allowed four thousand fish in a school to turn the same direction, the same amount and at the same split second. The magical sight filled him with awe.

Moments later, a small silvertip shark glided out from behind a growth of coral. After a good look at Rick, it apparently decided its hunger wasn't strong enough to risk an attack. A flick of its tail, and it too vanished.

The coral teemed with fish, feeding off the plankton-rich water and each other. Rick glided along easily on the surface, not thinking, simply enjoying the spectacle. The conflict with Dave, the fate of the mission, his doubts about the path to take in his career, Eloise topless on the beach—all were left behind, back on dry land. Even the need to keep an eye out for sharks and whatever other hazards there might be, including ski-boats, couldn't spoil the deep calm that came over him.

By this time the water was about fifty feet deep. As always, Rick felt challenged by the skindiver's urge to "Go deep and stay long." He took three deep breaths and put his head down and his feet up behind him.

The surface dive left hardly a ripple. He swam down to admire a pink and green seafan that was easily seven feet across. A bright yellow angelfish looked out at him from deep among the branches, then retreated out of sight behind a mass of gorgonians. Below them, Rick noticed a large overhang in the coral wall, about two feet above the white sand bottom. It looked like a good spot to hunt for tonight's dinner. The hotel chef would be happy to prepare it.

He put his left hand under the lip of the overhang, did a half twist, and pulled himself under the shelf. With his shoulder on the sand, he peered around for a target.

Suddenly he realized that he had spent too much time lollygagging and hadn't left enough breath for a serious hunt. Just as he was thinking it was time to leave, he saw what looked like about a twenty- or thirty-pound grouper in a scour, far back to his left.

He stretched out, aimed, and let fly. The sand at the back of the cave erupted into opaque clouds and he knew he had a hit. Rick pushed himself out from under the overhang and pulled on the line that linked the spear to the gun. He expected some small jerking resistance. Instead, he met a stone wall. No way was that spear going to follow him. He could see it vibrating, but the line wouldn't budge. He finally figured that the spear had gone through the fish, then jammed itself up past the barb in a coral crevice behind the fish.

He got in two more hard tugs before he decided he'd better head for the surface. He could come back down for the gun and, he hoped, for the spear and the fish too. After five deep, refreshing breaths, he dove to the bottom again and tried to make out, in the dim light, what his problem was. The sand was still stirred up in the back of the cave. He recovered the gun easily, but he couldn't see the spear. When he tugged at the line, it still wouldn't budge.

He tried pulling hard first to the left and then to the right. No good. He swam to the back of the narrowing space between the floor and ceiling of the cave, now in zero visibility because of the roiled-up sand, and still couldn't reach the spear shaft.

Rick hated to lose the spear, but he would if he had to. No way would he part with the gun. He'd break the line if necessary. But once again, it was time to leave. He'd have to ponder his predicament more casually topside, where he could breathe at the same time.

He backed out of the narrow spot and turned around as soon as possible, pulling the gun behind him. As he emerged from the shadows of the cave into the sunlit open water, there was a momentary interruption of the light. It was as if one of the shadows from the cave had followed him.

That's silly, Rick thought. I must be getting a little hypoxic from working too hard and being down too long. Then he glanced up instinctively and became very still.

He had a problem.

Most sharks look large when you see them in the water with you. This white-tip really was large. It had just passed above the cave entrance, at about the level of the shelf. Now he was circling to the left and heading back toward Rick.

Rick was running out of air, and his only weapon was firmly tethered and unusable. As for his very unfriendly companion, *he* had all the weapons he needed—whole rows of them—and had no need to come up for air. Not a fair match.

Rick braced his right foot on the shelf and pulled the gun with both hands. After a moment, the line parted suddenly, right at the stock. He remembered noticing some corrosion there. He had meant to replace the line. Now he was glad he hadn't.

He turned back. The shark had completed his circle and was now about ten feet away and coming directly at him.

Conventional wisdom among those knowledgeable in shark lore has it that when a shark is ready to attack, the pectoral fins drop, the back arches, and sometimes, as a precursor to a feeding frenzy, the body starts to shudder markedly.

Rick was not in a mood to count how many of these symptoms he saw. It was time to leave. He held the newly freed spear gun, minus its spear but with its attached bayonet, between the shark and his precious body while he headed for the surface, twisting as he went to keep the predator in view.

By the time he broke the surface at last, he realized he really was hypoxic. He heard a loud buzz and distant bells and couldn't see clearly. He longed to raise his head and gulp in precious air, but he forced himself to breathe through the snorkel instead. He needed to keep his face in the water and his eyes on the shark.

Shit. The white-tip had followed him to the surface. It was circling him to the left, still about ten feet away.

Rick began thinking about the long swim to shore. Somehow he would have to manage to swim backward, with his face in the water to watch the trailing shark, and his spear gun at the ready to fend it off. Not an easy evolution.

Suddenly he heard a loud crack. He raised his head just far enough to see above the surface. In the foreground, that ominous fin, the stuff of movie chillers, went on circling. It looked closer now. Farther off was a gray Zodiac rubber boat. A man in a wetsuit was leaning over the side, slapping the water hard with the flat of an oar.

Another crack, then another. Rick ducked under and scanned the area. He didn't see the shark anywhere. Apparently the sharp noise had convinced him not to attack.

Still keeping a sharp watch, Rick swam toward the Zodiac. When he surfaced next to it, he noticed that a Diver Down flag, red with a white diagonal bar, fluttered from a staff at the bow.

The young man in the boat looked Japanese. He helped Rick aboard and said, "It looked like you had some unwanted company. I think the noise I was making helped to scare him away. Are you all right?"

"I'm fine, thank you," Rick said. "But I'm glad you were in your boat instead of in the water with me. We might both have been in trouble."

"Yes," the man said. "I was diving also, but I had to return to my boat. I had terrible foot cramps. I shouldn't have gone out alone wearing these new long fins."

"They always say never to dive alone," Rick replied. "I guess we both got a lesson in why today."

"Very true. Please let me introduce myself. I am Kazuo Takauji."

"Nice to meet you. I'm Rick Tallman."

"Are you here on vacation, Rick? The waters around Guam are wonderful for diving. Almost every form of sea life in the Pacific can be found here."

"Yes, the reef and the visibility and the temperature are all great," Rick said, dodging the question about why he was on Guam.

"I belong to a group that might interest you," Kazuo went on. "It is called Project Ocean Friends. Have you heard of it?"

"Afraid not."

"Oh. Well, we are conducting a thorough study of the marine ecology of this region. Will you be here long? Perhaps you would like to come to one of our meetings."

"I'm going to be pretty busy," Rick said. "Thanks anyway."

"Anyone who enjoys diving should know about our program," the young Japanese continued. "I will send you some literature and a notice of our next meeting. You are not obligated to come, of course, but I think you would find it very enjoyable. Where are you staying?"

Reluctantly, Rick told him the name of the hotel.

"Ah," Kazuo said, nodding. "I will mail the material to you this afternoon. I would be happy to take you to shore. I do not think I will dive again today."

"Thanks," Rick said. "I think I've had enough for the day too."

As the Zodiac bounced through the breakers on its way to the beach, Rick found himself wondering about the young Japanese. The man's equipment, from the boat to the stainless-steel knife strapped to his leg, was first-class all the way. Rick had also recognized the instrument on his wrist. It was one of those new and very expensive gizmos that combined a watch, depth gauge, thermometer, compass, and decompression computer. Why would someone invest that kind of money in diving gear and then economize on a pair of secondhand fins? Because no matter what Kazuo had said, those fins he'd been using were too beat up to be new.

CHAPTER 8

BY LATE IN THE AFTERNOON OF HIS SECOND DAY ABOARD *Ocean Friend*, Tom was starting to wonder if he had made a big mistake. Not that anything had happened to upset him. That was the point. Nothing at all had happened. The morning before, the research ship had stood out from Guam to a position fifteen or twenty miles northwest of the island, then started a slow, deliberate search pattern. One mile west, 200 yards south, one mile east, 200 yards south, one mile west, 200 yards south.... The turns at each end had been very wide. He assumed that was to keep that winged torpedo-looking device they were towing at the end of a long cable from slowing so much that it dragged the bottom.

By sunset they had scoured two adjoining rectangles a mile wide by about ten in length. As far as Tom could tell, they had found exactly nothing. Although he didn't know for sure, because the door to the electronics room was locked and a curtain was drawn across the porthole. When Tom had tried to visit the bridge, Kazuo had appeared from somewhere, told him that the ship's officers needed to concentrate on their work, and had led him, politely but firmly, back down to the main deck.

The second day had dawned just like the first, as the ship continued its methodical attempt to treat the face of the ocean like a gigantic gridiron, and once again Tom had had nothing to do but stand by the railing with his hands in the pockets of his cut-off jeans and watch the seabirds riding the currents above the ship's wake. He had thought he might get a chance to try the submersible, but the craft never even came out from under its tarp. Its runners might as well have been welded to the deck. And the damned ship had never stopped its damned search pattern long enough for him to get in even a short dive.

His big excitement of the day had come a little before noon, when Kazuo had appeared on deck wearing his yellow and blue wetsuit, a canvas carryall bag over one shoulder.

Tom had hurried over. "I'll go suit up too," he had declared. "I'll just be a minute."

"No, no, my friend," Kazuo had said, with a smile that showed two even rows of very white teeth. "I have an errand that I must do alone. I'll be back very soon."

"But what's the point of my being here? I've done nothing but stand around since yesterday morning."

Kazuo's face had grown serious. "There is a point to everything we do in our Project," he had said. He had pointed over Tom's shoulder, toward the bulkhead. "Look at the fire extinguisher behind that glass door. It has never been used. Does that mean there is no point in its being there?"

"I didn't sign on to turn myself into a fire extinguisher," Tom had muttered.

"Perhaps you are being trained to greater patience," Kazuo had replied. Tom had heard a teasing note in his voice, but it hadn't masked a hint of irritation. "In any case, I must go—alone."

He had raised his hand over his head and gestured. Two deckhands came running. One of them had unlocked a little door in the pedestal between the portside davits, exposing a control panel. Kazuo had tossed his carryall into the Zodiac, climbed in himself, and nodded. The deckhand had pushed a button, then had begun to turn a knob slowly. With a groan, the powerful hydraulic cylinder at the base of the davit had started to lengthen. The steel C frame had uncurled, lifting the boat, its heavy motor, and its passenger and thrusting them out over the water.

The cable had begun to lower the rubber boat toward the water. Kazuo had pushed the button for the outboard's electric starter and rested one hand on a spoke of the boat's wheel. He had turned his head, looking over his shoulder to judge the relative motion of the ship and the sea. The ship had rolled to port, dropping the boat just even with the top of an approaching swell. As the keel of the boat had touched water, Kazuo had slapped the cable release levers, advanced the throttle, and spun the wheel to port. The motor had roared. Its bow riding high, the Zodiac had curved away from the ship's side and made a wide turn southward, casting up rainbow-colored arcs of spray as it skipped across the waves. Moments later it had been out of sight, hidden by a squall approaching from the southeast.

In the two hours since Kazuo's departure, Tom's mood had grown steadily bleaker. After another fruitless try at finding someone to chat with or something to do, he thrust his hands into his pockets and walked aft to the fantail. He slumped to the deck, his shoulders sagging.

What had possessed him to fall in with Hoshi and her Chicken Little tale of fast-approaching global disaster? Sure, she and Kazuo believed it, but so what? People believed all sorts of unlikely things. And even if they were right, their idea of placing an Ark on the ocean bottom was just plain kooky. And even if they somehow managed to do it, why should he be part of its crew? He wasn't sure that he would even want to survive the end of everyone and everything he knew in the world.

Maybe it was time to think about moving on. Truk was just a short hop away on one of the puddle jumpers of Air Mike, as everyone called Air Micronesia. He had been meaning to dive Truk for years. A whole fleet of Japanese ships, more than seventy of them, lay on the bottom of its huge lagoon. It was the biggest collection of divable wrecks in the entire Pacific, and many of them were at snorkel depths.

What was the point, though? He had already dived to

more wrecks, more coral reefs, more underwater caverns, than he could remember. What would one more, or seventy more, or a thousand and seventy more, do for him or anyone else? In the attic of his uncle's house in Honolulu was a big carton full of photos he had taken on dives, plus half a dozen notebooks full of notes on his unique underwater experiences. He had found them fascinating, and he had desperately wanted to share them with others who didn't know or appreciate the ocean. But one day he had realized that no one wanted to look at his pictures or listen to his stories. He hadn't carried a camera or notebook since. Why bother?

Tom leaned back against one of the uprights of the A-frame derrick and stared down at the propeller wash bubbling and splashing under the overhang of the stern. The noise and commotion were impressive, but what did they mean, after all? So what if you make a big splash? Soon enough you're dead, and the sea rolls on as it has rolled for five thousand years.

The sun was too bright. He pulled the bill of his cap lower and gazed out toward that perfect, unbroken, rounded horizon that can be seen only on the open ocean. The curve of the ship's wake, glittering in the sunlight, seemed to echo the shape of the horizon. He narrowed his eyelids against the glare. It seemed easier simply to shut them. Why not? There was nothing out there to look at.

Suddenly—a minute later? ten?—he opened his eyes, blinked twice, and straightened up. He hadn't imagined it. The wake of *Ocean Friend* was no longer a ruler line drawn across the face of the water. It curved, a great wide curve that could mean only one thing: The search was being called off for now. Maybe they were returning to port.

Tom felt like cutting loose with a Rebel yell. But he didn't. He didn't want to stand out, and no one aboard *Ocean Friend* spoke much louder than a whisper, when they spoke at all.

The Project compound came into view just a little before sunset. The captain used the bow and stern thrusters to maneuver the ship gently in to the seaward end of the pier.

Tom noticed a familiar-looking Zodiac tied up to a wharf nearer shore. So this was where Kazuo had come on his mysterious errand. . . . Tom had suspected as much. He shouldered his backpack and started up the pier. At the landward end, he had to wait at the electrified gate until someone came along with the right card to unlock it. He was wondering how to find a ride to Agana when a white Land Cruiser came barreling down the hill. It stopped a few feet away, in a sideways slide that flung up a choking cloud of dust.

The rear door swung open. Hoshi Ito was sitting in the back seat, looking at Tom. Waiting.

He took a deep breath and walked over to the car.

"Hello," he said, putting his head inside the open car door. "We're back."

"Yes. I called you back," Hoshi said. "An important part of your training is to begin this evening."

"Called us back?" Tom repeated. For a moment he thought she was talking about telepathy or something equally far-out. Then he thought of another possibility, though that too seemed unlikely. "Do you mean you ordered the ship to leave the search area and sail all the way back here, just to bring me?"

Her lips curved upward, so slightly that he wasn't sure he was seeing it. "Are you surprised?" she asked.

"Well, sure I am. It's pretty wasteful, for a start. Why couldn't I have gotten a ride back with Kazuo?"

The car's driver turned to face him. It was Kazuo. "I told you," he said. "I had an errand to do alone. You must listen and learn. That is your first lesson."

Hoshi made a slight gesture with her right arm. "Please get in."

Tom hesitated. "Tell you the truth, I was thinking about asking for a lift into town. Not that I don't appreciate everything you've done, but—"

"Please get in," Hoshi repeated, in exactly the same tone of voice. It was as if his words had been spoken on a lower plane of existence that she did not stoop to acknowledge.

He got in.

At the house, Hoshi went inside without a word or glance. Kazuo took Tom by the arm. "Time to bathe," he said. "Do you know Japanese baths? They are not so different from your saunas and hot tubs. People in many countries have discovered that heat draws out poisons from the mind as well as from the body."

"I don't really . . ." Tom started to say. Then he suddenly realized how grimy he felt. Some time soaking in a hot tub might be just what he needed. "Sure, good idea," he concluded.

Kazuo took him to a smaller building at the back of the house. They undressed in an anteroom. Tom left his cut-offs, T-shirt, and skivvies on a peg and followed Kazuo into the main room. The floor and three of the walls were tiled in subtly blending shades of blue and green. A fourth wall of screens had been slid aside to reveal a small Japanese garden. Dazzling white sand had been raked into intricate patterns that echoed the shapes of the three rugged stones that protruded from the sand. A wall of rough stone surrounded the garden.

The pool, about six feet by nine feet, was set into the floor. Steam curled up from its surface and hung just under the wooden beams of the ceiling. Tom took a step toward the pool, but Kazuo touched his arm and pointed to the near wall. Now Tom noticed that an area of the floor along that wall was set off by a low tiled ridge. He glanced upward and spotted what looked like shower heads near the ceiling.

"First we clean ourselves, then we bathe," Kazuo said with a laugh. "That must seem very silly to Westerners, who do exactly the reverse."

"No, it makes sense," Tom replied, accepting a sponge and a small bottle of body shampoo. "Besides, it's sort of the same in the U.S. You're always supposed to shower before going in the pool. It's just that a lot of people don't do it."

Kazuo touched an unobtrusive bronze button set into the wall. Tom gasped as a chilly waterfall suddenly descended on him. Once he was totally wet, he stepped aside, lathered up, and stepped under the shower again to rinse off. At what seemed like the exact moment when he finished rinsing, the shower shut itself off as suddenly as it had started.

"Now for the bath," Kazuo said, walking to the edge of the pool. "Here there are steps down. It is best to enter the hot water gradually."

"I know," Tom said. He didn't bother to hide a note of irritation in his voice. Did Kazuo think he was a complete hick?

"Forgive me, of course you do," Kazuo quickly said, with a slight bow. "Not everyone is as familiar with our customs as you are."

Tom stiffened. Now he felt on the spot, as if he had just set himself a standard that he couldn't hope to live up to. But how? He hadn't claimed to know Kazuo's customs, had he? All he had meant was that he had been in hot tubs before. Now he had himself in two kinds of hot water!

He took a first step into the pool. The water was hot, all right—*really* hot. If he had been alone, he might have changed his mind about going in. But with Kazuo there, judging him, he couldn't. He took another step, then another, pausing while his balls and ass and lower back got used to the temperature. When the frontier between scalding water and chilling air had reached his chest, his face broke out in sweat and he began to feel light-headed. Without thought, he let himself sink until the water reached the middle of his neck. After a few moments, it felt wonderful. All the tension in his muscles drained away, and he felt a delicious urge to take a nap. He moved to the side of the pool, leaned his head back against the curved tiles of the edge, and closed his eyes.

Kazuo was shaking his shoulder. Tom opened his eyes. Had he really gone to sleep? When he tried to straighten up, he felt as if the pool had drained not just the tension but the strength from his muscles.

"Come," Kazuo said, climbing out of the pool. Tom followed him around to the side of the room next to the garden. On the floor was a polished log that had been hollowed into a trough. It was filled with very cold water. Kazuo knelt down, filled a carved wooden dipper with the water, and

DEEP FLIGHT

poured it over his head. Then he stepped aside and motioned for Tom to do the same.

With a mental shrug, Tom got down on his knees and lowered the dipper into the trough of water. As he lifted the dipper, he raised his eyes. For the first time, he noticed a small opening in the stone wall that encircled the garden. Through it, he saw a tiny portion of the blue ocean, stretching to the horizon. He looked down at the water in the dipper, then again at the ocean, and it seemed to him that he no longer knew which was which. Or did it matter? Hadn't Hoshi told him that he—that they—held the fate of the ocean in their hands? And now he saw that it was true.

Bowing his head, he tilted the dipper. He blinked as the cold water seemed to bring all his senses back to life.

In the anteroom, Tom discovered that his clothes had vanished. In their place were a pair of loose pants with a drawstring waist and a tunic with wide sleeves, both in fine-textured gray cotton. A pair of new straw-topped *zoris* waited on the floor. There was nothing that looked as if it was meant to serve as underwear.

He looked over at Kazuo, who was pulling on a pair of pants that looked like Tom's, but in white.

Noticing Tom's glance, Kazuo said, "Special clothes help draw a line between special events and everyday life." He put on his white tunic and tied a soft white sash at his waist to hold it closed.

Like his costume, Tom's sash was gray. "Do different colors mean different ranks, the way they do in karate?" he asked.

"Yes and no," Kazuo replied. "All this will become clear."

He took Tom back to the main house, to a small room furnished only with a tatami mat. "Please wait here," he said. "Focus your thoughts on the vital importance of what we do."

Tom tried to do as he was told, but the hot bath had left him exhausted. He lay back on the thick straw mat and closed his eyes. When he opened them again, Hoshi was kneeling just a few inches away from him. Once again she was wearing thin white silk that caressed the lines of her body. He sat up hurriedly.

"It is time," Hoshi said softly, rising effortlessly to her feet. "Come. You are ready."

"Wait! Ready for what?"

She gazed down at him, as if from very far away. "Only the fittest can hope to survive the great trials that the world will soon face," she said. "You must be trained. Trained and tested, again and again, until you truly become what you were meant to be. Come. We have no time to waste. It is time for your training to begin."

She turned and glided out of the room, not looking back to see if he was following. He was.

At the far end of the hall was the big shrinelike room where she had first told him the real, secret, mission of Project Ocean Friends. About thirty people were sitting on the floor in two semicircular rows. They appeared to be of many races and nationalities. Japanese and American, of course, but also Polynesian, Indian, and Middle Eastern. One square-headed blond man was almost certainly German. All wore white pants and tunics like Kazuo's. No, *almost* all: A young woman who looked part Vietnamese and part African-American was in gray. She looked up as Tom entered the room and seemed relieved that he too wore gray.

Hoshi motioned to an empty spot in the outer row and waited while Tom sat down. Then she moved to the focus of the group and sank to the floor.

"The ocean is our mother," she said, in a tone that was almost conversational.

"The ocean is our mother," the others in the room repeated, in ragged unison.

"She gave us life."

"She gave us life."

"We give back that which was given."

"We give back that which was given."

"Who stands ready to die for our mother?"

"We do."

"Who stands ready to *live* for our mother?"

The response came in a shout. "We do!"

"She will protect her children from the perils to come."

That apparently ended that part of the ritual. Hoshi sat back on her heels, and a faint rustling filled the room as the others shifted to more comfortable positions. Tom found himself remembering childhood Sundays, just before the sermon.

At a nod from Hoshi, a gray-haired man with a faint Aussie accent began his report on the Project's outreach effort. He recounted the number of people approached, names added to the mailing list, and number of leaflets distributed to cars and homes. Tom's attention wandered, until the end, when the man began to call on people from his team to comment on their own activities. Each in turn accused himself or herself of not giving enough to the program, of letting possible converts get away, of taking too long a lunch or coffee break. It was as if they were competing with each other to see who could be most self-critical.

At first Tom was tempted to think of this as a weird game, but gradually their sincerity began to reach him. He began to understand. They were so certain, beyond any touch of doubt, that what they were doing was the most important thing in the world. That was why they criticized themselves so bitterly, because they had not given everything they could to that urgent, overwhelming goal. Their own weakness deeply hurt them and left them ashamed, but the admission of that weakness healed them.

When everyone on the outreach team had made their confessions, Hoshi looked silently at the gray-haired man who was their captain. He stood up, walked to the center of the semicircle, and let his white tunic slip down off his shoulders.

Hoshi got to her feet. She held a long, thin bamboo rod in her right hand. Her face as still as ever, she raised the rod high and brought it down across the man's shoulders.

Tom flinched and looked away just as the blow fell. When he looked again, he saw a red welt across the man's back, punctuated by bright drops of blood where the rings of the bamboo had broken the skin.

The man's face was pale, but he waited, unmoving, until

Hoshi gave a faint nod. Then he pulled his tunic into place and said, "Thank you, Hoshi." He returned to his seat.

Still standing, Hoshi said, "Aleesha?"

The girl in gray sat up straighter.

"You received a letter from Hong Kong yesterday," Hoshi continued.

"Yes, I did, Hoshi," the girl said. She sounded scared. "It was from my mother."

"The woman who calls herself your mother? Did you read it?"

"Yes, I had to. She . . . she is very ill. She has no money, no one to help. She asks that I come back, to help her."

"Have you told her of our work? Does she realize how important it is? What else did the letter say?"

Aleesha stared down at her lap. "That I was a foolish and ungrateful child. When I was last with her, she ordered me not to return to Ocean Friends."

"She set herself in opposition to the work?"

"Yes. And when I told her I was coming back anyway, she began to scream and hit me. She said that I would be better dead." A few tears began to trickle down the girl's face.

Hoshi sat down facing her, only inches away.

"Who is this woman who calls herself a mother and yet wishes her child dead?" she demanded softly.

Aleesha was silent, but her chest began to heave. She clasped her hands so tightly that the knuckles whitened.

"Tell us," Hoshi insisted. "Tell yourself. What sort of person is she? Tell us!"

"A whore," Aleesha said, almost too softly to be heard. Then, in rising tones, "A murderer and a whore. She sold her body to strangers and killed her children before they could be born. She would have killed me too, but she waited too long!"

"And this person now tells you to abandon your true mother and your true mission, to come back to her," Hoshi said, in a voice that was almost conversational. "Why did you not tell me of this yesterday, or even give me the letter unread? Why did you force me to ask you about it in front of everyone?"

"I was so ashamed," Aleesha whispered. "I hate her. But I don't know what to do. Should I go to her? She's my mother, and she's dying."

She raised her tear-streaked face and gave Hoshi an imploring look. In reply, Hoshi slapped her, with enough force to knock her over.

After a long moment, Aleesha pushed herself back up into a sitting position. Her left cheek was flaming red.

"When the meeting ends, you will go to your room," Hoshi said. "You will stay there two days and think about the meaning of what has happened. At our next meeting, you will share with us what you have learned."

"I understand," Aleesha said weakly. "Thank you, Hoshi." She began to slump to one side. The two people on either side of her put their arms around her and kept her from falling to the floor.

Hoshi returned to her place at the center of the semicircle and stood looking down for what seemed like a very long time. When she looked up, she slowly scanned the seated disciples, studying each face in the room.

"Nothing is more important than our work," she said in a low voice. "Nothing, except the task of making ourselves equal to our work. We all will have moments of weakness. Of course we will. We are human. But by our own efforts, we can train ourselves to become more than we are now. We can make ourselves worthy of the work. We can become strong enough to face the dangers we know will come. But that can happen only if we uphold each other without counting the cost. Brothers and sisters do that, and as children of our mother, the ocean, are we not more than brothers and sisters to each other?"

She spread her arms wide, as if to embrace all of them at once. "This is our family," she continued. "The family that we ourselves have created. No other tie on earth is as important or as strong as the tie that links us to each other. At every moment, we hold each other close. Even alone, we are never apart. We will sit in silence now, and focus our thoughts on that tie. See it in your minds, a rope of pure light that runs between you and every other son and daughter of our mother. Feed it all your energies, make it stronger still. That web of light will save us all when the day of need arrives. Cherish it."

A profound silence fell over the room. Tom felt himself grow warm, as if all the others really were holding him in their arms. He had been a loner, a wanderer, for a long time. Now he began to ask himself if, at last, he had found himself a home. He truly belonged to—and yes, he truly loved—Hoshi.

CHAPTER 9

RAY LAPHAM APPEARED ON THE TERRACE, GLANCED around, and walked over to the table where Rick and Will Ward were having breakfast with Eloise.

"Good news," he said. "I just got word that *Berkone* arrived on schedule this morning. She's anchored in the harbor."

Captain Ward set down his coffee cup with a clatter. "I'd like to go aboard as soon as possible. Can you lay on some transportation for us?" he asked.

"Already done," Ray replied, with a satisfied smile. "A chopper will be here in half an hour. Do you mind if I come along? I've got a yen to see this craft of yours."

"Not at all," the captain said. "Though I suspect you'll have plenty of chances before this project's finished."

"Have any of you seen Dave Collier this morning?" Ray asked. "He should be on this trip."

Eloise drained her coffee cup and stood up. "I'll tell him," she announced. "Dave's not much of a morning person."

"Good." Ray glanced at his watch. "We'll meet by the helipad in about twenty minutes, okay?" He went back inside the hotel.

Eloise returned a couple of minutes later. Rick noticed

that her face was pinker than it had been before she went up to Dave's room.

"Dave'll be right down," she reported. She took her seat and went back to browsing through the local newspaper. "Hmm," she continued. "You two might be interested in this. The Ocean Friends people are showing a new film tonight on coral reef formation. They've got some really fine underwater cinematographers working with them. I went to one of their programs a couple of weeks ago, about the effects of nutrient plumes on sea life near coastal river mouths. I can't say I understood it all—marine ecology isn't really my field—but it was fascinating all the same."

Looking straight at Rick, she added, "Would either of you like to go to the film with me?"

The captain stepped on any answer to the question by musing out loud, "Ocean Friends? Can't say I've heard of them. Sounds a little kooky to me."

"I suppose so," Eloise said. "They do have a very narrow focus, but within it they seem to do some good work."

Rick frowned. "That name rings a bell, but I don't—oh, of course. That Japanese diver I met yesterday said he was going to send me some of their literature. I tried to tell him not to bother, but . . ."

Eloise smiled. "They're pretty persistent. One of them stopped me at the mall the other day, and it took me a good ten minutes to tear myself away."

Out over the bay, from the direction of Agana, a dot in the sky grew steadily larger, revealing itself to be a helicopter. It passed noisily to the left of the hotel and settled behind a band of palm trees.

"Dollars to doughnuts, that's here for us," Captain Ward said, pushing his chair back and standing up. "Come on, Rick, my boy. We can't spend the day sitting around the pool, ogling this beautiful girl."

"Why, thanks for the compliment, Captain," Eloise said with a grin. "You can ogle away as far as I'm concerned."

"Later," Rick said, grinning back. "And I just might go to that show with you tonight, if we finish in time. I'll give you a call."

Eloise looked pleased. "Do. And I'll see if Dave can come too."

"Are you coming or not?" the captain growled, tapping Rick on the arm.

Rick gave Eloise a shoulders-up, hands-out shrug and followed the captain down the aloe-bordered walkway to the helipad, which was simply a corner of the parking lot marked off by low concrete curbs painted white. Ray was already there. As they approached the waiting chopper, Dave came hurrying down the path to join them.

"Ray, you could have given me a little advance notice," he said, red-faced. "I haven't even had breakfast yet."

"We just heard about the trip ourselves," Rick said, taking pity on the engineer. "And I'm sure *Berkone*'s galley will have a cup of coffee and some chow for you."

Dave looked at him warily, as though he thought Rick might have his own private reasons for wanting to get on his good side. Rick shrugged inwardly. If that was the way he wanted it, too bad for him.

The MV *Berkone,* of San Diego, was a big, beamy ship with a helicopter landing pad mounted on the foredeck. Their helicopter made a wide half circle and touched down at the exact center of the pad. Captain Ward was the first one out the door, the moment the chopper's skids touched the deck. Rick followed, leaving Dave to fend for himself.

Ward knew his way around the ship. He headed straight aft, to a hangar amidships. The padded cradle inside held a tarpaulin-draped form that made Rick's pulse beat a bit faster. Covered up that way, it looked almost as if it might be a half-scale model of a 1950s rocket plane—Yeager's X-1, for example. Then two of the crew untied the tarp and started pulling it off. The resemblance to an aircraft thinned quickly.

"Is that your *Steel Albatross?*" Dave asked, coming up beside Rick. "It's a weird-looking contraption. Not like any submersible I've ever seen, and I've seen most of the important ones."

Rick bridled. It was almost as if the young engineer had just bad-mouthed his girlfriend. "You're right, she doesn't look like any other submersible," he said tautly. "That's because she isn't like any other submersible."

"Hmm," Dave said. He took a step closer and carefully perused the craft, from bow to stern. Ray joined him.

Once he conquered his irritation, Rick could understand Dave's puzzlement. He had been puzzled too when he had first seen the mockup of the *Albatross,* in Captain Ward's lab at the Scripps Oceanographic Institution. The stubby wings looked much too short and thick for the slim, tapered fuse-lage. And why on earth were those two control surfaces attached to the nose, canard-fashion? As for the tail section, the vertical rudder was hinged at the center, so that the whole thing turned, and the horizontal stabilizers on either side drooped, as if tired of holding up the wingtank-shaped structures that clung to their tips.

Rick's mistake had been to look at the *Steel Albatross* as if it were an airplane. Now Dave was making the mistake of looking at it as an ordinary submersible. It was neither. It was the first of a totally new class of craft, as indicated by its designation, SA-1: Submersible Aquaplane, number one.

One of *Berkone*'s officers appeared and said, "Well, Captain Ward, we've taken good care of your baby for you."

"I see that, Bill," the captain replied. "And I appreciate it. You remember Rick Tallman, don't you? And this is Ray Lapham, the SeaVenture project coordinator, and Dave, um . . ."

"Collier's the name," Dave said. "Hi."

"Bill Mares," the officer replied, shaking hands all around. "Welcome aboard."

Captain Ward looked up from his inspection of the *Steel Albatross.* "How long will it take to move *Berkone* to 200 fathoms and get this machine into the moon-pool, ready to go?" he demanded.

"An hour or so," Mares said. "We'll get right on it." He took a walkie-talkie from its belt pouch and spoke into it. A few minutes later, the vibration of the deck announced that *Berkone* was underway.

Dave continued to circle the *Steel Albatross.* "What's this bird of yours made of?" he asked Rick in an undertone. "I can't help feeling that I'm having trouble seeing it correctly."

"Go closer," Rick said, smiling to himself. He had had the same reaction as Dave the first time he had seen the full-scale *Albatross*. "Go ahead, touch it. It won't bite."

The flat black surface of the craft seemed to drink up every ray of light that struck it, giving nothing back. But there was more to its blackness than a paint job. The whole skin of the *Steel Albatross* was pleated in tiny folds less than an eighth of an inch apart. The lines of the pleats followed the contours of the fuselage, wings, and control surfaces, in a way that always reminded Rick of the underside of the whale in the book of *Pinocchio* he had had as a kid.

Dave took a couple of steps closer, with his hands clasped behind his back, and bent over to peer at the *Albatross*'s skin. "I get it," he declared. "If somebody tries to find you using sonar, those little ridges bounce the signals back at funny angles and keep your bird from showing up distinctly on their screen. Pretty clever idea."

Ray chimed in. "Don't they use the same principle to make those new Stealth planes radar-invisible?"

"I really couldn't say," Rick replied self-consciously. Ray was right about the resemblance to Stealth aircraft, of course, but security was security, and he didn't elaborate.

"That must be why we're having a problem seeing the thing," Dave said. "The light rays must be bouncing off at strange angles."

He reached out a fingertip and touched the craft, then jerked his hand back. "What the hell!" he exclaimed. "It's soft. I'd almost swear the damn thing's alive!"

"It's not really soft," Rick said. "There's an honest-to-God pressure hull inside there. But you're right, the pleated skin does have a good deal of resilience."

Rick caught a warning glance from the captain, who wanted to make sure that Rick didn't say too much on the subject. On the *Steel Albatross*'s first sea trials, Ward's team had discovered that the resilient skin not only reduced the craft's sonar signature to near zero but dramatically reduced her hydrodynamic drag as well, for reasons that no one fully understood. It had something to do with boundary-layer flow control, but the whole topic was highly classified and nobody talked about it very much.

Dave backed up and looked over *Albatross* from bow to stern. "Let me see if I've got this straight," he said. "This machine is what amounts to an underwater glider, is that right?"

"Close enough," Captain Ward said.

"In other words, when you go down, the diving planes turn some of your downward motion into forward motion," Dave continued. "But what about heading upward? How do you manage— Never mind, that's a dumb question. I get it now. You drop your ballast or blow your tanks or whatever, until you achieve positive buoyancy. Then the diving planes do exactly the same thing in the other direction: convert some of your vertical motion upward to horizontal. That is really ingenious. Obvious, too—I can't imagine why no one thought of it before."

Rick rolled his eyes. Dave had a real gift for rubbing people the wrong way. Even his compliment to Captain Ward sounded as if it had an insult hidden inside it.

"Rick, why don't you give Dave a short cockpit checkout while we're getting into position," Captain Ward said as he lovingly opened the canopy. Rick and Dave obliged the captain by climbing in, but the checkout was interrupted just a few minutes later by Mares and his crew and their hoisting lines.

"Mind your backs," Mares warned. Rick and Dave clambered out, then they and the captain stepped back to let the riggers attach lines to the flush and shrouded pad-eyes fore and aft. An overhead gantry was already positioned to lift the craft and carry it through a pair of tall sliding doors in the aft bulkhead of the hangar.

"Where are they taking it now?" asked Ray, who had been watching from a position at the railing.

Rick grinned. "Come see for yourself."

The riggers took up positions on either side of the *Alba-tross,* each with a line to bow and stern to keep her from swinging as she rose from the padded cradle and moved slowly backward. Rick, Dave, Ray, and the captain followed.

Just on the other side of the doors, Dave stopped so suddenly that Captain Ward bumped into him.

"What the—!" the engineer said.

Rick understood his amazement. The aft section of the superstructure's interior was one big enclosed space, stretching upward at least three decks. The rails of the gantry ran the entire length overhead. But the most surprising feature was below them, not above. It was a moon-pool, enclosed forward by the monohull and on port and starboard by *Berkone*'s twin-hulled stern. The pool was bottomless, and at the very stern was a pair of steel doors, something like the gates of a canal lock, that could be opened to give surface access to open water.

Captain Ward looked ready to bite his fingernails as the crewmen, closely supervised by Mares, lowered the *Steel Albatross* into the moon-pool and stretched mooring lines from the sides of her new berth. Two technicians in white overalls climbed down, popped the top hatch of the *Albatross,* and disappeared inside. After ten minutes or so, they reappeared.

"Predive check is complete, sir," one of them told Mares.

Mares spoke again into his walkie-talkie, then turned to Ward and said, "She's all yours, Captain. We'll be on station in another fifteen minutes."

"Thanks, Bill," the captain replied. He looked over at Rick and Dave. "How about it, Ricky? Are you ready to take Dave for a little familiarization dive? And the answer had better be yes. I didn't come all the way out here to play cribbage."

CHAPTER 10

RICK FELT A THRILL GO THROUGH HIM. THIS WAS A MO-
ment he had been looking forward to for a long time, and
here it was at last.

"Come on," he told Dave. "Let's suit up."

He led Dave to the portside locker room where the gear
for the *Albatross*'s hydronauts—as he'd learned to call people who drove submersibles—was stowed. Ward and Mares
went with them. A man in khakis was already there. Mares
introduced him as Doctor Werringen, the *Berkone*'s new
medical officer.

"Glad to meet both of you," Werringen said. "Am I right
that you'll be staying in the vehicle on this trip?"

"Right," Ward answered for them. "This is a simple familiarization cruise."

"Good," the medico said. "Then we don't have to worry
about administering serums against high-pressure nervous
syndrome and hypothermia. But just for your information,
we do have the latest formulations of them on hand."

He motioned toward a small refrigerator in the corner of
the locker room. "I've already worked up weight-depth-
dosage charts for both of you, so it'll be easy and fast when
the time comes for a trip that involves extra-vehicular
activity."

"Thanks, Doc," Rick said. He stripped to his skivvies and pulled on a light, short-sleeved wetsuit, then added soft, insulated rubber-soled booties. Dave, with a dubious look, did the same. With the assistance of one of the crewmen, Rick climbed down into the tiny submarine's forward cockpit.

The two places were arranged one behind the other, each with its own set of instruments and controls, though the rear set of controls would not be enabled on this dive. Rick settled into the forward seat and felt the oil-filled cushions adjust automatically to his weight and contours. He chuckled to himself. Count on Will Ward to give some thought to the sore butts of his hydronauts!

From behind him, Dave said, "This thing feels more like a jet fighter than a submersible." He sounded nervous.

"It is, in a way," Rick replied. "Captain Ward and his team have used the *Steel Albatross* as a testbed for a lot of cutting-edge technology. Put on your headset now, please. You should find it hanging on a hook, right under the starboard canopy rail. You'll hear everything I hear, and your monitor will show you everything I see."

He picked up his own headset, a lightweight combination of earphones and bone-conduction microphone, and slipped it in place just in time to hear Captain Ward's voice say, "Sierra Alpha One, this is *Berkone*. Do you read? Over."

"Roger, *Berkone*," he replied. "Read you five by five. Commencing predive checklist now. Over."

"Sierra Alpha One, *Berkone*. Roger. Out."

In front of Rick was a cathode-ray tube that looked a lot like a computer monitor, only circular and somewhat larger. It was black and lifeless. Rick reached forward and touched the tip of his index finger to the screen. It immediately glowed dark red, a color chosen to help preserve the crew's dark-adapted vision.

Red letters appeared against a black background:

SA-1
COMMAND MENU
Do you require instruction?
Yes   No   Cancel

He touched NO and watched the two lower lines change to:

Do you want the predive checklist?
Yes No Cancel

"Proceeding with predive checklist," he announced, as he pressed YES.

Over the earphones, Captain Ward's voice said, "Roger, Rick."

It had been some time since he had flown this bird, but he knew it so well from before that now he found it all very familiar. It was as if he had never been away.

The monitor screen took him, step by step, through a check of all the craft's systems. Thanks to the thoughtful planning of Captain Ward and his team, the process wasn't much more complicated than using a cash machine to make a payment on his charge card. When it was done, the screen gave him a new display:

SA-1
CONTROL OPTIONS
DESCEND ASCEND
Monitor Cancel

Rick pressed DESCEND, then, on the next screen, STATUS. The screen background turned white. Rows of boxes contained such labels as MAIN HATCH, LOCKOUT TRUNK, and RADIO PORT. Some were in red letters, and some in green. As he watched, those in red turned green, one after another, as each system was cleared for underwater operation. When the last one had changed, he announced, "Green board! Sierra Alpha One is ready to dive."

"Roger, Sierra Alpha One," Captain Ward replied. "Casting off."

Rick looked up from the computerized display. The moon-pool became much brighter as the stern doors swung open. Members of the crew released the mooring lines and began walking the *Steel Albatross* backward. Two divers slipped into the water, preparing to detach the lines as soon as the craft was in the open.

"Sierra Alpha One underway," Rick said formally. "Departing *Berkone* at one-zero-two-four. Over."

As the *Steel Albatross* cleared the stern of *Berkone* and sunlight came streaming in through the canopy, Rick reached for the lower part of the CRT, which now read:

DESCEND ASCEND
Aux. Inst. Cancel

He pressed DESCEND. A new display came up:

SA-1
DESCEND CHECKLIST
1. Ballast blowers: OFF
Next Item   Cancel

He worked through the new checklist, system by system, readying the craft for submerged operation. Each item took only a couple of seconds, the time to read it and compare it with his mental checklist. At each step, the program gave him the option of canceling the entire evolution. Finally he reached the end and read:

SA-1
PARAMETERS CHECKLIST
Rate of Descent: 10 mpm
INCREASE   DECREASE
Select   Cancel

Rick kept his fingertip on INCREASE until the screen showed a rate of descent of thirty meters—just shy of a hundred feet—per minute. Behind him, Dave had obviously been following everything on his own monitor. Now he let out the first sound he had made since Rick started the first checklist.

"Thirty meters a minute!" he exclaimed. "Aren't you going a little overboard?"

Rick smiled at the engineer's choice of words. "Not really," he said, as he continued to work through the parameters checklist. "The kind of submersible you're used to, it might make sense to go down more slowly. But the *Albatross* is different. She needs a higher rate of descent to give her the flying speed needed for control. If we went down too slowly, we'd lost hydrodynamic control, like a stalled airplane."

"I can't say I like the sound of that," Dave said darkly.

"No sweat even then," Rick replied. "An airplane that stalls, falls. Not us. Unless we use auxiliary thrust, we just drift around aimlessly until we manage to get underway again."

The *Steel Albatross* was fifty yards astern of *Berkone* now. The electronic instrument panel showed:

```
SA-1
READY TO DIVE
Begin Descent Recheck
            Cancel
```

"*Berkone,* this is Sierra Alpha One. Leaving the surface at one-zero-three-niner," Rick reported. "Over."

"Sierra Alpha One, this is *Berkone,*" Captain Ward replied. "Roger. You're cleared."

Rick took the aircraft-style joystick in his right hand and touched BEGIN DESCENT with his left index finger. The intake valves opened to flood the ballast tanks, forcing the air from them in a foaming rush. For a moment or two, nothing seemed to happen. Then the *Steel Albatross* slipped quietly beneath the waves. The dive was on.

Rick pressed forward on the trim button set into the top of the stick, to give the *Albatross* a nose-down attitude. As the craft's negative buoyancy increased, and with it her rate of descent, the stubby "wings" picked up effectiveness. The *Albatross* started moving forward, slowly at first, then with increasing speed. Rick jockeyed the controls, trying to recover his instinctive sense of the craft's response rates. It felt very unfamiliar at first, but soon he was delighted to discover that it all came back. He had a feeling that he could almost fly the *Steel Albatross* blindfolded.

"Hey, why are those numbers blinking?" Dave demanded.

Rick glanced down. The monitor array now showed a simple instrument panel: compass, depth gauge, turn-and-bank, clinometer, artificial horizon, and rate of ascent-descent. It was the latter that had just spooked Dave. Their actual rate of descent was approaching thirty-five meters per minute, instead of the thirty that Rick had preselected, and the on-board computer was making sure that he knew about it. Rick eased back on the stick, bringing the nose up, then eased the stick forward again just before the numbers stopped blinking. One of the hardest things he had had to learn when he first flew the *Steel Albatross* was that everything happened more slowly underwater. If he had waited to ease forward again until their descent rate was on the button, he would have drifted to slower than the chosen rate and would have had to correct in the other direction.

The depth gauge indicated that they were at seventy meters. It was darker now around them, as the bright sunlight of the upper world was filtered out by the water. Rick changed hands on the stick and felt for the bank of light switches on the panel to his right. The front and side arrays of halogen lights blazed out, much brighter than he remembered them being, but the water at this depth was not clear enough to let him see as well as he would have liked.

Rick found himself wishing that he had a pair of the light-intensifying infrared goggles he had used on his last mission in the *Steel Albatross*. He made a mental note to ask Captain Ward if there were any around.

"How maneuverable is this thing?" Dave asked.

Rick felt a spurt of irritation. "This is the *Steel Albatross,* not a 'thing'!" he said tartly. Then he pushed the stick over to starboard. The *Albatross* banked, then leveled off as he brought her around to her new course. Rick waited a moment, then put her into a tight spiral to port.

As they started into their fourth complete circle, Dave said, "All right, all right! I get the idea! And I apologize for calling it a 'thing.' Now can we please straighten out, before I toss the breakfast I never got?"

Rick chuckled to himself. He was pretty sure that Dave would start treating the *Steel Albatross* with a little more respect after this.

"Er . . . how deep are you going to take us?" Dave asked.

Rick glanced at the depth gauge. They had already passed 150 meters. That was nothing compared to the depths they would be working at when they watched Dave's bottom-crawler in action, but it was deep enough for a familiarization dive.

"We'll level off at 200 meters, and you'll see how slowly we decelerate," he said, glancing at the changing numbers on the screen. Along the bottom of the display, set off by a background in a lighter shade of red, were the choices:

DESCEND ASCEND
Aux. Inst. Cancel

Rick pressed ASCEND and DESCEND at the same time, to level off and slow to a hover. As always, he was awestruck by how long it took the friction of the water to bring the boat to zero speed.

Dave noticed too. "This is some slippery boat, isn't it?" he remarked.

"I thought you'd be impressed," Rick replied, as he began to rig the boat for ascent. He pressed ASCEND by itself. The items on the preascent checklist came on the screen, one by one, followed by the items of the parameters checklist. At last—it was only thirty seconds or so, but it felt like forever—the screen read:

SA-1
READY TO ASCEND
Begin Ascent Recheck
          Cancel

"*Berkone,* Sierra Alpha One," Rick called. "All systems check okay. Beginning ascent at one-one-zero-eight, depth two-zero-four meters. Over."

"Roger," the captain's voice replied.

Rick pressed the BEGIN ASCENT box on the screen. At the same time, he pulled back on the stick. As the craft gained momentum, he used the diving-trim control to bring the nose up. The high-speed pumps were forcing seawater from the boat's ballast tanks, shifting her buoyancy from negative to positive. The craft wandered a little, then settled down as her motion upward gave the stick more authority.

Rick made a quick note on the clipboard strapped to his thigh. Something should be done about the *Steel Albatross*'s electronic control system. The system of extensive checklists made a lot of sense before a dive. It was even a reasonable precaution when the craft was sitting on the bottom, getting ready to return to the surface. But in "flight," it was cumbersome at best.

This dive was a good example. During the time it had taken him to shift the boat from DESCENT mode to HOVER mode, their downward momentum had carried them well past their target depth. He could have used the stick more aggressively, put the craft in a stall to stop their continued descent, but that would have spent all their forward momentum and left them adrift, with practically no effective control over the boat's movements unless he brought the auxiliary propulsion system on line. There had to be a better way, and he was beginning to have some ideas about what it might be.

He was bringing the boat around to a heading that would carry them back to *Berkone* when Dave said, "This doesn't feel like the right direction. Are you sure you know where we are?"

"You'd better hope I do," Rick said with grim humor. "Unless you think you can learn to fly the *Albatross* in the next fifteen minutes or so, I'm your only ticket home."

"I don't like the sound of that," Dave replied. "What if something happened to you? As soon as we get back, I'm going to tell your boss that I need to know how to operate this thing."

So Dave was back to calling the *Steel Albatross* a "thing"! But Rick comforted himself by imagining the moment when

Dave started telling Captain Ward that he intended to pilot the boat. The captain would probably set a new world record for going ballistic!

"Sure, you do that," Rick said. "But please hold the talk now till this evolution is completed."

He checked their forward speed and rate of ascent against their horizontal distance from the mother ship, did a quick calculation in his head, and spoke.

"*Berkone,* Sierra Alpha One. Estimate the surface at one-one-one-seven. Over."

Captain Ward acknowledged the message.

The *Albatross* was more responsive going up than she had been going down. Rick settled back in his seat and let his pilot's instincts take over. He kept his head up, watching the watery world flow past the canopy, only occasionally glancing down at the instrument panel to check his speed and heading. The experience was exhilarating. It didn't give the same adrenaline rush as pushing the edge of the envelope in an F-14, but hell, adrenaline wasn't the only thrill around!

He looked upward and picked out the distinctive catamaranlike stern of *Berkone* ahead, a few degrees to starboard. He nudged the submersible to head toward her.

One moment they were gliding silently through a blue-green world with a rippling ceiling of white light. The next moment the canopy broke through the ceiling and they had blue sky above them. The stern of *Berkone* was less than fifty yards away.

As the boat began to rock with the swell, Rick reported, "Sierra Alpha One, on the surface, fifty yards astern, awaiting tow." That was really a formality. A retrieval team of divers was already on its way out with towing lines.

Once the *Albatross* was safely moored in the moon-pool, Rick cracked the hatch and he and Dave clambered up onto the catwalk.

Captain Ward was waiting for them. "Good dive?" he asked gruffly.

"No problem," Rick replied.

"Well, not quite," Dave said, stepping up beside Rick.

"There's one problem: I don't like feeling so helpless. I want to know how to drive that thing. Just in case."

The cords in the captain's neck swelled up, but when he spoke his voice was mild, for him. "Well, mister, that's a reasonable request, even if it could have been put in a more respectful way."

Dave quickly hid a look of surprise. "Uh, sorry," he muttered. "But I'm not completely new to this, you know. I've piloted submersibles lots of times."

"The *Albatross* is different," Rick said.

"I see that. All I meant is that I'd like to know more about the boat and its systems. I don't expect to become an expert, just to learn enough to deal with an emergency. That would make any dive we make together safer for both of us."

"That's reasonable," Captain Ward repeated. "Okay, mister. How about this afternoon? The boat's onboard computer includes a pretty advanced simulation mode. Between that and the HELP program, you could start picking up what you need to know in an hour or two."

Dave blinked a couple of times and said, "Thank you, sir."

"That's okay, son. Now why don't we all go find a place to sit down and debrief the dive you just made."

Rick and Dave followed the captain to *Berkone*'s wardroom. They drew mugs of coffee from the urn and sat down at one of the tables. The captain pulled a notebook from his pocket and Rick produced his clipboard.

"Here are my notes on the dive," he said, handing the sheets to the captain. "The boat behaved like a little lady the whole time."

"Did you notice anything different when you turned on the lights?" the captain asked.

"Why, yes. They seemed a lot brighter."

"They are. We just replaced the tungsten-halogen lamps with HMI units, with a test depth of 20,000 feet. The H comes from the Hg symbol for mercury, M stands for the rare-earth metals named dysprosium, thulium, and holmium, and the I is for iodide and bromide. And I won't tell you how long it took me to memorize all that. The point is, HMI lights are about five times more efficient than the old tungsten-halogen bulbs."

Rick gave a low whistle. "That's quite a boost," he said.

"It's even better than that," the captain said. "Because these lamps are the first to use some newly developed high-efficiency reflectors."

"Well," Rick said, "they give out lots of light. But I wonder if the infrared gear wouldn't be a better bet for our particular mission."

"We'll keep that question open for now." Captain Ward glanced over the notes and asked, "What's this mean? DN/UP/DN?"

Rick hesitated. The captain was a submariner from way back, and the *Steel Albatross* was his baby. He had put all his intelligence and experience into the design of the craft. There must be some flaw in Rick's idea if Ward hadn't thought of it himself.

"Well?" Captain Ward demanded. "Spit it out, son."

"It was just something that came to me while we were going through the preascent checklist," Rick replied slowly. "We're in the habit of thinking of the *Steel Albatross* as something like a sailplane. But really, that's not a good analogy. Sailplanes don't go up on their own. Any time you want to gain altitude in one, you have to find a thermal updraft or get a tow from someone. The *Albatross* is more like a lighter-than-air craft, a dirigible, or maybe a cross between a dirigible and a glider, if there were such a thing. Depending on her buoyancy, she can go up, go down, or just hang in one place."

"Of course," the captain said. "But where are you going with that?"

"Just about anywhere I want," said Rick. "Because the boat gets the energy to move horizontally from its motion in the vertical plane, either up *or* down. Which means that, with a fast enough system for filling and emptying the ballast tanks, the boat could keep its forward motion while shifting from positive to negative buoyancy and back again, as often as you like, as long as your ballast and deballast energy holds out."

"Well, Ricky, you're on to something all right," the captain exclaimed, slapping his hand on the table. "It's just a question of packing more energy of both kinds on board. I've been doing some noodling on that subject myself recently, and there are some new developments along those lines that I'd like to try out. It'll take a pile of calculations to find out if it's practical, but the principle makes sense, I can tell you that."

"I'd like to make some changes in the controls," Rick added. "The touchscreen is neat, but it's a little too slow for the kind of action I've got in mind. Maybe you could rig something that would fill and blow the tanks quicker."

Captain Ward gave him a shrewd look. "I get the idea, son," he said. "And it's beginning to sound like what you want is an underwater F-14!"

CHAPTER 11

RICK WAS UP EARLY. HE POURED HIMSELF A CUP OF COFFEE from the self-serve buffet in the hotel dining room and took it outside, to a bench screened by bushes. A few minutes later he heard footsteps. Eloise came into view, wearing her skimpy one-piece bathing suit and carrying a beach bag and a snowy white towel.

She stopped in midstride and said, "Oh, rats!" Dropping her bag and towel on a nearby chair, she went back into the hotel.

Rick took a few more sips of coffee. More footsteps. He expected to see Eloise return. Instead, Dave Collier appeared, wearing tennis shorts and tennis shoes so white that they had to be new. He carried a tennis racket and a can of balls.

"Damn!" he suddenly exclaimed.

Rick craned his neck to see what the matter was, then grinned to himself. Dave had obviously stepped on one of the overripe tropical fruit that fell onto the terrace from time to time. One of this tennis shoes now sported a sickly yellow blob with green highlights.

Dave looked around furtively, then grabbed Eloise's towel from the chair and used it to wipe off his shoe. When he finished, he tossed the towel on the pavement, next to the squashed fruit.

Just in time. Eloise reappeared, with a tube of sun lotion in her hand. When she saw what a mess her towel had become, she said, "Yuck! Dave, what in the world happened to my towel?"

"Oh, is that yours?" Dave replied, shamefaced. "Er ... I don't know. Do you think it blew onto the ground?"

"Dave ..." Eloise said in a warning voice. "Will you ... Oh, never mind. I'll talk to you later. Right now I've got to go back to my room for another towel."

"I'll be glad to go get one for you," Dave offered. "Um— how about a game of tennis later?"

Eloise snorted. "I'll think about it, after I get over my mad."

They returned to the hotel together, leaving Rick to think about Dave's refusal to own up to what he had done. What went on between Dave and Eloise was none of his business. But what it said about Dave's character was. He wouldn't forget it.

Later, Ray appeared from the hotel and ambled over to Rick.

"No change, I'm afraid," he said. "That low-pressure system to the southwest is still making waves. Oops, bad joke. Sorry. Anyway, we're still on hold. Currently, we're shooting for tomorrow, if the sea calms down a little."

"Any chance you'll change your mind and send Rover down today?"

After a slight hesitation, Ray said, "No, no chance. You've got the day free. But I do want to tell you how sorry I am, and embarrassed too. You came halfway around the world just to help us out, and so far we haven't had a chance to use your expertise at all."

"Not to worry," Rick said with a grin. "I'm used to it. You know the motto of the armed forces: 'Hurry up and wait.' "

"Thanks for being such a good sport. Do you have any plans for the day?"

"Not yet," Rick said, with a shake of his head. "I heard

about a couple of dives that sounded interesting. Maybe I'll give one of them a try."

Will Ward came out onto the terrace just in time to hear Rick's last sentence. "Give one of who a try?" he asked.

"Not 'who,' 'what.'" Rick quickly explained about the further delay in mining operations.

"Hmmph," said the captain. "I guess we can't argue with the weather. Tell me, Ray: Based on your experience so far, how many days a month do you expect that rig of yours will be able to do its job?"

Ray's face tightened, and his cheeks turned a dull pink. "That's my worry, Captain, not yours," he said. "But just for the record, I'm confident we'll fulfill our mission. Especially if you and your team fulfill yours."

He turned and strode away without another word.

Rick raised his eyebrows. "I'd say he's some pissed off," he observed.

"Pissed off . . . and worried," Captain Ward replied. "He should be. This project is way behind schedule already, and he's the guy who's going to catch flak for the delay. If I were in his place, given the urgency of the mission, I'd take a few more chances."

"What urgency?" Rick demanded. "People have been talking about deep-ocean mining programs and trying to get them going for years and years. Ray showed me some clippings he saved about a project he was hooked up with back in the seventies. It didn't sound all that different from what our friends here are planning to do. If it could wait twenty years, what difference will a few more weeks or months make?"

The captain glanced around before saying, "Those earlier efforts you're talking about were intended to make a buck. Not right away, maybe, but sooner or later. When the projected return on capital stopped looking good, so did they. So their promoters pulled the plug on them. Free enterprise in action."

"Sure. So?"

"This program's different. Its goal is basically strategic. No one at the policy level really gives a damn whether it turns a profit or not, as long as it manages to beef up our stockpile of scandium and other rare-earth metals, as well as other elements—cobalt, chromium—that are strategically important and in short supply. What happens to our country in the next century just may depend on whether we have enough of those elements to meet our needs."

Rick shook his head. "Back in Honolulu, after you told me we were going to be going after scandium, I looked it up. As far as I could tell, about the only thing it's good for is making rechargeable storage batteries. What's so important about that?"

Captain Ward sighed and put his hand on Rick's shoulder. "Let's take a little stroll on the beach," he said.

"Before breakfast?" Rick replied, pretending to be shocked.

"Hell, yes. We need to work up an appetite," the captain said. He said nothing more until they were down at the water's edge, well away from any possible listeners. Then he said, "I finally got permission to tell you a little more about our mission. The way I figure, if you know exactly how important it is, and why, you've got a better shot at carrying it out successfully. By the way, Ray and Eloise and the others are *not* privy to what I'm going to tell you. They know what they're after, and they know it's important, but they don't know why. Understood?"

"Aye, sir."

Captain Ward turned to face the bay. "What do you know about buckyballs?" he asked, in a voice so low that Rick had trouble hearing it over the noise of the surf.

"Buckyballs?" Rick repeated.

"That's what everybody calls them," the captain said. "The stuff's official name is buckminsterfullerene. After Buckminster Fuller, the guy who invented geodesic domes."

Somewhere in Rick's mind a faint bell rang. "Wait a minute," he said. "Isn't that some newly discovered form of carbon?"

Captain Ward nodded and said, "Right. Or maybe several newly discovered forms of carbon. The lab fellows aren't quite sure yet. Instead of the carbon atoms hitching up with each other in the form of layers, the way they do in graphite, or in crystals, the way they do in diamonds, they form a hollow sphere that's supposed to look a hell of a lot like a soccer ball."

"Sounds cute. But what's it good for?"

"What isn't it good for?" the captain replied. "There must be a hundred labs around the world, working day and night, finding new uses. The problem is, there are so many possibilities that nobody can keep track of them. If you dope it with metals like lithium or potassium, you can make it act like an insulator, a conductor, a superconductor, or even a totally new kind of semiconductor. If you dope it with fluorine, you get one of the slipperiest substances ever. If you squeeze it, it gets smaller ... up to a point. But at that point the stuff is harder than diamonds. And when you let go, it springs back to its original size. One guy even tried shooting buckyballs at a stainless-steel wall, at about seventeen thousand miles an hour. They didn't shatter, they simply bounced off."

"They survived a collision at close to escape velocity? That's pretty amazing."

"You can bet that a bunch of your dad's old colleagues in the space program are staying up nights, trying to figure out how to put that particular property to good use."

"But that's not the part that's so urgent, is it? Not many people in high places seem to think that *anything* about the space program is very urgent."

Captain Ward rubbed his fingers and thumb over his cheeks and said, "Well, no. That's true enough ... and one of these days they'll wake up and realize their own unmitigated blind stupidity. But that's beside the point. Did I mention that buckyballs are hollow? They are. But it turns out that they don't *have* to be. You can sort of fold the net of carbon atoms around some other molecule. What you get is a buckyball with something inside it. Then, if you zap it with a laser, the buckyball gets smaller and smaller, until it just fits around the other molecule."

"Like using plastic film and a heat gun to shrink-wrap something," Rick observed.

"It's a lot like that," said Captain Ward. "And what's got everybody in the field gibbering like apes is that each type of filled buckyball seems to have different properties from all the others. And one—scandiofullerite—is very special. When you make a ceramic compound with it, you get a superconductor that apparently works at the kind of temperatures you find in your average home freezer."

Rick turned and stared at Captain Ward. "Are you serious?" he demanded. "Why, that could be the most important discovery since the steam engine or the transistor!"

Captain Ward nodded. "You can bet on it," he said. "Or even since gunpowder. How do you like the idea of a 500-mile-an-hour train, magnetically suspended a few fractions of an inch above the track? Or electrical generators with twice the efficiency of anything we've got now? Never mind my pet submarine propulsion system, ELMAHYDYD. With all the other possible developments, that's no more than a pimple on the ass of progress."

"There has to be a catch," said Rick. "What does it take to make these buckyballs of yours? A billion-dollar laser and the output of a couple of good-sized power plants, I bet."

"You lose," the captain replied. "Would you believe a glorified light bulb and about a hundred bucks worth of stock laboratory glassware, plus a few solvents? 'Course, that's just laboratory production, but before you know it, we'll be able to make the stuff by the truckload for a couple of bucks a pound. There's an old lampblack factory, outside of Odessa, Texas, that's already being converted for buckyball production. Of course, I'm talking about empty buckyballs, not filled ones. Those are just a tad more complicated to produce."

Rick frowned thoughtfully. "And the filled ones are what do all the science-fiction stuff. What was the name you mentioned? Sandy fluoride?"

"Close enough," Captain Ward said with a smile. "Scandiofullerite. You get it by wrapping a buckyball around a molecule of scandium."

"And to do that, you have to have the scandium. I think I'm starting to get the picture."

"Good," the captain said, turning back toward the hotel. "You can turn it over in your mind while we work on some breakfast."

"By the way," he added, as they took one of the tables on the terrace that was already set. "Your friend Dave is a determined fellow. He's been going out to *Berkone* every day, putting in time on the *Albatross* simulation program. I took a look at the tapes yesterday. He seems to be coming along pretty well."

"Good for him," Rick said, in what he hoped was a neutral voice.

"Um. Now he wants to solo."

"What! Captain, you're not thinking of letting that guy take the *Steel Albatross* on a dive by himself, are you?"

"By himself? Of course not. I doubt if I could get permission to do that, even if I did think it was a good idea. But he's already cleared to dive with a properly qualified hydronaut. Meaning, in this case, you or me. And you'll remember that I built the *Albatross* with dual controls."

Rick scowled down into his glass of pineapple juice. "No way am I going to play driving instructor for that guy. Forget it, sir. No way!"

"All right, Ricky," Captain Ward said cheerfully. "Let's drop it. Here comes the rest of our chow."

Rick was crossing the hotel lobby with Captain Ward when the desk clerk, a young Chamorro with very white teeth, called out, "Mr. Tallman? A package just came for you."

The manila envelope had no sender's name on it, only Rick's and the notation "By Hand." Rick tore it open and pulled out a videocassette, a glossy brochure with a stunning photo on the cover of waves crashing against a cliff, and a stack of stapled documents that were clearly the product of a desktop publishing program. Rick scanned the top one. The title was "Effects of Phosphate Runoff on Marine Life."

He looked inside the envelope and found a smaller piece of paper. The engraved letterhead read "Society of Ocean

Friends," with addresses in Guam, Tokyo, and Honolulu. The message was written in broad felt-tip:

Dear Rick Tallman,

As I promised when we met, I am sending you some materials that I am sure will interest you. If you would do us the honor to attend one of our soon-coming meetings, please give me a telephone call at the number on this page. I will arrange to bring you.

Kazuo TAKAUJI

P.S. Would you like to dive with me one day? I know many interesting sites in Guam waters.

"What have you got there?" asked Captain Ward.

"A note from the guy who saved my ass during that shark incident the other day," Rick replied. "Japanese fellow. He's with some bunch called Ocean Friends. This is some of their material he sent me."

He passed the note over to the captain and began to thumb through the color brochure. Whoever these people were, they had fantastic photographers working with them. Some of the underwater shots, of life on coral reefs, were really stunning, as good as anything Rick had ever seen.

"Huh!" Captain Ward said. "Takauji. I wonder if that's a common name in Japan. How old is this friend of yours?"

Rick looked up from the brochure. "Midtwenties, I guess. Why?"

"The age is about right," the captain said, seeming to be talking to himself.

"Who? What?"

"Oh, sorry, Ricky. I was just remembering something that happened a long time ago. Right here in the Marianas, as a matter of fact. I was serving on the old *Overhill*, a destroyer escort. We were on convoy duty, shepherding a bunch of freighters loaded with ammunition and stores for Halsey's Task Force 38, which was doing one hell of a job bombarding industrial targets along the coast of the Japanese home islands."

"Bombarding Japan itself?" Rick asked, trying to recall details from his naval history course at the Academy. "That must have been right at the tail end of the war."

"It was. Either just before or just after Hiroshima, in fact. The Imperial Navy had already lost the last of its important surface units, but their submarines were still in the game. The latest twist, I remember, was what they called *kaitens*, long lance torpedoes fitted with manual controls operated by a diver. We called them human torpedoes."

"Sort of the underwater equivalent of a kamikaze plane, you mean?"

"Exactly. We were keeping a very sharp lookout for them, especially after we heard that the heavy cruiser *Indianapolis* had just gone down in the Philippine Sea, sunk by a Japanese sub. We lost about 900 of the crew of 1200. May they rest in peace."

"Amen," Rick said. "But what were you doing serving on a DE? The way I always heard it, you've been a submariner since at least the days of Noah!"

"None of your guff, young man! I only went into pigboats after my time at the Academy, and that didn't happen until after V-J Day. I'd hitched up back in '42 by lying about my age. I went all the way through the war as a humble swabbie."

"You, Captain? Humble?" said Rick, grinning. "I'm trying to imagine it, but it just won't come to me."

"Well, maybe not all *that* humble," Ward conceded. "After all, I did manage to come out of the war with a rating and a hawsepipe appointment to Annapolis. But my years before the mast left me with some valuable insights, you might say. I've never been able to take some joker in the wardroom quite as seriously as he might like, just because he's got scrambled eggs on his hat. As far as I'm concerned, he's got to earn my respect."

"Sounds reasonable to me," Rick said, grinning at Will's use of the old expression for an officer's gold braids. "But you were about to tell me a story about the old days. Let me see, who was in command of the fleet back then? John Paul Jones? Or was it Decatur?"

"These little pissants got no respect for their elders," the captain growled at the ceiling. "No use trying to tell them anything."

"I'm sorry, Captain," Rick said. "I'd really like to hear what happened."

"That's better. I can tell you, it's quite a yarn. Let's go sit down someplace, and I'll spin it for you."

CHAPTER 12

"As I told you before," Captain Ward said, "*Overhill* was on convoy escort duty. We were supposed to leave Apra Harbor at 0900, but merchant ships are worse than yearling calves when it comes to keeping them herded together. One thing and another, we didn't get everybody underway until damn near sunset.

"Our skipper, a Reserve lieutenant commander named McCrary, didn't like it. He'd done a tour of duty on a tincan in the North Atlantic, at the height of the German wolfpack attacks. As far as he was concerned, a convoy, darkness, and the chance that there was an enemy sub out there was about the worst kind of mixture there was, practically guaranteed to blow up in your face. He passed out every pair of night glasses we had on the ship and promised a carton of Baby Ruths to the first gob who sighted something that shouldn't be there.

"Just before first light the next morning, the radarman reported a possible contact, five miles ahead and slightly to starboard. Then it vanished from his screen. A glitch? Or a sub that had just dived? The skipper was in no mood to take chances. He put the convoy on a zag to port, sounded battle stations, and we took off toward the contact with a bone in our teeth.

"Five minutes later, when we were halfway to the contact's last position, the sonarman locked in on it. A Japanese I-boat, for sure. It seemed to be trying to slip away from us to the eastward. As soon as we could, we made our first run on the target, throwing a standard pattern of depth charges. We were turning to start a second run when the bow of the Jap sub broached. It shot at least thirty or forty feet into the air, in a shower of spray, then fell back with an almighty crash.

"A few years later, when I knew more about subs, I found myself wondering what had happened there. The only thing I could think of was that our depth charges did double-duty damage to the boat, or maybe even triple-duty damage. The bow planes had gone to full nose-up and stuck there; the ballast tanks were fully blown, bow tanks first; and now there was a fire on board.

"In any case, there we were, with an enemy sub surfaced, dead in the water and now on an even keel, just four hundred yards away. Our three-inchers got her range pretty fast, but before they could hole her, the front hatch popped open. There was a cloud of greenish gray smoke that made me want to cough just looking at it, and a dozen sailors ran up on deck and jumped into the water.

"The skipper ordered our deck guns to cease firing, and he picked up the bullhorn to call on the Jap sub to surrender. But right about then, we noticed that the sub was sitting deeper in the water. More guys came running up through the front hatch and jumped into the drink. Then the boat started down by the bow, a big swell hit the open hatch, and that was all she wrote.

"We got our boats into the water to pick up survivors, of course. Some of them wouldn't let us rescue them. One big guy, we snagged his shirt with a boathook, but before we could haul him into the boat, he deliberately raised his arms over his head, slipped out of his shirt, and sank. From his insignia, he was a sergeant in the Imperial Marines. One hell of a tough outfit—ask any of our guys who helped take Iwo Jima from them.

"We bagged eight or nine swimmers, all the ones we saw,

then we had to hightail back to our convoy. One of the prisoners turned out to be an ensign, just a couple of years older than me, who spoke English. Back at the beginning of the war, right after Pearl Harbor, there had been a lot of rumors about captured Japanese flyers wearing UCLA class rings. Those rumors were all bullshit, but this kid we'd captured really had spent a year at UCLA just before the war, studying electrical engineering.

"I'd pulled guard duty, so I was spending two watches a day down in the brig with him and the other prisoners. They seemed pretty happy to be done with the war, but not him. He refused to eat, mostly refused to talk, and spent practically the whole time lying on his bunk with his face turned to the wall. It looked to me as if he'd decided to starve himself to death. Maybe the disgrace of staying alive after his boat had gone to the bottom was too much for him.

"We could see he was getting weaker every day, but there wasn't anything we could do about it. And to tell the truth, most of the guys didn't really give a shit. We'd been at war with Japan for four long, hard years, and a helluva lot of good men had died as a result. If one of the enemy wanted to kill himself, so that? He was just saving us the trouble.

"For some reason, I didn't feel that way about this guy. Maybe because he was close to my own age, or because his English made him seem less like an enemy, or because I got the feeling that he really didn't want to kill himself, that it was something he felt forced to do. That offended me. It's one thing to put yourself in the way of a danger for some purpose, but what he was doing was a pointless sacrifice. Worse than pointless, criminal. The war was as good as over, and whatever happened next, his country was going to badly need people like him.

"I wasn't supposed to talk to the prisoners, but my watches were too boring to just stand around with my thumb up my ass. I started saying some of the things I'd been thinking. The prisoner never said anything back, but I could tell he was listening. Sometimes, when I made a really good point, I could see his shoulders stiffen, as if he had to hold himself back from jumping into the argument. But he still wouldn't eat. When he came down with some kind of fever and refused to take any medicine for it, I was sure he was a goner.

"Then came August 15, the day of the Japanese surrender. The order came to cease all offensive operations, and at 1100 the sirens sounded for a full minute on every U.S. and Allied warship in the Pacific Theater. Admiral Halsey's radio message was piped throughout our ship, including the brig. I happened to pull the eight-to-twelve watch that day. When the announcement came, our prisoner struggled to push himself into a sitting position, and a look of hope came over his face. Then it vanished. He looked up at me and said, 'This is a stupid trick.' They were the only words he'd said in a week or more.

"I had to do something. Later that day, Emperor Hirohito broadcast a message announcing Japan's surrender and calling on his subjects to accept the peaceful and friendly intentions of the enemy. I talked our radioman into piping the message to the brig the next time it was repeated. This time our prisoner believed it. When dinnertime came around, he took his tray and managed to eat a few bites. By the time we transferred him and the others to a battlewagon, for transport to a P.O.W. camp, he was in pretty good shape, considering what he'd been through.

"Almost a year later, when I was stationed in Santa Barbara, waiting to take up my appointment to the Academy, I got a note addressed to 'Sailor Ward, U.S. Ship *Overhill*, U.S. Navy.' I can't imagine how it reached me. It was from our former prisoner, saying that he was well, that he was planning to take up his studies again, and that he owed his life to me.

"Well, hell, I couldn't let that go by. I wrote back that he didn't owe me a thing, but that I wouldn't mind hearing news of him from time to time. After that I got a card from him every year, around Christmastime. He usually managed to find out where to send it too. Nothing much, a few bits of news about the year past, a photo now and then, a birth announcement for his son. Just a way of keeping in touch. I sent him cards too, not every year, but most. Funny—I never looked him up, in all the time that I was in Japan. A card a year felt just about right.

"Then, three or four years ago, no card. And none since. I wrote a couple of times, but I never got an answer. I think he must be dead. I can't think of anything else that would have stopped him from writing."

Captain Ward fell silent and sat gazing out toward the water.

"You're right, that's quite a yarn," Rick said, stirring in his seat. "And it all happened right around here?"

"Not far away. Let's see, we'd been underway eight or nine hours when our radar picked up the sub, and the kind of convoy we were riding herd on was lucky to make more than about ten knots. Figure around seventy-five to a hundred miles from Apra Harbor."

"That must be what made you think of it, being on Guam again."

The captain turned and stared at Rick. "You haven't been listening too hard, have you, Ricky? Either that, or you've just turned dense on me. The thing that reminded me was that note you just got. Because the name was the same. Takauji. My friend's name was Yasunari Takauji, and he had a son who was born just about twenty-five years ago. It's probably just one of those coincidences, of course. But when you throw in Guam and an involvement with the sea, you begin to wonder. What if this young fellow you met is the son of the man whose life I saved in these very waters, over forty-five years ago? Wouldn't that be a hell of a thing?"

Rick nodded. "Hell of a thing," he echoed.

CHAPTER 13

"SEAVENTURE." THE NAME HUNG IN THE AIR. KEN Kirby watched his director's face, but nothing showed beyond a polite interest.

The silence stretched out. Finally, Harley said, "I give up. What is it?"

Ken riffled through his stack of index cards. "A corporate shell our friends in Virginia have had sitting around since their glory days in the 'sixties. They pumped some life into it a few months back, as an umbrella for an experimental deep-sea mining project."

"All right, I'm with you now," Harley said. "A report crossed my desk. They reactivated that boat Howard Hughes built for them way back when, correct?"

Ken nodded. "I think the right word is 'ship.' It's pretty big."

"Fine, whatever. But go on. How does that relate to your current investigation? I'd like an update on that too, by the way."

"You'll get it, but as for SeaVenture, all I can say is that Red Bell took a very curious interest in it, from even before the time that the project was officially announced. There may be nothing in it—he's been heavily involved in offshore drilling for years—but the combination of him and our colleagues caught my eye."

"As well it might," Harley replied. "You're not suggesting that Langley has something to do with this oil market manipulation of his, are you?"

Ken shook his head. "No, no. I wouldn't put it past them, but there's no evidence at all of that. I did notice something else, though. It may be a coincidence, but Bell has poured a lot of dollars—tax-deductible dollars, by the way—into an environmental group called Ocean Friends. And I found out this morning that the group's other major backer is none other than Cuichi Nishimura."

"Bell's Japanese partner? Very interesting. What do we know about this Ocean Friends group?"

"Not much," Ken replied with a shrug. "They sponsor educational programs about the ocean and pollution and so on, and they have some sort of scientific research effort going. What I've read of theirs struck me as a little off the wall: paragraphs of good, solid data about some problem, followed by a lot of mystical stuff about how we all come from our mother the ocean."

Harley tugged at his earlobe and said, "An environmental cult? Well, it wouldn't be the first one. Look at those people out in Arizona, who shut themselves up in what they claimed was an ecologically complete, working environment. But I don't see a hardnose like Bell sitting around, chanting and burning incense. What's in it for him and his crony? And how does it tie in with the oil business, if it does?"

"Good questions. I wish I had some good answers. By the way, judging by the action in oil futures, Bell and Nishimura may have started hedging their bets in the last few days. Maybe their plan, whatever it is, isn't going quite as smoothly as they expected. I still figure their exposure is pushing a billion dollars, though."

Harley blinked. "Men like that do not bet the ranch on anything less than a certainty. What makes them so sure that oil prices are going to fall through the floor?"

Ken pursed his lips to whistle a few notes from *Carmen*, then recalled that Harley hated it.

"I've managed to cross off most of the possibilities we thought of," he said hastily. "The most likely one that's left is some sort of imminent technological breakthrough that they've found out about and nobody else has. Something like a practical technique for extracting oil from shale, or a really cheap, effective solar cell, or an energy-storage device that would make electric cars twice as efficient and half as expensive as gas-powered cars."

"Yes, that *would* set the cat among the pigeons, wouldn't it? You don't have any reason to favor one of those ideas over the others, do you?"

"No, but I'm starting to think I know where to look. I mentioned that SeaVenture's deep-sea mining ship is in shakedown trials now, didn't I? She's operating just off Guam. And by a very peculiar coincidence, the headquarters of Ocean Friends is also on Guam."

Ken took a deep breath, then plunged ahead. "Did I ever tell you? I've always had a yen to see the Western Pacific."

Harley stared. "Out of the question," he snapped. "We're a research institution, not an operational agency. Our charter is crystal clear on that. If Langley caught even a whisper that we were sending our people into the field, they'd come down on us like an Alpine avalanche."

"Come on, Harley," Ken said, rolling his eyes theatrically. "I'm not talking about parachuting in with a Kalashnikov strapped to my chest! My research has raised certain issues, and to explore them properly, and in depth, I need to pose some questions to people in the field. It's still research, even if I'm not hanging out in my office. Who could object to that?"

"You know very well who. You also know that I find rhetorical questions a pain in the ass."

"Sorry," Ken murmured, hiding his glee. Whenever Harley started focusing on style, rather than content, it meant that he was preparing to retreat from his announced position.

"Still," Harley said slowly, as if thinking through a subtle point that had just occurred to him. "There's no real difference between asking questions of an expert who happens to be in Guam and, say, consulting a document that happens to be in the LBJ Library. Is there?"

Ken tucked his index cards in his shirt pocket. "None that I can see," he replied, getting to his feet.

"Not so fast," Harley snapped. "How long will it take you to get some closure on the other files you're working on?"

"Call it a week."

"See to it. Then I'll be willing to take another look at this cowboy project of yours. Mind you, I'm not saying I'll okay it."

"That's fine," Ken said. "I'll ask Joyce to find out about flights to Guam."

Will Ward let the telephone receiver drop back into the cradle, then walked out onto the balcony of his hotel room. The sun, just past the zenith in a cloudless sky, streamed down on the beach and the blue-green waters of the bay. The scene looked like the cover photo of a tourist brochure, but he was in no mood to appreciate it.

Another goddamned last-minute delay! This had to be the most screwed-up enterprise he'd ever had the misfortune to be mired in. Today, for a change, the weather report had been promising, but now there was a problem with the computers that controlled the operation. If Ward had known earlier, he could have hitched a ride out to *Berkone* and done some useful work. Too late for that now, though.

He went back inside. The desk was piled high with papers and drawings. He picked up a report on a super-efficient CO_2 scrubber that some NASA people had just developed. Was it something he might be able to adapt to *Albatross?* He read the first paragraph and half of the second. Then he dropped the report on top of one of the piles. It would have to wait for later.

He looked around the room, then crossed to the balcony door and stared out at the bay again. It looked as picture-perfect as before. He hated it.

He spun on his heel and went over to the dresser. The bottle of Wild Turkey was lying on its side, at the back of the second drawer, hidden by a stack of neatly folded shorts.

He held it up and studied it. Half empty, already? It was hard to believe. Was the chambermaid helping herself to a daily snort or two? Not much chance of that, and he couldn't put the blame on evaporation, either. No, he knew perfectly well where it was going, and how quickly too.

So what? What he did when he was off duty was nobody's business. If he let them, the continuous delays and constant inactivity would drive him nuts. Luckily, he knew a couple of effective cures for that. One was to throw himself completely into a new project. For the moment, that was out of reach. But the other ...

The bathroom door was five long strides away. He took a cellophane-wrapped glass from above the sink, poked his thumb through the wrapping, and tore it off. Sometimes he was tempted to dispense with a glass, but he always resisted. Drinking from the bottle was strictly for thorough-going drunks, and he was a very long way from being one of those.

Returning to the room, he unscrewed the cap on the bottle and started to pour. The glass was half full when he thought he heard a footstep in the hall, near his door. Someone coming to see him? He quickly replaced the cap, put the bottle back in the drawer, and set the glass on the desk, in the shelter of one of the stacks of papers. Then he took a deep breath and waited.

Nothing. False alarm. Both relieved and ashamed, he retrieved the glass and stared down into it, as if he could read the future in the tiny circle of amber light.

Back in his hotel room from an afternoon dive, Rick rinsed off in the shower, then, still naked, pulled a chair near the window and looked over the letter he had found waiting at the front desk. No return address, but it had been mailed in San Diego and forwarded from his mother's place in Palm Beach.

He ripped open the envelope and felt a grin spread across his face as he recognized Sam's handwriting. Dr. Samantha Deane, MC, USN, was a hot runner in her field. A highly skilled orthopedic surgeon, she was also one of the few women to have won the right to wear the dolphin insignia of a submarine medical officer. She was currently assigned to the U.S. Naval Special Warfare Center in Coronado, California, serving as medical officer to the SEAL teams training program. A lieutenant commander with several years' seniority, she considerably outranked Rick.

She also had gorgeous orange-red hair, high cheekbones, an upturned, freckle-dotted nose, a body that would stop traffic on a freeway, and green eyes that made Rick's knees wobble. They had both felt a spark the first time they'd met, and soon the spark had set off a blaze of passion that still warmed Rick's heart—and a few other parts as well—when he thought about their times together. Whenever he reminded himself that Sam was a widow with a six-year-old son, however, a chill that felt very much like fear started turning down the thermostat of his passion.

It wasn't that he disliked Sam's son. He thought Billy was a pretty neat kid, in fact, and they had a lot of fun together. As for Billy, he ranked Uncle Rick right up there with Batman and the Teenage Mutant Ninja Turtles. It was just that ... well, Sam had made it clear that she thought Billy deserved a full-time father, not just a drop-in uncle, and that she herself wanted a lot more commitment than occasional, even if wonderful, weekends.

Worse than that, Sam seemed to have serious and growing doubts about being involved with a Navy man on active duty. Rick couldn't blame her. Her father, a MedEvac chopper pilot, had bought the farm during the Vietnam era, and her husband, while serving as an instructor at Top Gun, had tried to bore a hole in the ground with his F-5 Talon. Then, only last year, her older brother, Mac MacDougall, a legendary figure in the SEALs, had gone off alone on a self-chosen, highly classified, and very deep dive from which he never returned.

The last time Rick had seen her, right after the operation on his arm, she had let him see both her confidence and her doubts.

"You'll be almost as good as new, unless you goof off with the PT and the exercises," she had said after examining the arm. "I imagine that when you come off medical leave you plan to ask for a return to flight status?"

"I guess so. That, or go back to finish SEAL training."

She had nodded. "Putting yourself in the way of danger. I know. Tell me, have you ever thought about taking yourself just a tiny bit *out* of the way of danger? You can serve your country and have a fine Navy career, without always choosing the riskiest duty around."

"I know. But I like stretching limits, including my own. And you can't do that without a little bit of risk," he had replied. There had been a touch of pride mixed with resignation to the hard facts about his own character. "It's challenges that make me feel alive."

"Uh-huh. Until you run up against one that makes you feel very, permanently, dead. Never mind," she had added, starting for the door. "Forget I mentioned it. But don't forget to do your exercises."

In their letters and phone calls since then, both of them had tiptoed around the issue—or bundle of issues—that threatened to sink their relationship. Rick knew that, sooner or later, he would have to decide how much he wanted what Sam offered and how much he was ready to give up for it. But not now; not yet.

He shook the cobwebs out of his mind and unfolded the letter.

Dear Rick,

I've been meaning to write for what seems like forever, but the latest training cycle at Coronado is nearing the end, and you know what that's like. I've been putting in what seems like 80-hour weeks watching over the condition of our "Baby SEALs"! And the day before yesterday, in the playground, Billy decided to use his face to stop a moving swing. No great harm done, just a couple of stitches in his lip and a chipped baby tooth, but it didn't do anything for my peace of mind.

The reason I have time to write is that it's Saturday and Billy's off at baseball practice this afternoon. Kiwi offered to take him and bring him home, and of course

I said yes. As soon as I finish this letter, I'll take some hamburger patties out to thaw and get the charcoal going. Wish you were here. I can still taste that barbecue sauce you whipped up one time. But of course Palm Beach is much too lah-di-dah to go in for charbroiled hamburgers, isn't it? Filet mignon au foie gras, a modest chardonnay on the terrace overlooking the sea, and rubbing shoulders with senators and millionaires, right? You ARE doing your exercises, aren't you?

Billy still talks about the way you taught him to body-surf (and I still haven't forgiven you for doing it!). His swimming is coming along really well. Last Sunday we spent the day at the beach with Kiwi, who taught Billy to swim underwater (at least three strokes!). Having a friend who's a SEAL instructor does have its advantages. Speaking of which, have you decided if you'll come back to finish the course and qualify, once your arm is fully healed? Kiwi says he'll hunt you down and do something awful to you if you don't, but that's just his way of saying that he misses you. I do too.

Oops! There's the front door, and the patties are still in the freezer, not to mention that the charcoal is sitting in a bag in the garage. And I still have to clean the grill from last weekend. Help!

Miss you—
Sam

Rick refolded the letter and let it drop to the floor next to his chair, then stood up and gazed out the window at the deep blue waters of Tumon Bay and the cloudless tropical sky. His reflection showed faintly in the plate glass. His jaws were clenched, his eyebrows were drawn together, and his tight-pressed lips protruded slightly. It was the face that his mother, who'd majored in French at Sweetbrier, always called "Ricky bouding." It was only when he himself was in college that he'd found out that *bouder* was the French word for "pout."

He picked up the letter again and skimmed it. What the hell did she think she was doing, spending every spare moment with Kiwi Kraus? And letting him give Billy swimming lessons, and take him to ballgames, and all the rest of it? Sure, she and Kiwi had had a few dates, before Rick had come on the scene, but that was ancient history.

Or was it?

They must see each other every day at the base, not to mention weekends at her place or the beach. That was no guarantee of romance—sometimes just the opposite—but usually, if the chemistry was the least bit right, close proximity helped a bunch. Rick had stopped believing in absence makes the heart grow fonder somewhere around tenth grade. And no matter what else he and Sam might have going for them, he was sure that he was a case of out of sight, out of mind.

There was something else. Kiwi was a SEAL, and fiercely proud of it, but his position as chief instructor at Coronado meant that he wasn't exposed to all the risks of active service with the teams. Was Sam starting to think that that was a lot better than being hung up on someone who, whatever direction he decided to take, was going to be courting danger at every turn?

And what about her letter? Had she really not noticed that it came out sounding like "Kiwi this, Kiwi that"? Or had she written it that way deliberately, to give Rick the message that he wasn't the only SEAL in the ocean? Either way, he wasn't thrilled. Either she was unaware of how he might be feeling, or she was trying to manipulate him.

He was itching to crumple Sam's letter into a ball and try for a carom shot off the wall into the wastebasket. He nearly did it. Then the part of his mind that he thought of as The Calculator put its two cents' worth in.

"Why burn your bridges before you come to them?" it asked.

It occurred to Rick, not for the first time, that The Calculator didn't always make total sense. Still, it had a point. When it came right down to it, he didn't want to break off with Sam, no matter how much gloomy satisfaction he might get from doing so before she could do it herself. What he really wanted was for her to say that she would wait for him, however long it took. It would also be nifty if at the same time she told Kiwi Kraus, very nicely, to piss off. But how did Rick get from here to there?

For inspiration, he called Room Service and asked them to send up a couple of beers. They asked if he wanted Budweiser, Kirin, or San Miguel. On the principle that a beer from the Philippines, a shorter distance away, was bound to be better, he asked for San Miguel. Ten minutes later the buzzer sounded. He pulled on a pair of shorts, opened the door, took the tray and signed the chit, then poured himself a glass of suds. It was okay—not terrific, but okay.

Glass in hand, he sat himself at the small desk and pulled open the drawer. Aside from a printed questionnaire about hotel service, it held exactly two postcards, two sheets of notepaper with the hotel crest at the top, and two small envelopes, also with the crest. Was there a maid who did an inventory between guests and brought the drawer up to regulation?

He pulled out a sheet of notepaper and started to write.

Dear Sam,

Your letter got to me today, after a lot of wandering around the globe. I'm glad it did. I've missed you (and Billy too), and it was nice to get some news about both of you.

As you see from the fancy stationery, I'm on Guam. Don't bother asking why—I couldn't tell you anyway. But if I mention that I'm here with a mossback that you know well (who thinks you have a terrific pair of legs), you'll get the general idea. I'll pass along whatever details I can after the job is done.

You sound like you see Kiwi pretty often. Give that old lobster catcher my best. I thought of him the other day when I heard a golden oldie from the Everly Brothers, called "Birddog." If he doesn't recall it, tell him to hunt up a copy and give it a listen. It's worth it.

Yes, Mommy, I've been doing my exercises, and washing behind my ears too, and (seriously now) I think the operation was a complete success. You know who I give the credit for that.

I've been doing a lot of diving since I got here, as much as the job gives me time for. The waters couldn't be better. In a few days, I'm going off with a young Japanese who saved my bacon from a hungry shark. He's here as part of some kind of environmental group. They make films, publish booklets, and so on. I promised that I'd go to a meeting with him too. I guess I should have been more cautious. They might be subversives, after all. But when I have to start worrying about going to a meeting and watching some slides of undersea life, I've gotten pretty close to the end of my useful services to the United States Navy. And I'd hate to think that I'm there already.

I'd give a lot to be there with you and Billy now, and have a frozen hamburger right off the grill—don't forget the pickle relish and chopped onions. But that'll have to wait until I've fulfilled my obligations out here and get orders and passage back to the States.

Rick put down the pen and looked at the letter for a long time. He took another pull at his glass of beer. Finally, he grabbed the pen again and scrawled "love, Rick" at the bottom of the page. The last time he could recall his hand trembling so much was in fifth grade, while he was addressing a Valentine's Day card to LouAnn Hermann, the blonde with the blue hair ribbons who sat two rows ahead of him in class, who had never given the least sign that she knew he was alive.

He addressed and sealed the envelope without giving himself any time to change his mind. And after all, what was there to change? He hadn't asked Sam to run away to Reno with him. He hadn't promised eternal fidelity. All he had done was show that he was still interested, and that he didn't much care for all that stuff about Kiwi Kraus. Sam could take that any way she liked. And if she didn't like it, t. s., amigo.

CHAPTER 14

Oɴ ʜɪs ᴡᴀʏ ᴏᴜᴛ ᴏꜰ ᴛʜᴇ ʜᴏᴛᴇʟ, Rɪᴄᴋ sᴛᴏᴘᴘᴇᴅ ʙʏ ᴛʜᴇ room that Ray had turned into an office. The project coordinator gave an admiring glance at Rick's tanned and finely muscled body in his cut-off jeans and tanktop, then looked at his diving bag.

"Going somewhere?" he asked.

"I figured I'd go for a dive," Rick replied with a grin. "Just for a change, you understand. Would you mind sending a fax to Washington for me?"

"No problem. You have it ready?"

Rick looked over the single sheet before handing it to George.

TO: LT ALBERT DEFORD, BUPERS
FROM: LT RICHARD TALLMAN, SEAVENTURE, AGANA GUAM

Al, could you make a photocopy of the War Patrol Report(s) of USS OVERHILL (DE477) for the last two weeks of July and the month of August 1945 and send it to me here? No big rush, just idle curiosity. Message ends.

Al Deford, a classmate of Rick's at the Naval Academy, had always had a passion for naval history. After he'd received his commission, his major professor had pulled several strings to get him posted to BuPers, where he did routine administrative work during the day and spent his evenings and weekends browsing through files and logbooks that no one had looked at in fifty years or more. Rick had passed through Washington and met him for a beer a few months before. At that time he was deep into a study of naval preparedness at the start of the Mexican-American War.

Ray in turn looked at the message and raised his eyebrows. *"Overhill?"* he asked.

"Someone I know served on her, in these waters, during World War II. I'd like to have a feeling for what it was like back then."

Ray nodded. "Yeah, that might be very interesting. I'll send it out right away."

After the first few days of depending on the SeaVenture people for transportation, Rick had rented a car, a peppy white Pontiac Sunbird convertible. He went out to the parking lot, tossed his bag in the backseat, and drove into Agana on Route 1. The road hugged the coast for most of the short trip. Soon he saw the Paseo de Susana Park jutting out into Agana Bay. At its outer tip, a small replica of the Statue of Liberty held up her torch by the entrance to the boat basin. As usual, a bunch of Japanese tourists was clustered around the base of the statue, snapping away with their cameras and getting the scene on videotape.

Rick eased over into the right lane and slowed down. Just past the Public Market, he spotted the entrance to the parking lot for the Agana Marina. He pulled in, found a vacant spot, and put the convertible's top up. He hated the inconvenience, but he knew he wouldn't be able to sit down when he came back to the car if he left the seat in the direct rays of Guam's midday sun.

From the small booths that ringed the Public Market came the aroma of steaming pots of seafood, frying chicken, and some pungent local delicacies he couldn't put a name to. He took a deep breath, then hefted his goodies bag and started down toward the water.

The gray Zodiac rubber boat was tied up halfway down the finger pier. Two men stood next to it. One was the young Japanese, Kazuo. The other, wearing faded red and yellow jams with no shirt or shoes, looked like an American. He was deeply tanned, and his long, shaggy blond hair was bleached almost white by the sun. A gold chain circled his neck. Rick immediately pegged him as a beach bum.

Kazuo was wearing trunks and a T-shirt that advertised the Nacogdoches Chili Parlor in Papeete, Tahiti. He noticed Rick's approach and raised his hand in a gesture that was between a wave and a salute. The other guy looked around. His cheek muscles contracted, pulling his lips into a replica of a smile that looked hopelessly forced and false.

"Rick!" Kazuo said. "I am glad you could accept my invitation. This is Tom, a countryman of yours."

"Hafa adai," Tom drawled.

"How ya doin'?" Rick replied. He thought he remembered the formal phrase for "How are you?" in Chamorro, but he was damned if he was going to get into a linguistic one-upping contest with this guy.

"Tom is also a very experienced diver," Kazuo said. "I asked him to come along today to stay with the boat. The first place we are diving, the Blue Hole, is very beautiful, very exciting, but there are sometimes very strong, sudden currents."

"Fine with me," Rick said, nodding to Tom. He climbed down into the Zodiac and sat down near the middle of the boat, just in front of the waist-high podium that held the controls. Kazuo took the wheel and started the big outboard, while Tom cast off and pushed the bow away from the pier and into the channel. A few moments later they were bouncing through the line of breakers into the open water outside the bay. Kazuo made a long curving turn to port, put the boat on a westward course that paralleled the shore, and opened the throttle.

Tom came aft and plopped himself down next to Rick.

Over the roar of the engine, Rick asked, "Do you know the dive sites we're headed for?"

Tom shrugged. "Not really. I dived the Blue Hole once, that's it. It's a good dive. Kazuo tells me you're real hot shit underwater. True?"

It was Rick's turn to shrug. "I've done some diving, but not in these waters. Do you know the area?"

"Pretty well. I've been sort of working my way around the Western Pacific for a while now, hustling to support my diving habit. It's a full life."

"I bet," Rick said. Just as he'd thought: a beach bum. "Are you here on vacation?"

"Not exactly. An outfit called SeaVenture brought me out as a consultant."

"SeaVenture? That's the deep-sea mining operation, isn't it?"

Rick hesitated before saying, "That's right."

"Huh. So you grab anything you find that you can make a buck off of, and you don't know or care what kind of damage you're doing to the seabed."

"That's a pretty extreme attitude," Rick said, biting back a more familiar expression usually abbreviated b.s.

Tom gave a bitter laugh. "Is it? A couple of months ago, I was down in the Bismarcks, northeast of Papua New Guinea. Those islands have some of the most amazing fields of hard coral, in every color you can imagine. But half the reefs are dead now. You know why? The lumber companies, mostly Japanese, want to log the islands, but they need to get permission from the local chiefs. So they offer the chiefs dynamite in exchange for logging rights, and the chiefs use the dynamite as a quick and dirty way to get their fishing done. One blast will take a reef out of action for at least twenty or thirty years—maybe forever—but the chiefs don't know that, not yet. And you can bet that the people who are making money off the operation aren't going to tell them."

"If you're asking for my opinion, that really sucks," said Rick. "But SeaVenture isn't that kind of operation. They're not going to be drowning dolphins in drift nets or dynamiting coral reefs. In the depths they'll be working, there's practically no marine life of any sort that could be put in danger."

"Would they care if there was?" Tom demanded. "Never mind. You work for the outfit. I don't want to put you on the spot."

Rick scowled. Was Tom suggesting that he was too cowardly to disagree with his employers? Did he think that marginal types like himself were the only ones who had the freedom or the guts to speak their minds?

"You're not putting me on the spot," he said firmly. "And I don't really know the top management of the company yet, so I can't speak for them. But from what I've seen so far, they've put a lot of effort into making it a low-impact operation."

"Sure, okay," Tom replied. "Let's hope you're right."

To bring the conversation to a close, Rick turned his shoulder to Tom and watched the coastline go by. The boat was just passing Cabras Island. The superstructure of a freighter peeped over the dunes from Guam's commercial port, on the other side of the small island. Just ahead was the thin ribbon of the Glass Breakwater, nearly three miles long, which enclosed Apra Harbor and protected it from the Pacific rollers.

Rick recalled that the breakwater was named for Guam's first American governor, Captain Henry Glass, USN, who had claimed the island for the U.S. during the Spanish-American War. The Navy still played a central part in the daily life of Guam. The island was covered with Navy installations, from the naval air station at Brewer Field and the big antenna arrays of NAVCAMS, which handled all naval communications for the Western Pacific, to the naval magazine, on hundreds of acres of hilly jungle in the southern part of the island. Above all, there was the naval station, which occupied the big peninsula that edged Apra Harbor on the south. It was just coming into sight past the end of the Glass Breakwater. This anchorage had always held an important place in Navy planning, but its strategic value had soared since the huge base at Subic Bay, in the Philippines, started being phased out. Guam now ranked as the single most important base in the Western Pacific.

"We're almost there," Kazuo shouted, just after they rounded the point of the peninsula. He backed off on the throttle, the note of the motor descended to a throaty burble, and the bow settled lower in the water. They puttered along for a few minutes more, then Kazuo killed the motor, went to the bow, and leaned over the side to peer down into the water. "No runoff here," he said over his shoulder. "Very good visibility."

The boat continued to drift slowly forward, until Kazuo hefted the heavy anchor and dropped it over.

He came back and squatted in front of Rick and Tom. "The Blue Hole is an opening in the coral shelf just below us at about sixty feet, that goes straight down to perhaps 300 feet," he explained. "Too deep for us today. But at 130 feet there is an opening, a window, that leads to the outer coral wall and the open sea. The wall goes much, much deeper, beyond the reach of any diver, but it is a beautiful sight. I think you will not forget it. It is fun to go down the shaft, then leave through the opening and return to the surface on the outside. I have prepared a diving plan," he added, reaching for a folder and pulling a sheet from it.

Rick looked it over. It was pretty straightforward, allowing them twenty minutes of bottom time at 130 feet, followed by one four-minute decompression stop on the way up, at ten feet. A second dive, listed as twenty minutes at sixty feet, worked out to require a seven-minute stop at ten feet because of residual nitrogen in their blood from the first dive.

Rick passed the worksheet back and indicated the instrument on Kazuo's left wrist. "I'm surprised you still work it out with the tables," he said. "I thought that gadget of yours kept track of elapsed time at each depth and automatically calculated your decompression stops."

"So it does," Kazuo said. "Also intervals on the surface and repetitive dive calculations. But I trust it more when I have an idea of what answers it should be giving me."

He stood up, pulled off his T-shirt, and took a lightweight

wetsuit from his diving bag. Rick had been thinking of the young Japanese as slight, even thin. Now he changed his estimate. True, Kazuo's ribs showed clearly, but so did the hard-ridged abdominal muscles that had to have come from constant, dedicated workouts. Rick glanced down and spotted the thick callus along the outer edge of Kazuo's hand. A long-time karate student too, and probably very good at it.

Rick stripped down and wriggled into his wetsuit, then donned his buoyancy compensator, SCUBA tank, weightbelt, and mask. Kazuo was ready before him. "We'll stop at the reef to check our depth gauges against each other," he said. He sat on the gunwale and rolled slowly backward into the water.

Rick was next. The water temperature was about eighty degrees—not quite a warm bath, but close. He floated free for a few moments, then asked Tom to hand him another three-pound weight, which he slipped onto his belt to "justify himself with Archimedes," or achieve neutral buoyancy. Apparently Kazuo had adjusted his buoyancy earlier. He was already on his way down, in a lazy spiral that kept him close to the anchor line but gave him a 360° view of the surrounding water. Rick followed.

When he reached the sloping surface of the reef, where Kazuo was waiting for him, Rick's depth gauge read fifty-seven feet. He pointed to his wrist and signed a five and a seven. Kazuo looked at his high-tech diving computer and made a circled thumb and forefinger okay sign, then pointed to his left.

The Blue Hole was well named. Against the paler blue-green of the reef, it showed up as a deep blue circular void with no apparent bottom. The sun was high and the tide was at ebb slack, so the hole in the shaft that led to the outer reef could easily be seen through the gin-clear water.

Kazuo swam over the edge, gave a couple of strong kicks with his giant fins, and began a quick descent through the shaft. Once more Rick followed, but slowly. Never had he seen such an explosion of underwater life. It began on the sloping approaches to the hole and increased with the depth in diversity and concentration, in a way unimaginable to a diver with no experience in tropical waters. Not only were there more varieties of gorgonian coral than he had ever seen, but the anemones with their attendant clown fish were simply beyond numbering.

At the mouth of the hole, Rick assumed a head-down position and began his own slow descent. He noticed that Kazuo was already at the window, waiting for Rick to join him, but Rick refused to rush. A large overhang at about eighty feet sheltered dozens of pearl-colored soldierfish. Some of them seemed to be swimming upside down. But then, so was he. Twenty feet farther down, he admired some bright red sea whips attached to the rocky wall and wished he had thought to bring along his camera.

All too soon, he reached the level of the window onto the open ocean. Kazuo was still hovering there, waiting for him. They started through the opening, waited to let a big dog-tooth tuna swim past, and began a gradual ascent to the surface. They hadn't been deep for the twenty minutes they had planned on, but Rick was glad to see Kazuo take the decompression stop at ten feet anyway. This was supposed to be a fun dive, not an occasion for getting the bends.

Back in the boat, Rick said, "Nice dive. I wouldn't mind coming back here for a longer one some time."

"You should try it at night," Kazuo replied. "There is a school of what they call flashlight fish, that comes out only at night. Each fish gives off a flickering light, from a small place on its head. Have you seen fireflies, tiny insects that fly in the evening, giving off a greenish light? I don't know if you have them in America. In Japan we have a festival at which the children try to capture them. These fish look very like them."

"Sure, we have fireflies," Rick said. "I used to catch them in a bottle when I was a kid. I can't remember seeing them in a while, though. Maybe they're getting rarer."

"Probably all those insecticides we use," Tom contributed. He gave Rick a look as if he held him personally responsible for the existence of Flit, Gulfspray, and DDT.

Rick ignored him. "Your worksheet mentioned a second dive, a shallower one," he said to Kazuo.

"Yes, Barracuda Cave. It is not at all a difficult dive, but it has much of interest." Kazuo pointed down the shore. "You see that large boulder sticking from the water, the one with the birds circling it? It is called Barracuda Rock, though I have not seen any barracuda there. The cave is in the cliff just behind it. Many fish school there: copper sweepers, goatfish, Moorish idols, parrotfish, and many Spanish dancers, which I love to watch. I have also seen morays and sea turtles, and occasionally a white-tip shark."

"Sounds like fun. Let's go."

They weighed anchor and motored closer to the rock, which turned out to be a pile of huge boulders. As they came near, dozens of the boobies that nested there took wing and began to circle the boat, filling the air with their raucous cries.

"Don't worry," Tom called. "We're not after your eggs!"

While Tom dropped and set the anchor, Rick and Kazuo changed to fresh air tanks and prepared to dive.

They left the boat together and slowly made their way shoreward through gentle swells. The roof of the cave opening was above water for the first fifty feet, so they swam on the surface, using their snorkels, until the lowering ceiling forced them to switch to their tanks.

Before they left the surface, they spent a few minutes paying homage to a time-honored cave diver's custom. They splashed water back toward the cave opening and watched the sparkling blue effervescence that erupted on the disturbed water surface. The interplay of blue lights and shadows in an underwater cave was something that any diver who truly loved the sea never forgot.

As they quit the surface and headed for the back of the cave, Rick found that he didn't need the light he had decided to bring at the last minute. The refracted sunlight gave plenty of illumination, and he felt less like an intruder without it. Had they been there as spear fishermen, it would have been different.

As advertised, a school of copper-colored fish swept

through the cave, glistening as they tacked one way, then another on their way out. Following them was a small school of bright purple fish with long, translucent dorsal fins. As they swam out of the cave close to the sandy bottom, Rick spotted what looked like a tunnel through the base of a coral finger that extended out from the shore. Curious, he swam over and was about to explore it when he saw, camouflaged by the rocks, a large spotted moray. He veered away. No point in disturbing the creature's nap.

Kazuo caught his eye and pointed shoreward. Near the sandy floor at the base of a large coral head, two big snappers were darting in and out of crevices. Rick watched their antics for a while, then caught a glimpse of his watch. To his surprise, the luminous hands showed that they had already overstayed their planned limit. He looked over at Kazuo, pointed upward, and added a questioning shrug of his shoulders. Kazuo checked his diving computer, nodded, and pointed up in turn. They left the bottom together for their scheduled decompression stop at ten feet.

Back at the boat, Tom took the helm while Rick and Kazuo doffed and packed their diving gear.

"Thanks," Rick said. "Those are nice spots."

"Guam offers many interesting dives," Kazuo replied. "The reefs, of course, with their variety of sea life, but also many sunken ships and warplanes."

The mention of sunken ships reminded Rick of Captain Ward's story about his rescue of a young Japanese naval officer from a sinking submarine.

"Do you mind if I ask you a personal question?" he said.

Kazuo's face became perfectly blank and still, like a 3-D hologram of himself.

"Not at all," he said, after a long pause.

"Are you any relation to someone named Yasamara Takauji, who was in the Japanese Navy during World War II? I might be a little off on the first name."

Kazuo blinked, just once. In a level, emotionless voice, he said, "My father's name was Yasunari, and he was a cadet officer in the Imperial Navy. Why do you ask?"

Rick was stunned. "That's just amazing," he said with a

big smile. "My godfather is Will Ward, who met your dad at the very end of the war. When he noticed your name on the note you sent me, he told me the whole story."

"Captain Will Ward is here, on Guam?" It was Kazuo's turn to be stunned. "I must go right away, to give him my respects. But why is your name not Ward, if he is your father?"

"No, no," Rick hastened to explain. "He isn't my father, he's my *godfather*. That's someone who's a friend of the family and who takes on a special responsibility for a child when it's born."

"*Ah so desu ka!* I should have remembered this, from the film with Marlon Brando."

Rick laughed, as he tried to imagine Captain Ward speaking in a whispery voice, making someone an offer he couldn't refuse. Then he said, "That's not exactly the kind of 'godfather' I mean. But he has known me all my life. He taught me to dive, as a matter of fact."

"My father honored him greatly," Kazuo said in a solemn voice. "Each year, as the New Year approached, he would take much care to select a card of best wishes for Captain Ward. He always showed it to us before he sent it. Once he told me that the Emperor had saved his life, but that Will Ward was the means the Emperor used to do it. I asked him to explain why the Emperor would use an American sailor, but he shook his head and would say no more."

"Is your father . . . ?"

"He died three years ago, after a long illness."

"I'm sorry."

"Thank you. One of my regrets after his death was that I wanted to send a card in his name to Captain Ward, but I did not know where to send it. Now I can give up that regret and carry out my duty."

"I know Captain Ward would be pleased to meet you," Rick said. "I'll be sure to tell him about this wonderful coincidence."

"Coincidence?" said Kazuo. "I wonder. For my father's son to meet the—what do you say, godson?"

"That's right."

"—the godson of Captain Will Ward goes far beyond co-incidence. Some things are meant to happen."

Rick said nothing. He didn't believe in luck, or fate, or the influence of the stars, and he didn't really understand people who claimed that they did, but he had been taught at an early age that a gentleman never argues about politics, religion, or someone's choice of a mate.

Rick glanced over his shoulder. Tom was standing at the wheel, staring forward as if oblivious to everything except the course he was holding. He wasn't. Something about the set of his shoulders told Rick that he had been listening hard to the conversation between Rick and Kazuo. And when his eyes flicked down for a moment to meet Rick's, the spark of anger in them showed that he didn't like what he'd heard one bit.

After dropping Rick at the marina, Tom pointed the Zodiac's bow southward for the short trip back to the Ocean Friends compound. During most of the voyage, Kazuo sat silent, gazing off toward the horizon.

The silence was stretching to the breaking point when Tom asked, "Who is that guy, anyway?"

Kazuo gave him a look as if he didn't quite remember who Tom was. Then his eyes narrowed. "Rick Tallman? An American spy, of course."

"Then why have you been sucking up to him?"

"He has an important part to play in the *Glomar Champion* mining project. He is also a highly trained diver who went through the American Navy's SEAL training program. That means that he can be a very valuable friend to our goals. He can also be a very dangerous enemy. I have long argued that it is surer and safer to win a friend than to defeat an enemy."

"What was all that stuff about your father and his godfather?"

For the first time that Tom could recall, a look of uncertainty, even puzzlement, showed on Kazuo's face.

"I must learn more of this," he said, as much to himself

as to Tom. "It may be a lie, a very subtle trap. But how could they know? If it is true, if Rick Tallman is indeed the godson of Captain Will Ward, then I have a much stronger reason to make a friend of him. In fact, I must. My honor, and the honor of my family, would never allow me to be his enemy."

CHAPTER 15

As THE BOSTON WHALER CURVED IN TOWARD THE PIER, the helmsman moved the power lever into reverse and added throttle. The throaty burble of the exhaust rose briefly to a roar, then settled back to its earlier level as the boat came parallel to the dock and gently nudged the piling next to the recessed wooden ladder that led to the top of the pier. The man in the bow stood ready to hold the boat off with his boathook, but it wasn't necessary.

Captain Will Ward, who had been standing poised at the gunwale, reached up over his head, grabbed a high rung on the ladder, and began to scramble up onto the pier. Rick was right behind him.

"Nice landing, guys. Thanks," Rick called, as the motor launch made a wide circle and headed back for open water, where *Berkone* rode at anchor. The man at the helm waved an acknowledgment.

Ward was already walking with purposeful strides in the direction of the parking lot. The set of his shoulders said clearly that he was not in a good mood. No surprise there. Rick quickened his pace and caught up to him.

"Another day down the tubes," he remarked, in as close to a cheerful voice as he could manage. "Still, I guess we deserve an *E* for Effort."

165

"Sure," Ward growled. "And Ray and his bunch deserve an *F* for *FUBAR:* Fucked Up Beyond All Recognition. If it weren't for the fact that those turkeys are picking up the tab while we field test and fine-tune the improvements in the *Steel Albatross,* I'd have us gathering our marbles and heading home by now."

At the car, Ward spun around and went on, "This is— what?—the fourth time we've gotten all ready to follow that contraption of theirs down to the bottom?"

"The third, I think," Rick murmured.

"Whatever. Too many, whatever the number. Don't get me wrong, Ricky," the captain continued, in a slightly milder tone. "I know how many things can go wrong with new and complicated machinery. When your daddy piloted the space shuttle, he and his crew had to sit around for weeks on end until everything started working right at the same time. But at least in his case, the ground crew knew what the problems were and had some idea how to deal with them. With this bunch, I am beginning to wonder if there's anyone in it who knows shit from shinola."

Rick chuckled. He unlocked the convertible, pushed the button to unlock Ward's door, and put the top down. As they pulled out of the parking lot, the uniformed guard waved from his glass-walled booth. By his expression, he was wishing he too could jump into a convertible and drive off somewhere.

At the highway, Rick waited a moment for a break in the light traffic, then turned left, in the direction of Agana. "I wonder," he said, picking up from Ward's last statement. Before he could say what he wondered, a rusty station wagon with two sailboards strapped to the roof rack roared past, enveloping the convertible in a cloud of blue smoke. The two guys in the wagon were deeply tanned, blond, and no older than seventeen. The one on the passenger's side gave Rick a grin that was half a sneer. Then the station wagon dodged back into Rick's lane, just in time to miss an oncoming truck.

"Assholes!" Rick muttered, tapping the brakes and dropping back a couple of car lengths.

Ward said, "I don't know that you ever qualified for a safe-driving merit badge, son. As a matter of fact, you've given me a good bunch of hair-raising rides over the years."

"That's different," Rick protested. "I always know what I'm doing. Those kids don't even *know* they're taking risks."

Ward gave him an ironic smile. "Then who's the asshole?" he asked. "The guy who takes some damn fool risk because he doesn't know it's dangerous, or the one who knows it's dangerous and does it anyway?"

"Okay, okay!" Rick exclaimed, laughing. He threw up his hands in a gesture of surrender, then quickly put them back on the steering wheel, before Ward could get on his case for that too. "But I know for a fact that you've never been much of a play-it-safe type yourself, Captain. I've heard a few stories from my dad."

"That'll do, Ricky. And I think you'd better start calling me 'Will,' if you don't mind. Ray said he doesn't want us using ranks in front of the public, and 'Will' sounds a lot better than 'that old fart Ward.' "

"Aye-aye, sir," Rick said, straight-faced. "I mean, Will."

Ward pretended that he hadn't heard. After a moment, he said, "You started to say you were wondering about something."

"Did I?" Rick cast his mind back. "Oh, yeah. All these delays aboard *Glomar Champion:* Don't you find them a little suspicious? Sure, you always need a shakedown period with new equipment, especially if it's loaded with cutting-edge technology. But they've had plenty of time to get the bugs out, if you ask me. Either they're all doing a half-assed job, or somebody on their team is doing a first-rate job of screwing things up."

"Are you talking about sabotage?" Will asked. "I can't say it sounds very likely to me."

"Why not?" Rick replied. "You're the one who told me that this project is vital to national security."

Will sighed. "Ricky, you know that, I know that, and a few dozen people in Washington and at a couple of hush-hush research labs know that. As far as the rest of the world is concerned—and that includes *everyone* working on the

SeaVenture project—what's going on here is a feasibility study for a new approach to deep-sea mining. Which, as a matter of fact, is exactly what it is. Why would it be worth anyone's while to sabotage it?"

Rick didn't have an answer for Will, except that there might be more people who knew or guessed the underlying purpose of SeaVenture than Ward knew about. But he wasn't convinced of that; he certainly didn't have any evidence for it; so he kept his mouth shut. Still, something about the SeaVenture project, or about the team that was running it, simply felt wrong to him. It was like walking into a beautifully decorated house and sensing that there were termites in the joists and rats in the walls.

"Never mind, Ricky," Will said, patting him on the shoulder. "We'll do what we came here to do, and do it damn well, once Ray and his crew give us the chance. But it's not up to us to do their job too ... or even to interfere with the way they choose to do it."

"Yes, sir," Rick said. With a grin, he added, "Will."

In town, Rick pulled over to the curb near a drugstore. "I'm nearly out of toothpaste," he explained. "I'll just be a minute."

When he came out of the store, Will was standing on the sidewalk next to the car, talking to a tall, slim woman in a pale yellow raw silk dress. Her back was to Rick, but both the dress and the golden blond hair that flowed over her shoulders looked very familiar. He hurried over.

Will saw him coming and said, "Rick, you son of a gun, you've been holding out on me! You never breathed a word about your lovely friend here."

The woman turned. Rick felt a grin spread across his face. "Hi, Natalie," he almost shouted. He hoped he didn't sound or look as goofy as he felt. "It's really great to see you again." He meant every word.

"Hello, Rick," she replied, with a demure smile. "I am very glad to see you. I remembered that you were coming to Guam, but I did not have an address for you. I could not believe it when I saw you drive by just now. I turned and followed, of course, but without much hope. There was traffic in the way. Then, by a wonderful chance, I noticed your car stopped at the curb here."

She turned to Will and added, "Rick saved me from a band of thieves last month in Honolulu. He was very brave and very gallant."

"Oh, that's our Rick, all right," Will said, giving Rick a sly wink. "Brave and gallant as they come. I've always admired his good taste too."

"He has very good taste in friends, that is clear," Natalie said. Her smile revealed two small charming dimples in her cheeks.

Rick noticed a flash of irritation. He was glad that Natalie and Will got along, but did they have to get along quite so well? He pushed the unworthy thought out of his mind and asked, "How long are you here for, Natalie?"

"This man!" she said teasingly. "Five minutes after I arrive, he is already trying to get rid of me!"

"Don't mind him," Will said. "He doesn't mean any harm."

Rick felt his cheeks grow warm. They were practically telling him to go off and play in the yard, and give the grown-ups a chance to talk. He started to make an angry reply, then realized that it would make him sound even more like a kid.

Natalie must have sensed his reaction. She moved next to him and slipped her arm into his. "I want to hear all about your adventures on Guam," she said in a silky voice. "Have you had time to do much diving yet?"

"Some," Rick said. He was very aware of Will's ironic glance. "Not as much as I'd like. You know how it is. New projects take a while to get off the ground."

"Does that mean that you have some free time?" she continued. She turned to Will and added, "You must think I am a very bold woman. But I am not here for long, and it would not be reasonable to waste the little time we have with coyness. Don't you agree?"

"Oh, sure," Will said, giving Rick another look. "Tell you what, Rick: I'll take a cab out to the hotel and leave you two to get reacquainted."

"You don't have to—" Rick began.

At the same moment, Natalie said, "Oh no, you must not—"

They stopped, met one another's eyes, and laughed.

"After you," Rick said, sketching the bow he had been forced to learn in sixth-grade dance class.

"Where are you staying?" Natalie asked.

Rick named the hotel and added, "It's out at Tumon Bay."

Natalie clapped her hands. "So is mine! I am at the Ocean Grove. Perhaps you will follow me there? Then I will join you and we can drive your friend to his destination."

Will said, "Good idea, Ricky. And that'll give me the excuse I've been looking for to sit in the backseat of this jalopy of yours and feel the wind in my hair." He chuckled and brushed a hand over his steel-gray crewcut.

Rick opened the door and pulled the seatback forward. "Do it now," he said with a grin. "But don't blame me if people think you're some bigwig on his way to collect the keys to the city. And if anyone starts picking things up off the ground and tossing them in your direction, duck. They might be flowers, but you never know."

Natalie returned to her car, a sporty red Japanese coupe, and waved as she drove past. Rick pulled out from the curb and got close in behind her.

"So that's the reason you were out until three A.M. in Honolulu," Will said, leaning his elbows on the seatback. "Very classy. What is she, French?"

"More or less," Rick replied. "She owns an art gallery in Tokyo."

"*Very* classy," Will repeated. "Did you really rescue her from a gang of muggers?"

"Well . . . more or less. With a little help from the automatic she was carrying in her purse."

"Oh? The lady is full of surprises. So what brings her to Guam?"

Rick said, "I'm not sure. She said something about hunting down Japanese antiques that got scattered during and after World War II. Ivory carvings, stuff like that."

"There must be an awful lot around," Will said. "Half the guys who served in the Pacific Theater went home with a souvenir or two. I've got one myself, a carved kimono button, what they call a *netsuke*. Never mind how I got it. It's back in San Diego, in a little cigar box with my short snorter and my ruptured duck."

"I know," said Rick. "This is where I'm supposed to ask what's a ruptured duck and a—what was it?—snort shorter."

"Short snorter. What it was, every time you hit a new port, you'd take a piece of whatever the local paper money was, get all your buddies to sign it, and paste it on the end of all the other pieces you'd collected. By the end of the war, I must have had better than two dozen bills taped together, along with the John Hancocks of a couple of hundred shipmates, some who'd been put out of the picture for good. I guess the custom's died out. Too bad."

"And a ruptured duck?"

"That's what we called the little gold lapel pins we all got on leaving the service right after the war. I was a civilian for a little while, you know, before I entered the Academy. Anyway, this pin was meant to be an eagle, I guess, but eagle or duck, he sure as hell looked like he needed a truss."

Rick laughed. Up ahead, the left-turn signal on Natalie's coupe began to blink. He slowed down and followed her onto a side road that curved to lead along the rear of a line of beachfront hotels. She pulled into one of the parking lots, using a card to raise the red- and white-striped wooden barrier. Rick made a U-turn and waited by the entrance. After a few moments, she came walking toward them, tying a red and gold scarf over her hair.

"*Very* classy," Will murmured once again. "Continental." As Natalie neared the car, Will settled back into his seat, draped one arm along the folded top, and basked like a lizard. Rick had the unnerving impression that the old seadog was planning to turn chaperon on him.

Will seemed to read his mind. "Don't worry, son," he said. "I'm not going to be the ant at your picnic. Just drop me by the hotel on your way to wherever you're going."

Natalie opened the door and arranged herself in the passenger's bucket seat. As she swung her legs in, Rick caught a fleeting glimpse of ivory thigh above the edge of her sheer hose. He swallowed, cleared his throat, and tried to distract himself by wondering if Natalie was the only woman on Guam who wore a garter belt. As an effective distraction, this turned out to rank near the bottom of the list.

"Well . . . where are we going?" he asked. "Any ideas?"

Natalie hesitated. "Would you be offended if I suggest combining business with pleasure? I promised to call on someone who lives near Talofofo, on the east coast of the island. I am told that the area around Talofofo Bay is very *pittoresque.* It isn't very far," she added, with an uneasy look at Rick's face.

"Nothing on Guam is very far," Rick pointed out. "Sure, why not? It sounds like fun . . . as long as we don't have to worry about snakes getting into the car."

"Snakes? What do you mean?"

Will leaned forward and said, "One of the guys we work with was telling us the other day about the snake problem on Guam. They're not native to the island, so they don't have any natural enemies to keep their numbers down. Like the rabbits in Australia. By now there are more than twenty snakes for every man, woman, and child on the island. In some areas they've gotten so thick that people keep bricks on the lids to their toilets, to keep the snakes from crawling into the house through the sewer pipes."

Natalie shuddered. "I think I would like to avoid those parts of the island, if that is possible."

"Simple, if I knew which parts they were," Rick said. "Don't worry, though. I'll fight them off with my bare hands if I have to!"

Natalie clasped her hands in front of her, in a gesture that looked borrowed from an old silent movie. "My hero!" she breathed. Rick gave her what he knew must be a goofy grin.

From the backseat, Will growled, "I'd like to get back to the hotel before this conversation gets any sappier."

"Sure thing, boss," Rick replied. He shifted to neutral, revved the engine, and moved the lever into drive. The light, powerful convertible took off like a scalded cat, leaving enough rubber and noise behind to make everyone within earshot look up to see what had happened.

"In one piece!" Will shouted in Rick's ear. Rick replied with a breezy wave of the hand.

Moments later he pulled up at the entrance to their hotel. Will shunned the car door, clambering over the side instead. "I can recall when cars had little steps built into the fenders for just that purpose," he huffed.

"That must have been right before you enlisted under Admiral Dewey," Rick said. "Or was it John Paul Jones?"

"Hmmph. No respect," Will grunted. He took Natalie's hand. "Watch out for this one. A man who doesn't respect his elders and betters isn't likely to know how to give a lady the treatment she deserves, either."

"I'll remember that," Natalie said solemnly. "It was a pleasure to meet and talk with you, *mon capitaine.*"

"The pleasure was mine, mademoiselle." To Rick's astonishment and delight, Will raised Natalie's hand and brushed it with his lips, with as much aplomb as if he had been a diplomat all his life, instead of a hardbitten old salt of a submariner.

Eloise was just coming out of the hotel. She was wearing white shorts and a brightly striped pullover shirt and carrying a tennis racket. Wide-eyed, she took in the scene, then gave Rick a look of amused inquiry. He shrugged and grinned in reply. Will, straightening up, intercepted their exchange. He didn't appreciate their mockery. His face seemed to swell up like an overinflated balloon. But before he could let loose with an old-fashioned quarterdeck blast, Rick took a hand.

"Eloise," he said, "I'd like you to meet Natalie Yussupov. She's just in from Tokyo for a few days. Natalie, this is Eloise Jackson, one of our co-workers."

The two young women exchanged hello-how-are-yous with cautious warmth, while eyeing each other carefully. That gave Will time to take a deep breath, count to ten, and go through whatever other evolutions he used to calm himself down.

"We'll be back later," Rick added. "Why don't we all meet for a drink around the pool?"

"Great idea," said Eloise. "I'll keep an eye out for you. Have fun."

With a wave that was more like a flip of the hand, she walked away toward the hotel's tennis courts.

"Well, I've got a lot of paperwork to catch up with," Will said. "Natalie, if I don't see you again on this visit, enjoy your stay on Guam."

"Thank you, but I know we will meet again," Natalie said. "I hold myself to it. *Au revoir.*"

"See you later, Will," Rick added, as he moved the lever to drive.

The drive to Talofofo took them up over the lush green spine of the island and down the other side to the eastern coast. From there, the road ran south along the upper edge of a continuous line of high cliffs thick with ironwood trees. Below, Rick could see a wide, empty beach of brown sand washed by powerful rollers. A bit offshore, half a dozen surfers defied the heavy seas. Beyond them, there was only the Pacific, stretching to the horizon, as limitless as the sky.

As they approached Talofofo Bay, Natalie, who had been studying a scrap of paper she had taken from her purse, directed Rick to turn inland, onto a narrow road that climbed into the hills. After a couple of miles, they turned left onto another dirt road that was little more than two ruts through the jungle. The road ended at a clearing around a tumbledown wooden shack that leaned precariously backward and to the left. The remains of an olive-drab Jeep and a '50s-vintage Chevy pickup decorated the garden. At the sound of Rick's car, three barefoot children, two girls and a boy, came out into the yard and looked at them with big eyes. They all had the glossy black hair and wide faces that spoke of Polynesian ancestors. The boy, about four, was barebottomed as well as barefoot.

"*Hafa adai,*" Natalie called. "We're looking for Mr. Sanjana."

The children exchanged a glance but didn't speak. The

little boy stuck his thumb in his mouth and tugged at his pecker with the other hand.

The door opened and an elderly man limped out onto the porch. His dark brown face was seamed with wrinkles, but his black eyes looked alert and shrewd.

Natalie repeated her greeting and introduced herself. The man—Rick assumed that he was Mr. Sanjana—nodded and beckoned them toward the house. The children shrank away as Rick and Natalie passed, but when Rick glanced back, the little boy was already climbing into the convertible. He hoped the kid was toilet-trained.

The front half of the cabin served as kitchen, dining, and living room. It was furnished with a chrome, plastic-topped breakfast table, four matching chairs, a two-burner stove with a big propane tank on the floor next to it, three broken-down rattan chairs, two rice mats, and an old army cot. At Mr. Sanjana's gesture, Natalie pulled out one of the chairs and sat down. Rick did the same.

"I got word that you might have an old weapon to sell," Natalie began.

"A sword," the man replied. "Very old and valuable."

"May I see?"

He left the room and returned two minutes later carrying a narrow package about three feet long, wrapped in a black plastic garbage bag. He placed it in the center of the table and stepped back.

Natalie stood up and opened the bag. Inside was what Rick instantly recognized as a Japanese samurai sword. The hilt was covered with a complex pattern of black braid. What looked like ivory peeped through the holes in the braid. The scabbard, in contrast, was drab-painted metal.

Leaving the sword in the bag, Natalie opened her shoulder bag and took out a pair of thin white cotton gloves, a rolled-up face towel, and a curious tool that looked a little like an awl with a small, removable hammer at the other end. After pulling on the gloves, she picked up the scabbard in her left hand and took the hilt in her right. She pressed a small button near the base of the hilt and slowly withdrew the sword. The blade resonated with a distant and magical whisper as it was moved, and even in the dim room, the polished steel caught and sent back the light in gleams that seemed to move by themselves.

Natalie carefully put the sword down on the table, with the subtly curved blade resting on the folded towel. She studied it for a few moments, then turned it over and studied the other side. Her face was impassive, but Rick sensed her disappointment. Whatever she was looking for, this didn't seem to be it.

She bent down to examine the hilt carefully, then picked up the little tool and separated it into its two parts. She placed the point lightly against a particular spot and tapped it with the hammer. A small steel pin popped out from the other side. She collected it and set it to one side, then took the sword in her left hand, holding it by the blade, near the hilt, with the point toward the ceiling. Rick was relieved that she held it with the sharp edge away from her palm.

Suddenly she clenched her right fist and struck the underside of her left wrist, three or four times in quick succession. Even as Rick wondered what she was trying to do, the braid-covered hilt fell to the table, followed by the ornamented metal disk that divided blade from hilt and served to protect the swordsman's hand.

The tang of the blade, the part that had been hidden by the hilt, was dark and rusty. Natalie held the blade up to the light and rubbed her gloved thumb across the tang several times, then brought it close to her eyes.

"Ah, so," she said, turning to Mr. Sanjana. "As I thought. This blade is not old. Many like it were forged during the 1930s, a time when the Imperial Army and its officer corps was growing rapidly. I needed to make sure, because occasionally an officer of samurai descent would disguise a blade that was a family heirloom with an Army-issue hilt and scabbard."

"Like General Patton and his ivory-handled .45s," Rick commented.

"Yes, if your General Patton's ancestors had been carrying those same guns into battle for eight or ten generations," Natalie said, looking over at him. The comparison seemed to offend her.

"How much for the sword?" the old man asked, poking his face forward. "I hear they are worth a lot of bucks."

"Some are," Natalie agreed. "This one isn't. There is nothing the least bit unusual about it. I might find someone in Japan who would buy it simply because having a real sword, one that has perhaps seen battle, confers status. But there are thousands of swords like this, and no one is going to pay very much for one of them."

"How much?" the man repeated, in a voice that rang with anger, suspicion, and disappointment.

"If you like, I'll take it off your hands for two hundred fifty dollars, cash," Natalie said. Before he could speak, she added, "You might be able to get twice that, if you yourself sell it directly to a tourist—one of the Japanese honeymooners over at Tumon Bay, or an American sailor with a few months' pay in his pocket. But it might take a long time to find a buyer. It will probably take *me* a long time to find a buyer. This way you have the money, and I have the risk."

"You have my sword too," Mr. Sanjana pointed out.

Natalie nodded. "Yes. And of course, I ask no questions about how it came into your possession." She pulled a small, smooth leather pouch from her shoulder bag, undid its drawstrings, and took out a roll of bills. Rick noticed that they all seemed to be used tens and twenties. She counted off ten twenties and five tens, put them on the table, and started to return the roll to the pouch. As an afterthought, she added two twenties and a ten to the stack on the table. "Three hundred, Mr. Sanjana. I wish I could offer more, but that is already more than I should pay for a blade of this quality."

Only the man's eyes moved, from the sword to the money and back again. Suddenly his hand darted out and snatched the little stack of bills. Then, to Rick's surprise, he smiled broadly.

"A friend of my cousin, down Inarajan way, sold a sword like this last year," he said. "My cousin says his friend felt lucky to get two hundred dollars."

"He was," Natalie said soberly. "And you are more lucky still to get three hundred." Briskly, efficiently, she replaced the guard and hilt on the blade, inserted the steel pin in its tiny hole, and tapped it into place with the hammer. Then she slid the reassembled sword into its scabbard.

"*Si yu'us ma'ase,* Mr. Sanjana," she added, with a slight bow. Rick recognized the words as Chamorro for "Thank you." "Adios."

The old man followed them out into the yard. The kids had gotten tired of playing in the convertible and were in the middle of a game of tag. The little boy was It, and he wasn't having much luck at tagging the two older ones. He stopped, panting and near tears. Rick felt like weighing in on his side. At that moment, the oldest of the three, a girl of eight or nine, came in close to tease the little boy. With a sudden lunge that would have done credit to a trained fencer, Barebottom darted forward, tagged her, and ran away, laughing.

At the car, Natalie put the sword in the trunk, then turned. "Adios, Mr. Sanjana," she repeated. "You have my address. I am not on Guam very often, but letters are forwarded. I am always glad to learn of people who have antiques they wish to sell, and I am always glad to reward those who help me learn of such people."

As Rick steered the car down the rutted track toward the road, he said, "Did you rip off the old guy?"

"What? I do not understand."

"How much is that sword really worth?"

She studied his face. "If I am lucky, I will sell it in a month, or two, or maybe six, for fifty or sixty thousand yen," she replied. "Between three hundred fifty and four hundred fifty dollars. If I am not lucky, I do not sell it at all."

"That's not much of a profit margin," Rick commented. "Why did you pay him as much as you did if that's all it's worth?"

Natalie gave an amused sniff. "For two reasons. Mr. Sanjana himself had a good idea of the sword's worth. By paying him a little more than that, I made him feel happy and superior. And now the word will go out to his friends, and the friends of his friends, that Natalie Yussupov pays good prices, in cash, for Japanese swords. And the next person who approaches me may show me a real treasure."

Rick laughed and shook his head. "You're a pretty shrewd businesswoman, aren't you?"

"I have to be," Natalie replied. "It is that, or starve."

CHAPTER 16

As THE GENTLE, BREAKER-EDGED SWEEP OF TUMON BAY came into view, on the far side of the naval air station and Guam International Airport, Rick pulled over to the side of the road and stopped.

"You've already said yes to cocktails at my hotel," he reminded Natalie. "After that, how about dinner and a night on the town?"

"Of course," she said simply. "I know a charming little restaurant in Agana, one of the few that serve authentic Chamorro cuisine. Have you ever tried *kelaguen* with fina-dene sauce?"

"No, but I have a feeling I'm going to," Rick replied. "On one condition: I'll be glad to let you choose the restaurant and tell me what to order, but this evening is my treat. Deal? After all, you bought my dinner back in Honolulu."

For a moment she looked mulish, then she smiled. "Understood. Did I mention that there is also entertainment? Authentic *Kantan Chamorrita* folksongs, accompanied on the *belembaotuyan,* which is a stringed instrument a little like the Indian sitar. Some of the songs have hundreds of verses and go on for hours. They are very droll."

"Really?" Rick said as he put the car in gear. "Sounds

like something we wouldn't want to miss." Mentally, he added, *Not!*

At the hotel, they found Eloise and Ray at a shady table with a lovely view of the bay. Rick made the introductions, and he and Natalie sat down.

"What would you like to drink?" Ray asked as he beckoned the waiter. "Eloise, as a good, patriotic American from the heartland, is having a Coke. She asked for Dr Pepper, but they don't stock it. Apparently Guam is not yet Channelview, Texas."

"Now don't you go badmouthing Channelview," Eloise drawled in an exaggerated po'boy accent. "Why, on a sunny day, all those colored fumes from the petrochemical plants make the most gorgeous rainbow you ever did see!"

Ray paid no attention. "I," he continued, "am sampling the Trader Vic special. They don't call it that, but I distinctly recall trying something that looked just like it at Trader Vic's in 'Frisco, back in 1964. I'm reasonably sure it contains rum. Aside from that, your guess is as good as mine."

He indicated a tall glass that held what remained of his drink and an assortment of fruit slices on a green plastic skewer shaped like a miniature palm tree.

"I already have dibs on the decorations," Eloise said.

Rick met Natalie's gaze. She looked relaxed and amused. Looking up at the patient waiter, she asked, "May I have a kir?"

"Of course, miss. One kir. And?"

"A San Miguel, please," Rick replied.

"You must be French," Ray said to Natalie as the waiter went off to get their orders. "Only the French would ask for a kir in the Western Pacific—never mind expect to get one. *Crème de Cassis* must be even scarcer around here than Dr Pepper."

"At least the waiter knew what I meant," Natalie pointed out. "But yes, I am French, although I now live in Tokyo."

Ray asked where she was from in France. When she said Montpellier, he told her that he had spent several months in the area. Soon the two of them were discussing favorite restaurants, shops, and beaches.

Rick looked over at Eloise and shrugged. "There's a great barbecue joint not far from Channelview," he said.

"There's a great barbecue joint not far from anyplace in Texas," she replied. "Not to mention a great Mexican restaurant. I get lonesome for them sometimes. But not a one of them serves kir, I'm sorry to say. Dos Equis or Carta Blanca, sure."

Rick grinned. "Sounds good to me, though I have to admit I'd take a long-neck bottle of Pearl over any Mexican beer. Just a born lowlife, I guess."

Eloise made a big show of looking him over.

"Something wrong?" he asked.

She shook her head. "Nope. I was just wondering what you did with the pack of Luckys you're supposed to keep tucked into the rolled-up sleeve of your black Harley T-shirt."

Rick's laugh was loud enough to make Natalie and Ray break off sharing recollections of the Plage de la Corniche in Sète. A moment later the waiter arrived, with a bottle of San Miguel and a pilsner glass for Rick, and a wineglass of some pinkish-purple liquid for Natalie. He poured Rick's beer, then retreated.

Natalie took a sip from her glass and made a wry face. "California chablis with grenadine," she reported. "But I've had worse. At least it's cold and the color is attractive."

She turned back to Ray and asked, "Are you one of the treasure hunters also?"

"Treasure hunters?" Ray repeated. "What do you mean?"

The caution and alarm in his voice surprised Rick. Why did the question bother him so much?

Natalie was surprised as well. "I apologize," she said in confusion. "I know that Rick is a diver, and when he said that you worked on the same project ... These waters are full of sunken ships, after all—some that go back hundreds of years."

"Let's hear it for Spanish galleons and pieces of eight," Eloise interjected. "I used to dream about them when I was a kid. I grew up just a few miles from Jean Lafitte's old stomping ground."

Natalie's face grew more confused.

"He was a famous pirate," Eloise added. "In the Gulf of Mexico."

"It's a natural mistake," Ray told Natalie, brushing Eloise's comment aside. "But we're not hunting for sunken treasure. Nothing so glamorous, I'm afraid. What we're doing is trying out a new approach to deep-sea mining. If it works, it could be the start of a very important industry, but for now, it's just a pilot project."

Natalie nodded. "I see. You are prospectors, like in the Western movies, but with a boat instead of a donkey. Will you find gold and silver?"

Ray shifted in his seat. "We're not really looking for precious metals. It's more humble stuff we're after: cobalt, manganese.... And we basically know where to look, thanks to Eloise. The point is to see if our new method of getting it to the surface is practical. Now let me ask you a question: What does it take to persuade a cosmopolitan Frenchwoman who lives in Tokyo to come to this godforsaken island?"

The abrupt change of subject was about as subtle as a trombone solo in a Christian Science reading room. Natalie blinked with surprise, then briefly explained her interest in, and search for, Japanese objets d'art. She didn't mention her expedition with Rick that afternoon, nor the purchase of the samurai sword, so Rick decided to keep his mouth shut about them too.

"Your work must let you travel a whole lot," Eloise said. "I can't tell you how much I envy that. Apart from Texas and Oklahoma, about the only places I've ever been are Aberdeen, and Caracas, and now Guam. Why can't they find a need for a marine geologist someplace glamorous, like Paris or Rome?"

"No minerals and no ocean," Ray suggested. Rick and Natalie laughed. After a fraction of a second, Eloise joined them, but without much enthusiasm.

After some general conversation about Guam, Ray turned to Eloise and began to talk about some unfinished problems with the project. Rick looked over, caught Natalie's eye, and made a tiny gesture with his head. Her nod in reply was just as tiny.

"Rick," she said, during a pause in Ray and Eloise's shop-talk, "would you mind taking me back to my hotel? I'm sorry to break up the party, but I've had a long day."

"Oh, sure!" Rick sprang up and pulled her chair back for her. "I'll see you," he told the others, as he dropped some bills on the table and Natalie made her goodbyes. "Are we going to make another try tomorrow?"

"We'll know more about that tonight," Ray replied. "I'll give you a call as soon as I find out how things went today."

"Thanks. If there's no answer, you might just have them slip a note under my door."

As he and Natalie left the table, Eloise wrinkled her nose at him. She obviously had her own ideas about why he might not be answering his phone that evening.

"I like your friends. I find them *sympa,*" Natalie said as they walked toward the car. "Easy to be with, I mean."

"Thanks. I don't really know them that well yet, but we get along. Do you really want me to drop you at your hotel, or was that just a polite excuse for leaving?"

She gave him a sidelong glance. "I *do* need to shower and change before our evening out," she said. "But if you care to wait for me, I promise not to be long."

"Sure thing."

At Natalie's hotel, Rick parked in the visitors' lot and opened the trunk. "Are you going to walk through the lobby carrying a three-foot-long sword?" he asked. "You might get some funny looks."

Natalie took off her silk scarf and wrapped it around the sword, then tucked it sideways in her shoulder bag. Most of it stuck out, of course, but at least it was less obvious.

"Will you wait by the pool?" she asked, sliding the straps onto her left shoulder. "Or would you prefer to come up to my room? There are magazines to look at."

"I'll come up," Rick said quickly.

Natalie's room looked like the twin of Rick's. Same pair of double beds, same long, low dresser-desk in dark woodgrain plastic, same TV set on a high shelf in the corner, and same view of Tumon Bay from the handkerchief-sized balcony on the other side of the sliding-glass doors. It didn't smell the same, however. There was a hint of perfume in the air, like flowers and herbs, but with a darker undertone. The scent grew stronger as Natalie collected some things from the dresser drawers and took a blue and white dress from the closet. She put the fresh clothes in the bathroom, then returned to hand Rick a glossy magazine with a photo of an elaborately carved and decorated chest on the cover.

"I won't be long," she repeated.

She returned to the bathroom. Rick took the magazine out on the balcony and flipped through the pages. The articles and the ads featured stunning color photos of paintings, furniture, Oriental rugs, and pieces of jewelry. All of it looked as if it might have come from the mansion of one of his mother's friends in Palm Beach—very expensive, and guaranteed to be in acceptable taste simply because it *was* so expensive.

An image flashed by that was a little different. He backtracked and found a full-page photo of a Japanese sword. The scabbard was covered with a deep red enamel, and there seemed to be some sort of small gold figure set into the black braid on the hilt. On the facing page, smaller photos showed closeups of the point and tang, with hilt removed, which was engraved with a column of Japanese characters. There was no written description or price, only in small, dignified type, the name, address, and fax number of a gallery on New York's Madison Avenue. Penciled lightly in the margin was the notation "Nagasone? $40–$50,000."

Rick whistled under his breath. Clearly, these swords weren't something you'd find in a Cracker Jacks box!

He looked through the rest of the magazine more carefully, but there were no more swords. He stepped inside and dropped the magazine on the desk. From beyond the bathroom door, he could hear the shower running. He suddenly found himself imagining Natalie naked, with water streaming down over her glistening breasts. Dry-mouthed, he took a step in the direction of the bathroom, then hesitated as Sam Deane's face, wearing a reproachful look, flashed across his mind.

He scowled. Sam? Who was obviously taking advantage of his absence to fool around with Kiwi Kraus? She was in no position to complain about anything he did. To hell with it! He strode over to the bathroom door, tapped on it, and opened it a crack.

"Hi," he called, over the noise of the water. "Do you need any help washing your back? I'm pretty good at massage too."

He couldn't make out what Natalie said in response, but he decided to assume that it was an invitation. In junior lifesaving, he had learned how to get out of his clothes while running to the rescue of someone who was drowning. Now he put the lesson to a use that probably would have shocked his scoutmaster. Kicking off his shoes and stepping out of his pants, he pushed the door open wider and stepped inside the steamy room.

"*Ooh la la,* the door! I am freezing!" Natalie called.

Rick pulled off his shirt, socks, and shorts and tossed them in the corner. "Don't worry," he said, reaching for the edge of the shower curtain. "I'll warm you up in no time."

"We should think about dinner," Natalie said a while later. She stood up and walked with a flowing grace to the closet. Rick leaned on one elbow and admired her firm, beautifully formed body. What would she say if he asked her to walk back and forth across the room a few more times? Too late: She was already slipping into a thick white terrycloth robe and tightening the belt.

She came back to the bed and leaned over to brush her fingertip across his lips. He darted his head forward and caught the finger in his teeth. "Mmmmm," he murmured.

She tapped his cheek with her other hand. "That is not the sort of dinner I meant," she said sternly. "Don't be naughty."

Rick released her finger and said, "People around here eat late. It's the Spanish influence. We have lots of time," he added, snaking his arm around her waist and pulling her back toward the bed.

She easily slipped out of his grasp and took two steps backward. "We'll have lots of time after dinner," she said. "Now I must dress and fix my hair. And you also, you must stir yourself and dress."

"Okay." Rick sighed. "You're the boss."

Natalie had chosen a restaurant in downtown Agana, not far from the Plaza de España. Rick parked the convertible on a side street. Nearby, the white form of the Basilica, lit by a three-quarter moon, loomed over a ragged fringe of palm trees. According to the clock on the Basilica tower, it was already 9:30.

The restaurant belonged to what Rick thought of as the exposed brick, hanging plants, and red-checked tablecloth school. About half the tables were occupied. One of the waiters led them past a low stage with two barstools and two mike stands and seated them at a table near the back of the long, narrow room. With sinking heart, Rick remembered that Natalie had promised him hour-long Chamorro folksongs. Was there any chance that the singer would trip over a fireplug and break his leg on the way to work? Probably not.

"Oh, good," Natalie said, scanning the menu. "They are serving *kelaguen* tonight. That is a spicy chicken dish made with lemon juice and grated coconut. It comes with taro leaves cooked in coconut milk. Very typical. If you prefer, though, there is octopus baked with vegetables."

Rick suppressed a shudder. "The chicken sounds fine," he said. "Is it really spicy?"

"*Comme ci, comme ça,*" she replied, holding her hand out horizontally and tilting it from side to side. "If it is not hot enough for you, you can always sprinkle it with finadene sauce, which has been known to eat holes in the plate."

Rick gave her a quick glance. Her expression was as serious as ever, but he caught the hint of a twinkle in her eye.

"What about drinks?" he asked. He glanced around. The waiter noticed and started in their direction. "I don't think this place is going to have kir."

"No matter, beer is fine," Natalie said.

Rick gave the waiter their order, then leaned forward with his elbows on the table and studied Natalie's face.

She shifted uneasily. "What are you thinking?" she asked.

"That I'd like to track down those guys who attacked you in Honolulu," he said with a grin. "They deserve a reward for getting us together."

"It is not a matter for jokes. I don't know what I would have done without your help."

Rick shook his head. "You would have been okay. The gardens are pretty crowded at that time of evening. As a matter of fact, I can't figure out why those hoods tried to mug you in a place with so many people around. It wasn't very smart."

"Perhaps if they were smarter they would not be crooks," Natalie suggested. "But these are unhappy memories. Let us talk of something else."

The waiter brought their beers. Rick took a sip of his, then said, "You seemed to know what you were doing today when you were looking over that sword. I was a little surprised to find out that you're such an expert on weapons. It doesn't fit, somehow."

Natalie sat up straight and folded her hands in front of her. She looked as though she was getting ready to deliver a lecture.

"That is because you are like so many of your countrymen," she said. "You look at a Japanese sword, and you see a weapon."

"Isn't it one?"

"Yes, of course, among the deadliest ever created. But it is much, much more. For over a thousand years, the sword has been one of the highest expressions of Japanese art. The great swordsmiths of the past are as much revered in Japan as Leonardo and Dürer are in Europe. You think I am an expert, but believe me, I have not lived or studied long enough to become a true expert in this field. There is always so much more to learn."

Rick was listening to her words, but he was also enjoying the play of expressions on her face. People were so much more alive when they talked about something they cared about passionately.

To keep her talking, he said, "I didn't know that."

"Of course not," she replied sharply. "We Westerners assume that all cultures are much like ours, but Japanese culture is very different. Do you know that when MacArthur and the Americans occupied Japan in 1945, they ordered all swords to be confiscated and destroyed as dangerous weapons? Some of the greatest art treasures of Japan were put onto barges and thrown into Tokyo Bay, as if they were banal, mass-produced revolvers! Fortunately, a great scholar succeeded in finding someone in authority who would listen and understand, and the destruction was stopped. But the confiscation continued, if only unofficially."

She paused to let the waiter set down two plates of chicken, a bowl of what looked something like creamed spinach, and a smaller bowl of dark brown liquid with red and white specks floating in it.

"That's the finadene sauce," Natalie said, pointing to the small bowl. "Treat it with great respect."

"I will," Rick promised. He took a small bite of his chicken. The spices warmed his mouth, but compared to some Indian and Mexican dishes he had sampled over the years, this was almost boringly tame. Natalie must have a different idea of spiciness than he did. He took a spoonful of sauce and sprinkled it over the chicken, then tried another bite. Instantly, he could feel his eyelids burn and his scalp start to itch.

"Woo!" he exclaimed, grabbing for his beer glass.

Natalie shook her head sadly. "You would not listen. Try the taro leaves. They are said to cut the heat."

He took a forkful of the spinachlike vegetable. It wasn't easy to chew, but it did seem to bring some feeling back to the inside of his mouth.

To distract himself, he asked, "What were you saying about confiscations?"

"I believe the word your soldiers used was 'liberate,'" she replied. "Some of the stories of those days are horrifying. There was one staff sergeant who would take a Jeep to one of the *daimyo* mansions near Tokyo, force his way in with a submachine gun, and fill the back of the Jeep with priceless swords and other antiques, which he then traded to the clerks at the PX for cigarettes and beer."

Rick frowned. "You'll find rotten apples in any outfit," he said. "If that sergeant had gotten caught, he would have been looking at a good long stretch in Leavenworth."

Natalie raised her eyebrows. "Perhaps. But what of other American soldiers who, in all kindness, traded food and fuel for swords? The people they dealt with were happy with the bargain; after all, they were starving. But they were giving up treasures worth many, many thousands of dollars in exchange for a few dollars' worth of rations. Was that fair?"

"It sounds like a pretty raw deal, but don't ask me," Rick said uncomfortably. "I'm not a philosopher, or a businessman either. In wartime, or even right after a war, everything's topsy-turvy. Things happen that aren't fair or right by ordinary standards. And anyway, don't you make your living from buying and selling those same swords?"

"Touché," she said, suddenly breaking into a smile. "Yes, I do, when I can find one that I can afford to buy. That is becoming harder and harder. Did you know that last year, a Japanese sword sold at auction in New York for almost half a million dollars? It was over six hundred years old and the work of one of the most celebrated swordsmiths in history. But even more ordinary blades bring many thousands of dollars, if they are fairly old and well documented."

Rick scraped most of the hot sauce off a piece of chicken and took a bite. It was tolerable—just. "It sounds to me as if you'd better find yourself a very rich backer," he said. "Either that, or look for a different line of work."

"Perhaps you are right," she said. "But there is always the possibility of a great *coup*. In Europe, Old Master paintings still turn up now and then in junk shops, sold for the price of the frame. With Japanese swords, such underestimation is even more likely. To the untrained eye, a blade that is a great treasure may look like just another sword, if it has been fitted with a nondescript hilt and scabbard. And we know that some of the greatest blades dropped out of sight at the end of World War II. They have never been traced. Some, no doubt, are rusting at the bottom of Tokyo Bay, but what of the others? Think of it: An immensely valuable work of art may be lying forgotten in someone's closet, not a mile from where we sit!"

"That's an exciting thought," Rick said, impressed by her fervor. "But why Guam? Did a lot of swords end up here for some reason?"

Natalie quickly said, "No, no. Not at all. One might find Japanese artifacts anywhere that American soldiers went after the Occupation. I know a dealer who once bought five very fine, very old *tsubas,* or hilt guards, from a woman in Denton, Texas. These are round or oval disks, usually of intricately patterned wrought iron, often decorated in brass or gold, much sought after by collectors. The woman was using them as drink coasters!"

Rick laughed with her. Then he said, "Still, stumbling across a really important sword isn't very likely, is it?"

"Perhaps not," she admitted. "But ... have you ever heard of the Emperor's Sword? This is a legendary blade that is said to have almost magical powers. In 1281, the Mongol ruler Kublai Khan assembled an army of over a hundred thousand soldiers and a fleet of 4000 ships to invade and conquer Japan. The Japanese emperor commanded Rai Kuniyuki, the greatest swordsmith of his time, to forge the finest sword he knew how to make. When the Mongol fleet anchored off Takashima, on the coast of Kyushu, the Emperor's Sword was on the shore to oppose them. At the very moment that it was drawn from its sheath, a great wind blew up and sent the Mongol fleet to total destruction. That wind, in Japanese, is called *kamikaze."*

"So that's where they got the name for those suicide planes they used toward the end of World War II," Rick said. "I never knew that. But I have a hard time swallowing the idea of a sword with magical powers. It makes an interesting story, but ..."

"About its supposed powers I cannot say, but the sword itself is no myth," Natalie replied. "It was still listed among the Imperial Treasures in 1938. At some point in the next eight years, it disappeared. One more casualty of the war, perhaps, but ..."

She stopped and toyed with her fork.

"But?" Rick prompted.

"Rumors, nothing more. Rumors and myths. There are still groups of fanatical nationalists in Japan who dream of reviving the Empire. Recently their newspapers have started to speak of the Emperor's Sword. They say that it will reappear, and that when it does, it will set in motion the events that will lead to Japan's ultimate destiny, which is to rule first Asia, then the world."

"Fairytales," Rick snorted. "You don't really believe that, do you? According to the English, King Arthur and his knights are sleeping inside a mountain somewhere. They're supposed to wake up and rally round when the country's in mortal danger. I guess things haven't got that bad so far, because they've never shown up."

"Yes, I know," Natalie said impatiently. "And in Germany the same story is told of Frederick Barbarossa, and in France of Charlemagne. But this is different. The Sword is real. It exists, or at least it did exist not so very many years ago. Why all these stories, and why now? Pure folly? Perhaps. But isn't it possible that these fanatics have somehow glimpsed a very small part of an important truth, that the Emperor's Sword is in a place where it might, one day soon, be found?"

Rick found her earnestness impressive, but he couldn't stop himself from asking, "By you?"

Natalie blinked, as if he had just awakened her from a dream. "No, perhaps not," she said sadly. "That would be too much to hope for. And even if I managed to find a trail, the fanatics would go to any length to keep a *gai-jin* like me from having any part in the reappearance of the Emperor's Sword."

CHAPTER 17

CAPTAIN WILL WARD SHOOK TWO ASPIRIN TABLETS AND A multivitamin capsule into his palm, tossed them into his mouth, washed them down with orange juice, then made a face. The juice tasted as if someone had dissolved a couple of spoonfuls of cigarette ashes in it.

Out on the water, a speedboat yammered by with two water-skiers in tow. Ward winced. The familiar racket drilled into his head like a crew doing street repairs next to his table. As the boat made a wide curve, to start another run parallel to the beach, its windshield caught the light of the rising sun and speared it straight at Ward's face. He squinched his eyes shut and reached into the pocket of his aloha shirt for his sunglasses. They weren't there. He must have left them in the room.

Was it worth going back for them? Probably not. Here came the waiter with his coffee. Besides, if he went up to his room, feeling the way he did, he would probably be tempted to try the old hangover cure, a hair of the dog that bit you, and it was against his principles to touch the stuff before noon at least.

He poured a cup and took a sip. His mouth turned down. The coffee was okay, if a little weak. He wished everything else was okay, but it wasn't, not at all. Funny: A lot of his old Navy buddies would give their left ball for an indefinite, all-expenses-paid stay at a luxury beachfront hotel on a tropical isle, with nothing to do but watch the girls walk by in their string bikinis. He had no objection at all to watching girls, with or without bikinis, but he preferred to do it in smaller doses and more private circumstances. Seeing so many of them, in public, without the chance to do anything about it, left him feeling frustrated and over the hill at the same time.

As for having nothing to do, that was no treat—that was his biggest problem. He was bored out of his skull and sensed that he was getting stale. In any case, if he wanted a vacation, which he didn't, Guam would be pretty far down on his list of places to go. If it made the list at all.

Should he pack up and move out to *Berkone?* He'd been turning over the idea for a few days now, and it was becoming more and more tempting. No beach and no pretty girls, a tiny cabin with zero frills, chow that was likely to be uninteresting at best, and no shops that carried Wild Turkey, but there were compensations. Just being on shipboard would make for a nice change. And if these delays continued, at least he could get some work done, instead of sitting around letting moss grow over his ass.

Berkone had well-equipped electronics and machine shops on board. With some help from the ship's technicians, he could jury-rig some of the improvements he had been thinking about for the *Steel Albatross*. Then he and Ricky could take the boat down for some deep-water testing, really put the new modifications through the wringer. A little activity would feel good. . . .

"Will?" a voice said. "Good morning. Do you mind if I talk to you for a minute?"

Ward looked up. Dave was standing there, looking as scraggly as ever.

"Nope," Ward grunted. "Pull up a chair, son. You want some coffee?"

"Oh, no, thanks. I already had breakfast." He fell silent and glanced around, as if expecting to find cue cards propped up against one of the palm trees.

"So, what's on your mind?" Ward asked.

Dave took a deep breath and said, "The *Steel Albatross*. I want to go for another dive in it."

Ward gave a snort. "You will, if that outfit you're with ever gets its shit together. That's why Rick and I and the *Albatross* and *Berkone* were brought to Guam in the first place."

Dave's cheeks reddened. "I haven't forgotten. But that's not what I mean. Listen," he continued in a rush, "I've put in hours and hours piloting the *Steel Albatross* in the simulation mode. There's hardly a day gone by that I haven't wangled a ride out to *Berkone* and put your craft through its imaginary paces. I don't know why it's so fascinating. Maybe because it's like diving and flying at the same time. I used to think about maybe taking flying lessons someday. But then I got totally wrapped up in undersea technology and forgot about flying."

Ward massaged his right temple and listened with half his attention. It occurred to him that he and Dave probably had a lot in common. Each of them, after all, had invested his skill and ingenuity, and a lot of hard work, in designing and building an undersea vehicle. The *Steel Albatross* and Dave's *Rover* had very different missions and configurations, of course, but they were also similar in a lot of ways. No surprise there: Most of the big problems were the same for any piece of equipment meant to function in deep water. If only he could manage to get past the younger man's hippie appearance and anti-Establishment cracks.

"I think I'm ready to try it for real," Dave concluded. His eyes were fixed on Ward's face.

Ward blinked. "Pilot the *Albatross?* You?"

The young engineer's face turned a deeper shade of red, but he didn't retreat. "That's right. Why not? I've been deep before, I'm experienced at piloting undersea vehicles, and after all the time I've put in on the simulator, I'm as qualified to handle your craft as anybody could be who hasn't actually done it."

"Yes, but—"

"Look, Will," Dave said. "If you're so against the idea, why did you encourage me to learn to pilot the *Steel Albatross* in the first place? Just to keep me out of your hair?"

"Good question," Ward admitted, nodding. "I guess the answer is that I'm a firm believer in backup systems. What if Rick took you down to five thousand feet—or three hundred, for that matter—and then suffered some kind of blackout? Unless you knew how to bring the *Albatross* back up, we'd probably lose both of you. Just the thought of it gave me fits. But now that you know which control does what, I don't worry so much."

"A backup system's no help unless you've tested it and know it works," Dave pointed out. "How can you be sure I know which control does what if you haven't checked me out?"

Ward chuckled. "Nice try, son, but no cigar. The SA-1 is an experimental craft. Whenever she's operational, every detail of her functioning, every nudged lever and pressed button, is recorded for later analysis. If I want to know how you've been handling her, all I have to do is look at the tapes. And I've been doing a lot of that.

"You do have a point," he added, after a moment's thought, "about checking out your backup systems. Simulator time can't give you the seat-of-the-pants feeling you get on a real dive. Am I right that nothing's scheduled for this morning?"

"Nothing for us," Dave replied, with a disgusted look. "Ray decided that we need to inspect the hose before it's lowered again."

Ward opened his eyes wide, then wished he hadn't, as the glare off the water reminded him of his headache.

"The big hose?" he demanded. "The one that's supposed to vacuum up the minerals from the bottom?"

"We're using the airlift technique," Dave said. "You couldn't possibly sustain an effective vacuum over that kind of range, and even if you did, the pressure differential would collapse the pipe."

"Fine, airlift," Ward said impatiently. "My point is, you must have eight or ten thousand feet of hose on board *Champion,* am I right? And Ray's planning to inspect every inch of it? That could take years!"

"It's not quite that bad. The hose is stored flattened, wound up on huge reels. What they'll do is watch while they run it from one reel to another, through an ultrasound rig that's supposed to detect any defects. They had some bubbling last time and want to see if they can find out where and why it happened. The rig can check more than fifty feet a minute. Even so, allowing for setup time, it's bound to take most of the day."

Ward pushed his chair back and stood up. "Hell of a way to run a railroad. Still, better safe than sorry, I guess," he grunted. "All right, Dave. Let me have a little palaver with Rick and see what we can do. Where will I find you in, say, half an hour?"

Dave's face lit up. "I won't budge from right here," he said. "And thank you, sir! This means a lot to me."

As Captain Ward walked toward the hotel, it occurred to him that Dave Collier had just called him "sir" for the very first time. Maybe there was something to be said for doing people favors.

Rick came back from his morning run along the beach to find Will waiting in his room.

"I'll just be a minute," he promised, ducking into the shower for a quick rinse.

When he reappeared, Will asked, "How's your friend Natalie?"

Rick made a face. "Gone," he replied. "She had to fly back to Japan yesterday, some important business deal that couldn't wait."

"Too bad. Oh—Ray asked me to give you this fax that came in for you."

Rick unfolded the single page. As he'd expected, it was from his friend at the Navy Bureau of Records, in Washington.

TO: LT RICHARD TALLMAN, SEAVENTURE, GUAM
FROM: LT ALBERT DEFORD, BUREC
The War Patrol Reports of USS OVERHILL for June, July, and August 1945 were properly logged in (in 1945) but don't seem to be filed with the ship's earlier WPRs, as they should be. By my count, that leaves fewer than eighteen million, four hundred three thousand other places they might be, assuming no one pulled them twenty years ago and forgot to log them out or send them back. How badly do you need them? And aren't you glad you didn't go into naval history?

"Huh," Rick said, tossing the fax on the dresser. "Typical."

"Problem?" Will asked.

"Not really." Rick explained that, after hearing Will's story about his ship's encounter with the Japanese sub, he had been curious to read the official account of the incident. "No luck, though," he concluded. "The reports must have been misfiled."

"Well, that's too bad. I wonder if there's anything in the Japanese naval archives. But I can imagine that, right after the surrender, they had more important things on their minds than keeping their records up to date."

Rick grinned. "For a true bureaucrat, *nothing* is more important than keeping his records up to date!" He slipped on a light blue polo shirt and a pair of chinos.

Will wandered over to the sliding doors and gazed out at the view of the bay with his hands clasped behind him. One of them slapped rhythmically in the palm of the other.

"What's up, Uncle Will?" Rick demanded teasingly.

Will hated being called that. As he had once explained, "If I were your uncle, that would make me a relative of your father. And I'll be screwed, blued, and tattooed before I let anyone pin that one on me!"

Now he turned and growled, "Listen here, sonny—" Then he saw Rick's face and realized that his leg was being pulled.

"Fact is," he said in a more subdued voice, "there's something I want you to do."

"Sure," Rick said cheerfully. "Name it."

"Take Dave Collier on a dive and check out how he handles the *Steel Albatross*."

"No." The refusal escaped Rick's lips before he even had a chance to think about the request.

Thunderclouds gathered in Will's face. "No?" he echoed, in a quiet tone that was even more ominous than a blast. "And just why not, mister?"

"I don't trust him. Also, I don't like him and I think his attitude sucks."

"That's frank, at least," Will replied. "But I'm not asking you to like him. The way you find out if you can trust somebody is by working with them, not by crossing them off your list without a fair trial. I admit Dave got under my skin some too, with his pseudointellectual leftwing remarks, but I've seen a change in his attitude in the last couple of weeks. I think he deserves a chance.

"Anyway," he continued, before Rick could respond, "I'm not asking you to give him a character reference. Our mission here requires you to take Dave down in the *Albatross*, deeper than you've ever gone. In my assessment, you need to have a trained backup pilot down there with you, someone who's already been checked out. It's a matter of safeguarding expensive government property. The boat only has room for the two of you, so that means Dave is it. Any questions?"

Rick turned away without replying. How could he tell Will Ward how deeply he resented sharing the *Steel Albatross* with Dave Collier and not, at the same time, reveal his pure, unvarnished jealousy? He could admit it to himself, but he was damned if he was going to confess it to Will.

He didn't need to. "Listen here, Ricky," Will said. "I know how you feel. Don't forget, I invented that baby. I cringe every time anybody else takes her controls—you included. I did what I could to make the craft idiot-proof, but there still must be a hundred ways to fuck up. During every dive, I pace the deck on *Berkone* and imagine all the dumb-ass moves the guy at the controls might be making. And at the same time," he added, "I agonize over all the design mistakes I may have made and don't yet know about."

He paused.

"Yes, sir," Rick murmured. There didn't seem to be much else to say.

"*But,*" Will went on. "You helped teach Kiwi Kraus how to fly the *Albatross,* at a time when you two were not exactly asshole buddies. It was a question of carrying out an important mission, and that came in way ahead of your personal feelings. The situation here is exactly parallel. I need your cooperation—your *full* cooperation—and I have a right to expect that you'll give it."

"I will," Rick promised.

"Good. I thought you would. Come on, let's collect Dave and see about promoting a ride out to *Berkone.*"

"Now? This morning?"

"And why not?" Will demanded, starting toward the door. "You can't have anything better to do, what with *Glomar Champion* calling in the usual delays and your lady friend gone off-island."

The two frogs untied the mooring lines from the *Steel Albatross* and swam back toward the open stern doors of *Berkone.* As the submersible rocked and pitched in the swell, Rick looked over his shoulder and said, "Your boat, mister."

Dave looked a little pale. "Er, thanks," he said. "It seemed to take a lot of people and a lot of time to get us underway. That pool on the mother ship is bottomless, isn't it? Why couldn't we just pull the plug and dive?"

Rick rolled his eyes. The beginning of an evolution was not the right moment for idle chatter. "We could, I guess, in theory," he replied. "But practically, no. Not enough clearance on either side. One bad move and you bump the side of the moon-pool and a wing is out of tolerance. You don't realize how totally dependent a boat of this type is on precise dimensions. Are you going to start the predive checklist, or do you want me to take the helm?"

"Sorry," Dave said.

The face of the monitor in front of Rick changed as Dave began to work his way through the items of the checklist. He seemed to hesitate over a couple of them, but soon enough, Rick heard him transmit, "Ah, *Berkone, Albatross* here. We're about to dive. Over to you."

Rick grinned. He could imagine Will Ward's face as he listened to this very unorthodox message. Civilians like Dave might believe that any way you got the information across was okay, but the Navy had long since learned that any departure from prescribed voice communication procedures could lead to costly, even tragic, misunderstandings.

"Sierra Alpha One, this is *Berkone*," Captain Ward replied. "Understand system is ready to dive. Is that affirmative? Over."

Dave didn't seem to understand that he had just been publicly rebuked. "That's right, *Berkone*," he said. "We're on our way. Talk to you later."

Rick's screen now showed:

```
SA-1
READY TO DIVE
Begin Descent  Recheck
              Cancel
```

A moment later it became an instrument panel. With a click and a muffled gurgle, the intake valves of the forward ballast tank opened and the craft took on a sharp nose-down attitude. Too sharp? Rick put his hand on the stick, ready to take control of the boat if Dave seemed to be biting off more than he could chew. But as the waves covered the canopy, he felt the stick ease back. The "bubble," which indicated the boat's angle of descent, slowly moved from forty-five degrees down at the bow to just shy of thirty degrees—still a steep descent, but well within the craft's design envelope.

As they passed the 150-meter level, the *Steel Albatross* suddenly banked sharply to the right. Rick caught his breath and got ready again to take the stick. Was this the time to step in?

"Sorry about that," Dave said as the boat leveled out. "Hoo boy! All I wanted to do was put it through a turn. I thought I knew what I was doing, from working in simulation, but the real thing is something else!"

"A simulation program is just someone's idea about how a craft will respond," Rick said. "It might be accurate, or it might not. We're working to make it better, but we're not there yet," he added.

"It sure can't give you that pit-of-the-stomach feeling I got just now. Or the spooky sense that any time you push the control stick one way, something out there tries to push it the other way."

"That's reality," said Rick. "The boat wants to keep going in whatever direction it's going at the time, and any change sets off a battle. The catch is, if you fight too hard, for too sharp a turn or too steep an ascent or descent, you end up defeating yourself. You have to get a feel for exactly how much change you can get away with."

Dave sighed. "I see that. Thanks for agreeing to take me on this dive. There's a lot more to this than I dreamed. It doesn't feel at all like other submersibles I've dived in."

"It's not, any more than a sailplane is like a blimp. By the way, we just crossed the 300-meter level. Are you still planning to take it all the way to 1000 meters? Don't forget, we've got a seamount in the neighborhood that tops out at 800 meters or so."

"I won't forget," Dave replied. "That's the idea. A thousand meters is just about the minimum depth for Rover's mining operation. I want to be sure I can handle the *Steel Albatross* at those depths. Otherwise, what's the point?"

Rick was tempted to point out that new drivers didn't start by entering a Formula One race. He held his peace, because he didn't want to say anything that might spook Dave. Besides, he had to admit that so far the engineer was doing a workmanlike job of flying the *Albatross*.

They were crossing 750 meters when the boat's bottom-profiling sonar kicked in. Rick studied the schematic on the screen and said, "That seamount is coming up on us, Dave. I make the top of it to be 300 meters off and about 50 meters below us. You should either start slowing our rate of descent or come around to a heading that will give us plenty of room to get by it."

"Oh, right. Thanks."

The stick inched backward and to the left. At the same time, the instruments on the monitor blinked out, to be replaced by:

```
SA-1
PARAMETERS CHECKLIST
Rate of Descent: 30 mpm
Increase Decrease
Select   Cancel
```

As Rick watched, the rate of descent changed to 25 meters per minute, then to 20. Dave seemed to know his way around the boat's control system, even if he hadn't yet gotten the feel of it.

Abruptly, with no warning, the screen went dark. Not quite dark—Rick could still see the dark ghosts of the letters that had been there a moment before. But then even those faded.

"What happened to the screen?" Dave demanded. "Did you turn off the screen?"

"Not me," Rick replied tautly. He leaned forward and touched the screen. Nothing happened. One of the buttons just below the screen was labeled STANDBY/RESUME. Pressed once, it put the onboard computer into a power-saving standby mode. A second press brought up the computer again. Dave must have accidentally pushed it. Rick made a quick note on the pad strapped to his thigh. Will should disable the feature, or at the very least add an on-screen "Really? Are You Sure? (Y/N)" prompt.

"Here we go," Rick said as he pushed the button.

"Well?" Dave said. "Go ahead."

"I did," Rick replied grimly, staring at the still-blank

screen. "I thought I knew what our problem was, but apparently I didn't."

"Here, let me take a shot at it. After all those hours in simulator mode, I think I know what may have happened."

"Sure, go ahead," Rick said. "Just be sure you don't make any dumb-ass moves that leave us in worse shape than we are already."

"Don't worry, I know what I'm doing," Dave said, almost cheerfully. "Hold on. I've got a hunch that—"

He broke off. A few seconds passed. "Nothing happened," he said. Rick heard a sudden note of panic in his voice.

It was time, and past time, to take charge. "I have the conn," Rick said, peering out through the canopy. At this depth, the effective range of the boat's spotlights wasn't much better than twenty yards. Where the hell was that damned seamount? The last thing they needed—

"Shit!" Rick exclaimed as he caught sight of solid, sloping ground directly ahead. Even as he pulled back the stick, he was sorting rapidly through alternatives and calculating the odds of success for each of them. The results were not comforting.

"What is it?" Dave demanded, the panic in his voice more obvious now. "What's wrong? Tell me!"

"Can it, shithead," Rick snapped. "I'm busy!"

The nose of the *Steel Albatross* came up and she went into the underwater equivalent of a stall. The stick took on a mushy feel, as the control surfaces started to lose their bite on the water. The forward motion of the boat was much slower now, but it was still drifting toward the gently sloping side of the seamount.

"What are you doing?" Dave cried. "We're going to crash!"

"Shut up," Rick said. Manipulating the stick with all the delicacy and skill he possessed, he steered the *Albatross* into an orientation that brought the hull parallel to the incline of the slope. The boat still had negative buoyancy; he hadn't had time to deal with that. It crept forward and downward, closer and closer to the seamount.

The impact, when it came, was even slighter than Rick had expected. *Too* slight, in fact. Rick frowned. In the glare of the spotlights, the surface of the seamount looked more like cottage cheese than rock. What was going on down here?

"Why did you land?" Dave demanded. "Tell me!"

Rick took a deep breath. "We didn't have enough searoom to miss the slope completely," he explained. "This way we can take the time to fix whatever went wrong before we start our ascent. By the way ... what was your hunch?"

"What do you mean?"

"You said you had a hunch how to bring up the computer again. What was it?"

"I ... never mind."

"You don't happen to remember what you did just before the computer went dead, do you?"

"Me? Nothing. Nothing at all!" Dave exclaimed. "What are you talking about?"

"You had the conn. What happened? Did you lean your elbow on one of the switch panels? Believe me, we'll both be better off if you tell me exactly what you did. If I don't know what's broken, I can't fix it."

"There's something wrong with the machine, that's all," Dave insisted. "It's not my fault, it's Will Ward's. He's the one who designed this thing!"

Rick noticed, in a corner of his mind, that Dave had gone back to calling the *Steel Albatross* a "thing." One of these days, the two of them were going to have to have a little conversation about that, out behind the barn.

"It happened on your watch, mister," Rick said aloud.

"That doesn't make it my fault," Dave insisted, in a voice raised in panic. "What's going to happen now? Are we ... do you think we'll get back?"

Rick took a deep breath. "Oh, hell, yes, sooner or later," he said. "If worse comes to worst, we can always drop the keel. We'd have the wildest ride you could ever imagine, but we'd still get back to the surface. That's a last resort, though.

"Now," he added, "shut up and let me work." He tried each of the banks of switches to the left of the monitor.

None of them had the slightest effect. "We'll try to go up under manual control."

The *Steel Albatross* was equipped with a complete set of manual controls and basic instruments. Captain Ward had insisted on that redundancy. Rick's eyes sought the luminous face of the mechanical fathometer. The needle had stopped at 805 meters. He groped with his left hand for the forward and aft mechanical ballast lever. The ballast levers were located about where the thrust levers would be in a fighter, but they were oriented vertically instead of horizontally. He moved them momentarily to the full up position and then back to half deflection when he heard the gentle hiss of high-pressure air forcing water out of the ballast tanks. He nodded to himself. Of course he had complete confidence in his craft, but he was also a firm believer in Murphy's Law. Any time things worked exactly the way they were supposed to, it was a bit of a relief.

By now the emptying ballast tanks should have changed the boat's buoyancy from negative to positive. Slowly, delicately, Rick pulled back on the stick and waited to see the ground slip away beneath them as they began to rise.

Nothing happened. The *Albatross* was still in exactly the same spot. Frowning, Rick returned the ballast control levers back to full up. The hiss increased, but nothing else happened. It was almost as if the boat were glued to the bottom.

"Shit!" Rick repeated, more quietly this time. He stared out through the canopy at the surface of the seamount. Was he imagining it, or had the *Steel Albatross* sunk deeper into the ground?

"Dave?" Rick said, as calmly as possible. "Didn't somebody tell me that these seamounts were covered with a rocky crust?"

Dave cleared his throat. "That's right," he said. "Why?"

"Because I don't think this one is," Rick replied. "This one is made of something more like quicksand. And it looks like we're stuck in it."

"Stuck? *Stuck?*" Dave's voice went up most of an octave. "That's impossible!"

Rick was sorting through, and discarding, alternative courses of action with a speed that owed much both to a naturally quick mind and his training as a fighter pilot. Now he put the process on hold long enough to say, "Nope, afraid not. Unlikely, but not impossible at all. This muck has a hold on us that gets tighter the longer we stay in it. It's like being in a heavy snowstorm and trying to pull a sled whose runners are frozen to the ground. And the buoyancy we're getting from our empty ballast tanks simply isn't enough to break us out. If it were, we'd already be on our way."

"But ... The keel! Why don't you drop the keel? That would save us!"

Rick took a deep breath. Dave's hysteria threatened to become contagious.

"True," he said, as calmly as possible. "And if we have to, we will. But that's totally a last resort. We'd have very long odds against ever recovering it, and fabricating a replacement would take quite a while. In the meantime, the *Albatross* would be grounded. I've still got a couple of tricks up my sleeve."

He moved his hand to the controls for the boat's attitude jets and started firing short bursts, alternating between left and right. The principle was the same as rocking a car that was stuck in deep sand, gradually increasing the momentum until it was enough to break them free. But after less than a minute, he knew that it wasn't going to work. The boat wasn't shifting at all. The attitude jets were designed to influence the direction of a free-floating craft, not move one physically that was mired in quicksand. He could keep trying, but it would simply be a waste of their dwindling energy supply.

The keel jettison handle was mounted on the deck, under Rick's feet, back near the seat pedestal, where no one was likely to pull it by accident. Rick released his shoulder harness and bent down to reach for it, but as his fingers touched it, he pulled back. As he had just explained to Dave, jettisoning the keel effectively meant the end of his mission. It was a radical confession of failure, on his part and on the part of the *Steel Albatross*. He simply wasn't ready to take such a step.

But what choice did he have? To sit on the ocean bottom, stuck in mud that shouldn't be here, until the batteries ran down and the oxygen-regenerator and CO_2 scrubber stopped working? Sacrifice himself and Dave, rather than sacrifice his pride? Ridiculous! This was supposed to be a sea trial, not a kamikaze mission!

Suddenly he remembered Will telling him about his new, untried submarine propulsion system, the one with the outlandish name. ELMAHYDYD, that was it. A reduced-scale prototype had been incorporated into this version of the *Albatross,* for emergency use only. And if this didn't count as an emergency, what did?

The two controls—a pushbutton that initialized the system, and a thumbwheel to regulate the amount of thrust— were mounted forward of the ballast control levers and protected by a latched cover. It was a long stretch. Rick fumbled with the latch and flipped the hinged cover back, muttered a quick, nondenominational prayer, and pressed the button.

The boat's headlights dimmed instantly, as the refrigerant system in the experimental drive drew down current from the boat's batteries. To ease the strain, Rick reached over and flipped off the lights.

"What are you doing?" Dave demanded, close to panic. "We can't see!"

He was right. At that depth, the blackness was close to absolute, relieved only by the luminous markings on the boat's mechanical instruments. Rick vowed to tell Will that the light-intensifying goggles he had used on his last mission in the *Albatross* were essential to this mission. The secrecy rules that barred them from being used would have to be bent.

"Calm down," Rick said. "I'm trying something else."

"What?"

As far as Rick knew, even the existence of ELMAHYDYD was classified information. If Dave hadn't discovered the secret drive during his simulation sessions in the *Albatross,* it wasn't Rick's place to let him in on it now.

"Something," Rick replied. "And if that doesn't work, I'll try something else. Now just sit back and enjoy the ride, okay? I'm busy."

The tiny LED telltale next to the drive's controls changed color from red to green. Presumably that meant that the drive was ready to operate. Rick put his thumb on the thrust control wheel, took a deep breath, and rotated the wheel to full on.

Nothing—no sound, no vibration, nothing. It was as if the control was a dummy, not even hooked up to anything. Rick felt his shoulders droop in disappointment. He had really expected Will's new gadget to let him pull a rabbit out of the hat—or, rather, an *Albatross* out of the mud. But maybe that was the problem: the mud. Maybe it was blocking the intake of the new drive and keeping it from working.

Whatever the reason, ELMAHYDYD's failure left Rick no choice. It was time to drop the keel. Or almost time. First he had to flood the fore and aft ballast tanks, to keep the buoyancy of the boat within reasonable limits once the weight of the keel was gone. Too fast an ascent would make the boat broach and fall back to the surface with massive impact. The collision would certainly damage it and injure or kill its passengers. Not what he'd call bringing the mission to a successful conclusion.

He was reaching for the ballast control levers when his eye fell on the vertical-speed indicator. It claimed that they were rising at more than thirty meters per minute. Broken, obviously; but when he looked at the fathometer, it read 728 meters. No, he corrected, make that 725. The *Steel Albatross* was ascending, and ascending fast. Will's new drive had freed them from the mud, so smoothly that Rick hadn't felt a thing!

The telltale next to the drive thrust control wheel changed back from green to red. Rick recalled that Will had told him the new drive was good only for a short burst—but boy, was it good for that! He moved the wheel back to the zero setting, and the telltale blinked out. Then he tried the first of the row of headlight switches. The lights came on, but with a sickly yellowish tinge, like the beam of a flashlight whose batteries are nearly kaput. Which, Rick thought, was a pretty accurate description of the situation.

"Hey, we're moving!" Dave exclaimed. "We did it!"

What do you mean, *we?* Rick thought sourly. Then he realized that Dave's response was too ridiculous, and too typical, for Rick to waste his energy resenting it. In any case, he still had a lot to do to bring them and the boat back safely.

He gave the stick a gentle wiggle and felt the resistance as the diving planes bit, fore and aft. Their vertical speed was now approaching fifty meters per minute, close to the boat's design envelope. He grasped the ballast levers and began flooding the tanks, lowering the speed of ascent to just above thirty meters per minute, then stabilizing it there.

Next problem.

"Can you give me a heading home?" he asked Dave.

"What?" said Dave. "No ... I'm sorry. I didn't notice. All my attention was wrapped up in handling the controls, and then when we crashed like that ... Is it important?"

"Only if you want to get back any time soon," Rick replied grimly. He studied the instrument panel compass and did some quick calculations. "Let's see, except for that turn to starboard of yours, we've been on pretty much the same 235° outbound heading the whole time. Figure the turn at 75°. We were on that heading for about five minutes. Add that to the westerly current of about three knots at this depth, and we come up with a return-to-*Berkone* heading of about 070°. Should be close enough for government work."

He established a hard turn to port and held it until the compass needle approached 100°. Then he eased off and settled on 070°.

"Are we ... is it all right?" Dave asked, in a quavering voice.

"Oh, we'll get back in one piece," Rick replied. He moved his lower jaw from side to side to relieve the tension, then added, "Whether we'll still be in one piece after Will Ward is done with us is another question altogether."

CHAPTER 18

WILL LISTENED IN SILENCE TO RICK'S REPORT. NOW AND then he made a note on the pad in front of him. Rick passed over his use of ELMAHYDYD. He would fill the captain in on that later, in private.

Will must have known that the report was incomplete, but when Rick fell silent, he said, "We've learned a couple of things today. It's good to know that the *Steel Albatross* is operational, even with the on-board computer down. But we also found out that we've got some unsuspected bug that can crash the computer and take it out altogether. It's better to know that than not know it, but I'm not going to rest easy until we isolate the bug and fix it. Dave, tell me again exactly what you did just before the crash."

"I don't know, I . . ."

Rick gave the young engineer a curious glance. Dave sounded not just nervous, but terrified. Why? The danger was over.

"Try," Will urged him. "I'll get it all off the tapes later, but I'd like to get a head start on this problem."

Dave looked at Ward with the frozen stare of a rabbit facing a snake. "I, uh; we were nearly as deep as we were supposed to go," he said haltingly. "I used the computer screen to lower our rate of descent, but I wasn't sure if it was working, so I adjusted the knob too. Then, *zap!*"

"Knob? What knob?" Will demanded.

"The one to the right of the screen, that sets the descent rate," Dave said. "*You* know. It's right over the rate-of-descent meter."

"Over?" Rick echoed. "You mean under, don't you? The knob over the meter sets rate of *ascent*. And both of those controls are supposed to stay at zero when the *Steel Albatross* is under computer control."

"Nobody ever told me that!"

"Let's leave that aside for a minute," Will said. "Dave, what exactly did you do when you thought you could bring the computer back up?"

"It doesn't matter. I was wrong."

"Apparently. But what did you *try?*" When Dave still hesitated, Will added, "If you really don't remember, I can get it off the tapes."

Dave's Adam's apple bobbed up and down, twice. He cleared his throat and said, "I turned that knob back to Off. Then I did the same with the one under it—turned it to On, then back to Off. When that didn't do anything, I pushed the Resume button. But that didn't work either."

Will frowned. "But you expected it to, didn't you? Why?"

"I don't know, I just—it seemed logical, that's all."

Will tapped his fingernails rhythmically on the tabletop and studied Dave's face. As the silence grew, Rick could feel a storm approaching. But why? What was going on?

Suddenly Ward pushed himself to his feet and leaned over toward Dave. "You already knew about the bug, didn't you?" he said quietly. "You must have discovered it during one of your simulated dives. And instead of telling me, so I could try to correct it, you kept it to yourself. Then, today, you deliberately disabled the computer, thinking you knew how to bring it back up. But you didn't. It's the only explanation that makes sense."

Dave's lips moved, but no sound came out.

Ward leaned closer, until his face was only inches from

Dave's. "Well, mister? Do you have anything to say? By God, you'd better!"

"Yes, I ..." Dave croaked. "Okay, you're right."

"You fucking asshole!" Rick shouted, springing up from his chair with fists clenched. "You could have killed us!"

He dived across the table at Dave, who cowered back in his chair, his hands raised to fend Rick off.

Suddenly a hand twisted itself in the neck of his T-shirt and stopped him in middive. "Rick," Will said warningly, "sit down. I'm handling this."

He pushed Rick back into his chair, then turned back to Dave. "Tell us about it—*all* about it."

Dave stared down at the table. "There's nothing to tell," he said in a low voice. "A couple of days ago, I tried to use the manual rate-of-ascent knob, while the computer display was still set to Descend mode. Everything locked up on me. But when I turned the knob off and pushed Reset, it was all right again. I thought about mentioning it, but it didn't seem like a big deal. Then, today, when I was about to bring us up again, I remembered what had happened. I didn't even stop to think. I just reached out and turned the knob. You know the rest."

"But *why?*" Rick demanded.

Dave didn't reply.

"Check me if I'm right," Will said. "You deliberately created an emergency that you thought you, and only you, knew how to deal with. Lots of brownie points in that—*if* it had worked as planned. When it didn't, you panicked. Is that about right?"

Dave looked up at him. "I just wanted to prove that I knew what I was doing. Do you think I don't understand the way you guys think of me? You haven't exactly kept it a secret. Do you think I like being treated like an irresponsible, helpless kid? I wanted to be given some respect!"

"Respect isn't given, it's earned," Will replied grimly. "And not by pulling foolish, irresponsible, and dangerous stunts like today's, either."

"What are you going to do?" Dave asked.

"I'll have to report what you did. You're not under my

command, so it's not up to me to decide what happens next. But if you ever—*ever*—do anything that puts the *Albatross* at risk again, I promise you that I will personally have your ass for a beefsteak!"

The chopper returned them to the hotel. Dave, still pale from being chewed out by Will Ward, vanished upstairs. Rick was delighted to see him go. It removed the constant, almost overpowering temptation to deck the turkey, a course of action that, as Will had carefully explained to him, would be prejudicial to order and good discipline.

Rick wandered out to the pool area, sat down, and asked the waiter for a beer. He had only had time for a couple of well-earned sips when Eloise appeared, carrying a battered leather attaché case.

"Dave just told me a peculiar story about your adventures today," she said, pulling a chair over next to his.

"I bet he did," Rick said dryly.

Under her tan, Eloise's face reddened. Apparently she had heard something fairly close to the truth. "Listen," she said, "Dave has some problems that— Oh, never mind. That's not what I wanted to talk to you about. What's all this about a seamount covered with mud?"

Rick shrugged. "It was a seamount covered with mud," he replied. "Or maybe the whole thing was mud, I wouldn't know."

"You didn't happen to bring back a sample, did you?"

"Sorry," Rick replied. "We were too busy figuring out how to bring ourselves back to worry about bringing back some mud."

Eloise put her attaché case on her lap and unlatched the lid. "How about your location?" she asked. "Or, rather, the location of this muddy seamount? Did you record it?"

"It should be in the electronic log, unless our computer problem crashed that too," Rick told her. "We've got a GPS locator on board—that's the Global Positioning System that works by triangulating signals from synchronous-orbit satellites."

"I know," Eloise said. "I've used it myself. But I didn't know it worked underwater."

"Well, it doesn't, as a matter of fact. The GPS gizmo is really a microwave transceiver, and microwaves only work line-of-sight. But what we do is get a GPS reading at the start of every dive, then feed it into our inertial tracking system. There may be a little slippage in going from one method to another, but Will Ward swears its median range of error is less than fifty feet. Unless you're searching for the gold ring you accidentally dropped overboard in 500 fathoms of water, that's close enough."

Eloise was beginning to look excited. "How do I get hold of this electronic log?" she asked.

"You don't, as far as I know," Rick replied. "You can try asking Will Ward, but I wouldn't put money on the odds of him saying yes. What's so interesting about a hill of mud, anyway?"

"Only that, according to what we know about marine geology, it shouldn't be there," she retorted. She opened her attaché case and took out what looked like a topographical survey. "Look," she said. "This is the Marianas Trench, just west of us. And here, about eighty kilometers farther west"—her finger traced a curved line to the left of the bluest part of the chart—"we've got a chain of seamounts called the Marianas Forearc. Some of them are known to be mud."

"There you go then," Rick said. "Now we've found another one."

Eloise shook her head. "Yes, but on the wrong plate. Do you know anything about plate tectonics?"

"That's the theory that the earth's surface is made of huge plates of rock that slide around and bump into each other, right?"

"Close enough," she replied. "Well, the Pacific plate, the one we're on, dives under the Philippine Sea plate at the Marianas subduction zone. It's the subduction that created the Marianas Trench. As the plate gets down to around fifteen kilometers below the surface, the enormous pressure squeezes water out the rock. Gradually, the water forces its way back up to the ocean floor, carrying dissolved minerals with it, and forms underwater volcanoes of cold mud. Okay?"

Rick chuckled. "Clear as mud, teacher," he remarked.

"That's just the brief course," Eloise said, grinning. "I'll go into detail if you want."

Rick held up his hands in a gesture of surrender. "No, no, that's fine. So today, what Dave and I landed on was the side of a mud volcano. I can't say that's a very comforting idea. Are there more of them around?"

"There shouldn't be any," she replied. "That's what I've been trying to explain. Guam and the other Marianas—Saipan, Tinian, Rota—are volcanic islands, part of the so-called Rim of Fire. And the seamounts we're planning to mine are too."

"How do you know?" Rick asked. "Isn't this the first time anybody's been down to look?"

"Yes and no. Volcanic seamounts usually have a strong magnetic signature. That's because magnetic minerals in the lava got aligned by the earth's magnetic field as they crystallized. We've done magnetometer surveys of the area, of course, and overlayed them on our depth-sounding charts. They agree, most of the time."

"But not always?"

"No, you're right. But we've got other kinds of evidence too." Eloise pulled more papers from her attaché case and sorted through them until she came to one that looked like a sidescan sonar chart.

"We've been assuming that features like this are lava flows," she explained, pointing to a crooked line that resembled a gully on a hillside. "But I just thought of another possibility. What if they're serpentine? That's a mineral that forms when warm water under pressure reacts with peridotite. That would fit with the idea that subducted water is seeping up to form mud volcanoes. Why it should be doing it on this side of the Trench instead of the other, I haven't the least idea."

Rick was impressed by her efficiency and expertise but

still puzzled by her obvious concern. "Does it really matter that much?" he asked.

"You'd better believe it does," she retorted. "First of all, it's a question of scientific knowledge. If some geological feature turns up where our theories say it shouldn't be, that means there's something about our theories that needs fixing. But aside from that, our program involves sending Rover and Junior down to scrape mineral-rich crust off the slopes of volcanic seamounts. Just what do you think would happen if, as chief geologist on the project, I choose the wrong kind of seamount and Junior lands on a thick layer of mud instead?"

"Bye-bye, Junior," Rick said.

"And bye-bye, Eloise, too," she added. "Now do you see why I want that log? I *think* I know which seamounts are good sites for us, but I want to be very damned sure I know which ones to stay away from too!"

CHAPTER 19

TOM FITZHUGH DIMLY SENSED THAT HIS OUTSTRETCHED arms were starting to sag downward. He tried to force them up to the level of his shoulders. It felt as if someone had just turned a blowtorch on the muscles at the base of his neck. He told himself to visualize rolling the pain into a ball, squeezing it until it was very small, and throwing it as far as he could. It seemed to work, a little. Slowly, a quarter inch at a time, he forced his arms back to horizontal.

Everything ached. His calves were knotted, a band of pain ran across his back from one hip to the other, and the arches of his bare feet were threatening to cramp. But all that was nothing, compared to the way his arms and shoulders felt. His muscles had long since gone past the "burn," to a stage of advanced oxygen starvation that sent ever more urgent alarm signals to his brain.

Those damned weights! When Kazuo first fastened them to his wrists he had almost laughed. They felt like nothing at all. One kilo each, just a little over two pounds? He could wear them all day, every day, and not even notice they were there!

How long had he been standing against the wall? It seemed like hours. All he knew for sure was that he couldn't do it much longer. Every time he made a slight move, the rough stucco scraped at the bare skin of his shoulder blades. Stinging, blinding sweat streamed from his forehead into his eyes. One chilly drop clung to the point of his chin, then dripped onto his chest.

He jerked his head back upright and opened his eyes wide. A deep breath helped. It would be so easy to let his arms fall to his side, to step away from the wall, to do a few stretches to quiet the swelling chorus of muscles in pain. This was a training exercise, not a punishment. All he had to do was stop. Nothing would happen to him, no one would even reproach him.

A dozen feet away, Kazuo had been hunkered down since the beginning of this trial, but he showed absolutely no fatigue. His arms hung loosely at his sides. His eyes were open but they seemed to focus on something far beyond the walls of the tiny garden. Around him, the white sand was raked into a pattern of subtle curves, interrupted by a single pock-marked boulder.

A sound that was close to a sob rose in Tom's throat and escaped before he could capture it. Kazuo turned his head and studied Tom's face. After a long moment, he said calmly, "You are strong. Stronger than you know. Hold out until the end. It isn't long now."

"I will," Tom croaked. His arms were beginning to sag again. He swallowed hard and forced them back into position.

Why was he doing this? To prove that he had the right stuff to become one of Ocean Friends' chosen few and help save the world? Not really. And all the talks he had heard, all the literature he had read about the environmental catastrophes that loomed, painted a very convincing and very scary picture. At some deeper level, though, he knew that he was neither convinced nor scared.

Oh, sure, it looked pretty certain that the world was going to come to an end very soon, and that pure dumb luck had offered him a chance to be one of the handful of survivors. Very heavy stuff, but emotionally it didn't move him. Like all those people who lived out their lives next to the San Andreas Fault, despite hearing experts tell them that an angry earth might swallow them up at any moment, he simply didn't accept that any of it could really happen to him.

So why was he standing here with his arms outstretched like the figure of a crucifix? Why had he gone for three days sitting cross-legged on the mat in his room, with nothing to eat but a small bowl of rice each day at dawn? Why had he spent a long time—how long he still didn't know—floating in a tank of blood-warm seawater, with his eyes and ears masked and only the rhythm of his heart to remind him of his own existence?

The reasons were simple, after all. Hoshi had asked him to, and Kazuo would have been disappointed if he'd refused. He would do anything Hoshi asked him to do, unless it was something that might cost him Kazuo's friendship.

From somewhere nearby came the low sound of a gong. Tom blinked the sweat out of his eyes and saw Kazuo rise to his feet in that simple, graceful motion that Tom was trying so hard to learn. He walked over to Tom.

"This trial is over," he said. "You have conquered. Now you may lower your arms."

Tom felt as though the balls of his upper arms had frozen in their shoulder sockets. As he tried to let his arms down slowly to his sides, they clicked and creaked. Above all, they hurt, more than they had at any moment until now. The sweat on his face and body turned clammy. He sensed that he was swaying and starting to fall face forward, but there was nothing he could do about it. He had already used up everything he had.

As he fell like a lightning-struck tree, he felt Kazuo catch him under the arms and lower him gently to the sand.

"Rest, now," Kazuo said in a neutral voice that was somehow comforting. "I will return soon and take you to the baths. A long soak will bring your strength back."

"Wait," Tom said as Kazuo turned to go. He forced himself to sit up, then, after a couple of ragged breaths, to lurch to his feet. "I'm ready now."

The group in the shrine room was smaller tonight, no more than ten people. Tom recognized most of the faces. It was odd that he had not yet met any of them one-to-one, but Ocean Friends had good reasons for everything that happened. He went to one end of the semicircle and managed to sink to a cross-legged sitting position without using his hands. He wondered if anyone had noticed, then realized that his pride in this new accomplishment was very childish. He felt his ears start to redden.

Hoshi had noticed. From her place at the center of the circle, she gave him a glance that praised him for succeeding and reprimanded him for showing off. The glint of amusement that came with those messages made him feel even more like a four-year-old, and, like a four-year-old, he vowed that next time he would *really* impress her.

Kazuo was the last to arrive. He padded in silently with a sort of gliding walk that looked effortless and covered ground surprisingly quickly, and he took the spot next to Tom. As soon as he was seated, Hoshi began the invocation.

"The ocean is our mother."

"The ocean is our mother."

"She gave us life. . . ."

This time Tom found that the response rose naturally to his lips. His mind drifted toward a centerless, boundaryless state that he recognized from certain moments underwater, when the wall that separated him from the ocean began to seem vanishingly thin.

Just at the moment when he started to lose conscious awareness of his surroundings, the ritual ended. He blinked and tried to put aside the feeling of regret and loss that washed over him.

Hoshi turned to the gray-haired man that Tom recognized from the earlier meeting. "Harlan? Please tell us of our successes with outreach."

Harlan bowed slightly and said, "The teams we sent to Manila, Taipei, Hong Kong, and Jakarta have made themselves known to the authorities and received permission to conduct educational forums. The Chinese authorities still won't give us visas, but negotiations are continuing. We are about to sign the lease on a former theater in Honolulu, where we will be able to mount exhibits and show our films about our Mother Ocean and the dangers she faces. Hoshi?"

"Yes, Harlan?"

"One thing I don't understand." He hesitated, fumbling for words. "Those who hear our message, many of them, ask how they can join our work. But they aren't allowed to. We're told to say that they should tell their friends what they have learned, nothing more. Shouldn't we, well, sign them up? Organize groups wherever we can? Why reach out, if we don't pull in those we reach?"

Hoshi nodded. "You ask an important question. Here is the reason: If we recruit members and form groups, people will begin to think of us as a political organization, which they must be for or against. Rulers will start to wonder if we threaten their power. Our message will be lost in the noise of controversy. And why would we look for numbers? Those who truly hear the call of our mother will find their way to us, as each of you found your way here. Those who do not, do not belong with us."

"Thank you, Hoshi," Harlan said, bowing again.

Hoshi's eyes traveled around the circle once more, pausing at each of the dozen people whose attention was focused entirely on her. When she reached Tom, she seemed to pause especially long. Under the pressure of her gaze, he found it hard to breathe. Had he done something to displease her? Was she about to single him out for criticism?

"Tom Fitzhugh," she said.

Tom straightened his back and met her eyes.

"Hoshi?"

"Is it now your deepest wish to join our circle and serve our mother?" she demanded.

Tom heard a voice, hoarse and with a hint of his grandfather's brogue, but undoubtedly his own, say, "It is."

"Will you pledge yourself to each of us and accept our pledges in return?"

"That I will."

Hoshi rose to her feet and walked toward the corner of the room. As she went, she rolled up the left sleeve of her robe to above the elbow.

On the floor near the door to the veranda was an enormous pottery bowl, the size, shape, and color of a small bolide. Its deeply pocked, mottled surface made it look as if it had traveled across many light-years to arrive at precisely that spot. Hoshi stopped next to it. From her sash, she drew a small knife with a cord-wrapped hilt. Blue-white light collected along the twin edges of the leaf-shaped blade.

"Stand with me now," Hoshi said, "just as you came from our mother."

Tom at once understood what she meant. He scrambled to his feet and walked over to her. Unknotting his sash, he shrugged off the tunic, then loosened the drawstring of his pants. As they slipped down to his ankles, he took a single step sideways, freeing his feet. There he waited, strangely at ease, for whatever might happen next. He was stark naked in front of a roomful of almost-strangers, and the oddest part was that he could not imagine being otherwise.

Hoshi held her left arm out, over the bowl, and bent her hand back with the wrist facing up. The flexed hand threw her tendons and veins into relief. Holding the knife with the same delicacy that he had seen when she held a writing brush, Hoshi lightly stroked the point across her skin. A thin line of red appeared in its wake, then swelled and widened. As the crimson liquid sluggishly collected on her delicate wrist and began to drip into the bowl, she said, "Our blood is but a tiny part of the greater ocean. Our mother lends it to us, and we are always ready to give it back to her."

Tom breathed shallowly, through his mouth. His face and palms felt clammy, and his stomach was churning. His cock and balls seemed to be trying to crawl up into his abdomen. Was he about to disgrace himself forever by passing out? The sight of blood had always, since he was a small child, made him feel faint. He didn't mind spearing fish underwater, because the gray-green clouds that spread from the wounds didn't look like anything more than ink, but he hated cleaning his catch afterward and having to acknowledge the pink stain in the water.

He turned his head and stared at his reflection, and

Hoshi's, in the glass doors of the veranda. That was better. The night outside sucked the colors from the scene, leaving Hoshi's wrist very dark but not distinctly red. As he watched, she took a narrow strip of material from her tunic and began to wrap it around her wrist. After a few turns, the darkness was no longer visible. He turned back and met her eyes.

"I stand here," she said, "for all the children who have found and joined themselves to our Mother Ocean. All of us have mingled our blood in the water of our mother, and now we are ready to welcome you."

She held out the knife, hilt first. Tom saw his right hand move toward it, though he was not aware of willing it to. The hilt was warm, almost hot, to his fingertips. He closed his hand around it and raised it until the small leaf-shaped blade was level with his eyes. Along the two edges was an irregular sheen, as if the blade had been given a microscopically thin coating of oil. He imagined—or was it real?—a tiny ruby-colored dot at the needle-sharp point. He swallowed hard and tried to blink it away.

He knew, without a word said, that they expected him to cut his wrist and let his blood drip into the enormous bowl. He understood what the act meant, and he wanted, even yearned, to carry it out. But how could he, who didn't even dare use a safety razor? His only choice was to apologize to Hoshi and the entire group, and then walk out of their presence forever. What use could they have for such a weakling?

No! If he carried out the rite, and then fainted, fine. Hoshi and the others could decide at that point whether they still wanted him in the group. But he did not want to—he wasn't going to—leave by his own act. If it was his blood they wanted, he would give it to them.

He stretched out his left arm at full length, rotated the forearm to bring the underside of the wrist into view, then bent his hand back as he had seen Hoshi do. The pale-blue veins, in their branching and joining, seemed to spell a message in an alphabet he had once known but forgotten.

He stared at them for a moment, then closed his eyes and raised the knife.

How long had it been since his last breath? It didn't matter anymore. His lungs, his leaping heart, the aching veins in his neck, all receded before the superior force of the impulse that was gathering strength in his mind. The muscles in his right arm were like a crossbow at full draw. Then something unseen released the trigger. His hand, and the razor-sharp blade it held, slashed downward toward his wrist.

"No," a quiet voice said in his ear. In that same instant, his plunging arm stopped abruptly in midair, held by a grip that was both gentle and invincible. He opened his eyes. Kazuo was standing close by his side. It was his hand that kept Tom's hand immobile.

Hoshi stepped forward and took the knife from Tom's hand. "We owe our mother our lives," she said. "But it is for her, not for us, to choose the moment when that debt is paid."

She took Tom's left hand in hers and drew the point of the blade along his wrist. He didn't feel its touch at all, and when the blood began to flow, he watched with no more emotion than if it had been ketchup squirting from a squeeze bottle. Before he could realize how odd this was, she was wrapping a length of soft cloth around his wrist and tying the ends neatly.

Hoshi turned and picked up a smaller bowl of the same rocklike material as the one that held the blend of seawater and blood. She came back to stand in front of Tom.

"Today you bind yourself to our Mother Ocean and accept her protection," Hoshi said. She filled the small bowl from the larger one and stood on tiptoes to raise the bowl over Tom's head. When she tipped it, the mixture of his blood and her blood and the water of the sea poured out and ran down his face and chest. He licked his lips and tasted salt. He felt his body begin to tremble all over. Only Kazuo's arm around his bare waist kept him from collapsing to the floor.

* * *

Rick wheeled the Sunbird into the hotel parking lot and found a vacant slot, then glanced at his watch. Ten twenty-five. He thought about seeing if anybody was hanging out on the terrace by the pool, then decided to go straight to his room instead. After spending two hours in a room full of Ocean Friends, he was a little tired of having people around him, and a little extra sack time would help set him up for the next day's activities.

Not that he thought of the evening as a waste of time. The meeting had featured a talk and film about "black smokers," the plumes of metal-rich geysers found on the ocean bottom of Baja California and elsewhere. The speaker, a professor of marine geochemistry, obviously knew what he was talking about. His film, taken at depths greater than ten thousand feet, showed strange albino species of shrimp, crabs, and anemones, against a riotous backdrop of yellow, orange, and red rocks. Rick had wondered, as he had once heard Jacques-Yves Costeau wonder in one of his films, why there is so much color where there is no light. The expert had explained that the colored rocks were sulphide deposits that had precipitated from the superheated mineral solutions of the geyser.

Rick had understood most of what the speaker had to say, and the film was gorgeous, but even so, he had felt out of his element. He was a diver, not a marine scientist. He was curious about what went on at great depths, but on the whole, the evening had reminded him of the note a little boy wrote after his birthday: "Dear Grandma, thank you for the book about penguins. It told me a lot more about penguins than I wanted to know."

As soon as the question period had started, he had given Kazuo a wave and slipped out.

He had reached the door to his room and turned the key in the lock, when he paused, frowning. Had he heard just the faintest whisper of movement inside? The noise might have come from another room, next door or across the hall, but he didn't think so. He flattened himself against the wall next to the door, pushed it wide open, and groped around the jamb for the light switch. It went on, but the light didn't.

That convinced him. Someone had sabotaged the light. Bending double, to present a smaller target, he charged through the doorway and flung himself to the floor on the left, in the narrow space next to one of the double beds. As he did so, he heard something strike the doorjamb. He wriggled around and peered past the foot of the bed. The interior of the room was black, but at the far end, the lights from the pool area made the door to the balcony show as a lighter rectangle. As his eyes adapted to the darkness, he thought he saw a silhouetted form slip past the doorway, onto the balcony.

"Damn! He's getting away," Rick muttered to himself. He jumped to his feet and dashed across the room toward the balcony. He was nearly there when some instinct made him throw himself to the side, just as something whistled past the place where his head had been only an instant before. He recognized the sound. His attacker was armed with a nunchaku, two deadly lengths of hardwood joined by a thin strong chain, which was a favored weapon of kung fu fighters and ninjas alike.

Rick had zero desire to fight barehanded, in the dark, against anyone with a nunchaku. He could think of lots less painful ways to commit suicide. But he wasn't offered a choice. As he rolled to the left, under the bed, the nunchaku smashed into the rug, just inches away. Rick kicked out with both feet and had the satisfaction of feeling one heel make powerful contact with his attacker's shin. Rick then wriggled to the foot of the bed, rolled over, and leaped to his feet. His hands, body, and mind were at peak preparation to attack or defend, whichever was needed.

Neither was. He caught a quick glimpse of a black form vaulting the railing of the balcony. He rushed outside in time to see a thin black cord, fastened to the railing with a trick knot, give a sort of shake and fall with a faint swish. He leaned over, very cautiously, and stared down into the darkness. By now he had a strong hunch what he would see, and he was right: nothing at all. The two burglars had vanished into the night as if they had never existed. He returned to the room and got one of the bedside lamps to work. He wasn't surprised to find that both had been unplugged. He went over to the door. Embedded in the doorjamb, at chest height, was a razor-sharp throwing star.

Rick found Will Ward at the hotel bar, chatting with Ray Lapham over a Scotch on the rocks. Rick ordered a beer, then told the two what had just happened to him.

"Here's the weird part," he concluded. "I got one glimpse of the second guy, the one who attacked me, as he was running out onto the balcony. You may think I'm a few bricks shy of a load for saying this, but I'd swear he was dressed up as a ninja. And he left this behind." He showed them the throwing star.

"Ricky, my boy," Will said heavily, "you've been watching too many of the wrong kind of movies. Maybe you should go back to skin flicks."

Ray stroked his chin and said, "I'm not so sure about that. It isn't the first time I've heard a story of this sort."

Will snorted. "Ninjas? At the tail end of the twentieth century? On Guam, for Christ's sake? Give me a break!"

"I'm not saying they *are* ninjas," Ray replied. "But look at it this way: If you're going in for hotel burglaries, a ninja costume makes good sense. Not only does it make you harder to spot in the dark, but if somebody does see you, he'll probably think twice about getting in your way. Remember, a lot of the tourists here are young Japanese honeymooners. They've probably seen more ninja movies than you've seen Westerns. They may think it's all nonsense, but when they run into a live ninja, at night, in their hotel room ..."

"Then you don't think they were after my room in particular?" Rick asked.

Ray shrugged. "I doubt it. Bad research and bad luck, more likely. Instead of a terrified young couple and a bunch of easily portable wedding presents, they found themselves up against someone who was both willing and able to fight back. I bet they're having one hell of an argument right this minute with whoever picked your room."

"I guess I should call the police," Rick said. "They'll know if there have been other break-ins like mine."

"Well, if you really—" Ray began.

"Cops?" Will said, interrupting him. "That doesn't strike me as a good idea. No real harm was done. Why don't we let it ride?"

Rick recognized that Will's question really amounted to an order, though he wasn't sure of the reason for it. He bit back an "aye-aye, sir," and noticed that Ray was glancing at Will sidelong, made curious by the old submariner's "command voice."

"Sure, Will," Rick said easily. "No problem. It's not as if I had anything in the room for them to steal. No codebooks or secret plans or diamond necklaces. Nothing but a spare pair of BVDs, in fact. And if they made off with those, I'll just buy more and send the bill to SeaVenture!"

CHAPTER 20

I'M SURE THIS IS A COMPLETE WASTE OF TIME," DAVE grumbled over the intercom. It was the third time he had said it since the beginning of the dive.

Rick ignored him and concentrated on his job. They were just passing the 500-meter level, and the *Steel Albatross* was descending at a very rapid rate of 50 meters per minute. Even so, it would be another quarter of an hour before they reached the depth at which Rover was supposed to be operating. Rick's hands automatically kept the *Albatross* in a wide clockwise spiral, with the big airlift hose and Rover's armored cable at the center, while he obeyed the fighter pilot's First Commandment: Thou shalt always look around you. Not that there was much to see at these depths, even with the boat's new, more powerful head- and sidelights. He wished he had the light-enhancing snooper lenses that Ward had adapted for underwater use. They were designed to use the bioluminescence given off by deep-sea organisms to illuminate the surroundings. They worked very well, as Rick had good reason to know. But like the gill that extracted oxygen from seawater, the snooper lenses were considered too sensitive to be shared with civilians like Dave and the other SeaVenture people.

"Rover's been working perfectly," Dave said, in a tone that dared Rick to disagree.

"According to the telemetry," Rick replied. "And you're the one who said that you didn't trust the telemetry. That's the reason Will and I and the *Albatross* are here. Remember?"

"Well, I've changed my mind. Whatever the problem was, it got fixed. We should start back to the surface right now, instead of wasting any more time on a pointless errand."

Rick kept his temper, but just barely. "A whole shitload of time and money has been spent to get you down to the ocean floor here, so you can watch your gizmo in action. Today's our first shot at accomplishing that mission. Turn back? No way!"

The fathometer on the instrument display read 1400 meters and the depth sounder showed a little over 300 meters to the bottom. Rick slowed the craft's descent rate and banked more sharply to the right. In a few moments, the vertical tube of the airlift apparatus came into view, looking like an infinitely long snake that disappeared from view both upward and downward. As the huge hose began to tend toward the horizontal, Rick rolled level and continued the descent, keeping the tube at about twenty meters to starboard. He didn't want to risk fouling the *Steel Albatross* on Rover's control cable.

Thumbing the Transmit button on the single-sideband radio, he said, *"Champion,* Sierra Alpha One. Do you read?"

Single-sideband reception was not as clear as amplitude modulation, or AM, but it had the big advantage of not being limited to line of sight. The return message began with what sounded like "Sezilexon" but then cleared up enough for him to make it out.

"Champion," Rick continued. "Request current depth reading on Rover. Over."

"Roger, Sierra Alpha One," he heard. "Current depth reading on Rover is one-five-niner-six meters. I say again, one-five-niner-six. Do you copy? Over."

"Roger, *Champion*. I copied one-five-niner-six meters. Out."

A glance at the fathometer showed that the *Steel Albatross* was less than sixty meters above Rover's reported depth. Rick changed the command angle of attack to just above a stall and pulled back on the stick. He was careful to keep his hand away from the manual rate-of-ascent knob. He had Captain Ward's assurance that the glitch Dave had used to lock up the computer had been located and fixed, but he was in no mood to test it.

The proximity alarm on the bottom-profiling sonar began to blink, and moments later, the bottom came in sight. So did the long, torpedo-shaped form of Rover. The craft was hovering about twenty feet off the ocean floor. A long cable ran from its stern to a metal harness near the bottom of the airlift tube. Rick maneuvered the *Steel Albatross* closer and came to a hover just off the bottom, with her bow and headlights pointing toward the other craft.

"*Berkone*, Sierra Alpha One is in position, at depth, ah, one-five-niner-three."

Dave's voice sounded for the first time in several minutes. "Before the dive, I programmed a whole series of standard maneuvers," he said. "The idea is to see whether Rover carries all of them out as instructed."

"I know," Rick replied. "Can we get on with it?"

"Oh. Sure. Uh, Charlie, are you there?"

A voice Rick didn't know said, "Roger."

"Great. Let's get this show on the road."

The voice read out a list of commands, beginning with Forward Slow and working up to Left, Right, Up, and Down Attitude Thrusters, Bow and Stern. At each command, Rover, like a very well-trained dog, did exactly as it was told. Rick found himself looking forward to tossing it a Milk-Bone after it did a good job of Shake Hands and Play Dead. At least it would make things a little more lively.

"That finishes the first series," Charlie's voice finally said. "I am now deploying Junior."

Rick looked toward the bow of the vehicle, expecting to see the smaller craft leave its dock and head for the bottom.

For a moment, nothing happened. Then he saw an opaque white cloud shoot out from one of the bow attitude jets, with much more force than it had during testing, a few moments before. Slowly—underwater, almost everything happened slowly—the submersible began to swing, pivoting on the cable at its stern. It picked up speed as it swung. With a growing feeling of horror, Rick realized that the immobilized *Steel Albatross* was directly in its path.

"Shut down all systems on Rover," Rick shouted into his mike.

"What's wrong?" Dave demanded, in a voice tinged with panic.

"Not now," Rick growled. His mind was racing through a list of alternatives. The list was very short. Ordinarily, the *Steel Albatross* derived the energy to move horizontally from the effects of positive or negative buoyancy. As Rick knew very well, those effects took time to work—too much time, given the present danger. One possibility was to pull the lever that dropped the boat's keel. That would certainly get them out of the way of Rover, but would they, or the boat, survive 1500 meters of uncontrolled ascent? Never mind the physical strain when the boat broached the surface like a love-sick orca and then fell back into the water. The impact would make that finely tuned little boat unusable without a complete overhaul. And even if they and the boat somehow survived all that, they would still have to abort the mission. Without its specially crafted keel, the *Albatross* was useless, and they would have zero chance of retrieving the keel from the ocean floor.

Okay, dropping the keel was the very last resort. But the seconds were ticking down, and Rover was swinging closer and closer, like one of those medieval weapons with a spiked ball on the end of a chain. Will had once talked of mounting caterpillar tracks on the boat's underside, which would have helped if he had done it and if they were on the bottom. But he hadn't and they weren't. Scratch that one. As for the secret drive that Rick had used to save their bacon when the boat got stuck in that mudmount, it would take much too long to get its superconducting coils down to near absolute zero.

The *Steel Albatross* did have sets of compressed-air attitude jets on the bow and stern, of course. Unfortunately, there weren't any that pointed due forward or aft. It hadn't occurred to Will that anyone might need to back up suddenly.

"Rover's going to crash into us!" Dave shouted. "Do something, quick!"

Rick wanted to tap him on the head and ask if there was anybody home.

"Sierra Alpha, *Berkone*. What is your situation?"

Dire, Rick thought, and getting steadily worse. Rover was less than twenty feet away now. It was moving more slowly than before, but that was no consolation. Even if it slowed to a molasseslike foot per second, it would still pack enough of a punch to badly damage the delicate skin of the *Albatross,* or even to breach the pressure hull.

The attitude jets . . . The *Steel Albatross* had the potential to move simultaneously in three dimensions, but Rover was swinging in a two-dimensional circle defined by the tether that linked it to the massive hose. If Rick could move his boat out of that plane of action or beyond the circumference of that circle—preferably both—the danger would be past.

Even as his hand fell on the manual controls for the jets, he was estimating an answer to a complex problem in solid geometry. He would find out soon enough if his solution was a good one.

He fired the ventral jets, bow and stern, at one hundred percent thrust and hit the switches that blew the forward and aft ballast tanks. The effect wasn't quite like sitting atop a Saturn booster, but the *Albatross* did begin to move upward. At the same time, Rick engaged the starboard-bow jet, swinging the bow away from Rover's line of approach.

Dave's runaway submersible was only a few feet away now. Rick got a clear view of the small crawler Dave had named Junior, in its cage on the bow. More than ever, the crawler seemed to wear a nasty, sneering expression. It had been the order to deploy Junior that set off this emergency.

Rick crossed his fingers and hoped that Junior didn't decide that this was a nice time to deploy.

As suddenly as it had started, the crisis ended. Rover drifted by the *Albatross* with at least three feet of vertical clearance and a couple of feet horizontally. Damned close, but Rick reminded himself that close only counted with horseshoes and hand grenades.

"Is it . . . Are we safe?" Dave demanded. His voice quavered.

"Safer than we were a couple of minutes ago," Rick said dryly. He switched off the attitude jets and shut down the ballast tank pumps, then got ready to explain to the indignant voices coming over his headphones exactly what had just happened.

"I'm glad," Dave said hesitantly. "Um . . . you really handled that well. I was so flabbergasted when Rover started acting crazy that I couldn't think what to do. I still can't believe it."

"Nothing like that ever happened before?" asked Rick.

"No, never. That's part of what's driving me batty. Intermittent faults are hard enough to handle when they always produce the same result. When you get different effects every time, how can you even start to work out what's causing them?"

"Good question." Rick pushed Transmit and said, *"Berkone,* Sierra Alpha." He went on to describe what had just happened. "Request a rerun of Rover's evolution. We'll watch from farther away this time," he added.

"Roger," Will's voice said only moments later. "Inform us when you are ready to commence."

Rick maneuvered the *Albatross* into a position slightly above Rover's plane of operation and at a distance well beyond the reach of the tethered vehicle, then radioed word to the mother ship. After a short pause, Charlie's voice again read the list of moves, from the top. As before, Rover did everything just the way it was supposed to.

As the moment drew closer to test Junior again, Rick felt his jaw tighten. Intellectually, he was certain the *Steel Alba-*

tross was completely safe, but his emotions apparently hadn't gotten the word.

"Deploying Junior," Charlie announced. A moment later, the smaller craft moved out of its docking cage and made its way downward to the seafloor. There, its caterpillar tracks took it forward, back, left, right, and in complete circles in each direction. When it finally returned successfully to its cage, Rick felt like applauding.

Dave apparently didn't. "I don't get it!" he exclaimed, pounding his fist on the top of Rick's seatback. "How can something go so wrong one time and work perfectly a few minutes later! I think I'm going crazy!"

"If it helps any, I saw it too," Rick pointed out. "We've seen what we came to see, haven't we? Let's go topside and hash this out with the others. Maybe someone will come up with an explanation. I'm starting to get an idea or two I'd like to toss at you."

"I'll take ideas anywhere I can find them," Dave admitted. "Personally, I'm fresh out of them."

Rick announced their intention to return to the surface, then initiated the ascent procedure. Once more the pumps began to force water from the ballast tanks. The craft began to move upward.

Oops! The *Albatross* was still pointing in the direction of Rover and its gigantic vacuum-cleaner hose. Already the wings were starting to derive some forward motion from their ascent, edging them toward a potential collision. Once more Rick reached for the bank of switches that controlled the forward attitude jets. He pushed the switch for the right jet and heard a satisfying hiss. The orientation of the bow shifted a few degrees to the left. He gave it another brief spritz, enough to let them clear the hose with a dozen feet to spare. As the hose left the cone of the *Albatross*'s headlights and became just another part of the surrounding blackness, Rick felt the stick trying to move in his hand. He waited for a few moments, to let the craft pick up more forward speed, then applied ailerons and rudder to put the *Albatross* into a banked right turn that would take them up in a wide spiral and bring them to the surface within shouting distance of *Berkone,* which was holding station a quarter of a mile from *Champion.*

A couple of minutes later, the instrument display beeped, not just once, but repeatedly. Rick sat up straighter and studied the dials. The depth gauge read 584 meters. Their rate of ascent was just over the 50 meter per minute he had targeted. Nothing wrong here, so what . . . ?

"What is it?" Dave demanded, leaning forward to look over Rick's shoulder. "Is something wrong with the computer?"

Rick gave a brief shake of the head. He wished Dave would sit back and leave him alone. Blocking out his fellow passenger, he touched a circle at the lower left of the screen, then studied the new display that came up.

"Someone's looking for us," he announced. "Looking for something, at any rate, and using the latest in side-scan sonar to do it too. The funny thing is that its signature doesn't match up with a ship-based unit. It looks more like somebody's towing it."

"Maybe it's the *Champion* or your ship," Dave suggested.

"Nope. The *Steel Albatross* doesn't recognize the signature. That means it's not one of ours, and not one of the Russkis', either. Not that they have what you'd call a big presence in these parts anymore."

"Who, then? The Chinese? The Japanese?"

"No idea," Rick said. "That's not my department. But I'd better pass the word about this contact. People don't put equipment like that on tuna boats."

Half an hour later, the *Steel Albatross* was bobbing safely in *Berkone*'s moon-pool. Rick and Dave had changed out of their wetsuits and joined Will Ward aboard a chopper bound for the *Glomar Champion.* They found Ray and Eloise waiting at the side of the ship's helipad, wearing glum faces.

"Well?" Ray demanded, while Dave was still a couple of yards away.

Dave silently shook his head.

"Why don't we go someplace quieter," Will said, shouting to be heard over the noise of the copter.

Ray nodded and shouted, "Follow me."

Below decks, in the wardroom, they were joined by Charlie Dexter, Dave's chief techie. The pocket protector in his rumpled short-sleeved khaki shirt made him look like a cross between a merchant marine officer and a Silicon Valley wonk.

Dave led off with a thorough and dispassionate report of the mission, one that didn't leave out a single important detail. Rick had to admire him for it. Charlie followed, presenting a printout that showed his every move, paired with the corresponding action on Rover's part. Everything matched up exactly, down to the first "Deploy Junior." The corresponding notation for Rover was garbage: a scramble of math notation, Greek letters, little arrows, and the symbols for diamonds, clubs, hearts, and spades.

Rick pointed to the line of symbols. "Does any of that mean anything to you? Or is it just the computer burping?"

"More like serious indigestion," Charlie replied. "It means *something,* all right. But nothing we're going to be able to figure out. If you know a shrink who treats computers, now . . ."

"It'll have to make do with us," Ray said. "We can't afford to give it years of therapy, anyway. Then, if I understand you, this gibberish is the computer reporting what Rover told it, right after the 'Deploy Junior' command? The problem must be somewhere in the vehicle then."

"We've run test after test," Dave said loudly. "This is the first problem we've had in weeks!"

The tiny seedling of an idea in Rick's mind was growing fast. "Was there anything different about this test?" he asked.

"Sure," Charlie said. "It was deeper than usual, and you guys were down there watching."

"What if the problem's depth-sensitive?" Rick asked. "The external pressure reaches a certain number of atmospheres, and *boom!* Two components get shoved against each other and cause a glitch. Is that possible?"

"In theory, sure," Charlie replied. "I thought of that myself, in fact. And it's true, the problems have come up only on dives that went deeper than eight hundred meters. But I couldn't find any sort of pattern to the problems, either mechanical or electronic."

"Of course not," said Dave. "Honestly, talking about parts of the control system getting pushed into each other, do you think Rover's something I built in my garage, using plans from *Popular Mechanics?* She's a thoroughly tested and proven deep-submergence vehicle, with dozens of missions under her belt and no problems at all until this one. And I hate to say it, but after today, I don't think these problems are accidents. I think somebody's causing them."

Charlie stood up. "If it'll ease your mind any, I quit."

"I didn't mean you, Charlie," Dave protested.

"Who else? I was the guy at the controls," Charlie returned. "And nobody snuck in while my back was turned and twiddled any of the knobs. But don't take my word for it, read the printout. There's not one damn thing wrong with the commands I gave Roger. They're exactly the ones we agreed on beforehand."

In a mild voice, Will Ward said, "Sit down, son. Nobody's accusing you of anything. We're just trying to get to the bottom of this."

"Well ..." Charlie sat down, but his expression stayed angry.

"Check me on this," Will continued. "These commands you're talking about: They're in digital form, aren't they?"

"Sure. What do you expect, semaphore?"

"I expect a civil response to a civil question," Will retorted. "Now, let's suppose there's something in your computer that adds some extra digits to whatever command you give every now and then. What would that do?"

Charlie scratched his head. "Sometimes it wouldn't do anything at all. And when it did do something, you'd have no way of knowing in advance *what* it would do."

"Doesn't that sound an awful lot like what's been happening with Rover?" Will suggested.

Dave broke in. "To me, it sounds an awful lot like a computer virus," he said. "That's how many of them work. They lurk undetected for periods of time, then do some kind of random damage before vanishing into hiding again. But that's not possible here. I thoroughly scanned our software for viruses before I left the States. It checked out one hundred percent."

"Have you scanned for viruses since you got here?" Rick asked.

Dave looked at him, frowning. "Why should I? I haven't downloaded any new programs. There's no way the software could get infected."

Eloise tapped her pencil on the table. "I don't know, Dave. . . . It might be worthwhile to do it again, just to be safe. And to check over the innards of your craft too. I know you already did," she added hastily, as Dave opened his mouth to protest. "But that was before today's events."

"Is all this really necessary?" asked Ray. "If Dave says he's checked out his software, should we ask him to spend the time and energy to go over his tracks again? What's the point?"

"The point," Will replied, "is that Dave and Rick found themselves in a very dangerous situation today, thanks to whatever bug we're dealing with in Rover. We came damned close to losing both Rover and the *Steel Albatross,* not to mention Rick and Dave. That would have been a real tragedy, and the end of this project."

The discussion continued for another half hour, but at the end of it, everyone came around to Eloise's suggestion. Rover would be returned to the surface, along with the mile-long airlift hose, and taken apart for testing. Meanwhile, every one of the command programs would be scanned for viruses and miscellaneous bugs.

"How long will this take?" asked Rick as the meeting broke up.

Dave shrugged. "A week to ten days, I guess. Why?"

"I'm planning to enter the All-Guam Thumb-Twiddling Championship," Rick said. "I just want to be sure I'm going to have enough time for training. It looks like the answer's yes."

Ray overheard and turned. "I'm sorry as hell about all these delays, Rick," he said. "If you can think of any better way to spend the next few days than hanging around the hotel, please go ahead. Oh, that reminds me: A fellow from the head office blew into town this morning. I gave him an update on the project, including your part in it. He seemed very interested in meeting you, especially after I mentioned that you've had some contact with the Ocean Friends people. Fellow named Ken Kirby. I imagine he'll get in touch with you."

CHAPTER 21

F ROM RAY'S OBLIQUE DESCRIPTION OF KEN KIRBY AS "a fellow from the head office," Rick had expected to find an upper-echelon spook, the kind who looked for listeners behind every tree, plots behind every event, and hidden meanings behind every word. The guy who was waiting for him by the hotel pool with a stack of colored index cards at his side looked and acted more like a professor at a small liberal arts college, the kind who knows everything about some obscure but interesting subject and a little bit about practically everything else.

After all that had happened, Rick felt the need for a calming beverage. He asked the waiter for a double Scotch on the rocks. Ken Kirby ordered a rum and exotic tropical fruit punch. As soon as the waiter left, he said, "Is piloting the *Steel Albatross* as much fun as it sounds? It must be a little like flying an F-14 in super slow motion."

Rick shot him an admiring glance. In one sentence—no, make that *two* sentences—Kirby had communicated that he knew a good deal about the *Albatross,* that he had had at least a glimpse of Rick's personnel file, and that he was someone who thought it was important to understand the feelings of people in the field.

"It has its moments," he admitted.

"What happened today?" Kirby asked. Noticing Rick's hesitation, he added, "You can talk frankly to me. Feel free to check that with anyone you like."

"The President?" Rick responded.

Kirby grinned. "As far as I know, he's never heard of me. But I doubt if he's heard of you either, so the chances that your call will go through are pretty slim."

"Just the same, I think I'll make one or two calls," Rick said, getting to his feet. *"Not* to the White House." A few minutes later, after talking briefly to Will, he returned to the table and said, "Okay, Ken, what do you want to know?"

"What happened today?" Ken repeated.

Rick told him everything, from the copter ride out to *Berkone* in the morning, to the debriefing session aboard the *Glomar Champion*. As an afterthought, he mentioned the anomalous sonar signal that the *Albatross*'s instruments had picked up during the ascent. Ken jotted some notes on a pale green index card, then tucked it in his shirt pocket.

"What about Ocean Friends?" he asked next. "I understand you've had some contact with them. How did that come about?"

"One of their people gave me a hand a couple of weeks ago, when I was having some trouble with a shark," Rick replied. "Later on, the same guy showed me some good diving spots and we just got to know each other. He's a good diver.

"After that, I went to one of their public meetings. By one of those weird coincidences, it turns out that the guy I met—his name is Kazuo—is the son of a man that Will Ward, my godfather"—he glanced at Ken, who nodded to show that Will's name meant something to him—"helped a lot back at the end of World War II. Because of that, Kazuo acts like he's under an obligation to me. It's embarrassing, sometimes, but I try not to pay attention. Kazuo is a nice guy and one hell of a fine diver."

"How about the others in the group? Can you tell me anything about them?"

Rick found himself describing Hoshi Ito, the guru of Ocean Friends, in great detail. He hadn't realized that he had paid her that much attention. Tom, the scuba bum, was next, followed by three or four people he'd talked to or noticed at the meeting he'd attended. Once again, Ken made lots of notes, this time on pink cards.

Rick broke off to ask, "Is any of this helpful?"

"Oh, yes," Ken said with a look of satisfaction. "Any information is useful, as long as it's reasonably accurate. It's just a matter of deciding where it belongs and what it connects to. Have you ever played three-dimensional chess? Too bad; it ought to be part of every fighter pilot's training. Well, thanks, Rick. You've been helpful. If I have any more questions, will I find you here?"

"Not for the next few days," Rick replied. "A friend asked me to come visit her in Tokyo, and the delay in our project makes this seem like a good time to take her up on it."

"Oh? Is this trip something that's been in the works a while?"

"Nope," Rick said with a smile. "As a matter of fact, I just thought of it this second!"

Impossible as it seemed, the terminal at Tokyo's Narita Airport was even more overcrowded than it had been on Rick's last visit. He changed some dollars into yen and made his way through the throngs to the Tourist Information Office, at the hub where the north and south wings of the terminal met. There he got a pleasant surprise. Unlike last time, he wasn't going to have to sit for two hours in stop-and-go traffic on what was laughingly called an express bus. There was now a train that left from a new station right under the air terminal and went nonstop to the heart of town.

Before buying his ticket, he hunted up Natalie's business card and telephoned her. She sounded very pleased when he told her that he was in town, but less astonished than he'd expected. Had she taken it for granted that he would come sooner or later?

"You are still at Narita?" she asked. "You know about the new JR East train line, yes? Take the Special Express to Tokyo Station. My gallery is near Sukiyabashi, in the Ginza, only steps from the Wako department store. Everyone knows where that is. It is one subway stop from the railway station, or you can easily walk." She gave him more explicit directions, which he noted carefully. Tokyo might be the second- or third-largest city in the world, and probably the richest too, but its maze of narrow, twisting lanes made it seem closer in spirit to a North African *souk* than to midtown Manhattan.

Once in town, he found the neighborhood easily. Locating Natalie's gallery was another matter. After wandering up and down several side streets, all of them apparently lined with galleries of one sort or another, he found a *koban*, or police box, and bowed politely to the officer on duty. Reading from his pocket phrase book, he said, *"Michi ni mayoimashita."* That was supposed to mean "I am lost." He hoped it really did mean that and not something like "Stick it in your ear."

He showed the policeman the side of Natalie's card that was printed in Japanese.

The officer studied it and let loose with a burst of Japanese. Seeing Rick's total incomprehension, he started over. Through a combination of pointing, holding up fingers, and basic English, he told Rick to go one block west, turn right for two blocks, then left. He finished by miming two sides of the street, then walking his fingers four buildings along the right side.

"Arigato gozaimasu," Rick said, after another glance at his phrase book. He smiled and bowed again. The officer, apparently pleased with his own performance, smiled, bowed, and said something that clearly meant either "You're welcome" or "Have a nice day."

Even with directions, finding the gallery was not easy. After walking back and forth in front of the fourth building on the right side, he noticed a carved wooden plaque with ideograms that looked like the ones on Natalie's card. Next to it was a low, narrow passage that led, tunnel-like, through the building. He followed it and found himself in a tiny hidden courtyard. On the far side was the front wall of a small, tile-roofed house that looked as if it might have stood there since the days of the shoguns.

The carved wooden door opened, and Natalie stepped out.

"Rick, *cheri*, you have found me at last!" she exclaimed. She came into the courtyard to meet him and kissed the air next to each of his cheeks, twice.

"It wasn't easy," Rick replied. He started to give her a real kiss, but she shook her head almost imperceptibly. He settled for his finest imitation of a Japanese bow. If any of the neighbors were watching for something scandalous, they would be disappointed.

One of Natalie's eyebrows twitched appreciatively. "Come," she said. "I want to show you the gallery."

He followed her inside and stopped in surprise. The room was tiny, no more than eight feet on a side. The walls were spotless white, as was the ceiling between heavy, age-darkened beams. The bare floor, of meticulously fitted cedar planks, looked as if someone had waxed and polished it every day for the last century.

Against the far wall, a lacquer stand held the traditional two swords—one long, one short—of a samurai. Behind, on a separate stand, was a battered iron helmet with a skirt of overlapping iron plates to protect the wearer's ears and neck. To one side, a porcelain vase of a pink so pale that it looked white held a single branch of lilac.

Natalie said, "Was it Gropius, the founder of the Bauhaus School, who said that 'Less is more'? I think he must have had Japanese blood."

"I don't know," Rick replied, with a mental apology to his art-history professor at Princeton. "I never went to that school."

Natalie tapped him on the nose with her forefinger. "You are deliberately being naughty. Admit it: You expected to find display cases full, full, full of art objects. Now you start to wonder if my—stock, you say?—is very low. Would you believe that some of my clients find this room overdecorated?"

"Sure," Rick said cheerfully. "Different places, different

customs. Those swords sure do dress up a room, though. Are they very valuable?"

"Not very," Natalie replied with a shrug. "This *daisho*—that is the name for such a matched pair of long and short swords—is a good example from the Edo period, around 1650, but it is not a masterpiece. I am asking six million yen for it and hope to get five."

Rick did some quick mental arithmetic, then let out a low whistle. "Between thirty and forty thousand dollars isn't very valuable? Let me know when you find one of these swords that *is* valuable! How about that tin pot behind them? I hate to think what it was like wearing one of those on a sunny day."

"The helmet is more valuable, because it is known to have been worn by one of the *daimyos* of Ieyasu Tokugawa, who as shogun became the real ruler of Japan back in the sixteenth century. It was he who made Tokyo—Edo, it was called then—the capital of the country."

"Sure, I read a book about him," Rick said with a grin. "Me and a few million other people."

Natalie gave him a sidelong glance. "I think you have had enough history lessons for one day," she said. "Come, let's go into my office. I have a bottle of decent Beaujolais that I have been saving for a suitable moment."

She slid one of the shoji screens aside. Behind it was a small room dominated by a massive desk with sinuous, vine-like contours. The computer and fax machine looked out of place on its dully gleaming surface.

"Magnificent, isn't it?" Natalie demanded, stroking the side of the desk. "It was made for my great-grandfather, when he was with the French Legation at Peking. He gave a Chinese woodcarver a drawing of a desk by Guimard, the great master of Art Nouveau, and told him to copy it. This was the result."

"It's very unusual," Rick said. "I'm amazed that you managed to keep it in your family for so long."

Natalie looked away. Rick noticed a dull rose flush in her cheeks.

After a hesitation, she said, "In fact, we didn't. My great-grandfather left it in Peking when he returned to France. In some way—easy to imagine how—it came to Japan, to the country home of a wealthy man. One day he discovered its link to my family, and he insisted on presenting it to me."

"That was quite a gesture."

"Yes." Natalie's usually grave smile developed a quirk. "Afterward, of course, I felt the need to present him with a gift of nearly equal value, an important *tanto* or dagger, but I admit it could not have had the same sentimental worth for him as the gift he had given me."

She opened a cupboard that was no more than four inches deep and took out two glasses and a bottle of wine with a flower-decked label.

"You treat your guests well," Rick said after she had uncorked the bottle and poured him a glass.

"For guests, I keep a bottle of excellent and rare cognac," Natalie replied. "It would be an affront to offer them something as uncomplicated as a *cru Beaujolais.*"

"They don't know what they're missing. Oh, can I use your phone? I don't have a hotel room yet. This was really a spur-of-the-moment trip."

Natalie looked at him steadily. "I believe this is the moment when I say, 'Oh, but you must stay with me,' " she said. "And you say—"

Rick interrupted. "No, no, I wouldn't dream of imposing."

"Exactly. Then I say, 'You're not imposing at all.' But I detest these games. What I truly say is that it would be a great pleasure to welcome you to my home. But for the comfort you are used to, a hotel might be better."

"You're all the comfort I need," Rick replied. He meant it too, but he couldn't help thinking that he sounded like the hero in a B movie from ten or twenty years before he was born.

Natalie's house was a fifteen-minute walk from the gallery, on an island in the Sumida River. Once across the bridge, she and Rick plunged into a maze of narrow alleys lined with tile-roofed houses. Every windowsill seemed to have its pot of multicolored flowers or contorted dwarf bonsai.

"All this was built up from mud flats a few hundred years ago," Natalie explained as they made another baffling turn. "Then it was a fishing village. There are still a few fishermen left, but not for long, I fear."

She stopped at a time-scarred door and opened it. Rick followed her in, then followed her example of slipping off his shoes and putting on a pair of cloth slippers. The room just beyond the foyer was bigger than Rick had expected and furnished in Western style. A few works of Japanese art—a scroll, a fan painting—hung on the walls, but the most prominent place was given to an oil portrait of a young man with heavy-lidded eyes and a brooding expression.

"That is my father," Natalie said. "A friend painted it during their university days in France."

"I can see the resemblance," Rick replied. "Nice place you've got here. From what I've heard about Tokyo real estate, I'd say the art business must be in very healthy shape."

Natalie smiled. "You Americans are so refreshingly frank. If you were Japanese, it would have taken you at least an hour even to think of hinting at such a personal question."

"I don't mean to pry . . ." Rick started to say.

"Of course you do, *cheri*. And you are right. To buy just the land under this house would cost more than most people could earn in two lifetimes. But it is not mine. A friend of mine owns much property here in Tsukudajima, which he holds as an investment. When he judges the time is right, no doubt he will tear down all the neighborhood, put up very ugly, very chic apartment blocks, and add greatly to his fortune. For now, he allows me to live here for a rent which, by Tokyo standards, is a great bargain."

"I see," Rick said. Privately, he wondered about the terms of the deal. Wealthy men who set up beautiful young women in secluded houses usually have more than real estate in mind.

Her smile widened. "No you don't," she said in a teasing voice. "Cuichisan is a friend and an excellent client, that is all. He is much too fervently Japanese to be attracted by a foreigner, and much too busy to do anything about it, even if he were. You have no reason to be jealous."

"Who, me?" Rick said. Then, as she gave him a roguish, sidelong look, he broke down and added, "Okay, I admit that the thought crossed my mind."

"Good. Frankness is very important to me." She wandered across the room and stood with her back to Rick, next to a brass-inlaid chest. She ran her finger along the edge of the chest, then shifted one of the objects on it, a small carved Buddha, a little to the right. Rick waited to find out what was coming.

Straightening her shoulders, she turned and said, "We should think about dinner. Here in Tokyo, people eat early. How do you feel about sushi? Some of the most celebrated sushi bars are not far from here, in the fish-market district."

"Well . . ."

Natalie gave a small smile. "Never mind, I have another idea."

The restaurant they went to was a short walk away, in a rustic old building. The waitress brought them the customary small decanter of hot saki and two porcelain cups about the size of shot glasses. She set half a dozen small bowls of various-colored sauces in the center of the table, then returned with platters of deep-fried morsels on wooden skewers. Rick followed Natalie's example, dipping bits from each skewer in different sauces. It was delicious, as long as he concentrated on the tastes and kept himself from wondering exactly what he was eating.

As they were finishing, Natalie suddenly asked, "Do you have any urgent business to keep you in Tokyo?"

He gave her a quizzical look. "No. Why? Trying to get rid of me already?"

"Don't be idiotic. I have just had a wonderful idea. Tomorrow I am busy. I have an appointment with a client who may be interested in that helmet you saw. But afterward, what do you think of two or three days at a *ryokan,* an old-style inn, on the Izu Peninsula? It is not far, less than a hundred kilometers, near the foot of Mount Fuji. We can go there very quickly by bullet train. There are hills and woods and some of the most beautiful hot springs in Japan."

"It sounds terrific," Rick said.

"Yes. Many newlyweds go there." She looked down at the table, and her cheeks slowly turned pink.

Rick shrugged, to get rid of the sudden tension in his shoulders, and said, "Maybe we ought to go back to your place now. It's getting late."

Natalie's sleeping room, on the second floor of the house, was in traditional Japanese style. The floor was covered with straw tatami mats, and the only furniture was a low black-lacquer table against one wall. From behind a shoji screen, Natalie took out a futon mattress and a heavy quilt. Rick helped her arrange them on the floor.

Natalie left the room. While she was gone, Rick took off his shirt but left his pants on. When she returned, she was wearing a thin cotton kimono.

"It is so fascinating to encounter another culture," she said, kneeling on the futon. She was close enough for Rick to smell a dusky scent she must have just applied. "In Japan, for hundreds of year, the inhabitants of the Floating World spent every moment studying the sources of human pleasure and the ways of magnifying it. We French think we understand *l'amour,* but next to them we are only naive children."

Naive child or not, Rick decided that it was time for him to take a more active part. He reached for the sash of her kimono and untied the elaborate knot. The kimono fell open. Natalie was not wearing anything underneath. He stretched out his hands, but she gently pushed him away.

"One thing I have learned from reading about the Floating World is that patience and care are repaid many times over," she continued. She put her hands on his shoulders, then ran them lightly down over his chest to his waistband. "Do you think you can be patient with me?"

Her fingertips were touching and stroking him in the most intimate way possible. He swallowed, then cleared his throat. "I'll do anything you want," he said hoarsely, trying to catch his breath. "Try me."

CHAPTER 22

NATALIE POURED TWO STEAMING CUPS OF COFFEE AND passed one across the small table to Rick. "Will you be able to entertain yourself today while I am with my client?" she asked.

Rick took a piece of toast and buttered it. "Don't worry about me," he said. "I'll just wander around and take in a few of the sights. Hey, you don't happen to know where the Japanese Imperial Navy archives are, do you?"

"For records from the war years, you mean?" Natalie frowned. "I have no idea. That is not a time that people discuss very freely. Much of Tokyo was destroyed by your firebomb raids, you know."

Rick felt his jaw tighten. "That's a damned shame," he said. "But I don't imagine they talk much about the rape of Nanking either, do they? The Japanese Army made a sport of tossing Chinese babies in the air and catching them on their bayonets."

"These are old but painful wounds that are better not reopened," Natalie said quickly. "As for the records, I have no idea, but if you like, I can try to find out where they are stored. Is there something in particular that you need?"

"Nope. Idle curiosity, that's all. Never mind. It just occurred to me: The naval attaché at the U.S. embassy can probably tell me what I need to know. I'll give him a call later. He should be at his desk by ten or so."

After breakfast, Natalie left for the gallery. Rick walked her as far as the end of the bridge across the Sumida, then took a side street to the left that led to Tsukiji, home of Tokyo's central fish market. Natalie had told him that the main action took place between five and six A.M., when the day's catch was auctioned off. Maybe so, but at eight-thirty the place was still bustling. On the street outside the fish-mongers' shops, retailers and restaurant owners haggled for what they needed, while wheelbarrows of iced fish, crates of crabs, and whole frozen tuna were trundled back and forth. Just as Rick was getting into the spirit of the scene, a store owner hosed down the sidewalk as he was passing, thoroughly soaking his socks. The store owner apologized profusely, but that wasn't much consolation to Rick as he squished on his way.

Part of his mind was taking in the exotic details of a foreign city, but most of it was still back with Natalie. Her lovemaking the night before had taken him to places and given him pleasures he had never even heard of. So why wasn't he swaggering and grinning like a sailor on leave who'd just had his ashes hauled? Was it simply some Puritan ghost, whispering that anything that felt so good couldn't possibly be right, and that anyone who knew how to make him feel so good had to be wicked?

Or was it more specific than that? Maybe the ghost wore the face of Dr. Samantha Deane. Not that Sam was a Puritan; their times together had given him plenty of proof of that. Still, he couldn't fool himself into believing that Sam would approve of his relationship with Natalie. Understand it, sure. She would probably pass it off lightly, under the heading of wild oats. But it would hurt her, and it would make her think less of him. It might even bring their romance crashing down. He didn't want that. But he didn't want to pass up this breathtaking time with Natalie either, even if the relationship didn't have much future.

Hell, why kid himself? Part of the attraction was that the relationship *didn't* have much future! So what? Natalie had made it as clear as possible that she was attracted to him, that she thought he was a fantastic lover, and that she could hardly wait to get back into bed with him. What more did he want? The Mormon Tabernacle Choir in the background, singing "O Promise Me"?

Rick stopped at a corner and shook his head. Maybe what all these questions and doubts came down to, after all, was that he couldn't believe his own dumb luck. Believe it, or trust that it would last. Maybe it wouldn't. Maybe, like all luck, it was bound to change on him. But until it did, he should stop worrying and try to enjoy it to the fullest. A good resolution, even if New Year's was long past.

His stroll gradually took him out of the fish-market district and into the southern fringes of the Ginza. Should he drop by Natalie's gallery, just to say hello? His pulse speeded up a little at the thought of seeing her, but he told himself that crowding her would be a very bad move. She had an important business deal to think about, and he would be a distraction at best. She might even feel that he was spying on her, like a jealous husband.

A pay telephone up ahead reminded him that he had a call to make. He located the number of the U.S. embassy and asked for the naval attaché.

"Lieutenant Commander Charles Burris," a voice said.

Rick grinned in surprise. Charles Burris was a former classmate at Annapolis and a one-time rival for the title of King of Demerits.

"Charlie, you old horse," he exclaimed. "It's Rick Tallman. I didn't know you'd let BuPers turn you into a cookie-pusher!"

"It's a tough job, but somebody's got to do it," Burris replied. "How they hanging, Rick? Didn't I hear that you were up to no good down Guam way?"

"You hear good. I'll tell you about it someday, over a beer or two. Listen, Charlie, I need some help. Do you have any idea where I could find records from the Japanese Navy during WW Two? It's nothing official, just idle curiosity."

"Hmmm ... that's a toughie. Whatever made it through the firebombings got scattered all over the map when the war ended. I'd say your best bet is the library at the National Institute of Defenses Studies. You have a pen? Take the Yamanote Line—that's the Japan rail loop that links all the major transit hubs—to Meguru, then ask for directions. When you find it, ask for a guy named Inagaki. You have business cards on you, don't you?"

"Sure."

"Good. Around here people think you must be an imposter if you don't have a card. Anyway, Inagaki should be able to help you, if anyone can. About that beer: Are you booked for tonight?"

Rick explained that he would be out of town and made a date for Sunday. After a quick exchange of news about mutual friends and acquaintances, he hung up, checked his map, and started walking toward the nearest station on the Yamanote Line.

At the Institute, Rick introduced himself to Inagaki, mentioning Charlie's name, and explained what he wanted.

Inagaki, a man of about forty, listened impassively. "The records of a JIN submarine, unit number not known, that was sunk off Guam in July 1945," he repeated. "Difficult, very difficult. The files here are very far from complete and not always in very good order, Commander. In any case, the log for the vessel's last voyage would still be on board, no? But let us see what we can do."

After two hours of digging through dusty files, Rick had had enough. "This is hopeless," he told Inagaki. "I have no right to impose on your time like this, just to satisfy my curiosity."

"No, no," the archivist replied. "We have learned a great deal. Of the I-class submarines still operating in June of that year, the fate of all but four is known. And of those four, one was dispatched to patrol off Indochina. It is difficult to imagine how it could have come to be near Guam. But how to choose among the three that remain ..."

Rick slapped his forehead. "What an idiot I am!" he exclaimed. "One of the officers on the boat I want was a young ensign named Takauji, who survived the sinking. Won't the crew rosters or personnel files tell us which boat he was on?"

"Of course," Inagaki said, with a gleam of excitement in his eye. "Come!"

They returned to the storage room. Over the next hour, Inagaki's excitement slowly evaporated, to be replaced by puzzlement.

"No one with the surname Takauji served on either the I-49 or the I-57 during 1945," he said finally. "Logic says that the boat you are seeking must be the I-53. But proof is another matter. I can find no records of the I-53's activities and no file for an Ensign Takauji who served on submarines. I apologize."

"No, I apologize," Rick replied. "I've taken up your whole morning with a wild-goose chase." Noticing Inagaki's blank look, Rick added, "That's an expression that means a pointless task. Anyway, thank you for your help. I appreciate it very much."

"Thank *you*, Commander Tallman," the archivist replied. "You have given me an interesting puzzle to consider in my idle moments. From what you tell me, we may now know what became of the I-53, but what became of all her records?"

The ride on the bullet train from Tokyo to a town called Mishima seemed to take no time at all, though Natalie insisted in a whisper that the very high-speed trains of France were much faster and more comfortable. At Mishima, they had to change to a local train that ran through the hilly center of the Izu Peninsula, stopping every five miles or so for no obvious reason. Now and then, through the trees, they caught a glimpse of the lower slopes of Mount Fuji, only a couple of dozen miles away. The top of the mountain was hidden in clouds.

A taxi ride from the end of the line brought them to a low two-story wooden inn, surrounded by evergreens. Behind it rose a sheer cliff, some fifty feet high, with a single twisted cypress at the rim, silhouetted against the late-afternoon sky.

From beyond a hedge of carefully shaped bushes came the purring of a mountain stream.

"This place looks great," Rick said as the taxi drove away. "I think we'll have a wonderful time."

"Oh, we will," Natalie assured him. "The *rotemburo,* or outdoor bath, is built around a natural hot spring. Many visitors come only for that. Others come for the cuisine, which features local wild pheasant and wild boar."

"Somehow I knew that food would come into it somewhere," Rick teased.

Natalie gave him a roguish look. "The pleasures of the table are among the greatest pleasures of life. There are others, of course."

"Of course." Rick picked up their bags. "Let's go check out our room, then hit the baths. Train trips always leave me feeling grimy."

At the entrance, they paused to take off their shoes and put on the waiting slippers. A maid in the traditional kimono bowed and led them along a covered walkway open on one side to a rock garden. She stopped at one of the shoji on the other side and slid it open. Natalie took off her slippers and entered the room barefoot, so Rick did the same. As he expected, the floor was covered with thick, soft, spotless tatami. On the far side of the room, a floor-length window looked out onto the river gorge and the cliffs on the other side.

The maid returned with two eggshell-porcelain cups and a dark iron teapot on a tray. She placed it just inside the door, then slid the shoji closed.

"Green tea," Natalie said. "To revive our vital forces."

Rick grinned. "I haven't noticed that our vital forces needed much help," he said, pulling her into his arms.

As they kissed, he felt his passion rising and hers growing to meet it. He pressed her against him, tighter and tighter still, as if by sheer pressure he could break through the barriers between them.

Suddenly she pulled her head back and gasped, "No, wait!"

He growled in his chest and leaned forward, trying to

recapture her lips, but she turned her face aside. "Later, *chéri*," she said. "Later. After our bath."

Rick took a deep breath and straightened up, opening his arms. He cleared his throat and asked, "How soon can we bathe?"

"After tea," she replied. "Are you so impatient?"

"You know I am."

Natalie carried the tray to a low table near the window and sank gracefully to the floor. Rick joined her. She filled one of the delicate cups and offered it to him in both hands, then poured for herself. As he sipped the delicate, astringent brew, he found his mood calming. What difference did it make whether he made love to Natalie now or two hours from now? The waiting would only enhance the pleasure.

"Rick?"

He blinked and realized that he had been gazing out at the river while his mind drifted off. For how long? The cup in his palm was barely warm. He raised it to his lips, but the tea had taken on a bitter overtone. He set it on the tray and gave Natalie a questioning look.

"It is time for the baths," she said. She handed him a folded kimono of blue cotton with a white pattern of stylized cranes and picked up another that looked like its twin. "After we wash off, we wear these *yukata* to go to the hot springs. The maid will bring our city clothes back to the room," she explained.

The indoor baths for men and women were next to each other. The men's side was empty. Rick sat on a low stool to lather and rinse. Then he put on the blue kimono and tied it at the waist. Just outside the door, he found a pair of fresh *zoris* and slipped his feet into them, then turned as Natalie came out.

The kimono clung to her curves and parted at the neck just enough to offer tantalizing glimpses of what lay within. "The *rotemburo* is this way," she said, with a gesture that widened the gap at the front of the kimono for a few seconds. When she met Rick's eyes, her expression said that she knew he had noticed.

Time-worn stone steps led down the hill. On either side,

the ground was covered with emerald-green moss that looked like the softest bed in the world. At the foot of the slope, next to the riverbank, was a steaming pool lined with large rocks and encircled by vine-draped trees. It looked much more natural than anything nature could have produced. At the far end, three adults, a man and two women, were soaking, submerged to the neck. On the bank near them, dangling their legs in the water, were a boy and girl of about ten. Both were totally nude. They looked up curiously as Rick and Natalie approached.

"Er," Rick said under his breath, "no swimsuits?"

"This is a bath, not a swimming pool," Natalie replied, laughing at him. "It is a grave breach of etiquette to wear anything into a *rotemburo.*"

"Got it. Well, okay. I'm game if you are."

At the edge of the pool, Natalie bowed to the others and slipped out of her robe. She neatly folded it and set it on a rock, then put one toe in the water. The face she made drew a friendly laugh from the rest.

Rick's turn. He turned his back while he took off and folded the kimono, but he couldn't very well back into the pool just to hide his privates. As he turned, he was very aware of their curious glances, quickly averted, but the serene and impersonal spirit of the moment made all that seem unimportant.

He joined Natalie at the edge of the pool. Kneeling, he bent down and dipped out a handful of water, which he rubbed on the back of his neck. The trick usually worked with cold water, so why not with hot? The spring water was hot, all right, and it smelled like a diluted mixture of old eggs and horse liniment. The palm of his hand puckered up as if he had coated it with styptic pencil.

"Is this stuff really supposed to be good for us?" he asked Natalie, who was now in to above her knees.

"Oh, yes. This hot spring has been celebrated for hundreds of years. It is said that the waters are particularly healthful for the skin."

Rick recalled his mother's tales about her stay at a world-renowned beauty spa. "We don't have to cover ourselves with mud or wrap up in sheets afterward, do we?" he demanded.

"Nothing of the sort, silly. Afterward we return to our room. And after that, we have a wonderful dinner before a blazing fire. And after that—"

"Let's leave some things unplanned," Rick said, breaking in. He lowered his legs into the water and was surprised to feel them immediately start to relax. Maybe there was something to this mineral hot springs business after all.

Soon Natalie was in all the way up to her neck. Rick was sorry to see her breasts disappear beneath the waterline. There was something very special about seeing human beauty unadorned, in an outdoor setting so full of carefully planned natural beauty.

As Rick lowered himself gingerly into the water, there was a burst of high-pitched laughter from the other end of the pool. He thought the kids must be laughing at his reluctance, but when he looked, he saw that the girl was flicking droplets of water at the boy. He seemed to be wondering if he could get away with dunking her. Neither of them looked particularly conscious of the fact that they were both bare-ass naked. The first time Rick had skinny-dipped, at about the age of the two Japanese kids, he had suffered from excruciating shyness, and that had been only with other boys!

Natalie was at the far end now, chatting with the three Japanese adults. A wave of feeling isolated, of being eternally a stranger, washed over Rick. Was that something left over from being a Navy brat who had attended half a dozen schools, in widely separated parts of the world, before sixth grade? Or was it more simply that he was in a strange land whose language and customs were still mysteries to him?

"Rick?" Natalie called, beckoning to him. "Mr. Iida teaches English and once lived in New York. Isn't that wonderful?"

Terrific, thought Rick as he waded over to join them. I get to hear all about his visit to the Statue of Riberty. But to his surprise, the Japanese spoke excellent English, with less accent than some guys Rick had served with who were native Americans. His observations about New York, and the contrasts between that city and Tokyo, were both funny and pointed, and the point wasn't always aimed at the Big Apple.

When Rick made a remark about trade, he said, "To understand what our government's trade policy means to us, you must go to New York, to 47th Street Photo, and see the Japanese tourists lined up to buy Nikon cameras and Sony disc players. I know this very well," he added, with an infectious laugh. "I was one of them!"

Rick was sorry when one of the women, who had been listening silently to the conversation, said something in Japanese that obviously meant it was time to go. The three, with the two kids, climbed out of the pool, toweled off, and put on their robes. A bow to Rick and Natalie, and they started up the steps to the inn.

"Nice people," Rick remarked.

"Yes. To be friendly and relaxed with other guests is part of the spirit of a *ryokan*. The result is that only those who are ready to be that way come to such a place."

Rick found a convenient underwater ledge on one side of the pool and sat down with just his head and shoulders above the surface. As he leaned back against the water-smoothed stones, he heard, as if from a great distance, the murmur of the river behind him. The water in the pool did not seem so unpleasantly hot or smelly now; in fact, it was having the same effect as spending a summer afternoon in a tree-shaded hammock, watching the branches sway with the breeze.

"Rick?" Natalie said, touching his arm. "I am going now, to take care of my hair."

"Mmmm? Oh, okay. I'll stay a little longer."

"Not too long. The evening meal is in an hour, and it is a very special part of staying here."

He watched appreciatively as she stood on the bank and dried off. Aware of his attention, she turned and moved in subtle ways that showed off her long sleek thighs and high firm breasts. When, finally, she wrapped her kimono around her, Rick felt a mad impulse to leap out of the hot spring, tear off her kimono, and carry her to the bed of soft green moss beyond the screen of trees.

"Don't be long," she repeated, in a voice full of invitation. Then she turned and started up the steps. Rick was inclined to follow at once, but the hot, mineral-laden water was leaching the resolution from his flesh. He leaned back again, closed his eyes, and listened to the music of the rippling water and rustling bushes.

Rustling bushes?

He sat up and looked around just as two men stepped through the hedge. Both had short-cut hair and wore dark trousers, dark zip-up jackets, and dark sunglasses. One held a Filipino balisong loosely by his side. With three graceful motions, he flipped the hinged halves of the hilt to expose the blade. The other was uncoiling a length of wire with wooden handles at each end. Both looked as if they could use a bath, but Rick had a hunch that wasn't the reason they had come to the spring.

Rick's first impulse was to move to the center of the pool, out of reach, and shout for help. Then he imagined Natalie running down the steps to rescue him and falling into the grip of the assassins. He couldn't allow that. No calls for help then. He was going to have to settle this bout on his own.

The two hoods were in no hurry. They approached the far edge of the pool and paused, staring wordlessly from behind their designer shades. Maybe they expected him to save them some trouble by passing out from fear and drowning himself. Instead, he put his palms on the bank behind him and pushed himself up out of the water to the edge of the pool, never taking his eyes from the two. For a moment, it bothered him to be facing armed men while he was both unarmed and unclothed. Then he reflected that Achilles had fought naked at the siege of Troy, and that his own ancestors, on the Scottish side of the family, had terrified the straitlaced English by charging into battle with nothing but their two-handed *claidh mor* and a thin coat of blue body paint.

As he expected, the two men separated and began to circle the pool toward him from opposite directions. Rick's expression and body language told them that he was indecisive and afraid. Inwardly, however, he let his mind see *saika*, the mental state that prepares for action by setting aside all distraction.

The knife wielder, on his left, was the greater danger. A garroting wire only works once it is fixed around the neck, but wherever a knife goes, it hurts. Rick looked from side to side at his approaching attackers with every sign of growing panic. Their steps slowed, then stopped. There was no rush. They knew he couldn't escape them.

The tiny ball of *ki*, or spiritual energy, in Rick's middle, just behind his navel, was whirling faster, building toward critical mass. As its strength spread through him, he made a feint as if to try to run to the right, past the strangler. That pulled the knife wielder forward, out of position and off-balance. Rick whirled around and sprang at him. The surprised hood raised his knife in both hands, aiming it at Rick's chest. Rick dodged left, put both palms on the ground, and launched a powerful roundhouse kick to the kishkes. His attacker staggered backward and fell. His head cracked against one of the stones bordering the pool, and his body rolled sideways into the water.

Rick had no leisure to see what became of him. He tucked and rolled forward, farther from the garroting wire, then did a half turn as he surged to his feet. The would-be strangler didn't look quite so confident now, but he was still pressing forward, the thin, deadly wire extended loosely between his outstretched and crossed hands.

Rick made the mistake of watching the hands and the wire too closely. His attacker's jumping side-kick took him by surprise. He recoiled, but not quickly enough to avoid a hard blow to the temple. The world darkened for a moment, but his defensive reflexes, honed by countless hours of training and practice in unarmed combat, saved him. When the man in black aimed a *nukite*, or piercing hand blow, at the throat, Rick ducked it and bored in, landing a forceful elbow strike to the solar plexus. That might have ended the battle, but his opponent managed a glancing handsword blow to Rick's bare and dangling balls.

Rick gasped and staggered backward, clasping his hands around his outraged family jewels. Through a red haze, he saw the man in black gliding after him, the garrote once more at the ready. Rick raised his arms to fend him off, but he sensed his strength draining out of him. He gathered himself for a desperate dive into the hot spring.

An angry shout. Rick looked around. Two men in blue kimonos were running down the steps from the inn, pushing their sleeves up to their shoulders as they came. The fluid way they moved spoke of many afternoons at a *dojo,* practicing the martial arts. Rick's attacker obviously reached the same conclusion. After a final menacing glance at Rick, he turned and fled through the bushes.

"The cavalry has arrived," one of the two said. "Are you injured?"

Rick recognized Mr. Iida, the English teacher he had been talking to earlier.

"No, I'm okay," he said. "But we'd better call the cops and a doctor too. There were two of those guys, and I think one of them's still at the bottom of the pool."

Lieutenant Akiyoshi spoke reasonably good English, but even so he conducted his interview with Rick through an interpreter. With extreme politeness and the directed incisiveness of a surgeon's scalpel, he went over the afternoon, the reasons for Rick's presence in Japan, his relationship with Natalie, and every detail in between, time and again.

Finally he said, not through the interpreter, "You have never seen these men before they attack you."

"That's right," Rick said, for the *n*th time.

"You say they are wearing sunglasses, and everything is happening very fast. Maybe you don't get so good a look?"

"Possibly," Rick admitted. "But they didn't look familiar."

"Please come with me." The police lieutenant took Rick to the back of the inn, where an ambulance was waiting.

Next to it, on the ground, was a blanket-covered stretcher. Akiyoshi took a corner of the blanket and pulled it back.

The drowned man's eyes were still open, staring blindly at the sky. From the corner of his mouth, a narrow trickle of water led past his ear and around his neck to make a dark splotch on the stretcher.

"Never saw him before," Rick said. "Sorry."

Silently, Akiyoshi unzipped the dead man's jacket and pulled it open. Rick gasped. Every inch of the man's bare chest and stomach was covered with finely detailed tattoos.

"Yakuza," Lieutenant Akiyoshi said. "You know what that is?"

"The Japanese Mafia," Rick replied. "I've read about them."

Akiyoshi lifted the corpse's left hand. The last joint of the little finger was gone. "This is proof," he said. "Why do yakuza attack you? I do not know. Maybe there is more you do not tell. But if you take my advice, sir, you will leave Japan at the soonest moment. You are in very big danger. You have killed a yakuza. His *kumi*, or clan, must take terrible revenge or lose face. Without face, they lose power. And without power, they are nothing, garbage."

"I understand," Rick said. "Thanks, Lieutenant. I'll take your advice very seriously."

When Rick returned to his room, Natalie threw herself into his arms. Her body was trembling. "This is all my fault," she said. "I am so frightened!"

Rick tightened his arms around her. "Your fault? Why?"

"Recently a man bought something from me, an important sword. Afterward he claimed that it was fake. I told him that I stood by my guarantee, that I would return his money, but he claimed that by selling him a fake sword I had damaged his standing far beyond anything money could repair. I didn't know when I dealt with him that he is important in the yakuza. If I had known, perhaps I would not have sold him the sword, but that too might have deeply offended him."

"You think he had his thugs attack me to get at you?"

"Exactly. They meant to injure or kill you, only to express this man's displeasure with me."

"Did you tell Lieutenant Akiyoshi about this?"

"No. What proof do I have? And if word got back to this ... person that I had named him to the police, he would never rest until he took revenge."

"You're in a dangerous business," Rick said. "First Honolulu, and now this. By the way, I didn't say anything to the lieutenant, but that thug who drowned *did* look familiar to me. I think he might have been one of the guys who attacked you in Honolulu."

Natalie stared at him. "No, that isn't possible," she said, her voice rising in pitch.

"Why not?" Rick asked. "If this gang boss is so mad at you, maybe he sent that bunch to Honolulu too. It makes sense."

"No, it doesn't," she insisted. There was an edge of hysteria to her tone. "It makes no sense at all! There is too much here I do not understand. Rick, I'm frightened! I don't want to stay here. Let's go away, tonight, right now!"

"Go where? Back to your house in Tokyo? You're safer here."

"I don't think I am safe anywhere in Japan," she replied. "Yakuza are everywhere. We'll go straight to Narita and take the first plane to Guam. Please, Rick, you must!"

Rick went on trying to calm her down and reason with her, but it was no use. Finally he agreed. With the help of the innkeeper, he found out that they could catch a bullet train to Tokyo from Atami, change to the Narita Express, and get to the airport in time for the last flight to Guam.

He was leaving the office when he remembered his date to meet Charlie Burris. He called him up and explained that he had to return unexpectedly to Guam.

"Too bad," Charlie said. "Next visit, okay? Oh, by the way, did you manage to get to the Institute archives today?"

"Yes, I did. Your Mr. Inagaki was very helpful, but we didn't manage to turn up much. Next time you're in touch with him, be sure to repeat how grateful I am."

"I can't do that, Rick," Charlie replied. "I just heard it myself a little while ago. Inagaki fell in front of a subway train this afternoon. I'm afraid he's dead."

CHAPTER 23

KEN KIRBY'S HOTEL ROOM OVERLOOKING TUMON BAY was starting to look a lot like his office back in Washington. The dresser and two borrowed card tables were piled with newspapers, magazines, and typed reports. He had done so much for the cash flow of his chosen newsstand in Agana that the owner was thinking of buying out his biggest competitor and becoming a chain.

Ken returned from the library of the University of Guam at a few minutes after three. He dumped several folders of photocopies on the spare bed and went to the bathroom to pour himself a glass of water. Sitting down at the writing table, he powered up his notebook computer and told it to dial the local access number for ARPANET, the worldwide computer network run by the Defense Department. When the log-on screen appeared, he entered his account number and password. A boxed, blinking message at the bottom of the screen told him that he had something waiting in his mailbox.

Using the trackball built into the keyboard, he moved the cursor to the mailbox and clicked for the table of contents, then groaned when it came on the screen. The file was huge, almost 500K, the equivalent of some two hundred single-spaced pages. It was his own fault. He had asked Joyce, by

E-mail, to round up whatever she could about the half dozen key people in the SeaVenture project, but he hadn't expected so big a response so soon. Joyce had been busy.

How long would it take to download the file, at 2400 baud, the fastest rate his pocket modem could handle? Half an hour or more, probably, with error-checking. Still, no point in putting it off. Whistling a bit of the Overture from "The Barber of Seville," he clicked on Receive File, then moved the trackball until the cursor pointed to the file name and clicked again to begin the transmission. A little box appeared in the upper right corner of the screen, with rapidly growing numbers that told how many bytes had been received so far. He found that comforting. It was so unnerving to start some program, then be forced to stare for minutes on end at an unchanging screen, with no way of knowing whether anything at all was happening inside the confounded machine.

He picked up one of the decks of index cards on the dresser and carried it with him to the balcony. Once Joyce's file was downloaded, it would take another ten or fifteen minutes for the encryption-decryption program to put the file *en clair,* even with the 80387 math co-processor he had on board. Still, it sure beat one-time pads or book codes, where decrypting a single page might take a whole morning.

The afternoon sun soon made the west-facing balcony unpleasantly warm. He went back inside and checked the byte-ometer on the screen. Up to 350K and climbing fast. As he waited, he considered a puzzle that was becoming increasingly perplexing. Why was he on Guam at all? This wasn't part of his job description. He was an intelligence analyst, someone with a peculiar talent for inferring patterns and trends on the basis of ridiculously inadequate evidence. His place, logically, was back in his office, sniffing at all the bits of information that flowed past him. Yet here he was, acting like a field agent, questioning informants, making site visits, looking enigmatic, and—face it—throwing his weight around. And loving every minute of it.

That was the key, of course. He was bored with taking in facts on paper, digesting them, and shitting them out onto other pieces of paper. Important work, sure, but ultimately dull. He wanted to be more than a backroom player in what Kipling had called the Great Game, to savor life in all its complexity. More prosaically, he was suffering from either unfinished wild oat sowing or a premature midlife crisis.

Now that he had a diagnosis, his obvious cure would be to follow the investigation to the end, after which he would realize that life in the field was really no more exciting than life behind a desk.

The computer gave a faint bleat. He checked the screen and saw a "Transfer Completed" message. After saving the still-encrypted file to disk, just in case something crashed, he called up the decryption program and set it to work, then lay down with his hand clasped behind his head and stared at the ceiling. He often got his best ideas that way.

Another bleat. He opened his eyes, yawned, and swung his legs over the edge of the bed. Time to get down to work.

He planned to read every word of the file at least once, preferably twice, before bedtime. But first the high points, if any. He saved and backed up the file, then started a key word search for "Ocean Friends." *Nada*. He tried "Nishimura," with the same result. Without much hope, he asked the machine to search for "Bell." He soon learned that at Princeton, Richard Tallman had been part of a group of freshmen who scaled the cupola of historic Nassau Hall and stole the clapper of the bell. Apparently this was a freshman tradition. A few moments later, he was delighted to find out that one of the officers on the *Glomar Champion* belonged to an organization devoted to playing Mozart on handbells.

Another match. Ken barely glanced at the screen, sure that it would be just as irrelevant as the others. Then his gaze sharpened. His hand groped blindly for a pen and a blank index card. *Come, Watson,* he thought. *The game's afoot!*

"You're beautiful," Dave said, propping himself up on one elbow. "You're the most beautiful thing I've ever seen."

Eloise snuggled next to him and playfully tugged at his ear. "Aw," she said. "I bet you say that to all the girls."

He reached down, very tentatively, to stroke her head. She looked at him and wrinkled her nose.

"No, I mean it," he insisted as he tucked a stray lock of hair behind her ear. "I still can't believe you're here with me like this. I started having dreams about you the first day we met, but it took so long to get up the nerve to say anything. Would you believe that I thought you and Ray—"

"Ray and me, we go back a long way," Eloise said. "He got me my first job, and a couple of years ago I was in a position to return the favor. But we were never close that way. Not the way you and I are."

She pulled his head down and kissed him passionately. Dave lost himself in the kiss and the caresses that accompanied it. He was about to roll over onto her again when she pulled back. "Hoo boy!" she panted. "You're way ahead of me this time. Let's take it a little easier, okay?"

"I'm sorry," he said, releasing his grip. "I can't help it. You're the only good thing that's happened to me in a long time. Ever since I got involved in this damned project, as a matter of fact."

"Come on now, honey. I know you've had some bad luck."

"Bad luck!" he said bitterly. "That's not the word for it. Have you ever had the feeling that somebody's out to get you? That they want to destroy everything you ever worked for?"

Eloise sat up in bed. The sheet fell away, but she paid no attention to it. "Dave, it's not good for you to think that way. You know it's not."

"Even when it's true?"

"But it's not," she replied. "Okay, the project's been delayed by some bugs in your gadget. It's been delayed by other things, too: bad weather, troubles with the airlift hose, bureaucratic fuckups, you name it. It's a complicated project, and complicated projects get delayed, that's all. You can't take it personally."

"The hell I can't! Listen, Eloise, there are *no bugs* in Rover. I know that! Rover is one of the most advanced and most reliable unmanned deep-ocean submersibles ever built. If she's acting crazy, it's because somebody sabotaged her."

"You've checked everything, more than once," Eloise pointed out. "You've practically taken that thing down to tiny pieces and put it back together again. Did you find anything?"

Dave sat up and reached over to pull her to him. He ran his fingers up and down her arm almost absentmindedly. "No." He sighed. "I didn't. But I was looking in the wrong place, and I was looking for something obvious. Do you know where the word 'sabotage' comes from? From the French word for a wooden shoe. A couple of hundred years ago, when the guys who worked in a factory got pissed off enough about the way they were treated, somebody would toss a wooden shoe into the gears and everything came to a halt. Pretty obvious. What they've done to Rover is different. Subtle. Maybe even indetectible, except by its effects."

"What are you talking about?" Eloise demanded. "You make it sound like somebody cast a spell on Rover!"

"Close," he replied as he lay back down and stared at the ceiling. "I hate to admit it, but I think Tallman and Ward came close to hitting the nail on the head. They may be too gung-ho straight arrow for my taste, but they're both bright, and Ward knows undersea technology from the word go. I'm surprised I didn't think of it, but I'm glad somebody did."

"Thought of *what*, for heaven's sake!"

"A depth-sensitive computer virus," Dave said. "You remember that Pan Am plane that blew up over Scotland a few years ago? It turned out there was a bomb on board with a trigger that was sensitive to altitude. The scumbags who made it wanted to be sure the plane didn't blow up on the ground, where somebody might have had a chance to survive. It's the same principle here. The on-board computer in Rover constantly monitors depth and transmits it to the surface. This virus must be written to kick in only when depth exceeds twenty-five hundred feet or so. We can test the programs until we turn blue, but if the depth reading isn't big enough, the virus stays safely hidden."

"That's just plain mean!" Eloise exclaimed. "Who'd do a thing like that?"

"Anybody who hates my guts, for a start," Dave said. "And I know I'm not the most popular guy around. I don't mean to, but I always end up rubbing people the wrong way."

"There's nothing wrong with the way you rub me," Eloise said. She rested her head on his chest and put her arm around his waist.

"Same here," Dave said, stroking her side. "But I've got a better question than who'd do such a thing. Who'd be able to? This isn't the work of some high-school hacker. I know enough about computers to do a pretty solid job of high-level programming, and I wouldn't even know where to start, creating a virus like the one we seem to be dealing with. But I think I'm getting an idea for how to trap it. Sure! That ought to—"

Eloise reached up and put three fingers across his lips. "Hush, sweetie," she said. "We've got better things to think about right now. You can go virus hunting tomorrow morning."

Later, Eloise and Dave drove down the coast to Umatac, where Dave had discovered a quaint cafe overlooking the town's famous black sand beach. The food was just so-so, but the view of the sunset across the bay was spectacular. On the drive back, Eloise sat close to Dave, with her head on his shoulder. She felt as if she were back in high school, on her way home after a beach party in Galveston.

As he turned into the hotel parking lot, he said, in a diffident voice, "Come back to my room?"

"I'm sorry, honey," Eloise replied. "I'm way behind in analyzing the magnetometer data. And I've got a couple of ideas I want to check out about that mud seamount you and Rick discovered. Once you get Rover fixed, everything's going to start happening fourteen to the dozen around here. I can't afford to be caught napping."

They said goodnight in the lobby. Dave clung to her in a way that was flattering and disturbing at the same time. Fi-

nally she tugged loose and went to her room. The red message light on her phone was blinking. She picked up the
receiver and pressed the pound sign.

"Eloise, this is Ken Kirby calling, at five-thirty P.M. Please
call me at my hotel as soon as you return. It's very
important."

Eloise frowned. What did Kirby want with her? They'd
already had two long talks, in which he asked her practically
everything except the name of her childhood orthodontist.

Well, only one way to find out. She punched his number.

"I need to talk to you," he said when she identified herself. "Some questions have come up."

"Fine, how about over breakfast?"

"I'm sorry, it can't wait. Please stay in your room. I'll be
right over."

Eloise hung up slowly and walked out onto the balcony.
The ocean was calm tonight. She wished she could say the
same for herself.

Pete Colon hummed to himself as he wheeled the serving
cart onto the terrace. Sunrise was his favorite time of day.
The air was cool and fresh, and the hotel guests were still
in their rooms asleep. Leaving the cart next to the pool, he
turned all the chairs right side up and sponged off the table-
tops, then took the stack of freshly ironed pink tablecloths
from the cart and began spreading them. The place settings
came next, followed by the fun part: fan-folding the pink
napkins and inserting one in each tall juice glass.

When all the tables were set, Pete stepped back and
looked over the scene. Too bad there wasn't a photographer
there from a big travel magazine, to snap a picture of him
standing by one of the tables in his white jacket, holding a
bowl of fresh fruit.

He wheeled the cart back into the kitchen and got a
broom from the utility room. The manager was a stickler
about having the walks swept every morning, though Pete
had never found anything on them but a dusting of sand
and a few flower petals. Still, the sooner he was done with

the walks, the sooner he could get the coffee urn going and sit down to his first breakfast of the day.

As he rounded the corner of the thatched-hut service bar, he muttered a curse. Some asshole had just about destroyed one of the bougainvillea plants. The walk was littered with blossoms and broken-off branches. Pete started to turn back, to get a gunny sack to put the rubbish in, but something caught his eye. On the ground under the bougainvillea was a large, dark bundle. It looked as if one of the guests had tossed a full laundry bag off his balcony.

Pete walked closer and squatted down to get a better view.

"Oh my God," he murmured, crossing himself. "Oh my God!"

For a moment, he stared up at the rows of empty balconies above him. Then he jumped to his feet and ran to wake the manager.

CHAPTER 24

Rick and Natalie's flight from Narita left over an hour late because of runway congestion. Arriving on Guam, they found that the airport taxi rank was empty. Another half-hour wait until a cab arrived. They used the time to reserve a room for Natalie at the hotel where she always stayed. Rick felt too exhausted to be overly gallant. He dropped Natalie at her hotel and went on to his. The front desk was unmanned, so he reached over the counter for his room key, went upstairs, and fell asleep within minutes.

He awoke at first light the next morning and lay in bed with his eyes closed, replaying his memories of the past two days. From the garden beneath his window came a sound like a crowd of people tiptoeing around and whispering to each other. He listened for a moment and decided it must be the wind agitating the bushes. Not his concern, anyway. He let himself drift back to sleep.

At seven-thirty he rolled out of bed, showered and shaved, and pulled on shorts and a sleeveless T-shirt. Downstairs, the terrace by the pool was set for breakfast, but no one was eating. Ray, Dave, and Will were standing near each other but not talking. A few feet away, Ken Kirby was sitting at a table, thumbing through some index cards.

Will was the first to notice Rick. "I thought you were in Tokyo," he said in a voice that, for him, was subdued.

"I was. Things got a little hairy there, so I came back."

"Things are pretty hairy here too," Will replied. "Eloise is dead."

"What!" Rick stared at him. "Eloise? When? How?"

"Some time during the night. One of the hotel staff found her this morning, in the bushes under her balcony with a broken neck. No way of knowing if she fell or jumped."

Dave overheard the last few words and turned, red-faced. "She had no reason to jump," he said fervently. "She had everything to live for. And there's no way someone of her height could have fallen over the balcony railing by accident. Somebody pushed her. And by Jesus, when I find the son of a bitch who—" His voice broke. Rick saw his eyes fill with tears.

A stocky man in khaki slacks and a tails-out sport shirt came from the hotel and approached the group. "I'm Sergeant Seguin," he said. He pulled a black leather case from his pocket and flashed a badge. "I've met Mr. Kirby already, but would the rest of you mind introducing yourselves and telling me your relationship to the SeaVenture project?"

They went around the circle. When they had finished, Sergeant Seguin thanked him, then said, "I came to tell you about my investigation, because I doubt if you'll see anything about it in the papers. In a case like this, publicity wouldn't do anyone any good. It's kinder to the memory of the deceased to keep things quiet."

"Hush it up, you mean?" Dave demanded. "Why?"

The sergeant eyed him coldly, then turned pointedly back to the others. "As her co-workers, you ought to know that Ms. Jackson probably took her own life."

"That's a lie!" Dave shouted. Seguin pretended not to hear. Ray took Dave's arm and said something softly in his ear. Dave shook his head from side to side, like a bear surrounded by yapping dogs, but he shut his mouth.

"We can't prove that she jumped," Seguin continued. "But we found a note on her dresser. It said"—he opened a battered notebook and read—" 'I'm sorry, I can't do anymore. It's become too much for me to bear.' It was signed with the initial E. We'll call in a handwriting expert, of course, but it looks like hers. One odd thing is that there was a computer disk sitting on top of the note. Maybe she was afraid a breeze would blow the note under the bed or behind the dresser, where it wouldn't be found."

A computer disk? Rick caught Will's gaze and raised a questioning eyebrow. Will scowled in reply. He had obviously had the same thought as Rick. And they weren't the only ones.

"Sergeant," Ray said, "could you release that disk to us as soon as possible? It may have information on it that is crucial to the success of our project."

"Oh? What kind of information?"

"Well—"

"I can tell you," Dave said, breaking in. "We've been having problems with the software that controls our undersea vehicle, problems that have created major delays. Ray is trying to say that Eloise sabotaged the computer somehow, using that disk. And that's a total crock, if I ever heard one."

"Yes, sir. Did any of you speak to Ms. Jackson last night?"

"I did," Ken said. Everyone turned and looked. They had apparently forgotten he was there.

"Mr. Kirby? You didn't mention that before."

"I wasn't sure it was relevant."

Seguin turned to an earlier page in his notebook and scanned it, then said, "I see. Can you tell me anything about the mood of the deceased when you saw her? When was this?"

Ken checked an index card. "She called me at nine-forty-eight, in response to a message I had left earlier. I came over here and met her in her room, arriving at shortly after ten. We were together about half an hour."

"For what purpose, if I may ask?"

"Something had come up that I needed to ask her about," Ken replied. "As for her mood, I'd describe it as upset and angry. Certainly not depressed, never mind suicidal. But that's simply my personal opinion. I am not a qualified psychologist."

"No, sir," the sergeant said. "Do you have any idea what Ms. Jackson was upset and angry about, or at whom?"

After a tiny pause, Ken said, "I couldn't say anything about that."

Rick caught Will's eye again. Ken hadn't really answered Seguin's question. Had he deliberately hedged? If so, he wasn't likely to get away with it. Seguin gave the impression of being a smart cop who wanted straight answers to straight questions and who wouldn't put up with fuzzy ones.

"I see," Seguin said. "Thank you for your help, Mr. Kirby."

While Rick was still recovering from his surprise, the sergeant looked around the little circle and added, "Did anyone else see Ms. Jackson last night?"

"I did," Dave said. "We had dinner together."

"Oh?" From Seguin's tone, Rick got the impression that he already knew this. "Was she in good spirits?"

"Wonderful spirits," Dave said defiantly. "That's why I know it's complete bullshit to say that she killed herself."

"When did you see her last?"

"We got back to the hotel about quarter to ten. She had some work to do, so we said goodnight in the lobby. If—"

Dave turned and stared out at the water for a few moments. When he turned back, his eyes glittered, but he had his voice back under control. "That's all," he said. "That was the last time I saw or spoke to her."

"I see." The sergeant consulted his notebook, then said, "Thank you for your help. If I have any more questions, I know where to find you."

He turned and walked toward the hotel.

"Well!" Ray said. "I can't say the local cops seem very efficient. Though heaven knows, this looks like an open-and-shut case. I'm shocked, I have to admit it. I can't imagine why someone like Eloise would try to wreck a project that she'd invested so much of herself in. Money, I suppose. Not many people can say no to it, if it comes in big enough packages. It really hurts me to think that Eloise didn't know she could come to me for help, though. No situation is so bad that the only way out is off the edge of a balcony."

"Eloise did not kill herself!" Dave said with quiet intensity. "Somebody pushed her. And it looks to me as if it was one of you. You're all part of SeaVenture, you're all staying in the hotel, and you're all taking it very calmly that someone you knew pretty well died a horrible death just a few hours ago. You all know more than you're saying too. Maybe you tell yourself that what you know has nothing to do with Eloise's death. Maybe you're afraid of being dragged into a messy court case. I don't know. All I know is, if you know something and you don't pass it on, you're a bunch of total shits!"

He turned and walked quickly into the hotel.

After a brief silence, Ray said, "Well. I think we have to excuse Dave's outburst. He must be badly shaken. Still, that doesn't give him the right to fling around wild accusations." He looked around absently and added, "I'd better go draft a report of this and get it off to Washington. I imagine we'll be needing another geologist now."

"Bureaucrats," Will muttered, as Ray walked off. "He sounds more concerned about writing the report of Eloise's death than he is about the fact that she's dead. She was a nice girl too. What a godalmighty waste."

Rick glanced around. Ken Kirby was sitting down again, riffling through those eternal index cards of his. Rick looked at Will and gestured with his head, then walked over to the table. "Mind if we join you?" he asked.

"Feel free. Ken put the cards in his shirt pocket and sat back with his head cocked to one side, looking at Rick and Will like a curious bird.

"This makes two violent deaths for me in less than twenty-four hours," Rick began. "What are the odds of that happening, I wonder?"

"In this part of the world, not very long," Ken replied. "What was the other death?"

Rick told him briefly of the attack by the two yakuza. When he finished, Ken scribbled a couple of notes on one of his index cards. Rick noticed that it was not a blank card.

"Natalie came back with me," Rick added to Will. "She didn't feel safe in Tokyo."

"Natalie?" asked Ken.

Rick explained who she was, mentioning the earlier attack on her in Honolulu and the fact that one of the yakuza may have been involved in that incident too. He also described his encounter with the two ninja in his hotel room. Ken continued taking notes.

When Rick finished, he said, "You and your friends live eventful lives, Commander. Sorry, I mean, Rick."

"Since you obviously know exactly who I am, and who Will is, and what level of clearances we hold, would you mind if I ask what you had to talk to Eloise about last night? I noticed that you didn't answer Sergeant Seguin when he asked you."

"No, I didn't." Ken brought his fingertips together to form a steeple, then rubbed the end of his nose with them. Then he looked around carefully, as if expecting to find a listener hiding under one of the other tables. It was the first time Rick had seen him act like a real spook.

"All right, in my judgment you have a 'need to know.' Here's the story," he said. "We think the SeaVenture project is being deliberately slowed up—sabotaged, if you like. We also suspect that one or both of two very powerful men are behind the sabotage. Yesterday afternoon, I discovered that Eloise Jackson once worked very closely with one of those men. Not very long ago, either. So I left a message that I had to talk to her. You know the rest."

"Like hell we do," Will said heavily. "Come on, Kirby. What happened when you went to see her?"

Ken rubbed his nose again. "I asked about her relationship with Bell—with the person I mentioned. She said she used to work for him. When I hinted that he might want to wreck SeaVenture, she seemed totally astonished. Her actual words were that he had never had the least interest in anything, unless it was black and smelly and worth a lot of money to him."

Will chuckled. "She had a lot of spunk, poor girl. I can practically hear her saying it. It doesn't sound much like somebody who's so overwhelmed with guilt that she jumps off her balcony."

Ken gazed thoughtfully in the direction of the hotel and the fatal balcony. "No, it doesn't, does it? When I left, I had the feeling that she was struggling with some difficult decision, but I never would have guessed that it concerned killing herself."

"I don't think it did," Rick said. "If you want my guess, you must have said something that gave her a clue to who the real saboteur is. After you left, she decided to check out her idea. She got in touch with him and made the mistake of letting him know what she knew. So he killed her."

Ken nodded judiciously. "It's possible. But as for evidence . . ."

"The disk!" Rick exclaimed. *"If* that was the disk that was used to sabotage Rover, then it must have been left in Eloise's room by the real saboteur. Right?"

"Unless she was the saboteur," Will pointed out. "We thought she was cute and funny, but that doesn't mean she was innocent. And don't forget that note."

"That note didn't say a word about sabotage or about killing herself," Rick pointed out impatiently. "How did it go? Something about 'I can't go on like this anymore.'"

Ken shuffled through his index cards and read them the text of the note.

"You see?" Rick demanded. "What kind of suicide note is that? It sounds a lot more like she was bowing out of some project or relationship than bowing out for good. If Eloise wrote it at all, I'll give odds she didn't write it because she was planning to kill herself."

"Good point," Will said. "But where does that leave us?"

"With a very narrow field of suspects," Rick said. "It had to be someone who worked with Eloise and who had the opportunity to sabotage the computer on board the *Champion*. It could be one of the ship's crew, but he would have had to be ashore last night, and Eloise would have had to know how to get in touch with him. Someone here at the hotel is a much better bet. And if we leave you out, Will, that basically means either Dave or Ray. My money's on

Dave. He was involved with Eloise and could have received that note from her. He has a history of lying and sabotage. And who would know how to screw up Rover better than the guy who designed it?"

Will frowned. "Now just hold on, Ricky. I know you and Dave have had some set-tos, and I know he's done some dumb and even dishonorable things. That doesn't make him a murderer. And why would he wreck his own boat, and his reputation at the same time?"

"You heard Ray's answer to why: Money. Ken's mysterious Mr. X offered Dave a lot of money to make sure that SeaVenture is a failure. And as for his reputation, that disk the sergeant found in Eloise's room may hold proof that Rover was deliberately sabotaged. In that case, who would blame Dave for the problems? He's the victim, isn't he?"

Rick opened his mouth to reply, but Ken interrupted. "What 'dumb and dishonorable things' did Dave do?"

Rick told him about Dave's stunt at the controls of the *Steel Albatross,* as well as the earlier episode with Eloise's towel. "I know the thing with the towel sounds incredibly trivial," he added, "but it shows what kind of guy he is. He'll do anything to duck responsibility for his own actions if it looks like they're going to get him into hot water. Right now he's probably feeling sorry for himself because Eloise forced him to give her the shove. Excuse me. I think I'll just go have a word with him."

As he got to his feet, Will said, "Just wait a goddamn minute, Rick. Who pinned a badge on you? You go messing around in a criminal investigation and you're the one who'll end up in hot water."

"What criminal investigation?" Rick replied. "You heard Sergeant Seguin. Eloise committed suicide. The investigation is closed. No damage to the reputation of the hotel, Guam's tourist trade, or the secrecy of the SeaVenture project and its godfathers in Washington. Everybody's happy ... except Eloise, and she's dead, so she doesn't count. Corpses don't have a vote in this."

Ken started to say something, but Rick turned and walked away. The more Rick thought about Dave's behavior earlier, the madder he got. What incredible gall, to pretend to be the chief mourner for somebody you just gave the ax!

Rick had to knock twice on the room door before Dave came to open it.

"What do you want?" he asked listlessly. "Why doesn't everybody just leave me alone?"

"Did you leave Eloise alone?" Rick replied.

Dave turned away. "Whatever Eloise and I had is none of your fucking business," he said. "Go away."

Rick followed him into the room. "Uh-uh. That note of hers that was supposed to be a suicide note: She wrote it to tell you it was over between you two, didn't she? And you couldn't stand that. When she accused you of sabotaging the project as well and threatened to expose you, you lost your head. Did you mean to kill her, or did it just happen?"

Dave's expression of open-mouthed astonishment was almost convincing enough to make Rick wonder if he had just gone off half cocked. But before he could start running back over the grounds for his accusation, Dave gave a strangled cry and came charging blindly across the room, head down and arms swinging wildly.

"You cocksucker, I'll kill you for that!" he screamed, burying his head in the pit of Rick's stomach and pummeling Rick's back and sides.

Instinctively riposting, Rick started to bring up his knee and smash Dave's face. He stopped himself. Dave clearly had about as much knowledge of unarmed combat as a kindergarten kid. Why use a sledgehammer to brush off an ant? An elementary aikido move sent Dave spinning across the room. He fell backward across the bed and lay there stunned.

After a few moments, he pushed himself up on one elbow and said, "I never dreamed you could be such a stupid asshole, Rick. Do you really think I killed Eloise, then left that note so people would think she killed herself?"

Rick hesitated before saying, "Well, yes. I guess I do."

"Then answer me this," Dave continued. "If I went to all that trouble to convince people it was suicide, why am I doing my goddamnedest to persuade the cops that some-body murdered her?"

Rick stared at him for a long time. Then he said, "I don't know. I didn't think of that. If I'm wrong about you, I'm sorry."

"You are," Dave said, flopping back on the bed and turn-ing his head away. "But your apologies are about as much use to me as a bucket of warm piss. Just get out of here, will you? I need to be by myself."

Rick left.

CHAPTER 25

THE COFFEE KEN HAD ORDERED FROM ROOM SERVICE was lukewarm when it came. By the time he got around to drinking it, it was cold. Cold as death. He had gotten a look at Eloise's body before it was taken off to the morgue—a professional courtesy on the part of Sergeant Seguin. The recollection sent a little shiver up the back of his neck. He had always disliked the thought of violence, but the reality of it was far, far worse than anything he had expected.

To distract himself from the memory of those open, sightless eyes that had been so lively only hours before, he turned on his computer and continued reading the file that Joyce had sent him the day before. After forty-five minutes, his eyes were tired from staring at the LCD screen, but he had gathered some interesting, and possibly relevant, facts. The captain of the *Glomar Champion* had recently shifted most of the money in his retirement account to the stocks of companies that would benefit from SeaVenture's success. That probably qualified as illegal insider trading, but it also gave him an excellent reason to want the project to succeed. Ray Lapham was several months behind on child-support payments and he subscribed to a newsletter that explained how to buy a Costa Rican passport and hide your money from the IRS in Austrian banks. Dave Collier was a steady contributor to Greenpeace, Friends of the Earth, and a couple of smaller environmentalist organizations with an activist orientation. Ocean Friends was not one of those listed, but Ken made a note to have Joyce do a further search of his bank records.

The computer beeped, and the little letterbox icon started to blink. Some E-mail had just arrived. He checked the directory and felt a smile of satisfaction cross his face. Before leaving Washington, he had asked his reporter friend in Japan to search out anything he could about the most prominent members of Ocean Friends. This, presumably, was the result. He got the downloading process started, then went on reading Joyce's file until another beep told him that the new file was now in memory. He exited the material about Ray and the others and brought up the Ocean Friends file.

The first section concerned Hoshi Ito, who apparently qualified as the guru of the group. She had succeeded brilliantly in high school, then, as was more or less traditional in Japan, she coasted through her years at a prestigious university. While there, she had had some contacts with several fringe nationalist groups (Ken noted the names for further investigation), but she had apparently not belonged to any of them. In her last year at the university, she had founded one of the earliest chapters of Ocean Friends and soon became the group's most important spokesperson. Since then, all her time had been devoted to that group's activities.

Ken shrugged. Not much there, after all. He started to skim the next section on Hoshi's family background. After a couple of sentences he backed up and began reading more carefully. It made quite a story. She was of samurai descent. In fact, one of her paternal ancestors had been among the Shogitai, the diehard defenders of the Tokugawa shogunate who'd fought a last-ditch battle against the Meiji Restoration in 1868, then committed mass ritual suicide on Tokyo's Ueno Hill when their side lost. Ironically, another of her ancestors was a leader of the Meiji forces.

Her grandfather, an officer in the Imperial Japanese Navy, was listed as missing in action at the end of World War II, and her grandmother, pregnant at the time, was living near

Nagasaki when the second American atomic bomb fell. Whether there was any connection with this exposure to radiation or not, the baby—Hoshi's father—was born blind.

Ken's informant added a note at this point explaining that for those of Hoshi's caste, any sort of physical disability was generally treated as a deep personal disgrace. Despite this dual handicap, of blindness and social prejudice, Ito had eventually become a respected Shinto scholar, married well, and fathered Hoshi. His second child, a boy, had been born with severe birth defects and died before his second birthday.

Ken wondered if the second child's fatal problems were connected to Ito's prenatal exposure to radiation. Maybe not, but the idea would have certainly occurred to him and his wife. If anyone had a good excuse for harboring anti-American feelings, Ito did. He had given in to his hatred? Even more to the point, had he passed it along to his daughter? Nothing in the file indicated one way or the other.

Disappointed, Ken moved on to the report on Rick Tallman's diving buddy, Kazuo Takauji. This turned out to be much less thought provoking than Hoshi's. On the face of it, Kazuo was simply a bright, intense young man with a passion for diving, who had gotten hooked up with Hoshi and her group simply through his love for the ocean. There was no evidence of political beliefs or involvements of any kind. At the university, he had hung out mainly with other sport divers. His only other interest was *kendo*, traditional Japanese swordsmanship.

Ken was about to go on to the next report when he stopped, his fingers still poised over the computer keyboard. Where had he seen the name Ito lately? It was a fairly common Japanese surname, as far as he knew, but the context in which it appeared had been unusual, he was sure of that.

He pushed his chair back from the desk and got up to go to one of the document-laden card tables. For the next twenty-five minutes, he riffled through one report after another, sure that he would somehow know when he got to the right one.

He did. It was a document he had requested before leaving Washington for Guam, on actual, rumored, and theoretically possible breakthroughs in the production and use of oil resources. The stiff cardboard cover was thick with red classification stamps, and each page was headed "TOP SECRET—THIS IS PAGE xx OF 137 PAGES." Ken, no great fan of classifying documents, thought it made good sense this time. In the wrong hands, the material in the report could set off major economic, political, and diplomatic flaps around the world.

He was sure the reference he wanted was somewhere toward the front, in the historical background section. Even so, he almost went right by it the first time. Not too surprising, as it consisted of one short paragraph:

> During WW II, the research bureau of IJN funded a secret laboratory in Nagasaki under charter to develop techniques for increasing the energy yield from hydrocarbon fuels. The head of this effort was a Captain Toshiro Ito. The lab was obliterated in the Nagasaki bombing, and records of laboratory activity are unavailable. Rumors persist that the researchers were successful in enhancing the energy density of oil, by using what is described as a rare form of carbon with very peculiar characteristics.

Ken let the report fall on the table and walked out onto the balcony, whistling the "Habanera" from *Carmen*. Nagasaki; a naval officer named Ito; oil. A string of coincidences? Possible, but he doubted it. Take it a step at a time. Suppose that that lab *had* discovered a technique for increasing the energy yield of oil. Suppose that, seeing the end was near, Captain Ito, true to his diehard samurai background, carried off a description of the technique but died before he could do whatever he intended to do with it. And suppose that his granddaughter somehow found out about it.

How had she gotten through to Nishimura? It didn't matter. The old fox must have immediately realized what he was looking at: a revolutionary decline in the cost of energy and, of course, in the value of oil. He and Red Bell were betting billions that the results would come within the next few months too. They must be starting to feel a hot wind at their backs. Even if they did manage to rediscover, and keep control of, the new technique, unless oil prices dropped a hell of a lot in the next six months, they were likely to find themselves tapped out.

How were Bell and Nishimura going about it? There wasn't even a hint that they were bankrolling any big petrochemical research projects. In fact, the only trace of cooperation between them was their joint financing of the Ocean Friends group, which didn't have any connection with oil. Maybe that was the payoff Hoshi Ito had demanded, in return for whatever information she passed on about the secret process her grandfather had discovered. It made a kind of sense: Here, take this revolutionary technology that's worth billions. All I ask is a tall world-class oceanographic research ship, and a star to steer her by.

That still left a big question: Why were Bell and Nishimura so concerned about halting the SeaVenture project that they were willing to engage in high-risk sabotage and, perhaps, even murder? There didn't seem to be much connection between mining mineral-rich crusts from the ocean bottom and a process for potentiating oil. Could the process (if it really existed) require some rare-earth metal as an ingredient or catalyst, one that was found mostly on the ocean floor? If so, they might be worried that SeaVenture, otherwise known as the U.S. government, would corner it and jack up the price to a point that ate into the ungodly profits Bell and Nishimura were counting on. Ken found himself wishing he had taken a few more science courses in college.

Back at the computer, he drafted a memo to Joyce, telling her to get more details, if possible, on Captain Ito and his secret lab. He was about to send the same request to his Japanese informant when he remembered Rick's curious tale of being attacked by yakuza thugs. Rick had said that the attack was aimed at his friend, Natalie, but he could be wrong. The attack might easily be part of the campaign against SeaVenture. If so, it was definitely time to give Natalie a much closer look.

Tom was about to enter his room when he collided with Kazuo, who was just coming out of it.

"Where have you been?" Kazuo demanded. "I have been looking for you a long time."

"I got tired of sitting around and decided to do a little snorkeling. Why? What's up?"

"We may have to make an important dive very soon. Maybe even today. Get yourself prepared." Before Tom could reply, Kazuo hurried away, in the direction of Hoshi's room.

The way Kazuo had ordered him around left Tom more than a little pissed off. He was a member of the group, after all, not a serving boy. And anyway, what was Kazuo talking about? Prepared? For what kind of dive? How deep? How long? In the submersible, or not? And what the hell was so urgent about it? The global warming wasn't going to happen overnight!

He decided to ask Kazuo some of these questions, in a nice, polite way. He walked down the hall to Hoshi's room but the screen was closed. He knew the rule. No one disturbed Hoshi when the screen was closed. He was about to turn and go when he heard Kazuo speak his name. He went closer and listened.

Kazuo was speaking English. ". . . take *Ocean Child* below three hundred meters without a partner. Tom must come. We have enough of the drugs for both of us. The only alternative is to take *Ocean Child* down from the ship."

"No!" Hoshi said. "There are too many people aboard *Ocean Friend* who might tell tales. The ship has already accomplished its most important task. I thought of sending a signal that would detonate the concealed charges in her hull, but it would draw too much attention, so I ordered the ship to meet us at the site, then return here. Here are the coordinates of the site."

As she read the numbers to Kazuo, Tom scribbled them on his forearm with a felt-tip pen. Whatever was at that location, Hoshi thought it was important enough to consider sacrificing a million-dollar ship and all her crew.

As he started to back away, he heard Hoshi add, "Use Tom on the dive if you have to. But he must not return. It is a shame. Personally, I like him as much as I could ever like an American. But our mission is more important than his life. We must allow no one to know that we have recovered the sword until the time comes to unleash its power on the world."

Tom stood as if frozen, then turned and walked almost blindly in the direction of his room, his path blurred by a veil of tears. He had been a fool, an idiot, a dupe. And the terrible part was that he wished with all his heart that he had never learned the truth. A pointless wish: His loyalty and devotion to Hoshi were shattered like a brightly colored but hollow Easter egg. Nothing could put it together again.

As he passed the telephone in the hall, he hesitated and glanced over his shoulder. No one. Kazuo was still in with Hoshi, plotting to murder him. Tom picked up the receiver and punched a number. When the call was answered, he murmured, "Rick Tallman, please."

"Sorry, sir, Mr. Tallman is out. Would you like to leave a message?"

"Yes," Tom said after a moment's thought. "Please take this down very carefully. He will find something very important at . . ." He read off the coordinates on his forearm, then asked the hotel clerk to repeat them back.

"Yes, sir," the clerk said. He read back the numbers correctly, then asked, "Anything else?"

"Yes. Just put 'Goodbye' and sign it, 'Thomas Patrick Fitzhugh.'"

His keycard was still in the hip pocket of his cutoffs. He left the house and walked down to the pier. As he let himself through the gate, he thought he heard Kazuo call his name. He didn't turn to look. The launch was tied up at the end of the pier, a thirty-five-footer powered by twin diesels, as well as a waterjet drive interfaced with the GPS receiver for dynamic positioning. He could be over the horizon before Hoshi and Kazuo even knew he was gone.

But then what? All his life he had loved the sea. He knew that terrors lurked in its depths—he had faced many of them at close range—but still the ocean remained a haven, a symbol of peace. Hoshi had won his love because the passion she claimed to feel was already in his heart. But she had lied, lied, and lied again. Nothing in the ocean was as terrible as the horror he had just seen in her.

"Tom! What are you doing?"

Tom turned. Kazuo was standing about twenty feet away. His body looked relaxed, but Tom recognized in his stance the alertness of a martial artist preparing for combat. Tom had picked up a few back-alley techniques himself over the years, but he knew he was outmatched. Still, what did it matter?

"I asked you to get ready for an important dive," Kazuo continued. "Why haven't you done it?"

Tom said, "I don't go on one-way dives."

The stillness seemed to silence even the waves. Then Kazuo said, "You were listening."

Tom nodded.

Kazuo spread his hands out in a pleading gesture and took a few steps toward Tom. "You must understand, Tom," he said. "We are all warriors in a great cause, and warriors must always be prepared to give up their lives for the cause. You freely offered your life to our mother when you took the oath before us all. Remember? Then why are you disturbed when your offer is accepted? It is a great honor!"

"Bullshit," Tom retorted. "You and Hoshi don't give a flying fuck about the ocean. All you're interested in is salvaging some crappy sword that's three hundred meters down, and you think I'll help you do it. Well, think again. Find your stupid sword yourself. Then take it and shove it up your ass."

Every muscle of Kazuo's face seemed to tighten, outlining the skull beneath the skin. "You are speaking of things you cannot possibly understand," he said, forcing the words out through clenched teeth. "The Emperor's Sword is a sacred object. It has been worshiped by my ancestors for a thousand years. To return it to the world is a holy quest, more precious than hundreds, even thousands of lives."

"Bullshit," Tom repeated. He knew his coarse words were goading Kazuo, but he didn't care. He could see no good way out of this situation, and at least he could go out fighting.

"Anybody who worships a hunk of steel is too dumb to live," he continued. "And if you've spent all this time and energy trying to recover it, you're as much of an asshole as your fucking ancestors were. Well, count me out. I'm—"

"Aieee!" In a blur of motion, Kazuo launched a flying kick that would have torn Tom's head from his shoulders if it had connected. But Tom, expecting some sort of attack, fell to his hands and knees, then sprang up in time to land the point of his elbow to the spot where Kazuo's neck met his collarbone. After that, the fight got hairy. Tom was overmatched, as he had known he would be, but he had the satisfaction of getting a few good licks in before he found himself on his back, helpless, with Kazuo's forearm pressing relentlessly against his throat.

"I am sorry, friend Tom," Kazuo said as Tom's vision blurred and started to darken. "I wish this could have ended another way."

Tom's last conscious thought was a fervent, bitter hope that Rick Tallman would understand his message and somehow even the score.

CHAPTER 26

RICK CARRIED HIS NIKES IN HIS LEFT HAND AS HE WALKED along the line of the surf toward Natalie's hotel. The righteous anger he had felt on the way to confronting Dave had drained away, leaving only a sour taste behind. *Had* he been unfair to Dave? It certainly looked that way. Eloise's death had shaken Rick more than he'd realized. She had been so full of energy, so gutsy, and now all that energy had vanished, leaving nothing but a *thing* on a slab in the Guam General Hospital morgue.

Death was all around him, and it was starting to close in. The yakuza who had attacked him was no loss to the world, but what about Inagaki? Would his successor care enough to learn his way around those mountains of files and documents? Doubtful. The next person who asked an obscure question, as Rick had of Inagaki, would get nothing but a perfunctory apology for an answer.

A stronger wave than usual raced up the beach and soaked Rick's jeans to the knees. He started to let out a curse, then shrugged. What did wet jeans matter? They would dry, sooner or later. The condition wasn't permanent, like death.

He stopped abruptly. Why did he assume that Inagaki's death was an accident? And why did he take Natalie's word that the yakuza attack was aimed at her? In Tokyo Rick had been asking questions about a Japanese submarine whose records were mysteriously missing. Before the day was over, someone had tried to kill him, and the man he had asked the questions of *was* dead. A coincidence? The more he thought about it, the less likely that seemed. It was much more reasonable to assume that someone—someone with an impressive intelligence network—was willing to do anything, even murder, to stop any inquiries about the I-53 of the Imperial Japanese Navy, lost off Guam in July 1945. But why? What was so important about the I-53?

A circuit closed in Rick's mind, and he recalled the sonar probe he had intercepted on his last dive in the *Steel Albatross*. Someone was using cutting-edge equipment to search the waters off Guam for *something*. The sunken I-53? Possibly, but it still made no sense. It was just a World War II Japanese submarine, not a Spanish treasure galleon, loaded to the gunwales with gold doubloons and jewel-encrusted idols.

Treasures. . . . Hadn't Natalie talked about a legendary, immensely valuable Japanese sword that had vanished at the end of World War II, and that rumor linked it to Guam? What if the sword had been on board the I-53 and was still in the sunken hull of the submarine? That would explain a lot.

Rick shook himself out of his spell and hurried down the beach toward Natalie's hotel. He found her in her room. In the background was a table with breakfast for two. It looked as if it had been waiting there a long time.

"I'm sorry I'm late," Rick began after giving her a kiss. "Something awful happened this morning. One of our people fell from her balcony and was killed."

Natalie stared. "What? Who?"

"Eloise. You remember her, don't you?"

"Of course I do. She was very lively and charming. What a terrible thing!" A shiver ran through her. She moved closer and put her arms around his waist, resting her head on his chest. "Hold me, Rick. I feel as if death is all around us!"

This echo of his own thoughts startled Rick. He closed

his arms around her tightly. After a few moments, he said, "Natalie? I've been wondering about something. The Emperor's Sword."

She leaned back from the waist to stare up into his face. "The Sword? Why do you bring that up?"

"Remember? When you were here on Guam before, you told me about it and said you dreamed of finding it someday."

"That is true," she said. "But why—"

"I've been thinking about what happened yesterday at the guesthouse, and the explanation you gave me, about a yakuza boss who felt you had cheated him."

Natalie became very still.

"I guess what I am trying to say," he continued, "is that I don't really believe it. Something is going on, something much bigger than a gangster's revenge, and I suspect that it has something to do with the Emperor's Sword."

Though Natalie was still enfolded in his arms, Rick had the feeling that she had suddenly moved a great distance away.

"Level with me," he begged. "If you're in trouble, maybe I can help. What's the real story with the Sword?"

She pulled away from him and walked over to the window. When she looked back, he saw both caution and fear in her eyes.

"Very well," she said softly. "I will tell you what I know. It is not much. A few years ago, someone told me a story he had heard from someone else who knew someone who . . . The usual thing with rumors. He said that, in the closing days of the war, a group of fanatical officers stole the Emperor's Sword and spirited it out of Japan. Perhaps they hoped to rally some of the bypassed Japanese garrisons in the Central Pacific for a last-ditch defense of the Empire. I don't know. Whatever they intended, it didn't work. The Sword vanished from sight, but its memory is still very much alive among the extreme nationalists in Japan."

"How did the Sword leave Japan?" asked Rick. "Do you know?"

Natalie gave a shrug that recalled her Gallic roots. "Japan

is an island nation," she said. "Evidently, it left by ship or by plane. By the end of the war, your country had complete command of the air and the sea. No Japanese plane or surface ship would have had much chance of escape. If there is any truth to the tale, I suspect the guardians of the Sword took it away by submarine."

Rick slapped his fist into his palm. "So *that's* why the Ocean Friends—"

"What is that you say?" Natalie asked.

"Nothing, just muttering to myself," Rick said quickly. "And that story about the gangster who wants revenge?"

"That is true, every word," she insisted. "But if you are right—that one of those men was among the ones who attacked me in Honolulu—there may be more going on than I realized."

"Oh? Why?" Rick probed. "Why couldn't the yakuza chief have sent his thugs there too? Honolulu is practically a suburb of Tokyo these days."

The question obviously disturbed her. "Rick, how . . ." she began to say, then broke off and turned away.

Rick felt everything he knew about Natalie being shaken, like the shards of colored glass in a kaleidoscope. He hated the new pattern they formed. "You've been lying to me from the first moment, haven't you?" he said. "That attack in Waikiki—no wonder I scared those thugs off so easily. I'm pretty good at unarmed combat, but I'm not *that* good. They were following a script. The whole idea was to get you next to me, wasn't it? To spy on me and the project. No wonder you so conveniently turned up on Guam like that!"

"Rick!" Natalie turned to face him. "You don't—"

"Mind if I use your phone?" he asked. He dialed the number of the hotel where Ken Kirby was staying and asked for his room.

"Ken Kirby," a barely audible voice said.

"This is Rick Tallman."

"I've been trying to reach you," Kirby replied. "I want to give you a warning. I told you this morning that two men were behind the plot against SeaVenture. Keep this to yourself, but one of them is a Japanese named Cuichi Nishimura. And I just found out that your Natalie Yussupov has had very close ties to him for the last couple of years."

Rick slowly replaced the receiver without a word.

"I do not think the person you called is a friend of yours," Natalie observed. "You have a look of thunder and lightning."

Rick strode over and took her by the shoulders. She seemed to shrink into herself.

"So that's it," he growled. "Your great good friend Cuichisan is the one who sent you to spy on me, isn't he? That explains something that puzzled me yesterday. I thought it was pretty amazing that those hoods found us so easily. But it wasn't really, was it? In fact, it was simple. Yesterday morning, you met Cuichisan at the gallery and gave him all the details of our plans. The yakuza probably got to the inn even before we did. Then they simply waited near the hot spring until I was alone. It should have been an easy kill, but it didn't work out like that. By the way, you might be interested to know that a very nice man, an archivist at the Institute for Defense Studies in Tokyo, was shoved in front of a train yesterday because of you."

Natalie flinched with each word. When Rick paused, she said, "You don't know what you're saying! Someone has been telling terrible lies about me!"

"Maybe," Rick replied. "But I doubt it. You were sicced on me in Honolulu, and I fell for it. Then lo and behold, you turn up conveniently in Guam and just happen to cross my path. I fall for it again. Then Tokyo, and the inn, and then you are so frightened that you have to come back to Guam with me. And little Ricky falls for it yet again. Ladies and gentlemen, in this corner, wearing cutoff jeans and weighing in at 187 shattered illusions, Richard Tallman, the heavyweight chump of the world!"

Tears were trickling down Natalie's cheeks. "All right, yes," she said, her eyes downcast. "When we met in Honolulu, it was not by accident. A man to whom I owe much—"

"Cuichisan," Rick contributed in a hard voice.

She gave a nod so slight that he was not sure he had seen it.

"This man," she continued, "asked me, as a favor, to get acquainted with you. He told me that he was in partnership with another man, an American, whom he did not trust. He wanted to have his own sources of information. A tremendous fortune was at stake, and you were important to the success of the venture. I agreed, of course. But what happened after that, what happened between us, was not part of his plan or mine. It happened because we both wanted it to happen."

"And your arrival in Guam?"

"Was his suggestion, but I would have come anyway. I wanted to see you again. And yesterday, at the inn, I realized that I was putting you in terrible danger. While the policeman was interviewing you, I called my friend and told him I could not give him any more reports on you. He understood at once and freely released me from the task I had taken on."

"The task of spying on me," Rick said.

"Yes!" she cried. "Yes, and yes, and yes! But not to harm you or the people you work with, only to protect his interests. You must believe me!"

Rick gave a hard laugh. "Believe you? Give me one good reason to. Not harm me? Your boss is the same guy who sent a couple of thugs to kill me yesterday. And for all I know, he's not just your boss, either. I'd sooner trust a timber rattler than you and your Cuichisan."

Natalie stared at him. Her cheeks were still wet with tears, but her expression was hard. "You!" she said. "What do you know about it? You were born a male, into a family with riches and power, in the richest and most powerful country on earth. You have never had to fight for anything in your life! Do you know what it is like to be an independent woman, in a country where the only women whose independence they recognize are whores? To have dignified gentlemen consult me for my expertise, then end the meeting with a pinch and a lewd suggestion?"

"You could have gone back to France," Rick pointed out. "Or to your family in New Caledonia. You didn't have to stay in Japan."

"No, this is true. I didn't have to stay, I *chose* to. I decided to fight on the terrain of my choice, with whatever weapons I had at my disposal. Neither you nor anyone else has the right to judge me."

Rick realized that he wasn't angry anymore, only tired and sad. "I'm not judging you," he said. "But we had something nice going, and you blew it. Ask yourself why, and if it was worth it. But don't bother trying to ask me. I won't be around."

He turned on his heels and walked out of the room, taking with him the image of her stricken face.

For a few minutes, the room was quiet. Then Natalie picked up the phone. "Yes, operator," she said. "I would like the number for an organization called Ocean Friends."

At the locked gate of the compound, Natalie stopped her rented car and gave her name into a weatherproof intercom unit. The gate buzzed and swung open. She followed the drive to the house and parked at the rear, as she had been told to do on the phone. A young Japanese man was waiting for her by the door. He led her down a long, silent hall to a doorway closed by a shoji, slid it aside, and gestured for her to enter.

The first thing she noticed when she entered the empty room was an antique celadon vase that, if authentic, was probably worth as much as four million yen. Near it, on the wall, was a masterful fan painting in Edo-period style that belonged in a museum. She couldn't begin to estimate its value. Whatever this organization was up to, it obviously did not have to scrabble for pennies.

"I am Hoshi Ito. You wished to see me?" a voice said from behind her.

Natalie turned. The leader of Ocean Friends looked very young, barely out of university, and very beautiful, but her face, for all its perfection, reminded Natalie of an Indian bronze in the Louvre that portrayed Kali, the Goddess of Destruction.

"Yes," Natalie replied. "I explained who I am to the person I spoke to earlier."

"But not what you wish with me. Please sit down."

Natalie sank easily to the floor, as she had painfully taught herself to do in her first months in Japan, and had the satisfaction of seeing a tiny flash of surprise on Hoshi's face.

"Can we be overheard?" she asked. Hoshi shook her head. "Good. Well, then: I know what your goal is, and I believe I can help you."

"Everyone knows our goal," Hoshi said. "To save our mother the ocean from the ravages of heedless man. We welcome everyone's help to achieve it, but I do not see how you in particular will help."

Natalie gave her a world-weary smile. "I speak of the real goal, of course," she said. "You are searching for a certain lost object, and I believe you are very close to finding it. When you do, I may be in a position to help you restore it to its rightful place in the world. I deal in great treasures all the time, it is my work."

Hoshi gave a tinkling laugh that was no more genuine than the puzzlement on her face. "You are telling me riddles," she said. "A great treasure? The health of our Mother Ocean is a great treasure that may soon be lost if our work fails, but I do not think you speak of that."

"Very well," Natalie said with a sigh. "You are searching for the Emperor's Sword. I have no idea if you seek it for its value in money, or its historical and artistic value, or its value as a political symbol. Your motive is a matter of no concern to me. *My* motive is simple: I wish it known that I had a role in the recovery of a great Imperial treasure. I already have some reputation and standing among those who know Japanese antiquities, but I want more. I want every owner of some forgotten treasure to think of *my* name when the moment comes to part with it, woman and Westerner though I am."

Hoshi had listened impassively to what Natalie said. Now she gave a smile that barely disturbed her lips and did not touch the rest of her face at all.

"If this wonderful tale were true," she said, "if we were looking for the Emperor's Sword, or if we had even found it already, I still do not understand your proposal. What would we need of you?"

Natalie gathered her nerve for the hardest part of her presentation. "To begin with, my silence," she said. "You would never have gone to such lengths to hide your true purposes if you did not know that they would set off much controversy and opposition. Therefore you will wish to continue to conceal them. Second, the reappearance of such a legendary treasure will cause a great stir. It must be handled with the very greatest discretion. I have had much experience in affairs that require discretion. I am prepared to place that experience at your disposal."

"Experience, discretion ... I am very sorry. Your experience is not required. And your discretion cannot be relied on. By coming here, you have proved that. In any case, you misunderstand our purpose. The Emperor's Sword is a great and powerful symbol, yes. But the secret that is hidden inside its hilt, engraved on the tang, is powerful enough to shake the entire world."

A terrible doubt began to grow in Natalie. Hoshi was being too frank, too confiding. But at the same time, Natalie felt her expertise challenged. "The tang?" she said. "I fear you are mistaken. I have read detailed descriptions of the Sword. The only mark on the tang is the *tachimei* of the maker, Rai Kuniyuki, founder of the Rai school of Yamashiro swordsmiths."

"That *was* true once," Hoshi replied. "No longer. My grandfather placed a secret there that is as powerful as the Sword itself was at the Battle of Takashima. He and many others with him died to save the Sword and its secret from the enemy. But we are wasting time. I must take steps to ensure your silence."

Hoshi raised her hands to clap. Fear washed over Natalie as she realized how badly she had misjudged the situation.

"Wait," she said urgently. "I must tell you that I have powerful friends and protectors. You surely know the name of Cuichi Nishimura. Would you make an enemy of him?"

This time Hoshi's smile looked genuine. "I do not think there is much danger of that," she said. "Cuichisan has known me since I was born, and we have been very close since I was ten years old. When he told me of your association with him, it was I who suggested he aim you at the American Navy diver. You see, I am frank, because I know you will never tell this to anyone."

"I left word that I was coming here," Natalie said, trying to keep her panic at bay. "If I don't return—"

Hoshi made a graceful gesture of brushing this aside. "A childish bluff. And even if not, it is of no concern. By the time anyone comes to look for you, he will find only an empty house. You must resign yourself to your fate."

Natalie's thoughts circled her skull like caged beasts. Had it been this way for her father, the day when he left their home in Phnom Penh with a briefcase full of gold Napoleons? She was barely six years old, and it was to be the last happy day of her life. What had he done when he reached the rendezvous and found, not the priceless Khmer-period idol he had been promised, but cold-eyed men with guns? Had *he* resigned himself to his fate? Or decided to battle it out to the very last?

"Sale petite garce!" she screamed. "Filthy little bitch!"

She hurled herself at Hoshi, aiming the long nails of her outstretched fingers at her tormentor's eyes. She missed, but only by a few millimeters. Three red lines sprang up on each side of Hoshi's face. Then a powerful arm encircled Natalie's neck and lifted her from the floor. Hoshi, still unmoved, met her eyes, then looked past her at the man who held her in a stranglehold. As a red film darkened Natalie's vision, she saw Hoshi stretch out her open hand, as if gathering up the threads of Natalie's life, and close it abruptly into a fist.

CHAPTER 27

AFTER LEAVING NATALIE, RICK TURNED AWAY FROM HIS hotel and walked north along the beach. He needed a little time alone, time to sort out his thoughts. This wasn't easy. He knew he was in the right. Natalie had been working for the other side all along. Using both sex and the maiden-in-distress routine as lures, she had hooked him in Honolulu, played him masterfully on her visit to Guam, and come very close to reeling him in when he went to Japan. Why, he didn't know. It seemed like a lot of trouble to go to, just to delay the SeaVenture project. But the facts were inescapable.

Then why did he have the queasy feeling that he had just acted like a true-blue bastard? Was it simply a vestige of his boyhood devotion to the ideals of the Knights of the Round Table? Even Sir Lancelot du Lac hadn't felt obliged to act courteously toward women who betrayed him. Still ... Natalie may have met him by design, but hadn't a real attraction, even a feeling of affection, grown up between them? She *couldn't* have been faking the whole time. Could she?

At the northern end of the beach, high, thickly wooded cliffs came right down to the water, blocking his way. At the entrance to a footpath was a small wooden sign that read "Puntan Dos Amantes." Point of the Two Lovers. It seemed like an omen. He turned onto the path, which began to wind upward. It was a tough climb, but when he reached the top, he found himself at the edge of a cliff with a dizzying view of the whole sweep of Tumon Bay, the Philippine Sea, and the highlands of central Guam. Agana was partly hidden by a light haze, but elsewhere visibility was excellent. A couple of miles offshore, he spotted a ship that he thought must be *Berkone*.

To one side, supported by two posts, was a weathered wooden marker. The deeply carved letters read:

PUNTAN DOS AMANTES
POINT OF TWO LOVERS

Alt. 410 ft. According to legend, two star-crossed Chamorro lovers came to this spot after learning that the girl's father had betrothed her to a Spaniard. They exchanged tender vows, then tied their hair together and jumped to their deaths.

What a way to go, thought Rick. Had either of them had second thoughts halfway down? Not that it would have made much difference if they had. Jump off a cliff, and you've just committed yourself all the way to the bottom.

He should have stayed with Natalie a little longer, given her a chance to explain, to defend herself. What would it have cost him? Nothing—except, maybe, his chance to make a big dramatic exit. Sure, his pride had been hurt. So what? He was a big boy now, he could live with hurt pride.

With all the confusion of events swirling around them, one thing was clear: The people on the other side, whoever they were and whatever they were after, were killers. The attack on him at the inn proved that, and so did the deaths of Inagaki and Eloise. If Natalie really was one of them, she would just have to take care of herself, and surely she could. But what if she wasn't? What if her connection with Cuichisan and the others was as innocent, or nearly as innocent, as she said? Then Rick had just walked out when she needed him most, abandoning her to real and great danger. The magic between them was probably gone forever, but surely he still had some obligation—if not to her, then to his own sense of personal honor.

He turned and retraced his steps, walking more quickly now. But when he reached Natalie's hotel, the desk clerk told him that she had gone out an hour or more earlier. No, she hadn't said when she expected to return.

Rick scribbled a note, asking her to call him when she came in, and left it in her box, then walked back down the beach to his own hotel. He was headed for the elevator when someone called, "Mr. Tallman?"

He turned.

"Some messages for you." A young guy, barely more than a boy, was holding out a little stack of paper.

"Thanks."

Rick glanced at the top slip. Who the hell was Thomas Patrick Fitzhugh? Then he recalled Kazuo's friend, Tom, the beach bum, and his attention sharpened. But why would Tom be giving him a set of coordinates and telling him they were important? Did he want Rick to meet him there for some reason? It made no sense.

With a shrug, he put Tom's note on the bottom of the stack and looked at the next. Sergeant Seguin would like to ask him a few more questions: Would the next morning at ten be convenient?

Another shrug. Why would Seguin want to question him? From what Rick had heard, he was still at the airport with Natalie, hoping for a taxi, when Eloise fell from her balcony. Chances were the police sergeant was simply spinning his wheels, hoping the smoke and dust would make it look as if he was going somewhere.

The next message was in a sealed envelope, with his name on the front in a spiky handwriting that looked European. He knew, even before he ripped it open, that the note was from Natalie. An apology and plea for forgiveness? A Go to Hell you SOB?

It was neither.

Dear Rick,

You have a right to hate me, though I swear I did not know that anyone meant you harm. Yes, the way we met in Waikiki was planned, but what happened later that night *was not* planned, by me or anyone else. Everything since has come sincerely from me. Believe me or not. It does not matter any more.

I write this because I may need your help. I have no one else to turn to. After I leave this at your hotel, I am going to the Ocean Friends compound, south of Agat. I have an appointment with Hoshi Ito, the leader of the group. If all goes well, or even if it goes badly, I will call you at your hotel before four o'clock without fail. If you are not there, I will leave a message that includes the word *relish*. Any message without that word does not come from me.

If you do not hear from me, it will mean that I have met with some important difficulty. Please use your judgment on next steps, but *be very careful*.

All the love I have to give is not much, perhaps, but such as it is, it is yours. Remember me fondly if you can.

Natalie

There was one more slip of paper, in the handwriting of the desk clerk. "Natalie has to return to Japan today on urgent business. She will get in touch in a few days."

Rick went over to the desk and held up the message. "Do you remember when this came in?" he asked.

"Sure. Just a few minutes before you returned," the clerk replied.

"Is this exactly the message the lady left, word for word?"

The clerk's face shut up. "She didn't call herself," he said. "Some man called for her. That's the message he gave me."

"I see. Thanks."

Grim faced, Rick went up to his room and waited. By the time the hour hand on his watch pointed to four, he had convinced himself that Natalie had run into big trouble, more trouble than she could handle by herself. And that fact in itself showed that she had been telling at least part of the truth when she'd protested her innocence. Rick had misjudged her. Worse, his accusations and anger had driven her to try whatever rash plan had taken her to the Ocean

Friends compound. If anything happened to her it was his fault. Not entirely his fault, he added to himself, but more than enough.

He knew where the Ocean friends complex was. He had driven past it a few days before with Kazuo, who had pointed it out. And he remembered noticing the high wall and the electrified gate with razor-wire topping, probably backed with infrared, ultrasound, and strain-gauge alarm sensors and a Doberman or two. A lot had been spent on securing the property against intruders. But just as France's fortified Maginot Line had stopped at the Belgian border, leaving its left wing anchored firmly in midair, the perimeter defenses of waterfront estates almost always stop at or a little past the low-tide line. Sensibly so: They were meant to keep out burglars, not mermaids. Or frogmen. Rick was betting that, Ocean Friends or not, the security people at the compound hadn't reckoned on an intruder from the sea.

As he moved around the room, collecting the gear he thought he might need, he kept glancing at his watch and listening for the ring of the telephone. The phone stayed silent. By four-twenty he knew that something or someone had kept Natalie from calling. Time to put Plan B into effect.

He stuffed most of the equipment into a nondescript canvas bag. Stripping, he pulled on a pair of Speedo trunks, then put jeans over them. The last item on his list was a knife. In the top drawer of the dresser was a very nice diver's knife, handmade, signed, and numbered. It was perfect for slashing through entangling underwater vines or making a hungry barracuda an offer he couldn't refuse. The knife had been one of his birthday presents from his mother. He wouldn't be surprised if she had commissioned it specially from the maker. It was a magnificent tool. But as a weapon it wasn't so hot.

Next to it in the drawer was another knife, with a hilt of slip-proof rubber, a seven-inch black-anodized blade, and a black plastic sheath with Velcro straps. It looked as if it had been run up on Sunday afternoon by a factory that made Saturday Night Specials. One glance would have sent an experienced cop reaching for his .38 with one hand and his cuffs with the other. Other knives might pretend to be for skinning deer, opening bottles, or carving whistles out of beech twigs. This knife was frank. Its obvious and only purpose was to do the other guy before he could do you. Rick balanced it in his hand for a moment, then tossed it into the carryall.

The drive to Agat took longer than he'd expected because of a truck that had spilled several crates of oranges onto the highway just south of Agana. As he drew near the Ocean Friends compound, he began looking for an inconspicuous place to leave his very noticeable convertible. He checked out a couple of dirt tracks that led down toward the water. Judging by the number of rusting beer cans on the shoulders, they served as lovers' lanes. His car would be out of sight from the road, but wouldn't an empty car—a new convertible, at that—on one of these tracks arouse exactly the curiosity he was trying to avoid? And more important would the car still be there when he came back?

Finally he recalled Poe's story about the purloined letter and pulled into the parking lot at Nimitz Beach. None of the people on the beach paid the slightest attention as he donned a full-coverage black wetsuit and scuba gear. Even the knife strapped to his thigh was apparently accepted as the usual thing. He gave a friendly wave to a family grilling hot dogs and waded into the surf.

The Ocean Friends compound was half a mile south of the beach, on the other side of a small rocky point. No boats were tied up at its private pier, and cautious glances did not reveal anyone patrolling the grounds. In fact, from fifty yards out, the place looked deserted. Rick studied the shoreline, searching for the best spot to go ashore, and decided on a tiny cove between two boulders. Thick bushes hid it from farther inland. Submerging, he swam in close and waited for a good-sized wave to sweep him into the cove. As the wave retreated, he scurried up the bank and into the shelter of the bushes and held his breath, listening for any shout of challenge.

Nothing, only the wind soughing through the leaves and

the lap-lap of the surf. Rick shoved the scuba tank under a bush, stripped off the wetsuit, and pulled on a pair of shorts and a T-shirt from a waterproof bag. The knife went into his waistband, under the T-shirt. If a guard spotted him before he spotted the guard, he could try pretending to be a recent recruit to the organization. That might give him an extra few seconds to make his move.

SEAL training had concentrated on underwater skills, of course, but Rick had been taught a good helping of stealth tactics on land as well. Using everything he had learned, he moved quickly and silently toward the house, from one place of concealment to another. The time of day, near dusk, created long shadows that made his progress easier. He was about to leave the shelter of a palmetto bush when a movement caught his eye. He froze. A door giving onto the veranda of the house swung open and two men stepped out. Between them, they carried a long, limp bundle wrapped in black plastic. It could have been a rolled-up carpet, but Rick was sickeningly sure that it wasn't.

The men started across the lawn, toward a dark, forbidding stand of trees. Rick followed them on a parallel course through the undergrowth. When they stopped, in the middle of the trees, he crept closer. They were standing in a tiny clearing, no more than five feet by eight feet. Tiny—but big enough for the long, narrow hole they had dug in the sandy soil.

"Let's get this over with," one of the men, a young Japanese, muttered. "I hope this is the last one."

He edged past the far end of the hole, positioning the bundle over the opening. His partner, his back to Rick, did the same at his end. "Okay."

They let go. The bundle dropped into the hole, with no more ceremony than a bag of garbage tossed into a landfill.

The second man, who looked Chamorro or Filipino, picked up a small entrenching tool and began shoveling sand into the hole. The blade of the tool didn't hold much. After a couple of minutes, the other man said, "Leave it. We'll come back later, after we finish with the house."

Rick waited until he couldn't hear their footsteps, then

slipped into the clearing. He used his hands to brush the sand off one end of the bundle, then tore open the thin black plastic.

"Oh my God!"

He had been ninety-eight percent sure of what was inside the bundle, but actually seeing it was different. Natalie's head flopped on her shoulder, and there were angry red marks on her cheek and neck. One eye stared defiantly at nothing. The other was closed. Rick reached down and felt for a pulse, but he knew it was only a gesture. She had probably been dead for an hour or more. Even if he had come the moment he got her message, he would have been far too late to save her. He moved his hand and gently closed the lid of the open eye. It was little enough, but it was all he could do for her now.

Then he noticed the second plastic bag, under hers. When he tore it open, he recognized the bluish, contorted features of Tom Fitzhugh.

He knew exactly what he should do: swim back to Nimitz Beach and use the telephone outside the snack bar to call Sergeant Seguin. He would have to explain why he had sneaked onto private property, but compared to a couple of murders, a little trespassing was not going to upset the authorities. By the time the police arrived, the two thugs and their bosses might have vanished, but that was part of the price you paid for going by the book. This was U.S. soil, after all, not enemy territory.

Footsteps. Rick straightened up and faded quickly into the shadows, knife at the ready.

The two men entered the clearing. The Chamorro carried a long-handled shovel. He took a heaping shovelful of sand and started to pour it in the hole, then stopped suddenly.

"What the fuck!" he said. "Look! Something's been at her, a dog or something. You can see her face! The other one too!"

The big man had his back to Rick's hiding place. He took a step toward the open grave and glanced down, then pulled a snub-nose revolver from his belt. "No dog did that," he said, peering into the woods. "There's a snooper around here somewhere. We better find him and shut him up."

Rick bent down and picked up a sizable rock. This stunt always worked in Westerns. Why not now? He lobbed it to the left, into a thick clump of bushes.

The bad guy bit, whirling around and firing two shots into the bushes. Before the echo of the second shot had died, Rick was on him from behind. His left hand clamped the thug's head, at the level of the temples, and forced it back and to the left, exposing the right side of the neck. One stroke with the razor-sharp knife was all it took. Rick let the suddenly limp body slump to the ground and jumped back, just in time to dodge a whistling shovel blade.

Before his opponent could recover for another swing, Rick leaped over Natalie's grave and grabbed him around the shoulders, then drove his blade upward, between the ribs, just at the level of the breastbone. The man gave a convulsive shudder as Rick forced the knife hilt sideways. Then he was still. Rick pulled the knife out and let the man fall, then bent over to wipe the blade on the man's shirt.

Before leaving the clearing, he leaned over for a last look in the shallow grave. Tom was totally in shadow, but a tendril of fading light touched Natalie's face. She looked more at peace. Rick picked a blossom off a nearby bougainvillea and dropped it into the grave.

"You'll have company for your voyage to the other world," he murmured. "That's about all I can do for you now."

CHAPTER 28

ANYONE AT THE HOUSE WOULD SOON START TO WONDER where the two gorillas were and come to look for them. It was time to execute a tactical regroupment, otherwise known as a retreat. Rick took as much care returning to the shore as he had taken on his way in. When he reached the small hidden cove, he stooped to retrieve his wetsuit and discovered that his knees were too weak to support his body. His hand was shaking as if he had been chain smoking and drinking strong coffee for thirty-six hours straight.

He sat down on the ground and waited for the fit to pass. He had killed before. He had chosen to become a professional warrior, and killing the enemy was part of the job. But that didn't make it come easy. He hoped it never would.

Had he really needed to ice those two thugs? Even after they knew that there was an intruder around, his skills would have probably allowed him to withdraw safely. Yet he hadn't even thought of it. Instead, he had created a situation in which he was forced to defend himself against their attack. Okay, it had been two against one, and one of them had had a gun, and neither of them was exactly an upstanding citizen. Still ... he had never had the least doubt that he could take them. And after seeing Natalie's face, he had never had the least doubt that he *would*. That didn't exactly

313

make him a murderer, but he didn't think his professor of ethics back at Princeton would want to crown him with a laurel wreath, either.

He took a deep breath and tried to focus his mind on more immediate questions than the extent of his own guilt. Why had Natalie come here, and why had they killed her? He had to shoulder part of the blame. He had mentioned Ocean Friends to her, during their final confrontation, and tipped her off that they were searching for the Sword, just as she was. After he'd walked out on her, she had obviously tried to cut a deal with them. In the process, she must have convinced them that she knew too much and posed a deadly danger to their plans. *Deadly* was the word.

But what was the reason for the urgency that made them kill rather than string her along? Were they so close to accomplishing their mission that they could not afford to take any risks? Had they actually found the sunken I-53?

The note from Tom! Rick gave himself a whack on the side of the head with the heel of his hand. How could he have been so dense? True, he had had some more pressing matters to attend to, which had taken all his concentration. Even so, when a member of a group that's conducting a high-tension, hush-hush search for something passes along a set of coordinates and says they're important, then gets himself murdered, chances are he's not giving directions to the nearest rest area on the turnpike. *Why* he had done it was a mystery, but *what* he had done seemed pretty obvious.

Tom's note was back at the hotel. The first step was to retrieve it and check the coordinates against a chart. Time enough to formulate a plan of action after the basic parameters of the situation were clear. Rick pulled on the wetsuit and scuba gear, glanced up the hill to be sure that he wasn't observed, and waded into the surf for the swim back to Nimitz Beach and his car.

The people on the beach paid no more attention to him when he came out of the water than they had when he went in.

As he drove up Highway 1 toward Tumon Bay, a few

things became clear in his mind. Kazuo and his gang were probably on their way to the site of the I-53 right now, and they were probably well prepared to handle any interference that might show up. Anyone who hoped to screw up their plans had to be ready to act *now,* and had to do it without attracting their notice. How could anyone creep up unnoticed on a boat in the middle of the ocean? A boat that was probably fitted with state-of-the-art sonar?

By a wonderful coincidence, the perfect tool for that purpose was just a couple of miles off Guam: the *Steel Albatross.* Unfortunately, the key to the tool locker was closely guarded. Rick imagined himself explaining his train of reasoning to Will and Ray (would he mention Natalie's murder and Tom's? How about the deaths of the two thugs?). And he should probably mention it to Ken Kirby. What then? Phone calls to Washington, probably, but it was now very early morning in Washington, so the whole matter would have to wait until somebody showed up to answer the phone. Then the request to use the *Albatross* on an operational mission would be bounced around from one agency to another. Sooner or later, someone would decide to cover his ass by saying no. That was always easier than saying yes.

Meanwhile, the Ocean Friends would have dived to the wreckage of the I-53, recovered the Emperor's Sword, and gone merrily off to do whatever it was they intended to do with it. Mischief of some kind, that was obvious.

No way!

Rick thought of the attack on him by the two yakuza as an occupational hazard, but the murder of Natalie made this a personal matter. He was going to stop Hoshi and Kazuo and their gang, by any means necessary. And it looked as if the only way to do that was to steal the *Steel Albatross.* Well, "borrow" it for a few hours. He certainly intended to bring it back.

The next question was, How? Ordinarily, launching the *Steel Albatross* involved at least two crewmen to walk the craft out of the moon-pool, two frogs to swim out and detach the lines, and God knows how many people hovering around the radio giving advice or just biting their nails. Rick had an idea how he could manage without most of the auxiliaries, but it depended on getting aboard *Berkone* and then into the pilot seat of the *Albatross* without raising any suspicions. Not easy.

What if he took Will aside and explained the situation to him? Will had a well-founded reputation in the Navy as a man who was willing to find a way around and through the Rocks and Shoals (as the Navy Regulations were known)—or even flat-out break them—if he thought it was important enough. But could Rick convince him that *this* was that important? At the least, he had to try.

At the hotel, he parked the Sunbird in the lot and went directly to Will's room. A discreet tap on the door produced no response. He rapped harder. From somewhere behind the door came a noise that somewhere between a grunt and a snort. In his mind, Rick saw Will Ward lying on the floor with a bloody head, the victim of an attack by one of the thugs that Ocean Friends had at its command. He rapped again, then tried the knob. It turned, and the door swung open.

"Oh, shit!" Rick hissed.

Will was lying—not on the floor, but sideways across the bed. He was in his stocking feet, and his Aloha shirt was unbuttoned, revealing a thick thatch of gray hair. On the desk near the bed was a bottle of Wild Turkey, two-thirds empty, and a glass with a finger of amber liquid still in the bottom. That was surprising. Most of the real boozers Rick had known drank straight from the bottle. Maybe Will wasn't that far gone—yet.

Rick closed the door behind him, walked over to the bed, and leaned close to Will's head. He was breathing regularly, through parted lips, and his color looked okay, though there was a row of tiny sweat drops along his hairline.

"Will?" Rick said, shaking the captain's shoulder. "Will, damnit, wake up!"

The only answer was an incoherent mutter.

Rick wondered if he should drag Ward into the shower. In movies that was what people always did with passed-out drunks. However, he had once seen it done in reality to a guy at a reunion of carrier pilots. The only result had been that the poor dope almost drowned.

What the fuck was he supposed to do now? Here he was, facing a major emergency that required immediate, drastic action, and his superior officer was totally out of commission. This was not the first time Rick had faced such a dilemma. The last time had been in the Persian Gulf, when the rustbucket LCU he was on came under attack from an Iranian gunship. Rick had saved the situation, but in the process he had screwed the pooch royally and come within a hair of getting his ass busted out of the Navy.

The answer came to him in a burst of logic. He had already been willing to steal the *Albatross,* which in the eyes of the Navy would be worse than piracy, mutiny, barratry, and jerking off in the head. He had wanted Will Ward's help—not to cover his ass but to carry out a difficult maneuver. He still intended to carry out the maneuver, and he still needed help, but he obviously wasn't going to get it from Will. Consequently, he had to get it somewhere else.

The answer wasn't one he much liked, because it involved eating a generous helping of crow. Still, he told himself, the mission came first. And in any case, he had only himself to blame. Both Will Ward and Ken Kirby had tried to stop him from going to Dave with his asshole accusations. Had he gone ahead anyway? Does the bear shit in the woods?

Before leaving Will's room, Rick put the Wild Turkey bottle on the closet shelf, rinsed out the glass at the bathroom sink, and opened wide the double doors to the balcony. If Rick's plan worked, someone was bound to come urgently looking for Will in the next hour or so. There was no point in letting the whole world know what Rick had just found out about him.

Five minutes later, Rick was knocking on Dave Collier's door. Once again he had to knock a second time before he heard sounds of life within.

The door swung open. Dave stood there, wearing faded jeans and a sleeveless T-shirt. His face had sagged since that morning, and he had blue-gray bags under his eyes.

"You again," he said listlessly. "What the fuck do you want this time?"

His breath smelled as bad as Will's.

"I need your help," Rick said simply. Was Dave too going to pass out on him? "Can I come in and explain?"

Dave backed away to make room, then closed the door behind Rick. "Well?"

"Rover was sabotaged by the same people who killed Eloise," Rick began. "It'd take too long to explain how I worked that out. But here's the point: I think I know how to really give them the shaft, if you'll help. What do you say?"

"I say you've got your fucking nerve," Dave replied. "A few hours ago, you were accusing me of killing a woman who was the best thing that's ever happened to me. And now you come around with some kind of cock-and-bull story about needing my help. Shove it in your ear."

Rick's first impulse was to deck the turkey and walk out. Then he reminded himself that Dave had a point, and anyway, the mission came first.

"Look, I said I was sorry," he said. "I meant it. I only had a few pieces of the puzzle, and I fit them together the wrong way. But now I've got a lot more pieces, and they're starting to make a very scary picture." He told Dave about his confrontation with Natalie and what he had found at the Ocean Friends compound.

"So you're not the only one who lost someone to those creeps," Rick concluded.

"At least you got back at them," Dave said.

"So can you, if you help me."

"How?"

"The only way I can sneak up on them is to use the *Steel Albatross*," Rick said. "And I don't have time to go through channels. I want you to help me borrow her for a few hours."

Dave stared at him for a moment, then gave a short laugh. "It's called hijacking secret government property, and it's worth a few years in scenic Leavenworth, Kansas."

"I'll take the rap," Rick replied. "I'll swear that I coerced you. In fact, you can blow the whistle on me the minute I'm underway. That'll put you totally in the clear."

"Screw that. If I agree to this nutty idea—and I haven't yet—I'm in all the way. How do you think you could swing it?"

A very big question, but Rick thought he had an answer. "When you were putting in all that time in the *Steel Albatross* in simulation mode, how did you do it?"

Dave shrugged. "I got out to *Berkone* somehow, told whoever was in charge why I was there, and did it."

"Where was the *Albatross,* in the moon-pool?"

"The first couple of times she was on deck, in that special cradle. Then they must have figured it would be simpler to leave her moored in the moon-pool."

"So you would just show up and climb aboard? No passes, no formalities, no one keeping an eye on you?"

"That's right," Dave said, giving Rick a shrewd look. "And I think I'm catching your drift."

"Do you think it'd work?"

Dave looked over his shoulder, toward the balcony and its view of the bay. "It might," he said at last. "It just might."

At the Agana marina, Dave hailed a kid who was sitting in a sixteen-foot boat with a fifty-horse outboard on the transom. "Want to take us out to *Berkone?*" he called.

"Sure. Twenty bucks, same as last time?"

"You got it." He and Rick climbed down from the dock and sat side by side on the middle thwart while the kid fired up the outboard and eased out of the slip. The ride out took less than ten minutes. As the boat drew close to the Jacob's ladder hanging down the port side of *Berkone,* a crewman peered down at them from the deck. Apparently he recognized Dave or Rick. He sketched a little salute and disappeared.

"One down," Dave muttered from the side of his mouth. He balanced on the gunwale and made a spring at the rope ladder, then scrambled up before the swell got him. Rick followed. As they arrived on deck, a ship's officer came toward them. Rick tensed up. This was the next hurdle. He recalled meeting the guy, but what the hell was his name?

"Welcome aboard," the officer said. "More simulations?"

Dave made a face. "Refresher sessions," he said sourly. "As if it's likely I've forgotten anything in the last couple of weeks. Bill, do you know Rick Tallman? Bill Mares."

"Sure," Bill said. "Hi, Rick. I've heard a lot about you."

Rick forced a grin. "Lies, all lies. Is the *Albatross* in the moon-pool?"

Bill nodded. "A lot less wear and tear on the craft that way," he said. "You know your way, don't you? I've got a stack of unfilled reports on my desk."

"Sure. Thanks," Dave said.

Rick and Dave walked aft to the massive superstructure that covered the moon-pool. In the locker room, Rick stripped to his skivvies, then checked the small refrigerator where the drugs were kept. Just as he recalled, on the top shelf was a folder with weight/time/depth/temperature dosage nomographs. He quickly scanned them, then loaded three syringes with the indicated quantities. There was a transdermal injector in the drug locker, but he wasn't absolutely sure how to work it. This was not the moment to find out.

"You're really going to dose yourself with that stuff?" Dave asked in alarm.

"I have to," Rick replied. "No way I can operate outside at those depths without protection. If high-pressure nervous syndrome didn't get me, hypothermia would."

He pointed to two of the syringes. "And there it is: protection. Better living through chemistry."

"What's the third one for?"

"It's supposed to help me tolerate the rapid compression," Rick said as he stuck the first of the needles into the muscle of his left arm and depressed the plunger. "I hope it works. Ah, Dave, would you mind giving me a hand with this one? Sticking a hypodermic in your own butt is a little tricky."

As the massive chemotherapeutic doses began their work, Rick suited up with an economy of motion that came from long practice. Then he and Dave returned to the moon-pool and walked over to the ladder.

"You'd better fill me in on what to do," Dave said.

"Are you a good swimmer?" Rick asked.

Dave bridled. "I lettered three years running at Northwestern," he retorted. "Hundred-meter freestyle."

"Good on you. But today's going to be more like two-meter freestyle. Once I'm in the boat and set to go, I'll give you the thumbs-up. You jump in and unclip the mooring lines, then climb out fast, before I pull the plug. I don't want to be bothered with trying to miss you as well as *Berkone*'s underwater structure on my way down."

"Thumbs-up, jump in, unclip, climb out," Dave repeated. "Then while I dry off, I can try to think of a good story to tell all the guys who come running to find out what I did with their pet submersible aquaplane. I just hope to hell Will Ward isn't one of them!"

Rick made a face. "Not much chance of that," he said. He didn't explain why.

In the cockpit, Rick activated the on-board computer and took the shortcuts through the predive checklist until he reached the screen that read:

SA-1 PARAMETERS CHECKLIST
Rate of descent: 10 mpm
Increase Decrease
Select Cancel

After a moment's thought, he changed it to fifty meters per minute. Apparently the program was upset by such a big change. *"Are you sure (Y/N)?"* began to blink at the bottom of the screen. He touched Y, and the parameter obediently shifted from ten to fifty.

As he grasped the stick and tested its movements, he glanced out through the coaming. Dave had stripped and was waiting on the side of the moon-pool for his signal. After one more swift but comprehensive scan of the instrument panel, Rick met Dave's eye and gave him a thumbs-up. Moments later Dave was in the water, casting off the lines that held the *Steel Albatross* fixed in the center of the moon-pool. Rick watched until the last mooring line was free, then pressed "Begin descent" and pushed the stick all the way forward.

Water rushed into the ballast tanks, encouraged by the pumps Will had added to this version of the boat, and air rushed out with just as much enthusiasm. For a long moment, nothing happened. Then, abruptly, the boat was underwater. When the nose dropped, Rick moved the stick back to meet it. Until the *Steel Albatross* was well clear of *Berkone*'s hull, he didn't want her to take on any forward motion.

He studied the depth gauge. Five meters, seven, ten ... As soon as he was sure that he was well below *Berkone*'s keel, he pushed the stick forward once more, to pick up the forward motion that the *Albatross*'s speed of descent entitled her to. At the same time, he gave her a touch of left rudder, to bring the nose around to a course that would take the *Albatross* to the coordinates Tom Fitzhugh had given him. He was on his way.

CHAPTER 29

RICK SETTLED INTO THE STATE OF RELAXED ALERTNESS OF an experienced pilot. His eyes constantly scanned the instrument display and the area ahead, above, and on either side of the *Steel Albatross,* but his mind was free to wander through the events of the last two days. It was clear now that he and Natalie had both been unknowing actors in a drama written by people who had their own hidden purposes and no scruples whatsoever about how to achieve them. Hoshi and the Ocean Friends, Natalie's Japanese patron Cuichisan . . . What were they really after, and what made them think they had the right to kill to get it? Rick might never know the answers to those questions, but he did know one thing: After what they had done to Natalie and Tom Fitzhugh, and tried to do to him, Rick was going to have to stop them, whatever it took.

Thirty-seven minutes out from *Berkone,* and about two-thirds of the way to the spot designated by Tom's coordinates, a light began to blink in the lower left corner of the computer display. Someone was trying to communicate with him. He reached down beside the seat for his headset and put it on.

"Alpha One, Sierra Alpha One, this is *Berkone,* do you

read? Sierra Alpha One, this is *Berkone*, do you read? Over."

Rick's eyebrows shot up. No mistaking that voice. How had they managed to rouse Will from his stupor and get him out to *Berkone* so fast? The veteran seadog sounded as if he were in the seat next to Rick, and his tone suggested that he was on the point of ordering his insubordinate subordinate to be keelhauled, as a preliminary to being tarred and feathered and ridden out of town on a rail.

First you have to catch me, Rick thought. Not easy, considering that the *Albatross* embodied everything Will knew about building an undersea craft that would be next to impossible for someone to find and track. He considered telling Will what he was about, but there simply wasn't time to give Will all the details required to justify what he had done.

Still, it wasn't right to leave his godfather totally in the dark. Rick thumbed the Transmit button and said, *"Berkone*, this is Sierra Alpha One. Status normal. Observing radio silence following this transmission. Out."

Will Ward started to squawk like Donald Duck. Rick reached over and turned the volume down to zero. He was within five thousand yards of his destination now, and he needed to concentrate. He activated the *Steel Albatross*'s low-band sonar and immediately got a contact: a small surface vessel at almost exactly the position on Tom's note. Doppler data indicated that the vessel was holding its station. He redirected the sonar to scan the ocean floor and keyed in the approximate dimensions of the target, three hundred feet by thirty feet. Those were more or less the specs for an American *Gato*-class submarine from early World War II, so they were probably a close enough fit for a Japanese I-boat. He turned on the magnetometer as well. A hunk of steel that size should register, even if heavily silted over.

The depth meter showed 280 meters, and the fathometer showed another 120 meters of water under his keel. Ordinarily, he should be plotting out a plan of attack by now, but what was the point? He knew nothing about the situation that lay ahead of him. His goals were to find the sunken hulk of the I-53, neutralize the opposition, and recover the fabled Sword. Any more detailed program would have to wait for additional information.

Suddenly the sonar contact light on the panel flashed. He studied the readouts. The position of the object was almost directly beneath that of the boat he had spotted earlier, and the size fit well with his estimate for a sunken submarine. And there was a second, smaller object as well. He knew that Ocean Friends owned an up-to-date deep-ocean submersible. Was that it? It made sense. And yet, if the submersible was there to deliver divers for EVA aboard the sunken sub, what about compression rates and decompression times? What about hypothermia? Could Ocean Friends possibly have access to drugs like those with which Rick had just injected himself? If so, the U.S. Navy no longer had an exclusive franchise for that super-secret corner of diving technology, and he was dealing with a much more sophisticated opponent than he had thought.

Rick sat up straighter. He pushed the stick forward and gave the *Albatross* a touch of right rudder, to put her on a course directly toward his new find. The only question in his mind was whether to turn off the head- and sidelights. By now it was after dark on the surface, but even if it were still daylight topside, little sunlight would reach this depth. He needed the lights on the *Albatross* to see anything at all. But what was the point of a stealth vehicle if you crept up on the opponent while putting out enough lumens to power the ad on the side of the Goodyear blimp? You might as well fax him an announcement of your impending visit.

Will Ward's snooper goggles, which worked off the faint bioluminescence found in deep water, would have solved the problem. But Rick didn't have the use of them on this mission, and there was no point in sitting around wishing for them. He would have to use the lights. He couldn't afford to charge blindly into an unknown situation, even if it meant losing the advantage of surprise.

Three minutes to target, according to the course computer. He eased back on the stick and changed the descent rate to just short of a stall. The controls started to feel mushy. Just as he was wondering if he should start climbing, to give the craft steerageway, the lights picked out the ocean floor. At the limit of the pool of light was a moss-softened form that was too regular to be natural. With a thrill, he recognized the contours of a Japanese long-lance torpedo. The I-53 must be nearby.

With no warning, a shape that had to be the bow of the Japanese sub loomed out of the darkness. Just beyond it, on the ocean floor, was a contraption that looked a little like a steel septic tank. Obviously the Ocean Friends submersible.

Using auxiliary power, he made a slow pass alongside the little sub, just skimming the bottom. He wasn't surprised to see that the outer hatch of the ventral lock-out chamber was open. Every few seconds, the chamber vented a few bubbles off whatever breathing gas that boat used. A faint turbidity running down current and the disturbed sediment along a trail leading to the Japanese submarine told Rick that he would have to deal with at least one unfriendly diver in the water.

Rick applied power for a climbing turn to port and brought the *Steel Albatross* to a halt about fifteen yards from the wreck and five yards off the bottom, with the bulk of the big sub between him and the Ocean Friends craft. He craned his neck to get an idea of the surface below. It looked reasonably solid and not too bumpy. He put the boat into a slow descent. Moments later, the oil-filled struts touched down and he heard the muffled whine of the self-leveling servos. A green light flashed when the boat was level.

Time to finish getting ready for his own dive. An extravehicular activity, or EVA, like this was one of the diciest evolutions in deep-ocean diving. Rick had carried them out before, but never with so little preparation, and never— *never*—alone. He was shattering the Eleventh Commandment of the SEALs: Never lose sight of your buddy. First, of course, you had to have a buddy not to lose sight of, and Rick didn't. In any case, by taking the *Steel Albatross* without authorization, he had committed piracy as well, so maybe one more broken commandment didn't matter much.

DEEP FLIGHT

He reached over his shoulders for the backpack straps. The pack contained the tanks of helium, hydrogen, and oxygen for the trimix his closed-circuit breathing apparatus would supply while he was outside the boat. At these depths, mixed gas was absolutely essential for survival. He would carry the breathing bags, the electronics that kept the gas proportions within very tight critical tolerances, and the miniaturized radio gear on his chest.

The packs showed Will at his cleverest. Space in the cockpit was extremely tight, and donning all the gear needed for a sortie from the vehicle required the contortionistic abilities of the Rubber Man in a circus sideshow. Will's innovation was to make the pack for the trimix tanks in the form of a detachable seatback. It not only solved the problem of where to store them when not in use; once they were on and detached, the cockpit became amazingly roomy.

Rick fastened the straps, attached the breathing-bag unit, and hooked up the two feeder hoses. Then he reached down on the floor for his helmet, which was automatically pressure-regulated by the breathing controls, and incorporated an oral-nasal mask that allowed him to speak into the built-in voice-activated microphone. He was planning to continue guarding radio silence, but if he had to break it, this gear sure beat hell out of trying to mumble a message around a rubber mouthpiece.

After inserting the tiny phones in his ear canals, Rick put the mask in place and strapped on the helmet, then instructed the computer to flood the cockpit. The water level and the pressure started to rise. Half a minute later, the cockpit was full and the pressures were equalized. It always amazed him that the magic potion in those predive shots completely eliminated the need for the val-salva maneuver to clear his ears on compression.

Rick cracked the hatch and eased himself upward, pausing only to grab a high-intensity handlamp from its clips under the instrument panel. His buoyancy felt okay: just enough weight on his belt to make him slightly negative, but not so much that it made swimming an effort.

A few kicks of his fins brought him up level with the deck

of the submarine. The Japanese boat was listing about twenty degrees to port, enough to make exploring her tricky but not impossible. An open hatch yawned on the foredeck, black against the gray-green vegetation that covered the wreck. As he swam closer, Rick saw that some of the plants had been scraped away near the hatch. Someone had passed that way very recently.

Rick switched the lamp to his left hand and drew his knife before descending, headfirst, through the open hatch. He had never seen a schematic of this class of boat, but all World War II boats were pretty much alike, with a torpedo room in the bow, officers' quarters near the control room amidships, and the big diesels and storage-battery compartments aft. American subs from that era featured a second torpedo room all the way aft, but he had no idea if the Japanese mounted stern torpedo tubes. Not that it was likely to matter. A valuable object like the Sword would almost certainly be kept in the captain's quarters.

Submarines had another standard feature, Rick recalled, as he flashed his torch around the torpedo room. They were incredibly cramped, with every cubic inch put to use. The passage between the torpedo racks was barely two feet wide—less now, because of the debris that filled it. Bundles of wires dangled languidly from the bulkheads and overhead, threatening to snag anything that passed by. Rick swam very slowly down the center of the passageway, pushing the obstacles aside with his knife hand and scanning ahead and to either side with the powerful torch.

Ahead, a watertight door stood open, as it must have stood for forty-five years. From among the debris on the deck, a skull gleamed whitely in the torchlight. Rick shivered as a tiny orange fish came swimming out through the eye socket.

Rick pulled himself carefully through the center of the opening. At these depths, there was no room for error, even with a buddy to cover for your mistakes. He recalled his own version of the aviator's maxim: Diving, like flying, is not inherently dangerous, but both are mercilessly unforgiving of human error.

He was probably in officer country now. The companionway was lined with cubicles that seemed barely big enough to serve as lockers. Rick flashed his light into each one as he swam past. Another skeleton, with something that gleamed in the midst of the tangled ribs. A gold button, probably. If it weren't 400 meters down, this wreck would be a bonanza for souvenir hunters.

Another cubicle, larger, with a tiny desk fastened to the aft bulkhead. And bobbing in the center of the room, like the piñata at a kid's birthday party, was Kazuo. His eyes were closed, and he didn't react when Rick shone the light through the glass of his facemask. Rick moved closer. What had happened to the Japanese diver? A minor malfunction in his breathing apparatus? That would be enough to put him under, even to kill him. Or perhaps he had been given too much, or too little, of one of the drugs. At these depths, the margin of error was vanishingly small. Rick thought he could see Kazuo's chest moving under his wetsuit, but he couldn't be sure.

Rick could not leave him there. Once back on the surface, he might wish he had, especially if Kazuo had any part in murdering Natalie. But down here, in an environment that was so essentially hostile to humans, Rick felt a deep kinship with and a deep responsibility for *any* member of his species. Still on guard, he moved closer to Kazuo. As he did, he saw something lying on the deck. It was a long, narrow metal box covered with tatters of rubberized canvas. He swam down to pick it up. The canvas shredded under his fingers, but the box was still intact. For the moment, he ran a short strap from the metal handle of the box to one of the D-rings on his harness. Then he turned his attention back to Kazuo.

Towing the young Japanese and the long awkward metal case out of the captain's quarters and back up the companionway to the forward torpedo room and the open hatch took just over eight minutes by Rick's wrist chronometer. Without that evidence, he might have been tempted to estimate it at closer to eight hours. Every foot of the way, jagged-edged bits of wreckage reached out to snag them. Any attempt to move faster threatened instant disaster, yet every time Rick stopped to disentangle himself, or Kazuo, or that damned metal case, it cost him twice the energy to get them moving again.

At last he towed his two burdens up through the hatch into open water. The cost to him was nothing worse than a long rip in the calf of his wetsuit and, he suspected, an equally long cut on his own calf. But for Kazuo? Once again, Rick aimed his torch at the young diver's face. His eyes were still closed, and his lips were starting to take on a bluish tinge. It looked more and more like a problem with the drug dosage.

Rick took Kazuo by the armpit and swam him across to the *Steel Albatross*. The aft seat in the cockpit was an even tighter fit than usual, because of the tanks strapped to Kazuo's back. Rick moved very carefully. After taking off Kazuo's fins and letting them drift away, he worked the unconscious diver's feet and legs under the aft instrument panel and gently forced him down into the seat. Kazuo's breathing apparatus kept threatening to snag on the corner of the canopy. Break any part of it, or even bend it slightly out of shape, and it would be goodbye, Charlie.

Finally, Kazuo's limp body sagged against the seat and Rick bent over the side to strap him in. The next order of business was to find someplace to put a three-foot-long metal case. Why hadn't Ward thought of including a trunk in the *Steel Albatross?* Or at least a little compartment for golf clubs, like the one Rick had once seen in a 1934 Packard roadster at a classic car show? Rick was tempted to leave the case behind, but he had a strong intuition that it contained the key to all the deadly events of the previous few days. He finally managed to wedge it alongside Kazuo. It was a tight fit, but not much worse than tourist class in a 747, and it wouldn't be as long a flight.

He fit himself into the forward seat and turned his trimix pack into a seatback again. He had practiced this maneuver a dozen times, but never under field conditions, near the edge of exhaustion, and with fingers that had decided not to cooperate. By the time he finished, his arms were starting to tremble.

Rick closed the canopy and initiated the procedure to flush the water from the cockpit. This was not a simple matter. It required the combined effort of powerful electric pumps and a substantial part of the boat's stored supply of high-pressure air. Rick forced himself to relax his muscles and breathe slowly and evenly. He had no idea what the result would be if he hyperventilated on trimix, but he suspected that it wasn't a good idea.

While he waited, he considered his next move. He could turn around and go back to *Berkone.* No question that was the responsible thing to do. But Kazuo might not survive that long without first aid. Still more compelling, someone was on the surface, waiting for the Japanese diver and the treasure he had sought. Rick was convinced that that person was Hoshi and that she, more than anyone else, was responsible for Natalie's murder. Rick needed to see her close up, to hear her story if she had one, to ... He wasn't going to think beyond that point. Not yet.

The water in the cockpit was down to waist level now, exposing the touch-screen display of the computer controls. As Rick reached out to press it, he wished he had some wood to knock on. He settled for crossing his fingers instead. In principle, the *Albatross*'s electronics were hermetically sealed, proof against any pressure the boat might encounter. Even so, monkeying with any kind of electrical gear while sitting ass-deep in salt water was probably frowned on by the Underwriters' Laboratory. If the high-pressure immersion had created a short anywhere in the system, Rick might find himself lighting up like one of the signs on the Las Vegas Strip.

A comforting red glow spread across the display, followed by:

> SA-1 COMMAND MENU
> Do you require assistance?
> Yes No Cancel

Rick pressed No, then entered a short-form command that put the boat directly into Ascent mode, without having to go step by step through the pre-ascent checklist. That was a new feature with this version of the *Albatross*'s software, one he had insisted on. He understood why Ward had done everything possible to idiot-proof the controls, but an experienced pilot needed the option of bypassing the safeguards, especially in situations that required a prompt response.

He punched in an ascent rate of fifty meters per minute. Pretty fast, but even so, it would be almost half an hour before they were back on the surface with pressures equalized. As the water was forced from the cockpit and ballast tanks, the *Steel Albatross* stirred fitfully, rocked, and began to lift off the bottom. Rick relaxed a little. Breaking loose from the suction of an ocean-floor landing was always a questionable business, as his experience with Dave on the mudmount had shown.

By now there was enough breathing mix in the cockpit for life support. He took off his helmet and oral nasal mask, then turned and removed Kazuo's facemask and mouthpiece. By the light of the handlamp, his color wasn't good, but at least he was still breathing.

Rick turned back, grasped the stick, and gave it a few tentative tweaks. It moved freely, but it had no effect on the boat's orientation. That was to be expected. They would need to reach an ascent rate of at least thirty meters per minute before the controls became effective without auxiliary power. He waited as patiently as he could, then, when he felt the boat start to respond, he steered her into a wide spiral calculated to bring them to the surface very near the launch from which Kazuo had dived.

CHAPTER 30

As the *Steel Albatross* rose past the fifty-meter level, Rick thumbed the Transmit button on the stick. The crew of the Ocean Friends launch might learn of his presence in another few minutes anyway, so why keep his friends in the dark?

"*Berkone,* Sierra Alpha One. Do you read? Over."

"Sierra Alpha One, *Berkone,*" Will's voice replied immediately. He must have been hovering over the mother ship's radio. "What is your condition?"

"*Berkone,* Sierra Alpha One condition normal. Preparing to surface at . . ." He read off the coordinates, then repeated them. "Request immediate helicopter support."

"Roger, Sierra Alpha One." Will read back the coordinates and added, "Your support will be there."

Will obviously wanted to know more, but Rick ended the communication. He needed to concentrate on bringing the boat to the surface as close as possible to windward of the Ocean Friends launch. The sail area of the *Albatross* was so tiny in comparison to practically any surface craft, that a position to windward was necessary to cut the risk of the sub drifting into a collision with the Ocean Friends boat.

From the aft seat came a muttered sentence in Japanese. Rick looked over his shoulder. "You're okay, Kazuo," he said. "I'm taking you to the surface. We'll be there in a minute."

"You, Rick Tallman?" Kazuo said in an exhausted voice. "You rescued me?"

After a long silence, Kazuo continued, "Half a century ago, Will Ward rescued my father from that accursed boat. When I felt myself failing, I was sure I was doomed to pay the debt for my father's life. I was resigned to that. Then you, Will Ward's godson, saved me. The paths of fate are very strange."

Rick couldn't help agreeing.

It was dark and moonless when they broke the surface, but starlight was enough for Rick to make out the form of the launch a few yards away, riding without lights. He doused all the cockpit lights and engaged the *Steel Albatross*'s deballasting pumps, to take care of any water that slopped in while the canopy was open for them to exit the boat.

"Can you swim across to your boat?" he asked Kazuo.

"Oh yes, I think so. But . . . Ah, wonderful! You brought the, ah, the object from the submarine. I will carry it with me."

Rick was about to object, but this was obviously the last act, and he was determined to find out how the story came out.

"Here, I'll undo your weightbelt," he said, twisting in his seat. "You'll need all the buoyancy you can get without your fins and breathing rig."

The boat took on a pronounced list to port as Kazuo clambered out of the cockpit, then rocked back to starboard as he let himself slip into the water. Rick checked that his knife was loose in its sheath, then followed, carefully closing the canopy behind him.

As he approached the launch, he saw, silhouetted against the field of stars, Kazuo handing the sword case up to a second slighter figure, then hoisting himself up the diver's ladder attached to the stern. Rick swam silently along the starboard side of the boat, looking for some less obvious entry point. Finally he dived, swimming quickly under the launch to the port side. As he surfaced next to the boat, he sensed, more than saw, someone bending over him and striking downward. He tried to duck, but too late. Something hard struck him just behind the left ear. Then the world went black.

From the jumpseat between the chopper jockey and his co-pilot, Will Ward looked out at a midnight-blue sky and a sea that was several shades darker, and damned himself to hell. He knew plenty of saltier expressions—at need, he could curse like a bo's'n's mate—but in this case he was using the theologically exact term. Somewhere out there, his godson and his brainchild were both in some sort of danger, and the fault was entirely his own. That was unforgivable.

He reached up and massaged his eyes with his fingertips. His eyeballs felt as if they were slowly retreating into his skull, while tiny hammers pounded sixty times a minute against his temples. Still, he felt a little closer to human than he had an hour earlier, when one of *Berkone*'s officers came to his room to tell him that someone had stolen the *Steel Albatross*. Had young Mares noticed anything unusual? Maybe every retired naval officer stumbled into the bathroom, splashed his face with cold water, and swallowed a couple of aspirin when he was roused from his afternoon nap. At least someone—almost certainly Ricky—had hidden the bottle.

The circumaural headphones built into his helmet blocked out most of the engine whine, but even the little that filtered through felt like a dentist's drill. It came as a relief when the pilot announced, "We've got a radar contact, sir. The position checks out with the coordinates you gave us."

"What does it look like?" Will asked.

"Hard to say, sir, at this range. Whatever it is, it's not very big. Under fifty feet."

"What's our ETA?"

"Call it seven minutes," the pilot responded. "What kind of opposition are we likely to run into when we get there, sir?"

"I wish I knew," Will replied heavily. "All I can tell you

is that Commander Tallman asked for helicopter support. I don't think he'd do that if he just wants us to hold his hand while he pees."

"No, sir. Are we trying to sneak up on them, or scare the shit out of them?"

"How about first one, then the other?" Will suggested.

"Can do," the pilot said, chuckling. "I'll take her down to wave height now and throttle back to quiet mode. Then when we're about three hundred yards out, I'll take her up to a hundred feet and switch on the searchlight. Look straight at that baby for a couple of seconds, and you'll see nothing but spots for the next week. And just in case, we'll ready the .50-caliber Gatling gun mounted in the nose blister."

"What, one of those Vulcans?" Will asked, impressed. "That's more than enough firepower to take on anything we're likely to run up against. This just may turn out to be a milk run after all."

A strong hand—Kazuo's?—grabbed Rick's upper arm and pulled him up into the boat. He fell to the deck as limp as a half-empty sack of flour. He might have been able to keep his head from hitting the planks, but he didn't try. The more helpless his captors thought him, the greater his tactical advantage once he saw his chance to act.

Opening his eyes a slit, he saw Hoshi kneeling next to the metal case, fumbling with its latches. After a few moments, she drew a knife and forced it into the crack where the lid met the body of the box. Nothing happened. Then, so suddenly that she recoiled, the lid flew back. Hoshi reached inside and withdrew a long slender object swathed in heavy cloth.

"The Emperor's Sword," she whispered reverently. She untied the wrappings and folded them back, then produced a small tool that Rick recognized. Natalie had used one just like it to remove the hilt of the sword she had bought. Like Natalie, Hoshi used the pointed end of the tool to push out the plug that held the hilt to the blade. Then she removed the hilt altogether.

"A torch," she said urgently. "This light is too dim."

Kazuo ducked into the cabin of the boat and returned with a small flashlight. He held the light steady on the bare tang of the sword. Hoshi lowered her head until her nose was almost touching the blue-tinted steel.

"Yes, there is Kuniyuki's mark," she muttered. "This is the blade it was said to be. And here, on the other side, just as I was told—"

She suddenly raised her head and stared coldly at Kazuo. "Take that light away," she ordered. "We have seen what we need to see."

Kazuo blinked in surprise, then said, "Yes, Hoshi."

Carefully, she replaced the hilt on the tang and hammered home the little peg. Then she stood up with the scabbarded sword in her left hand. Her right hand grasped the hilt, then hesitated, as if dismayed by its own audacity.

"Put it back in the case," Kazuo told her. "You said yourself that we have seen what we need to see. This is not for us."

"I have the right," Hoshi replied between clenched teeth. "My grandfather paid with his life, and the lives of his comrades, to save this weapon and its secret for the Emperor. His bones lie beneath us at this very moment. In his name, I claim the Sword!"

The blade flashed from the scabbard like a lightning bolt, gathering to itself every quantum of starlight. For a moment, Hoshi seemed daunted. "I never dreamed it would hold such power," she whispered. "I am not worthy to touch it."

"Put it away," Kazuo repeated.

Hoshi looked at him, as if seeing a stranger, then shook her head. "No," she said. "Once drawn, this blade must always be slaked with blood before it is resheathed. Otherwise its power departs."

She took a slow, almost drugged step toward Rick, then another. Suddenly Kazuo sprang in front of her.

"I told you, Hoshi," he said. "My honor requires me to defend this man's life with my own. Doubly, now, because he has just given me back my life. Enough blood has already been spilled. We have what we sought. Give me the Sword."

Rick, though still half dazed, used the rocking of the boat to cover for bringing his arms and hands under his chest. Later, he would wonder if Hoshi sensed his movements. Were they what set her off?

With a swiftness that defied the eye, the Emperor's Sword swung in an arc parallel to the deck, at shoulder height. Kazuo had no time to react or even to shout. His severed head made a graceful parabola, bounced once on the gunwale, and hit the water with a tiny splash. Hot blood rained down on Rick, then sprayed Hoshi, as the headless trunk sank, still twitching convulsively, to the desk.

For a moment, the whole universe seemed to stand still. Rick could barely make out Hoshi's expression in the faint light, but he thought he saw both grief and horror. Then her face changed. She glared down at Rick and said, "You! You are to blame for this!"

She raised the Sword high in the air, ready to deliver a stroke that could not help but be fatal. Rick took a deep breath. He heard a growing roar in his head and saw lights flash before his eyes. But the lights, and the roar, were real. Hoshi glanced over her shoulder at the rapidly approaching chopper, then turned back to Rick. But in that instant, he had scrambled to his knees and picked up Kazuo's headless corpse in both arms. As Hoshi swung the deadly Sword, he heaved the body at her, then jumped frantically to one side.

The razor-sharp blade sliced through Kazuo's body at the waist. The hips and legs fell back to the deck, but the upper half struck Hoshi in the chest. The two lifeless arms seemed to grasp her around the neck. Almost demented with terror, Hoshi backed away, trying to raise the Emperor's Sword for another blow at the remains of her victim.

Rick jumped to his feet, but he slipped on the blood-slick planks and fell heavily, catching a glancing blow on the forehead from a steel equipment box. At that moment, Hoshi succeeded in pushing what was left of Kazuo away from her. Her eyes, now quite mad, searched the deck and met Rick's. She nodded slowly, as if confirming some inner certainty, and began to pick her way carefully, almost daintily, across the gore-soaked deck toward him. As she came, she raised the Sword in both hands, high above her head.

"Good Christ!" Ward exclaimed, lifting himself up off the jumpseat to get a clearer view. "What the hell's going on down there? That boat looks like a slaughterhouse!"

The chopper came to a hover with the boat dead ahead. The pilot reached for the loudhailer mike and pressed the button on the side.

"Ahoy, the boat," he said. "This is the United States Navy. Stand by to be boarded. Keep your hands in sight and do not make any sudden moves."

"That's Rick, lying on the deck," Will exclaimed. "He's been hurt. And that nut with a sword is about to slice him into little pieces. Do something, for chrissake!"

In response, the pilot said into the mike, "You have been warned." Then he fired a brief burst of .50-caliber rounds across the bow of the boat. The sound of the ultra-rapid-fire gun was one continuous roar, and the tracer rounds stitched a line of orange across the darkness.

"What the fuck's she doing now?" Will demanded. Below, the woman had turned away from Rick and was advancing in the direction of the helicopter. What did she think, that she could conquer a .50-caliber machine gun with a samurai sword? Apparently so. When she reached the edge of the deck, she stepped up onto the gunwale and balanced there, holding the Sword aloft in her right hand. She opened her mouth in a shout. The wind from the chopper blades blew her words away, but her face and body screamed defiance.

"Oh, sweet Jesus!" the co-pilot said under his breath.

In a movement so swift that Ward's brain registered only its beginning and end, the woman turned the Sword, shifted her grip to the blade itself, and ripped open her own belly. Her face became a mask of agony. As she began to fall over the side, she lifted the bloody Sword and flung it, end over end, into the ocean. A moment later, it vanished into the depths and she was floating facedown on the waves.

CHAPTER 31

THE WARDROOM TABLE ABOARD *BERKONE* WAS LONG enough to seat eight. Will Ward was sitting at the head of the table, with Rick on his right and Ken Kirby on his left. The rest of the seats were empty.

"And that's it," Rick concluded. "When she saw that all was lost, she followed the way of her samurai ancestors and did her hara-kiri number. But she did her best to make sure that we wouldn't capture the Emperor's Sword by deep-sixing it in twelve hundred feet of water. For all I know, the Sword's back aboard the I-53 by now, along with her grandfather's bones."

"This business is weird enough without embellishments," Will growled.

"Agreed," Ken said. He began rearranging the dozens of colored index cards on the table. "Far too weird. We need a more sensible version of what happened."

Rick stared at him. "A sensible version? We've got half a dozen bodies to explain," he said. "What do you call a sensible version of that?"

Ken took the bridge of his nose between his thumb and forefinger and squeezed gently. "Fortunately, that one is fairly easy," he said. "A radical environmental cult, an internal dispute that leads to violence . . . That's the sort of thing that happens all the time in cults. The two leaders try to flee in a small boat and have a falling out. One kills the other, then, horrified by her deed, kills herself. An explanation that has the virtue of being true, if slightly incomplete."

"And the Sword?"

"Why even bring it up?" Will said heavily. "It's just a myth, of course. An ancient sword with secret magical powers? Come on!"

"From what you say, Rick, it sounds as if the Emperor's Sword might actually conceal an important secret," Ken mused. "If so, I have a wild idea of what it might have been. Have either of you ever heard of buckminsterfullerene, sometimes called buckyballs? It's a recently discovered form of carbon with some very interesting and peculiar properties."

Rick met Will's eye and burst out laughing. Ken looked offended.

"Sorry," Rick apologized. "Private joke. What about buckyballs?"

"Never mind," Ken replied. "If I'm right I shouldn't say anything, and if I'm wrong there's no point in saying anything. I'd just remark that once you know that a secret technique exists, you're a fair part of the distance toward uncovering it. I predict that a lot of petrochemical labs are going to be very busy in the near future."

Rick waited, but Ken didn't elaborate on this statement.

"So it's all wrapped up in a nice tidy package," Rick finally said. "But you forgot about Eloise. Dave Collier is never going to accept the story that she killed herself."

"He doesn't have to," Will said. "Sergeant Seguin found Ray Lapham's fingerprints on the railing of Eloise's balcony. After some vigorous questioning, Ray confessed. He's had the hots for Eloise for years, but she was never interested. He couldn't standing seeing her with Dave. The other night he watched them when they came back from a date and just saw red. He didn't mean to push her, it just happened."

"What! What about that computer disk? What about the sabotage of Rover?"

Ken shrugged and looked embarrassed. "We'll turn the disk over to our experts for examination. But proving that

Ray used it to install a virus in Rover's control program ... Well, why bother? Ray is already facing a homicide charge, and proving that he's also a saboteur would simply open a new can of worms. Just among us, it looks like Eloise introduced Ray to her former boss in Oklahoma and that Red Bell used Ray as his pipeline into the SeaVenture project. That must be how he and Nishimura found out that you and the *Steel Albatross* were being called in, in time to set up your 'accidental' meeting with Natalie in Honolulu. But I don't have any proof of that. The best thing to do, publicly, is to accept Ray's tale of a crime of passion."

"Does that mean that the two big guys who set up the whole business are getting away scot-free?" Rick demanded.

"I wouldn't put it quite like that," Ken replied. "Based on what I've been able to piece together about their financial shenanigans, I'd estimate that Bell and Nishimura stand to lose about half a billion dollars apiece. That'll still leave them with walking-around money, but it's bound to hurt a lot."

"Listen, Ricky," said Will. "You've done one hell of a job. I'm even willing to overlook a few instances of insubordination, piracy, and mutiny, since they were in a good cause. And since they succeeded. It doesn't really matter what story comes out about all this. The people who count will know what you've done. I'll see to it."

"I see," Rick said. He slumped down in his chair. Apparently he had just won a big battle. So why did he feel defeated?

Will clapped him on the shoulder. "What you need, son, is a good rest. You've been through a lot in the last couple of days. And while you're getting yourself back together, I'll see what I can do about reconfiguring the *Steel Albatross* for deep-ocean prospecting. It should be quite a challenge, finding something two and a half feet long and less than an inch wide, twelve hundred feet down."

"The Sword?" Rick whispered.

"What else?" Will replied. "If it really does hold some powerful secret, I'd rather we get it than someone else. And it's nothing more than a valuable antique sword, we can win a few points with our Japanese friends by returning it to the Imperial Treasury. How about it, Ricky? Are you game?"

Rick tried to dredge up some enthusiasm, but the best he could manage was a half-hearted, "Sure, Will."

"Fine," Ward said. "We'll have a ball. Oh, I almost forgot. This is for you. The guy at the hotel shoved it in my box by mistake." He handed Rick an envelope.

Rick looked at it listlessly. The postmark was San Diego. He ripped it open and recognized Sam's handwriting. Glancing over it, he saw the word "marriage," and, later in the same line, Kiwi Kraus's name. He let the letter fall on the table. "You read it," he told Will. "I don't think I want to."

Will gave him a shrewd glance, then picked up the sheet. After a few moments, he let out a surprised snort of laughter. "Well, what do you know?" he exclaimed. "That damned clamdigger is full of surprises. He's gone off and gotten himself hitched, to a lady chopper jockey!"

"A . . . what?" Rick sat up straight and reached for the letter. "Here, let me see that!"

He read it through once, fast, then again, more slowly. He spent a long time over the last line:

Billy and I both miss you. We know you have an important job to do, but once it's done, please come see us.

love,
Sam

Rick suddenly realized that there was nothing in the world he wanted more.

More Thrilling Adventures of the U.S.
Navy's Most Controversial Warrior—
Top-secret True Exploits That Can Only Be
Told as Fiction!

RICHARD MARCINKO
and John Weisman
present

ROGUE WARRIOR

(available)
ROGUE WARRIOR II
RED CELL

Coming in paperback mid-November

And look for. . .

ROGUE WARRIOR III:
GREEN TEAM

Coming soon in Hardcover from
Pocket Books

POCKET
B O O K S

915-02

New York Times Bestselling Author

STEPHEN COONTS

Stephen Coonts, the author of five consecutive *New York Times* bestselling novels, has taken the country by storm, by capturing the American imagination and fulfilling the American dream.

☐ **FLIGHT OF THE INTRUDER**
70960-7/$6.50

☐ **UNDER SIEGE**
74294-9/$6.50

☐ **THE CANNIBAL QUEEN**
74885-8/$6.50

☐ **THE RED HORSEMAN**
74888-2/$6.50

and **THE INTRUDERS**
coming in Hardcover mid-September from

POCKET BOOKS

Simon & Schuster Mail Order
200 Old Tappan Rd., Old Tappan, N.J. 07675

Please send me the books I have checked above. I am enclosing $_____ (please add $0.75 to cover the postage and handling for each order. Please add appropriate sales tax). Send check or money order-no cash or C.O.D.'s please. Allow up to six weeks for delivery. For purchase over $10.00 you may use VISA: card number, expiration date and customer signature must be included.

Name _____

Address _____

City _____ State/Zip _____

VISA Card # _____ Exp.Date _____

Signature _____

879